TARAN MATHARU

SUMM⬟NER

— THE OUTCAST —

Hodder
Children's
Books

HODDER CHILDREN'S BOOKS

First published in Great Britain in hardback in 2018
First published in Great Britain in paperback in 2019
This paperback edition published in 2020

1 3 5 7 9 10 8 6 4 2

A CIP catalogue record for this book is available from the British Library.

ISBN: 978 1 444 95828 7

Typeset in Garamond by Avon DataSet Ltd, Bidford-on-Avon, Warwickshire

Printed and bound by Clays Ltd, Elcograf S.p.A.

The paper and board used in this book are made from wood from responsible sources.

Hodder Children's Books
An imprint of Hachette Children's Group
Part of Hodder and Stoughton
Carmelite House
50 Victoria Embankment
London EC4Y 0DZ

An Hachette UK Company

www.hachette.co.uk

SUMM✪NER

Also by Taran Matharu

SUMMONER
The Novice
The Inquisition
The Battlemage
The Outcast (The Prequel)

The Summoner's Handbook

CONTENDER
The Chosen

To my readers

The Outcast: Character List

Arcturus – orphan and summoner

The Pinkertons – lawmakers from the city

The Nobles

King Alfric – ruler of Hominum, founder of the Inquisition, leader of the Pinkertons, overseer of Judges
Lord Royce Faversham – Charles's father
Lady Ophelia Faversham – Charles's mother, teacher at Vocans
Lord Lovett – ruler of Calgary
Lieutenant Elizabeth Cavendish – graduate, teaching assistant at Vocans
Provost Obadiah Forsyth – head of Vocans, Zacharias' father
Lord Scipio – summoning teacher at Vocans

The Army

Sergeant Caulder
Private Rotter (Rotherham)
Sergeant Percival – leader of the twenty-fourth platoon
Sergeant Daniels
General Barcroft – commands the south-western portion of the front lines; leader of the rebels

Celestial Corps – branch of the army

Vocans Academy

Crawley – head steward and rebel
Charles Faversham – noble whose demon scroll Arcturus stole
Zacharias Forsyth – noble
Prince Harold Corwin – prince of Hominum

Edmund Raleigh – noble
Damien Rook – noble
Alice Queensouth – noble, twin sister of Josephine
Josephine Queensouth – noble, twin sister of Alice
Baybars Saladin – noble
Fergus Lovett – noble
Carter Lovett – noble
Arthur Lovett – noble
Elaine Lovett – noble

The Dwarves

Ulfr – servant at Vocans
Uhtred Thorsager – blacksmith

Demons

Sacharissa – Arcturus's demon (Canid)
Satet – Lady Faversham's demon (Peryton)
Anansi – Lady Faversham's demon (Arach)
Hubertus – Lieutenant Cavendish's demon (Peryton)
Reubens – Provost Obadiah Forsyth's demon (Mite)
Valens – Elaine Lovett's demon (Mite)
Kali – Lord Scipio's demon (Felid)
Anansi – Charles Faversham's demon (Arach)
Trebius – Zacharias Forsyth's demon (Hydra)
Jet – Edmund Raleigh's demon (Mite)
Athena – Edmund Raleigh's demon (Gryphowl)
Gelert – Edmund Raleigh's demon (Canid)
Reynard – Alice Queensouth's demon (Vulpid)
Unknown – Orc shaman's demon (Phantaur)
Kerit – Prince Harold's demon (Nandi)

1

Arcturus shrank deeper into the stable's shadows, waiting for the dead of night. The clamour of the tavern next door had reduced to a gentle murmur, but it was not safe to come out yet.

If all went as planned, his master would ring the midnight bell soon, announcing to patrons that it was time to wend their drunken way home, or if they were lucky, to a room in the inn upstairs. Only then would Arcturus make his move.

It was a plan ten years in the making; almost two thirds of his young life. He was going to escape the beatings, the endless hours of toil and the meagre rations that were his only reward.

As an orphan, Arcturus's value was determined by the yield of his work, rather than the quality of his character. The ox in the stock next to him was fed better than he was; after all, it had been purchased at several times the price his master had paid for him at the local workhouse. He was worth less than a beast of burden.

The bell chimed, disturbing Arcturus from his thoughts. There was a creak as the tavern door swung open, then the crunch of gravel signalled the departure of the drinkers, their coarse laughter fading until silence reigned once again. Even so, it was a full ten minutes before Arcturus padded from the shadows and into the night air of the stables. He adjusted his pack and wondered if he had everything he needed.

Escaping was not as simple as running away, something that Arcturus had learned from bitter experience. In the early days, before he was sold to the innkeeper, children often ran away from the workhouse. They always returned a few days later, starving, beaten or worse.

There was no work for scrawny, uneducated children who had nowhere to go. Arcturus knew that if he ran away unprepared, he would end up begging for scraps before returning, hat in hand, to the inn. In all likelihood he would be sent back to the workhouse. Back to hell on earth.

Arcturus knelt in the straw and checked his pack one more time. Forty-two shillings: his life savings from tips, loose coins and charity. It would last him a few weeks, until he found a new source of income. A thick fur, discarded by a passing trader for the wine stain that adorned its centre, but still fit for Arcturus's purposes; he would not freeze if he needed to camp overnight. A serrated knife, stolen from the tavern kitchen at great risk. Although it was not much of a weapon against a brigand, it gave him peace of mind. Two candles, some bread, salted pork and a few spare garments completed his supplies. Just enough to give him a fighting chance.

The neigh of a horse in the darkness reminded him why he had chosen that night. An opportunity unlike any he had seen before. A young noble had arrived only a few hours earlier, exhausted from a long day's riding. He had not even bothered to unpack his saddlebags, simply throwing the reins disdainfully to Arcturus and trudging into the inn to book a bed for that night. Rude enough that Arcturus only felt a twinge of guilt about robbing the young man.

Arcturus knew where the noble was going. When they came of age, first born children attended Vocans Academy, to learn the art of summoning demons. The academy was all the way in the capital city of Corcillum, on the other side of the Hominum Empire. With any luck, the saddlebags would contain everything Arcturus might need for a similar journey, not to mention the fact that the wealthy young noble's possessions might be extremely valuable.

He sidled up to the horse, clucking his tongue to calm it. As a stable boy, he had a way with horses. This one was no different, nuzzling his palm as if searching for a handful of feed. He stroked it on its muzzle and unclipped the saddlebags, letting them fall to the ground.

Arcturus searched through each pocket, his heart dropping as he discovered that the vast majority of them were empty. No wonder the noble had left without them.

Still, the noble's steed was the real prize. Many horses passed through here, but this was a fine stallion, with long legs, muscled haunches and clear, intelligent eyes. It could outpace any riders who might follow him, be they thieves, brigands or even Pinkertons, Hominum's police force. It was not unknown for them to chase down a runaway orphan if the reward was high enough.

Arcturus rummaged in the last pocket and smiled as he

grasped something solid. It was hard to see in the dim light of the stable, but he could tell by touch it was a roll of leather. He unravelled it on the ground and felt the dry touch of a scroll within.

A thin stream of moonlight cutting through the slats in the roof allowed Arcturus to see printed black letters on the page. He held it up to the light and examined them more closely.

Arcturus's reading ability was poor; his education had been limited to the one year of learning at the workhouse. Fortunately, the books that travellers abandoned in their rooms often found their way into his possession, allowing him to practise over the years. His reading was now better than most, but he still had to sound the words out as he read.

'Do rah lo fah lo go . . .' He whispered the syllables. They made no sense, yet he could not stop, his eyes glued to the page. As he spoke, a strangely familiar sensation suffused his body, starting as a dull giddiness and gradually growing in intensity as word after word rolled off his tongue. The grey of the stable seemed to become brighter, the colours intensifying in his vision.

'Sai lo go mai nei go . . .' The words droned on. His eyes roved back and forth across the page as if they had a mind of their own.

Heart pounding, Arcturus felt something within him stir. There was a flicker in the darkness of the stable. Beneath his feet, the leather wrapping glimmered with violet light, patterns flaring along its surface. Out of the corner of his eye, Arcturus saw the outline of a pentacle, surrounded by symbols on each point of the star. The glow pulsed like a beating heart, accompanied by a low hum.

As he reached the last line of the page, a spinning ball of light formed in the air, growing into a brilliant orb that seared his vision. His ears popped as the humming turned into a roar, growing louder with every second.

Arcturus spoke the last words, then tore his eyes away and dove to the ground, clamping his hands over his ears. He could feel a fiery heat washing over him, as if he were lying beside a great bonfire. Then, as sudden as a lightning strike, Arcturus's world went still.

The new silence fell upon the stable like a cloak, only broken by Arcturus's deep, sobbing breaths. He shut his eyelids tightly, shrinking into a ball on the ground. He knew he should be moving, gathering his things and riding away before anyone arrived to investigate. Yet the ice of fear had taken hold, leaving him petrified on the cold soil of the stable.

There was a snap as the noble's horse broke its tether, then the thunder of hooves as it bolted into the night. The light, heat and noise had been too much for the well-trained beast. Realising his best chance at escape had just galloped out of the door, Arcturus's terror turned to despair.

Straw rustled in the darkness, followed by a low growl. Arcturus froze and held his breath. He kept his eyes shut and remained perfectly still. If he played dead, perhaps whatever it was would move on in search of more interesting prey.

The noise intensified, moving closer and closer, until he could feel the hot, moist breath of the creature in his ear. A tongue slid across his face, leaving a trail of saliva as it tasted him. Arcturus tensed, knowing he would have to fight.

With a yell, he leaped to his feet, striking out with a clenched fist. It met a furry muzzle, rewarding him with a yelp as the creature fell back. Emboldened, Arcturus struck out again, sending the creature skittering into the shadows. It was clumsy, stumbling and tripping over itself as it ran.

Arcturus grabbed his pack and sprinted to the door. The inn was dark still, with no signs of movement. He grinned with relief, realising he might still have a chance to escape. If he was lucky, the horse might not be far away.

But as he began to leave, a strange feeling came over him. Pain and . . . betrayal. He shook his head and took another step, but the feeling intensified. On the edge of his consciousness, Arcturus felt something stir. The creature was connected to him somehow, as if by a mental umbilical cord. Suddenly, Arcturus was overcome with an immense feeling of loneliness and abandonment, emotions that were all too familiar to him.

He turned and stared into the darkness of the stables. In the light of the moon, the entrance yawned like a cave mouth, shrouded in shadow. The creature was whining, like a dog whose master had kicked it. He felt guilty, for the demon had only been licking his face. Of course . . . a demon. The noble was on his way to Vocans Academy to learn the art of summoning them after all. Had Arcturus just done that? Summoned this demon? But that was something only nobles could do . . . wasn't it?

As if it could sense his guilt, the demon tumbled out of the stable, blinking in the moonlight. It was not as huge as he had thought, only the size of a large dog. In fact, it had the head of a dog too, with a pair of large blue eyes, followed by a second, smaller pair behind them. It was entirely black, with a shaggy ridge of hair along its spine. This ridge continued on to a bushy, fox-like tail, though it swished back and forth much like an eager pet. Strangest of all was its body, muscled like a jungle cat with sharp, dangerous claws and powerful limbs.

'What are you?' Arcturus whispered, holding a calming hand out. He could feel the demon's fear dissipating, replaced with an eager desire to please. The demon took a wary step forward, and licked his hand with a rough, wet tongue.

Arcturus examined it more closely, stroking its head. Despite its size, the creature looked young, with an overlarge head and clumsy, thick limbs that gave it a puppy-like mien.

'Do you want to come with me?' Arcturus asked, rubbing the creature under its chin. It closed its four eyes and nuzzled back, panting with pleasure. With each scratch Arcturus felt a keen sense of satisfaction on the edge of his consciousness.

'I bet any passing brigands would think twice before attacking us, eh?' Arcturus murmured, smiling. 'Let's just hope you don't scare the horse too. We're going to need him tonight.'

He turned, just in time to see a cudgel lashing towards his face.

Pain.

Then nothingness.

2

Arcturus awoke in darkness. For several agonising seconds, he thought the attack had blinded him. It was only the thin sliver of light at the end of the room that told him otherwise.

The air was stale and heavy, as if it had not been disturbed for some time. The stone underneath him was chilled, devoid of any warmth or comfort. Pain twinged through his skull with every turn of his head, and a tentative feel of his temple revealed a lump the size of a goose egg.

He lay in the gloom, bracing himself to stand and explore his confines. Perhaps if he crawled to the light, he could call for help. He tried to speak, but couldn't manage more than a raw croak. A thirst he had never known was raging inside him, leaving his swollen tongue cleaved to the roof of his mouth like a slab of salt pork.

Footsteps, loud and purposeful, echoed from the source of light. The door, for that is what it was, swung open, blinding him with the glow of a torch. He blinked in the new light, shading his eyes with a hand.

'Awake already, are you?' a cold voice snapped, lifting the flame higher.

Arcturus squinted, revealing brass buttons on black cloth: the uniform of a Pinkerton. The man had a handsome face, but his eyes were cruel and devoid of empathy. He approached Arcturus and crouched down to examine him.

Arcturus spied a tankard of water in the man's hand and snatched it, all sense of decorum forgotten. He took deep, noisy gulps, filling his belly until the liquid sloshed inside of him like a half empty gourd. The man chuckled and lifted him to his feet, his grip like a vice on Arcturus's shoulder.

'Thank you for the water,' Arcturus gasped, dizzied from standing so suddenly.

'It wasn't for drinking. It was for throwing over you to rouse your lazy carcass. Two days you've been in and out of consciousness. That noble must have hit you something fierce.' The Pinkerton laughed again, then pulled Arcturus out of the cell and down a narrow corridor.

'Where are we going?' Arcturus slurred, his gorge rising as a bout of nausea overcame him.

Forks of pain spread through his brain with every step, as if his skull was full of lightning. He felt the demon on the very edge of his consciousness, awash with confusion and terror.

Arcturus preferred the sensations in his own mind. Pain he was used to, for his master would knock him about when the mood took him. It was the demon's fear he could not abide, though he was getting flashes of his own as the Pinkerton ignored his question, dragging him up some stairs.

The stairs opened into a small hallway with a set of double

doors at the end carved from dark oak and stamped with the insignia of a noble house. They spoke of wealth and power, the old kind that was passed from generation to generation. Paintings lined the walls: portraits of old men with beady eyes that seemed to follow him as they went by.

'You're to go in alone. Be quick about it. It doesn't do to keep a king waiting,' the Pinkerton snapped, then grinned at the shock on Arcturus's face. 'That's right, boy. You're in *that* much trouble.'

He shoved Arcturus through the doors, then slammed them shut behind him.

Arcturus stumbled and collapsed to the floor, meeting the soft down of a bearskin rug. Bookshelves lined the walls, broken only by the door behind him and a crackling hearth in front. It was uncomfortably hot in the room, as if a sick man was being purged in a sweat lodge.

There were two armchairs and a stool by the fireplace. The young noble was in the smaller seat, eyeing Arcturus with trepidation. Behind him sat two middle-aged men, both with silver dusting their black hair at the temples. One appeared as the portraits did, his eyes beady with a hooked nose. He bore some resemblance to the young noble, and Arcturus guessed that he was his father.

The other wore a circlet around his head and a scowl, twisting an otherwise handsome face into a savage expression. He could only be King Alfric, ruler of Hominum. The three wore expensive clothing, all velvet, silk and silver lacing.

'Tell us exactly as it happened, Charles,' King Alfric growled at the young noble, his voice low and angry. 'Leave nothing out.'

'I told you already. I left the summoning scroll and leather in my panniers and bedded down in a filthy inn just outside Boreas. I woke up to a great racket from outside, so I went to investigate. Next thing I see is this . . . hoodlum . . . petting my demon!' Charles pointed a wavering finger at Arcturus, spitting as he spoke. 'I knocked him out with my blackjack and got the innkeeper to fetch the Pinkertons while I trapped the beast in the stable. It's not me you should be questioning. Ask the delinquent.'

'You will speak to your king with respect!' the father bellowed, leaping to his feet and slapping Charles across the face. He lowered his head and bowed to the king, who waved a languorous hand in acceptance.

'Calm yourself, Royce. We have more important things to worry about than petty niceties.' The king turned to Arcturus and gave him a forced smile, trying to put him at ease. It had the opposite effect.

'Listen carefully, stable boy. You are the only witness to the theft of Lord Faversham's demon . . . or should I say, his son's demon. The scroll and leather Charles mentioned are a way of transferring a demon from one noble to another, usually a parent to a child. Now, I want you to think very carefully. Who was it who took the items from the bag and summoned the demon in the stable? Did you see an insignia on their clothing, or perhaps a distinctive colour?'

King Alfric turned back to Lord Faversham before Arcturus could answer, which was just as well. His mind was still reeling.

'Lord Lovett has been blessed with four adept children, rather than the usual firstborn. His youngest daughter is joining Vocans

11

Academy this year, just like Charles. Providing a fourth demon for her would be difficult, especially for a weak summoner like him. You don't think . . . ?'

'My king, he would not dare. The Lovetts are rulers of Calgary, a poor fiefdom by all accounts. It is nothing more than a few farms and rivers. It would be too great a risk for him. If he was caught, my bodyguard would storm Calgary and take back what is ours, and more besides. With your permission, of course.' Lord Faversham inclined his head respectfully.

'Of course.' Alfric nodded, his eyes settling on Arcturus once again.

'Who was it then?' Charles asked, his voice low and threatening, the imprint of his father's hand blazing red across his face. 'Who stole my demon from me?'

Arcturus was struck dumb, unable to answer. Lying seemed the best option. Blame it on a mysterious figure, some faceless noble who came in the dead of night. The question was, would they let him live, in light of what he knew? And even if they did, what then? Back to the workhouse, to starve with the other children that nobody loved.

Perhaps it would be better to roll the dice, see what the truth would bring. A commoner being able to summon a demon was unheard of – it could turn his life upside down. But when you're at the bottom of the pile, it always makes sense to reshuffle the deck.

'It was me,' he announced, his voice as confident as he could make it. 'I summoned the demon. I can feel it now.'

There was a pause, then a cackle as the king and Lord Faversham burst into laughter. Even Charles snorted, though

12

the malice never left his eyes. Arcturus sat in silence, setting his jaw.

The king held up his hand, cutting the laughter short. His smile narrowed to a pursed slit.

'Charles, come here.' He beckoned the young noble over, then leaned in and whispered in his ear. Charles hesitated, then strode from the room, slamming the door behind him.

The king steepled his fingers, levelling his gaze at Arcturus. His grey eyes revealed nothing, but Lord Faversham drummed his fingers on the armrest, betraying a sudden nervousness. Despite the heat, Arcturus shuddered under the king's scrutiny.

'You're playing a dangerous game here,' Lord Faversham said, narrowing his eyes at Arcturus. 'Did they pay you to feed us this cock-and-bull story? Because if you think for one moment that you'll be able to lie and leave this castle alive, you are much mistaken.'

'It's true,' Arcturus replied, cursing the quaver in his voice. 'I read the scroll aloud and the demon appeared.'

'Commoners cannot summon demons,' the king snapped, impatience getting the better of him. 'The gift is passed down in the blood, always for the firstborn and sometimes for the siblings. The noble houses have been the only summoners in Hominum for two thousand years. Now, I will give you one more chance. If you tell me the truth and identify the thief, I will give you four hundred shillings and transport to Corcillum. You can't say fairer than that.'

But Arcturus could feel something new, screeching through him like nails on a chalkboard. It was pain, distant but fierce, emanating from the psychic thread that held him to the demon.

13

A fresh throb made him fall to his knees, clutching at his skull. The dual sensation of this new pain and his earlier injuries was almost too much to bear.

'You're hurting it!' he cried, burying his head in the fur of the bearskin rug.

'When will you end this farce?' Lord Faversham growled, kicking at Arcturus. But the king held up a bony finger, before pointing it at the entrance to the library.

'As we speak, your son is whipping the demon downstairs as I instructed him. I was hoping to merely cause the thief some discomfort. Instead, it seems we have revealed him.' The king smiled as Arcturus whimpered in agony.

He was barely able to comprehend the king's words, fresh waves of pain robbing him of all sense.

'Who are you, boy?' Lord Faversham growled, lifting Arcturus from the floor by the collar and holding him up in the air. 'Your stable-boy disguise has been found out. Tell us which house you belong to now and perhaps your punishment will be less severe. Are you a Sinclair? A Fitzroy?'

'No . . . house . . .' Arcturus choked.

'Put him down, Royce,' the king ordered, tearing Arcturus from Lord Faversham's grasp before his command could be obeyed. 'This boy is no impostor. Can you not tell by his accent, his demeanour? His body odour alone reeks of a common upbringing.'

'What are you saying?' Lord Faversham asked, breathing heavily. 'That this boy is telling the truth?'

'I am saying,' the king murmured, tapping his chin with a long finger, 'that this boy is . . . something new.'

3

Arcturus was thrown back into his dark cell, but this time with a bucket of water and some fresh bread. Arcturus devoured it, revelling in the warm chewy texture. On the other hand, the demon was given no such sustenance, and its thirst and hunger plagued Arcturus for hours on end. He banged on the door and demanded it be fed and watered, but received nothing but curses from the Pinkerton, then silence.

Finally, when the water bucket was empty and hunger began to gnaw at his stomach once again, Arcturus was dragged from his cell then marched through a side door and into the courtyard.

Lord Faversham and his son were waiting for him, their faces dark and broody with ill humour. A large box lay on the ground beside them, with a strange leather harness wrapped around it.

As Arcturus trudged towards them, he took in his surroundings, scanning for an escape route. The courtyard was surrounded by a cobbled stone wall, thick with ivy. An elaborate archway curved over the entrance and it was blocked by a heavy iron gate.

'Still alive, are you?' Charles said, kicking at the gravel on the ground moodily. 'I had hoped you would have died in—'

'No, Charles,' Lord Faversham cut him off. 'The king has made . . . arrangements for the boy, as you well know. No harm will befall him whilst he is in our care, is that understood?'

'Yes, Father,' Charles sighed.

Arcturus remained silent, his eyes on his feet. Where were they taking him? Somehow, he didn't feel afraid. Anything was better than going back to the inn.

He could sense the demon now, so close he could almost smell it. The box beside him trembled. Arcturus turned his eyes towards it and gasped.

The demon – it was trapped inside. He kneeled and laid his hand against the wood, sending it feelings of calmness and safety, despite his own misgivings about the future. Slowly, the trembling stopped. The sound of lapping inside gave him some relief as he realised they had finally given it some water. It seemed, for now, the Favershams wanted both of them alive.

'They're here,' Charles said, pointing at the sky.

Two dots hovered in the heavens, like birds circling above a cornfield. Slowly but surely they grew in size, until two winged beasts landed before them in a flash of feathers and fur.

Arcturus had to step back as they flapped and folded their enormous wings, the tawny feathers fluttering in the wind. They looked like winged, horse-sized stags, with majestic antlers branching from their foreheads. Their front legs ended in hooves, yet their back legs were clawed like a falcon's, complete with deadly talons that dug into the ground. Instead of the traditional bob that all deer had, the demons had long, elegant tail feathers.

Both were fitted with polished leather bridles and saddles, in which two riders sat, resplendent in navy-blue uniforms adorned with golden epaulets and shining gold buttons. They removed their leather caps and dark goggles and shook their hair out with audible sighs of relief.

One of the riders dismounted and embraced Charles, kissing him on the forehead. She was beautiful, with golden hair that fell about her face. Arcturus shuddered as he realised she was Charles's mother, Lady Faversham, renowned for her great beauty across all of Hominum.

Even so, as she turned to Arcturus, her expression was hard, the pretty face as cold and cruel as winter.

'He is the reason we are here?' She narrowed her eyes at him. 'We flew through the night.'

'The boy, and the fact that Charles couldn't get half a day's ride from here without losing his demon!' Lord Faversham growled. 'He needs to be flown to Vocans since he can't be trusted on his own, not to mention that he is already late starting the academic year as it is. You shall have to provide him with a new summoning scroll, or he won't be allowed to attend.' He paused and tapped his chin. 'It is a shame you need your Peryton demon for the Celestial Corps. It will have to be the other one.'

'You lost your Canid? Do you have any idea what your father risked to capture her for you?' Lady Faversham hissed, seizing Charles by the ear, her anger as sudden as her arrival. 'Now I will have to give you my Arach, and I caught it only weeks ago.'

Charles wailed like a baby, pulling at his mother's hand until she released him with a grunt of disgust.

Arcturus absorbed the information, taking note of the names

of the various species of demon, and the fact that his own was female. It appeared that demons could somehow be gifted through scrolls and had to be captured first. If he was to survive the coming weeks, he would need to learn all he could.

His understanding of the world of summoning was vague at best, given that he lived so far north of the jungles on Hominum's southern border, where most of the skirmishes took place.

Though they were not officially at war with the various orc tribes that inhabited it, the nobles, their retinues and the king's army would patrol along their borders, keeping Hominum safe from the occasional orc raiding party. Boreas, the city in which Arcturus lived, was far to the north, near to the border with the elves.

The next rider dismounted, a brunette with long tresses that came down to her waist. She nodded respectfully at Lord Faversham then went about attaching the box to a leather lead, before securing it to the bottom of her mount. She grinned at Arcturus's wary expression and gave him a wink. He responded with a hesitant smile, which was swiftly wiped away when Lady Faversham clicked her fingers at him.

'You, boy. If the king did not have such an interest in you, I would have you hanging from the gallows in a heartbeat. Nobody steals from the Favershams, especially not some filthy stable boy.'

Charles smiled hatefully at Arcturus from behind her back, drawing a finger across his throat. Arcturus responded with a cool stare, though tendrils of terror gripped his heart.

This time, it was the demon that calmed *him*. Waves of encouragement and support flowed through their mental link as it sensed his discomfort.

'Watch your back, boy,' Lady Faversham said, unimpressed by Arcturus's apparent lack of fear.

A servant scurried past them, dragging a heavy trunk behind him and attaching it to Lady Faversham's Peryton.

'Be careful with that,' Charles ordered, striding over to survey the fastenings. 'I don't want my clothes all rumpled.'

The servant bowed, a flash of fear passing across his face. He was barely older than Arcturus and he looked half starved. Arcturus felt fortunate he didn't have to work in this household.

'Ophelia, are you sure Lieutenant Cavendish's Peryton can carry the Canid?' Lord Faversham asked his wife.

'It's only a pup,' Lady Faversham responded. 'If she was full grown it might be a struggle over such a long distance, but thankfully you caught it young.'

'Aye, Hubertus is as strong as an ox!' Lieutenant Cavendish called, tying one last knot on the thick leather leads that were now attached to the demon's cage. She winked at Arcturus again, and he marvelled at how young she was. She could barely be older than eighteen, yet she wore the uniform of an officer. The Lieutenant jumped on to her mount in one fluid leap, then patted the saddle behind her.

'We'd better get going if we're to reach Vocans by nightfall. Since my luggage is heavier than yours, we might get a bit of a head start on you, if that's all right, Captain Faversham?' she asked, rubbing Hubertus's neck.

Vocans . . . was he to be a student there? The thought filled him with both excitement and dread in equal measure.

Lady Faversham gave Lieutenant Cavendish a curt nod then, with one final glare at Arcturus, she strode into the manor house. Arcturus hesitated before striding to the Peryton and holding up his hand. Lieutenant Cavendish gripped it firmly and pulled him up behind her with surprising ease. He could feel the Hubertus's muscles bunching beneath his legs, as the demon unfolded his wings.

'Hold on tight,' she murmured, grasping his hands and putting them around her waist. 'I hope you have a strong stomach.'

The wings flapped once. Twice.

And they were flying.

4

The world was spread below Arcturus like a patchwork quilt, the fields of crops splitting the earth into squares of green, yellow and brown. With every beat of the Peryton's wings, the fuzzy white cloud bank above them loomed closer. Soon they were in the mist, surrounded by a haze of the purest white Arcturus had ever seen. He revelled in the cool air, opening his mouth to catch droplets on his tongue. It was over all too soon, for they burst clear of the other side into the bright sunlight moments later.

'You've got a strong grip there, lad!' Lieutenant Cavendish chuckled, before clucking her tongue at Hubertus. The Peryton slowed down, until they hung above the clouds, rising and falling with each wingbeat.

'Sorry,' Arcturus breathed, realising he was squeezing her midriff tight. He relaxed his grip and gazed at the cloudscape around him. It was if they were floating above a sea of cotton, soft and welcoming as a feather bed. He had a wild urge to dive into them, but a gap revealing the ground far below reminded him of where he was.

'You'll get used to it,' Lieutenant Cavendish said over her shoulder. 'The first time I flew, I threw up over the side.'

'I wish you hadn't said that,' Arcturus groaned, feeling his stomach give a sudden lurch. He was not the only one feeling ill. Below him, he could sense that the demon was feeling nauseous as its box swung back and forth, and the hunger that gripped its belly was not helping matters.

Lieutenant Cavendish swivelled in her seat and flashed him a grin.

'You know, we're going to be travelling together for the rest of the day so we might as well get to know each other. My name is Elizabeth Cavendish. And yours?'

'Arcturus. Good to meet you,' he said, proffering his hand and shaking hers awkwardly. He hesitated, then asked, 'You're very young to be an officer, aren't you?'

'My, my, aren't you the forthright one!' she laughed, tossing her hair from her face. 'Actually, I've just graduated from Vocans, so I'm twenty years old. All graduates go on to become officers, but I'm just a second lieutenant, the lowest rank possible. I'm glad of it to be honest, what with the baby on the way. The less responsibility the better!'

'You're having a baby? Shouldn't you be resting, instead of fighting in the army?' Arcturus asked, loosening his grip around her midriff.

'Nonsense,' she scoffed, giving him a prod. 'Maybe in a few months, but I'll go home when I'm good and ready, thank you very much! Of course, most nobles my age have children as soon as they graduate, if not before, so the army are very understanding.'

'What's the hurry?' Arcturus asked.

22

'Don't you know anything?' Elizabeth asked, smacking her forehead. 'I keep forgetting you're just a commoner. Very strange business – you'll have to fill me in on the way.'

Arcturus bristled at the word 'just' but forgave her for it almost instantly. Of all the nobles he had met, she was by far the nicest, and didn't seem to mean any offence.

'Nobles have children early because only our firstborn are guaranteed to inherit the ability to summon. If I was to die in battle tomorrow, the Cavendish line would be cut off for ever! Better to leave a successor, just in case. Luckily for me, the Celestial Corps is a pretty safe job at the moment. We do a bit of scouting, keep an eye on Hominum's borders, avoid the occasional orc javelin here and there. Pretty simple stuff.'

It made a lot of sense, but for a brief moment Arcturus felt almost sorry for the nobles. Imagine having to marry so young, even if you hadn't met your soulmate yet.

As if she could read his mind, Elizabeth smiled and clicked open a heart-shaped locket that hung around her neck. A tiny painting of a handsome, mousy-haired man sat within.

'I was one of the lucky ones. I found the love of my life early on. He was a servant at Vocans and a commoner, like you. You're probably the only person I can tell who won't judge me for that. It is custom for the firstborn nobles to marry the second or third born from another noble house. It's caused quite some controversy at the academy, I can tell you. I guess I'm lucky that you're going to Vocans now. Maybe they'll have something else to gossip about.'

As far as Arcturus knew, a noble marrying a commoner was unheard of. He was glad in a way, for it meant that perhaps not all nobles viewed commoners as the Favershams did. At the same time, Elizabeth's talk of gossip made him anxious about how he would be received at the academy.

'Come on, we have a lot of ground to cover if we're to get there before sunset. You can tell me your story on the way.'

They flew through the day, the endless cloudscape broken by glimpses of the ground below. Arcturus tried not to look down, for the lurching of the Peryton's wings made his stomach uneasy. Instead, he distracted himself by telling Elizabeth Cavendish his story.

He found himself going all the way back to his childhood, from the early years of starvation and back-breaking labour in the workhouse, to the endless beatings and abuse at the hands of the innkeeper. Elizabeth spoke very little, but he knew she was listening for she would occasionally interrupt to ask him to describe something further. She was as fascinated by his life as he was by hers, and he suspected that she was unaware of the plight the orphans of Hominum faced, despite her common husband. For a moment he thought he saw a tear trickle down her cheek, though whether it was the harsh winds that tore at their faces or his words that brought them forth, he did not know.

As the sunset cast a rosy glow over the cloud bank and Hubertus began his descent, Arcturus reached the end of his story. Somehow, it had felt good to let it all out. He realised she probably knew more about him now than anyone in the world.

He was about to ask where Vocans was, but his mouth fell open, speechless, as it came into view. Four crenellated towers stretched into the sky, one on each corner of a vast, shadowed castle. It was a perfect square but for a crescent-shaped courtyard surrounded by high walls. A band of murky black water encircled it, a moat that could only be crossed by a heavy drawbridge. In the dim light of dusk, Arcturus could see hundreds of lights glowing from behind thin windows. It was a giant building, larger than anything he had seen before, as vast and immoveable as a mountain.

They glided expertly into the courtyard, spiralling until they landed on the cobblestones. Arcturus felt a flash of relief from his demon as the box thudded into the ground behind them.

A half circle of steps led up to a thick set of oak double doors, higher and wider than ten men. Behind them, an arched gatehouse loomed, shadowing the open drawbridge beneath it.

'I can't stay with you long, Arcturus,' Elizabeth said, unclipping the leather lead from his demon's crate. 'But I have some advice. Don't trust anyone, not even your teachers, for they are cut from the same cloth as their students. Study hard and take advantage of every opportunity you are given – the nobles will only respect you if you are better than them. Even then, some will hate you. But it is better to be hated and respected than their prey.'

'I will, Lieutenant Cavendish,' Arcturus said, lowering his head in deference. She tutted and lifted his chin.

'Keep your head up and give as good as you get. Your old life is over. Reforge your soul in the fires of Vocans Academy.'

Her eyes burned into his and he knew that she meant every word. He set his jaw and nodded.

'I won't let them push me around. I have my demon now. We have each other.'

For the first time, Arcturus didn't feel alone. It was a strange feeling . . . like a weight being lifted from his shoulders.

'What's its name?' she asked, pointing at the box beside them.

'I haven't thought of one yet.'

'Well, you'll need one. It's bad luck to leave a demon unnamed for too long.'

Arcturus was taken aback. He racked his brain, trying to think of a female name for his demon. The women in his life had rarely been kind to him, for the serving girls at the tavern had their own problems to deal with and the innkeeper's wife was as cruel as her husband. But there was one.

There had been a skinny waif of a girl, abandoned by her parents when they could no longer afford her. Sacharissa. Arcturus had taken her under his wing, teaching her the ways of the workhouse. They spent their nights together, sharing body heat in their freezing cot and talking about the lives they would make for themselves when they were older. But it was not to be. She had died of pneumonia a year later.

'Sacharissa,' Arcturus whispered. He felt the sting of tears in his eyes but wiped them away, furious with himself.

'It is a good name,' Elizabeth said softly. She let him have a moment to gather his emotions, then spoke again.

'I have a feeling you will need a weapon,' she said, rummaging in a pack at the back of her saddle. She removed a blade, still in its sheath. The scabbard was beautiful, the outer edge inlaid with gold and the leather embossed with the whorls and symbols of a summoner. She knelt at his feet and secured it to his left boot, for it came with two leather belts attached. Arcturus heard the scrape of metal as Elizabeth grinned at him and withdrew the

26

blade. It was too long to be a dagger and too small to be a sword, but it felt good in his grip when she handed it to him. He gave it a practise swing, feeling the balance of the weapon.

'This is a dirk. When you battle with an orc shaman's demon in the sky, you need a blade long enough to do some damage, but with enough speed and manoeuvrability to defend yourself from all sides – an attack can come from any angle. This is the perfect compromise. For a young boy like you, it will do just fine.'

She mounted Hubertus as he gazed at his weapon. It was an expensive piece, beautiful in its design and sharp enough to shave with. He wondered at Elizabeth's generosity. Nobody had ever given him anything before – and he definitely had never owned something so precious.

He only realised she was leaving when he felt the breeze from Hubertus's wingbeats against his face.

'There is greatness in you, Arcturus,' Elizabeth called, her voice almost snatched away by the wind. 'Remember what I told you!'

Arcturus watched until she faded into the darkness of the sky, wishing he had thanked her.

Then he set his jaw and turned to the double doors.

'Well,' he said, laying his hand on the box beside him. 'Let's get started.'

5

Arcturus stabbed his dirk into the crack on the edge of the box and heaved. The wood creaked under the strain, then the nails gave way and the lid crashed to the ground.

There was a low growl from inside before Sacharissa bounded out. Her fur stood on end and she snarled, spinning in a circle to scope out her surroundings. It was only when she saw Arcturus that she calmed, snuffling at his feet before lapping his hand with a rough, wet tongue.

'It's OK, Sacha. The Favershams won't hurt us here. Not if I can help it.' Arcturus brandished his dirk so she could see the blade, then slipped it back into the scabbard on his boot.

A cloud drifted across the moon, casting the courtyard in a shroud of darkness. Arcturus could barely make out the doors, but he stumbled up the stairs regardless, his hands outstretched in front of him. Sacharissa followed behind, bumping against his shins in her attempts to keep close by.

Before he could knock on the doors, they swung open unexpectedly. The inside was brightly lit and he shielded his eyes as a figure stepped out brandishing a torch. Arcturus gaped when his eyes adjusted to the glare. It was a dwarf.

Of course Arcturus had heard of the dwarves, though they were rarely seen in the north of Hominum, where he had grown up. This one appeared almost exactly as he had imagined, standing as tall as his midriff. The dwarf was stockily built, as all his people were, with long, red hair kept in a ponytail and a braided moustache and beard. He wore a simple servant's uniform, plain green with a red sash around the middle.

'Welcome to Vocans, my lord,' the dwarf said in a deep, respectful voice. 'Please, come in out of the cold.'

Arcturus did as he asked, speechless. Sacharissa gave the dwarf a suspicious sniff before entering, then sat protectively beside Arcturus.

'I see you already have a Canid. A fine specimen, if you don't mind me saying so.' The dwarf held out a thick, calloused finger for the demon to sniff. Sacharissa snorted disdainfully and flicked her tail, then walked further into the castle.

The room they were in was an enormous hall, with identical winding staircases on either side. They stopped at intervals on five levels, each one complete with a long balcony bordered by gilded metal railings. The ceiling was supported by giant oak beams, and Arcturus could see a dome of glass in the very centre that would allow natural light to illuminate the room in the daytime. All around the walls were sconced torches, casting pools of flickering light that made the marble floor look like shifting water.

'We call it the atrium. Beautiful, isn't it?' the dwarf said proudly.

'It is,' Arcturus breathed. At the very end of the hall, there was another set of doors, just as large as those behind him. But it was the archway above that took his breath away, for it was intricately carved with the twisting figures of a hundred or more demons.

Their eyes were set with a myriad of glittering jewels, and the shifting shadows of the torchlight made it appear as if the creatures were alive. He tried to spot a Canid like Sacharissa among them, but it was near impossible, given the countless species that danced along the stonework.

'Come with me, my lord. I have to take you to your quarters. Most of the other nobles are sleeping, but you'll get a chance to meet them in the morning. Do you have baggage?' the dwarf asked.

'No baggage,' Arcturus said, spinning to show the dwarf his rucksack. 'But hang on, I'm not a—'

'Follow me,' the dwarf interrupted, before he could finish. 'And keep your demon quiet if you please – we wouldn't want to wake anyone.'

The dwarf led him up the east staircase, holding the torch aloft to light their way. They continued to the top floor, though Arcturus caught tantalising glimpses of tapestries and paintings as they passed each level. He was disappointed to find the walls relatively bare when they finally left the staircase and made their way down a long corridor, but was fascinated by the suits of armour that lined the way. The occasional crumpled breastplate or crushed helmet revealed that they had once seen battle, and he realised with a gulp that he might someday face the creatures that had broken them. Sacharissa sensed his fear and began to whine, but he settled her with a scratch behind the ears.

Once or twice he saw orcish javelins and arrowheads, preserved on velvet cushions behind glass cabinets, but the dwarf walked surprisingly fast for one with such short legs, and Arcturus could not pause to examine them further. After what seemed an age, the dwarf stopped by a door and pushed it open.

'I will let the Provost know you have arrived. Your uniform is on the bed, although I know most of you like to have a tailor make a fresh one. Still, it's there if you need it. If you require anything else, ask for me, Ulfr. I'll do my best to assist you.' Before Arcturus could open his mouth, Ulfr had ushered him inside and closed the door behind him.

The room was enormous, almost the size of the stable Arcturus had worked in, with high ceilings and a chandelier lit by a ring of thin candles. The walls were lined with awnings of red and gold, and the carpet beneath his feet was a deep, white shag that Sacharissa immediately began to roll around on, rubbing her back against the fabric.

The bed was a king-sized four-poster, with a mattress so thick and plush that it would be difficult to climb into. Arcturus wasted no time in diving across it, revelling in the springy bounce and the silky, satin sheets.

'Up you come, Sacharissa. There's room for both of us,' Arcturus laughed, patting the space beside him. Sacharissa yapped with excitement, bounding on to the bed in one fluid leap. Her feet caught in the uniform at the foot of the bed, and Arcturus untangled it and held it up for them to inspect.

'Fancy,' Arcturus said. The jacket was double-breasted, made from a deep-blue velvet and held in place by shining gold buttons. It looked too showy to be a military uniform, but then Arcturus was no expert and Elizabeth's clothing had been just as ornate. He let his feet dangle off the side of the bed and undressed, before shrugging on the uniform. He was pleasantly surprised to find that it fit him well and the material was as soft as the bed sheets he sat on.

'I could get used to this,' he murmured, rubbing Sacharissa under the chin. Life wasn't so bad after all.

The echo of footsteps from outside disturbed his thoughts, then the door slammed open. This time, it wasn't a dwarf.

A man stood in the doorway, so tall and brawny that he had to stoop to enter. He was resplendent in the red uniform of a General, with tasselled epaulettes on his shoulders and rows of medals pinned to his chest. His hair was made up of blond curls, which tumbled across his shoulders in an aureate mane. The man was smiling when he stepped into the room, but as soon as he laid eyes on Arcturus he froze. His face was handsome, with chiselled features and a square jaw, but it turned ugly as it twisted into a furious scowl.

'Ulfr!' the man bellowed, balling his hands into fists. 'Come here, immediately.'

'What is it, Lord Forsyth?' Ulfr asked, scurrying in behind him. He kept his eyes low and gave a half bow as Forsyth turned on him.

'Why is this peasant in Charles Faversham's room?' Forsyth's voice was deep and threatening.

'Is he . . . but he . . .' Ulfr stuttered, his eyes flicking nervously from Arcturus to Forsyth.

'But nothing!' Forsyth growled, grasping the dwarf by his

beard and lifting him so he had to stand on tiptoes.

'Hang on a minute,' Arcturus interjected, standing up. 'I didn't tell him who I was—'

'I'll deal with you in a minute,' Forsyth snarled, his grey eyes flashing with anger. Arcturus fell silent, lost for words. The venom in the man's voice had turned his insides cold.

'My lord, it was an accident. You told me Charles would be arriving tonight, so I assumed . . .' Ulfr trailed off.

'You assumed this filthy urchin was the son and heir to Lord and Lady Faversham, did you?' Lord Forsyth said, lifting the dwarf still higher.

Suddenly, he hit the dwarf across the head, grunting with effort. There was a sickening crack of knuckles against skull and Ulfr sprawled across the carpet.

'Hey!' Arcturus yelled, rushing to Ulfr's side. The blow would have knocked the senses from any human, but the dwarf was only stunned for a moment, before cradling his head in pain.

'A halfwit and a half-man. Though the two often go hand in hand.' Forsyth laughed, rubbing his hand. Arcturus recognised the racist term 'half-man' and felt disgusted. Sacharissa gave a low growl as she felt his anger and padded towards Forsyth, but Arcturus calmed her with a thought. He did not want to make the situation any worse.

'When you've recovered your wits – if you had any to begin with – take the peasant to the empty room at the top of the north-eastern tower,' Forsyth commanded. He swept out of the room without a backwards glance.

'Are you OK?' Arcturus asked, trying to lift Ulfr to his feet.

'Get off me, human,' the dwarf barked. Arcturus released him as if he had been stung.

'And you wonder why the dwarves rebel against you so often,' Ulfr muttered bitterly, rubbing his temple. Already, a large lump was forming on the side of his head.

Arcturus understood the hatred that dwarves felt towards humans, for even he knew how the humans had overthrown the dwarves millennia ago, reducing them to second-class citizens in their own homeland.

'I'm not like him,' Arcturus whispered.

'There's nobody like Obadiah Forsyth,' Ulfr replied, hauling himself to his feet. 'But he is the black to your grey. In the end, you are all stained with the evil that is the human condition.'

Arcturus bit back a retort and started gathering his things together. Ulfr was already walking out of the room when he had finished.

'I hope there's a bed where we're going,' Arcturus said, tugging a reluctant Sacharissa behind him. She clearly didn't want to leave the plush carpet in Charles's room.

'It has all the essentials. It's where the Provost sends students as a punishment if they break the rules. Solitary confinement and all that,' Ulfr replied, turning into another stairwell at the end of the corridor.

'What's a Provost?' Arcturus's voice echoed in the tight confines of the staircase.

'A headmaster of sorts. He runs the academy, decides who graduates and sets the curriculum. You might say he's the highest authority at Vocans.'

'When do I get to meet him?' Arcturus asked. Ulfr ignored

him and turned into an empty chamber with two doors. He took him down the left one and they entered a narrow corridor.

'Storage rooms,' Ulfr grunted, pointing at the identical doors on either side. He pushed open a door at the very end and showed Arcturus a bare room with a thin pallet bed in the corner, with a simple desk and cabinet crammed against the far wall. An arrow slit allowed a cold gust of wind into the room and Arcturus felt the hair on his arms stiffen with gooseflesh.

'Home sweet home. If you need anything, keep it to yourself. I'm paid to serve the noble-born children, not freaks like you. Common summoners. It's not natural!' Ulfr shook his head and began to walk away.

'I want to tell the Provost how poorly the servants are treated here. When do I get to meet him?' Arcturus asked again, hoping to make peace with the dwarf.

Ulfr turned and gave Arcturus a bitter laugh.

'You've already met him. The Provost is Obadiah Forsyth.'

6

Arcturus woke feeling refreshed, despite the cold draughts of wind that gusted through the glassless window. Sacharissa had wrapped herself around him like a musty fur coat, keeping him warm and comfortable all night.

She whined in complaint as he extricated himself from her embrace and stood shivering in the room. He yanked the threadbare blanket from beneath her and wrapped it around his shoulders.

'Come on, lazybones, we're going to go find the baths and get ourselves cleaned up. First impressions are important.'

Sacharissa rolled over, then blinked her four eyes at him sorrowfully.

'None of that,' Arcturus grinned. 'Your puppy-dog act won't do you any favours here.'

She snorted with feigned annoyance, before padding to the door and nudging it open with her nose.

Arcturus followed her out into the corridor, past the storerooms and down the stairs. She snuffled at the ground, as if she was hunting for something.

'I hope you're not taking me to the kitchens,' Arcturus murmured, trailing behind her. 'We need to find the baths.'

As if she could sense his meaning, she turned and looked at him. When his eyes met hers, he felt the connection between them flare, and for a brief moment his senses swam with a new awareness. Sounds became more acute, smells were intense and vivid. Only his vision suffered, the blue-white light of the morning outside turning into shades of grey and shifting strangely in front of his eyes.

He staggered at the sensation, steadying himself on the wall. As quickly as it came, the feeling left him, but not before he sensed the scent that Sacharissa was tracking. Water.

'Lead on,' Arcturus smiled, shooing her forward. He grinned, relishing the memory of his new power. It was fascinating to learn that Sacharissa might not be able to see colours. Who knew?

She turned down the spiral staircase, taking him to the atrium while snuffling at the ground. It was obviously still early, for the castle was as lifeless and silent as a tomb, so he almost jumped out of his skin when a voice hailed him from the balconies above.

'Arcturus!' Obadiah Forsyth snapped, his face peering over the metal railing from the floor above him. 'Who gave you permission to leave your quarters?'

Before Arcturus could answer, Obadiah's head disappeared and footsteps echoed in the stairwell behind. He emerged red-faced, an accusatory finger pointed at Arcturus like a weapon.

'Sir, I am sorry, I needed to use the facilities,' Arcturus said, layering his voice with as much respect as he could. 'I did not mean to break any rules.'

It was an almost automatic response, for he had learned from his time with the innkeeper that deference could save him from a beating, or worse. It had the desired effect, for Obadiah paused mid-stride.

'Well . . . I guess that is a fair excuse,' he grunted begrudgingly, dropping his hand to his side, before walking around Arcturus, examining him.

Arcturus lowered his head and watched Obadiah through half-closed lashes, ready for any sudden moves. Instead, the noble lifted Arcturus's chin with a knuckle and nodded approvingly.

'Well, I'm pleased that you know to respect your elders. And betters for that matter,' Obadiah said, laying a hand on his shoulder and propelling him away from the doorway.

'Your morning ablutions shall have to wait. The king has asked me to find out what level of summoner you are. Come with me.'

Arcturus bit back a groan and followed Obadiah up the stairs. Sacharissa pattered behind them, whining as she sensed Arcturus's agitation. After a moment, Obadiah spun on his heel and kicked at Sacharissa, but she skipped out of the way with a growl.

'If you can't control your demon's infernal noise, I will shut her up for good,' Obadiah snarled.

'Sacharissa, stay,' Arcturus said hastily, pointing at the ground. She cocked her head at him, as if to ask, Are you sure?

'Be a good do—' he caught himself, '. . . demon, and wait

here for me. I'm sure it won't take long.'

She stared at him pitifully, then settled down and laid her head on her front paws.

'Good girl,' Arcturus said. Obadiah grunted, then continued on down the corridor.

They walked for a few minutes in silence, before curiosity overcame Arcturus's fear.

'What do you mean by "level"?'

'Different species of demons have different levels of demonic energy. For example, a Canid is a level-seven demon. That means, to have been able to summon her, you are at least a level-seven summoner,' Obadiah replied, without turning around.

Arcturus realised they were heading towards the south-west tower. As they turned into what Arcturus expected to be a stairwell leading to the top of the tower, they entered a large circular chamber with a ceiling that stretched hundreds of feet above them to the roof of the tower.

In the centre of the room was a strange column, made up of different segments of multicoloured crystals. It was so tall it reached the very top of the room, and Arcturus had to crane his neck to see the tip of it.

'Put your hand against the fulfilmeter,' Obadiah ordered, then pushed Arcturus to his knees before he could respond. He seized Arcturus's hand and pressed it against the cool gemstones.

Immediately, Arcturus felt something sucked out of him, flowing through his hand. It felt cool as ice and to his surprise, he could see a cobalt-blue glow around the edges of his palm.

'What you are feeling now is your mana being sucked into the fulfilmeter.'

'M-mana?' Arcturus stuttered. He could feel it roiling in his blood, cold under his skin.

'Yes, mana is the power you use when performing a spell. You will learn more about that soon, perhaps today if you keep your ears open.'

The last of the mana drained out of him, then the flow was reversed. But this was very different. It was hot and violent, a sharp contrast to what he had experienced just a moment earlier.

'Demonic energy, what all demons are made from. The more you can absorb, the higher your fulfilment level,' Obadiah murmured, tightening his grip on Arcturus's wrist.

The segment of gemstone Arcturus was touching lit up with a hum. The others above lit up soon after, each one emitting a dull thrum as they did so. Seven times the room flashed with new light, then the humming began to slow. It was just as well, for Arcturus felt full to the brim with the caustic energy. It felt like he was boiling from the inside out. Just as he thought it was over, the eighth segment flickered into life.

'A level-eight summoner,' Obadiah said, with a hint of surprise in his voice. 'That is . . . above average . . . especially for a summoner as young and as new to his demon as you. The usual for an untrained noble who has just arrived at the academy is seven, which is what I assumed you would be. I find this very interesting. I'm sure the king will share that sentiment.'

'What does it mean?' Arcturus said, massaging his wrist as Obadiah released him. He felt a flash of dread. Would it have been better if he were a weaker summoner?

'It means that you are unusual only in that you are a commoner, neither too high nor too low in level. You fall within the normal range of what we can expect from a novice. It also means that you could summon a level-one demon, such as a Mite, on top of your level-seven Canid. Of course, as you train in the various arts of summoning, your fulfilment level will improve over time, and you will be capable of summoning more powerful demons.'

Arcturus relaxed. Normal was good. He was unusual enough, without being something the king might see as a threat. As Obadiah began to lead him out of the room, Arcturus couldn't resist one more question.

'A Mite?'

Obadiah gave an exasperated sigh, then turned back to him. He reached into his pocket and pulled out a roll of leather. As he unravelled it, Arcturus realised it was identical to the leather mat he had found in Charles's saddlebags, a brown square with a black pentacle embossed on both sides. Obadiah dropped it to the floor and touched the leather with his fingertip.

The pentacle flared with violet light, just as it had in the stables. This time, instead of an orb expanding above, ethereal strands of white light blossomed from the glowing symbol, merging together like threads on a tapestry. It was not long until an insect-like form materialised and the glowing white faded to reveal the true colours beneath.

The demon looked like a giant beetle, so large it would barely fit on a man's hand. Its carapace was a dark red colour, with a sting not unlike a bee's on its behind and a pair of sharp mandibles that clashed as it stared at Arcturus through two black eyes. With a flutter of insectile wings, it buzzed into the air, before settling on Obadiah's shoulder.

41

'Beautiful, isn't he?' Obadiah said, stroking the Mite's shell. 'Rubens is one of my weaker demons, but perhaps the most useful. He's my eyes and ears at Vocans – step one toe out of line and he'll come straight back to me. Unless I've already seen it of course.'

He reached into his pocket once again and pulled out a shard of crystal. It was flat, like a broken piece of glass, yet Arcturus could see the room reflected on the polished surface. Obadiah tapped it on the Mite's shell and held it out for Arcturus to see. For a moment Arcturus thought he was looking at a piece of mirror, but as Rubens buzzed into the air, he realised that the image on the crystal was exactly what the beetle demon was seeing.

'The scrying stone and summoning leather are the two most important items in a summoner's tool chest,' Obadiah lectured, pocketing the crystal and rolling the leather up once again. 'Your demon usually resides within your body and can be summoned into existence, then infused back into you using the leather. The scrying stone lets you share your demon's senses, including sound and smell, though you need to look at the stone to be able to see what they do. Of course you will only be able to see black and white with yours. Canids and their various cousins are all colour blind.'

Arcturus smiled, glad to confirm his suspicions. Still, it was strange that he had been able to do it, if briefly, without a stone at all. He would have to investigate that later. The fact that Sacharissa could somehow be 'infused' into his body filled him with both excitement and apprehension. Could that really be possible?

'Right, that's enough for one day. I'm your Provost, not your teacher,' Obadiah said, shaking his head as if surprised he had shared so much.

'Thank you, Lord Forsyth,' Arcturus said, holding out his hand. 'I look forward to learning more. May I ask, would it be possible for you to take me back to Sacharissa and then show me how to find the baths?'

'I'm not your servant, insolent boy,' Obadiah snapped, ignoring the hand and stamping out of the room. 'We can collect your demon because it's on the way, but there's no time for a bath now – you'll have to wait until later. It's breakfast time. All the students are there. It's time for you to meet them . . .'

7

Obadiah led Arcturus to the dining hall, taking him into the atrium and beneath the carved archway. Sacharissa paced protectively beside them, sniffing with excitement as they passed through the doors and the scent of food pervaded the air.

The room was filled with low stone tables, surrounded by a dozen servants who scurried around with platters of food. Some of them were dwarves with thick braided beards and long ponytails. Ulfr was among them, marked out by a purple bruise that must have blossomed on his forehead overnight.

An enormous statue dominated the centre of the room: an armoured man with a powerful build and short beard. His stony gaze seemed to fix on Arcturus, following him as he walked deeper into the room. The level of detail was extraordinary, as if a giant had been turned to stone.

Despite the size of the dining hall, only a few tables were occupied, with an assortment of boys and girls who had turned to stare at them. Arcturus could see bacon and eggs piled high, the rich scent filling his nostrils and flooding his mouth with saliva.

'Good morning, students,' Obadiah said, striding ahead of Arcturus to stand beside them. He paused, looking at them expectantly.

'Good morning, Provost Forsyth, sir,' the students echoed back dutifully, though the tone was one of exasperation rather than respect.

'I would like to introduce you to our newest student . . .' He paused and Arcturus realised that Charles Faversham was seated with the others, staring at him with hatred in his eyes. 'Ah, I see that Charles has arrived at last. Has he filled you in?'

There were several nods from the table and Obadiah smiled.

'In that case, I shall give you a brief summary of the events that have led to a commoner joining Vocans. On his way here, Charles mislaid his summoning scroll. It was stolen by young Arcturus here.'

Charles shifted in his seat uncomfortably before shooting Arcturus another malicious look. Arcturus realised that the young noble must have neglected to mention that part in his version of the story. Obadiah didn't seem to notice Charles's embarrassment and carried on blithely.

'By some quirk of nature, he was able to summon the demon Lord Faversham had captured for Charles. After proper interrogation, King Alfric decided that it would be in Hominum's best interest to train the boy.'

One of the nobles stood up, a tall, heavyset lad with a square jaw and a cap of blond curls.

'Father, how is this possible?' the boy asked, giving Arcturus a disdainful look. 'The gift is passed through the blood, it is not some randomly occurring ability.'

'Do not interrupt, Zacharias,' Obadiah said mildly, pushing him back into his seat. 'But you have cut right to the heart of the matter. King Alfric has posed that very question to me. In fact, I have another announcement to make. I will be leaving Vocans as Provost, short though my tenure has been here. The king has requested that I lead an investigation, to find out whether Arcturus is a freak or if there are others like him out there.'

Arcturus looked from Obadiah to Zacharias, suddenly seeing the family resemblance between them. The Provost's son's face had become crestfallen, before twisting into a scowl as his eyes fell on Arcturus.

'Being Provost is far more important. This task is beneath you, Father,' Zacharias muttered.

'You think you know better than your king?' Obadiah asked, giving his son a withering look. 'Prince Harold, why do you think your father has sent me away?'

Arcturus's heart leaped in his chest as a pale-haired boy with piercing grey eyes stood. His brow was ringed by a silver circlet, studded with rubies. The king's own son was studying at the academy.

'Lord Forsyth, the reasons are threefold. The first is that in the last dwarven rebellion, the noble families suffered several deaths, and this could happen again if the ongoing altercations with the orcs become any worse. With commoners to swell our ranks, we will be able to take fewer risks, giving the more dangerous missions to them.'

Charles smiled at the prince's words and whispered in Zacharias's ear. Arcturus heard the words 'meat shields'.

'Very good, Harold. The second?'

'With commoners capable of summoning demons, they become a threat to us. By keeping them close, we limit their ability to cause us harm.' The prince spoke matter-of-factly, though he avoided Arcturus's gaze, as if ashamed of his words. 'This threat has grown of late, ever since my father increased taxes to cover our recent expenses.'

'Excellent! Now, explain the most obvious reason to my idiot son so he learns to keep his trap shut,' Obadiah said, narrowing his eyes at his son. Zacharias's face flushed red and he twisted his hands in his lap.

'A commoner being able to summon means that there may be a way to give the ability to a person who cannot. Therefore, it is possible that we can make all noble children summoners, rather than just the firstborn. We already know that this is possible, given that the Lord and Lady Lovett's second, third and fourth born children are summoners, which was highly improbable. We just don't know why it has happened. Perhaps the commoners are the key to finding out.'

Harold glanced down the table at a group of four students sitting a little apart from everyone else. Three were dark-haired boys of varying ages, while the other was a younger girl with long black tresses and round grey eyes that gazed at Arcturus with frank curiosity. He remembered King Alfric had mentioned the Lovett family, accusing them of paying Arcturus to steal the summoning scroll on their behalf. If he remembered correctly, it had something to do with not having enough demons for all of their children.

'I hope that this is reason enough. Now, Lord Goodwin will be leaving his role as your spellcraft teacher. We will bring in a new teacher to replace him.'

There was an audible sigh from the table, though whether that was because Lord Goodwin was popular or unpopular was unclear.

'Arcturus, please join your fellow students. After your first lesson, come and see me. There are some questions I must ask you before I leave.' With those parting words, Obadiah spun on his heel and strode out of the room.

Arcturus stood for a moment, cringing under the gaze of the nobles. There was a gap between the Lovetts and Zacharias, so he squeezed in and spooned some bacon on to his plate. Sacharissa installed herself beneath the table, searching the floor for food that might have fallen.

'Something reeks,' Zacharias complained, shifting away from him. 'Is it the Canid or the pleb?'

'Both,' Charles said gleefully, pinching his nose with his fingers. 'They smell exactly the same. Like wet dog.'

'Dog breath. That's what we should call him. Much better than Arcticunus, or whatever it was,' Zacharias laughed, and Charles snorted, spraying the table with egg. Another boy joined in with them, a sallow-faced noble with lank black hair tied in a ponytail.

'Good one, Zach,' the sallow noble guffawed, slapping Zacharias on the back.

'Oh, leave him alone,' Prince Harold moaned, rolling his eyes at the bullies. 'Last time we went hawking together, you three smelled twice as ripe, especially after the hike back. Sweating like pigs you were.'

Arcturus smiled gratefully at the prince, realising the young royal was very unlike his father. Harold gave him an apologetic shrug and went back to his meal. The other three glowered at him, but Arcturus ignored them and began to eat, trying to stop himself from demolishing it like a wild animal.

It had been a while since he had last put food in his belly, and though he was used to hunger, he knew he needed to keep his strength up for the challenging days ahead.

Both at the workhouse and inn, his meals had been made up of stale bread, watered-down gruel and bruised fruit. He had only tasted bacon once, when the innkeeper had allowed him table scraps from an unfinished meal instead of feeding them to the pigs.

As for eggs, he wasn't even sure how to eat them, and was forced to take furtive looks at the others as they mopped up the golden yolk with hunks of buttered toast.

It was not long before the rest of the table began to talk amongst themselves. Arcturus was keenly aware of the fact that he still needed to wash, especially after the comments the others had made. He looked up from his food, wondering if there was time to go before the others had finished breakfast.

A fair-skinned boy with scruffy black hair sat across from Arcturus. He noticed Arcturus's gaze and leaned forward.

'Edmund Raleigh,' the boy said, offering a firm handshake. 'We've all known one another since we were toddlers, so don't worry if some of the conversation goes over your head. Let me introduce you to everyone. You've already met Charles, Zach and Harold. The boy on the end with the ponytail is Damian, but everyone calls him Rook. It's his surname.'

'Like the chess piece, not the bird,' Rook said, then wrinkled his nose. 'You probably don't know what chess is anyway.'

Edmund pulled a face at him, and turned to two girls on his right. 'This is Alice, and this is Josephine, from the Queensouth family. Don't bother trying to tell the difference between them, you'll just get confused.'

'Hello!' the girls chorused. They were twins, with long blonde hair and large expressive eyes, giving them a doll-like appearance. Edmund was right, they were almost identical. But the one Edmund had introduced as Alice had given Arcturus a bright smile before going back to her meal. Edmund wrapped his arm around her and kissed her on the cheek.

'We're sweethearts, so don't get any ideas.' He winked, before turning to the remaining students to his left.

'This is Baybars Saladin, the fiercest swordsman you'll ever meet,' Raleigh continued, pointing to a dark-skinned boy beside him. The boy gave him a polite nod before returning to his meal.

'As you've probably guessed, these four are the Lovetts. This is Fergus, Carter, Arthur—'

'And I'm Elaine!' the girl piped up, beaming up at Arcturus. 'I love your demon! Is it a boy or a girl?'

'A girl – her name is Sacharissa.' Arcturus smiled at her. She looked too young to be a summoner, no older than thirteen. Most joined Vocans at Arcturus's age, fifteen years old. Perhaps her parents had sent her there early, to be with her brothers.

'She's so cute!' Elaine said, snatching some bacon from the table and holding it out for Sacharissa to eat. The demon immediately forgot her animosity to everyone who wasn't Arcturus, and lapped it up greedily.

'Elaine, that's not polite,' said Fergus, the oldest of the Lovett boys.

'Oh, all right. You're such a worrywart, Fergus,' Elaine moaned, before sneaking a rasher from Arcturus's plate and dropping it surreptitiously to the floor. A few seconds later, Arcturus heard snuffling and chomping from under the table.

'That's OK. She's barely eaten in days. I wasn't even sure that demons ate our food.'

'Gosh, you do have a lot to learn,' Edmund laughed, standing up. 'Good thing you're here! Come on. It's time for our first lesson of the year. Let's find out who our new spellcraft teacher is.'

8

Arcturus was expecting them to lead him up one of the winding staircases when they left the dining hall, but instead they only took a few steps out into the atrium where the others stopped and began to talk among themselves. It was very dark in the room, for the servants had yet to light the torches. The only source of light came from the dining hall behind them, and a broad column of sunlight from the glass dome embedded in the atrium's ceiling.

As he wondered at the darkness of the room, the other students pointed their fingers into the air, releasing balls of strange blue light that floated around the room, drifting this way and that as if they had a life of their own. They cast a dull cobalt glow in the darkness of the atrium, shifting the shadows and illuminating the gloomy cavern above their heads.

It was the first time Arcturus had seen a spell, and he gazed as the strange blue lights glided around the darkness like overgrown fireflies. He stared at his own fingers, wondering if he would ever be capable of creating such wonders. Sarcharissa whined, frustrated at his lack of attention. He tore his eyes away from the spectacle and put his hands to better use.

'What happens now? Shouldn't we be getting to the lesson?' Arcturus asked, rubbing Sacharissa's head.

'This *is* where all the spellcraft lessons are,' Elaine replied, crouching in front of Sacharissa and examining her with interest. 'I love her eyes – they're so blue! Can I pet her?' she asked, reaching out a hand.

'Elaine!' her brother Fergus snapped, jerking her away. 'You know you're not supposed to touch another person's demon!'

'Why not?' Arcturus asked, wide-eyed.

'It would be . . . unbecoming,' Fergus said, his face reddening. Even as he said it, Arcturus could feel the waves of satisfaction from Sacharissa as he scratched her between the ears. Fergus was right. It would be strange if Elaine were to do the same. It was too personal – touching another person's demon was almost like touching *them*.

'Sorry . . .' Elaine said, kicking the ground with the toe of her boots.

'Cheer up, I'm only looking out for you. You're far too young and even if you weren't, well . . . it's a commoner's demon.' Fergus frowned. 'No offence,' he added hastily.

Now it was Arcturus's turn to redden.

'None taken,' he replied, though his insides seethed with anger.

'Why don't you play with Valens? You only got him yesterday,' Edmund interrupted, strolling over from the others and giving Arcturus a sympathetic smile.

'I thought we're only allowed to have our demons out in lessons,' Elaine said, sticking out her bottom lip.

'Well, the teacher's late, but the lesson's started. I'm sure they won't mind, whoever they are,' Edmund replied.

She looked to Fergus for permission, who rolled his eyes before giving her an exasperated nod.

Arcturus tried to look disinterested but took a surreptitious step closer. A new demon – now that was worth seeing.

'Brilliant!' she grinned, before reaching into her pocket and pulling out a Mite, half the size of Obadiah's Rubens and brown as an autumn leaf, yet clearly of the same species.

'Hey, you're supposed to have him infused, not just out of sight!' Fergus remonstrated.

'What's the point of having the smallest demon here if I can't hide him in my pocket? Come on, Valens, let's practise hunting!' Elaine giggled, letting the demon fly from her palm to hover in front of her face.

Hunting . . . why would Valens need to practise that?

Arcturus couldn't help but smile as Elaine capered around the room, leaping and dodging as she and her Mite, Valens, played a strange game of tag.

As she neared the front doors, they blasted open and swung against the stone walls, sending Elaine scurrying back to the others.

For a moment Arcturus's heart leaped when he saw a Peryton outlined against the harsh light from outside, but his joy was short-lived as he recognised the icy beauty who sat astride it.

'Oh no,' Arcturus muttered, shuffling behind Fergus and Edmund.

Lady Faversham clopped into the room, her back ramrod straight as she surveyed the students. She dismounted, before slapping her Peryton's rump, sending it swooping back out of the front doors in a thunder of beating wings.

'So many familiar faces. It brings me such joy to see you all again,' Lady Faversham said, though her cold eyes showed only disdain as they skipped over Arcturus and the Lovetts.

'Aunt Ophelia,' Prince Harold said, walking over and shaking her hand. 'I had no idea you would be our replacement! Welcome to Vocans.'

Aunt? So the Favershams were closely related to the king. Arcturus knew it was only the king's curiosity that kept him safe. If Lady Faversham were able to convince him otherwise, Arcturus was as good as dead.

'I'm not your only teacher, Harold. I have brought an assistant teacher, Lieutenant Elizabeth Cavendish. She has managed to get herself pregnant by a common servant, so she might as well make herself useful. She can teach the youngster,' she nodded at Elaine, 'and the commoner. The rest of you are already far too advanced, so we will focus on the four battle spells of shield, lightning, fire and telekinesis in my classes. Please stand in a line over there.'

'Golly, she's something,' Arcturus heard Edmund whisper as they hurried to do her bidding. 'She's not even unpacked and she's already getting started.'

A second Peryton swooped through the front doors, wheeling around the atrium before landing with a clatter of hooves beside Lady Faversham. Elizabeth grinned at Arcturus, before dismounting and sending Hubertus out again with a click of her tongue.

'Elizabeth, take the little one and the common boy to the

summoning room and teach them the basics. I shall remain with the older students.'

'I'm not a *little* one,' Elaine pouted, scowling at Lady Faversham. 'I'm thirteen years old. Me and Arcturus should stay!'

The noblewoman's nostrils flared, but before she could respond, Elizabeth swiftly took Elaine by the arm and led her through a set of heavy doors a few steps away. Clearly, Lady Faversham did not take kindly to being contradicted.

'You too,' she snapped, clicking her fingers at Arcturus, 'and infuse your demon while you're at it. Don't you know you're not allowed your demon out other than in your room and in lessons? If I catch you again, I'll have you sent to the punishment room to think about what you've done.'

'I don't know how to infuse my demon yet,' Arcturus replied matter-of-factly, 'and the bedroom I've been given *is* the punishment room.'

Lady Faversham's eyes narrowed and she took a step towards him. Arcturus met her gaze as calmly as he could, though his heart thundered in his chest. Sacharissa bumped her side against his thigh, but he calmed her with a thought before she could let out a growl.

'I don't like your tone, boy,' she snarled, jabbing her finger at him. 'You will call me ma'am when you speak to me. Is that understood?'

'Yes, *ma'am*. Should I go now, *ma'am*? I wouldn't want to keep Lieutenant Cavendish waiting, *ma'am*.'

'Get out,' she hissed, pointing at the door, 'and take that stinking mongrel with you.'

Arcturus hurried to the summoning room, his courage suddenly failing him. He had been stupid to speak to her that way for she held all the power and he had none. But it had felt good to fight back. *Give as good as you get,* that was what Elizabeth had told him.

As he and Sacharissa passed by Lady Faversham, she darted forward and drew him closer, so he could feel her hot breath on his ear.

'The king's curiosity will only last so long,' Lady Faversham whispered. 'When it fades, I'll have the skin whipped from your hide, and more besides.'

Arcturus tore himself away, trying to stop himself from sprinting out of the room.

'See you later, Dog Breath!' Rook called after him.

9

Arcturus stumbled into the summoning room, slamming the door behind him. He leaned against it with his eyes closed, taking a deep breath. Sacharissa nuzzled him and he slid down, burying his face in her fur. He waited until his heartbeat returned to normal, and after a few moments, he lifted his head to find a bemused-looking Elizabeth watching him.

'You know, when I said stand up for yourself, I didn't mean to the teachers!' she chuckled, walking towards him. 'Lady Faversham is the king's cousin, not to mention that her husband is the king's best friend . . . well, second best, after Provost Forsyth. Then again, it's not like she was particularly fond of you to begin with, what with you taking her son's demon.'

'I had to show everyone I have a backbone. Who better to make an example of than Lady Faversham?' Arcturus said, more to himself than to Elizabeth.

'Let's just hope she doesn't make an example out of you,' Elizabeth whispered softly, lifting him to his feet.

The summoning room had a high ceiling, with heavy oak

floorboards covered in a spiral of pentacles, varying in size and shape, from the size of a man's hand to twice the length of a horse. There were lockers lining the walls on either side, and Arcturus could see leather gloves and aprons on hangars inside. The only source of light came from flickering torches in embrasures above the lockers, giving the room a smokey scent.

'Elaine tells me her brothers got most of the attention when her father taught summoning and you're completely new to all this, so I think it only right I give you both a crash course in summoning,' Elizabeth said, sending a blue ball of light into the air and allowing it to float aimlessly around the room. Elaine was sitting cross-legged on the floor, stroking Valens's carapace.

'Elaine, please explain to Arcturus how to create a wyrdlight,' Elizabeth asked, crouching in front of the young girl.

Elaine groaned and sent Valens fluttering into the air, then scrambled to her feet.

'Every demon has a source of *mana* within them. Mana is the power source for all spells and every demon has a different amount, depending on their species.' She spoke in a bored voice, as if reciting from a textbook. Arcturus stared in rapt attention, trying to memorise as much as he could. If King Alfric considered him a threat he might need to escape from Vocans and go on the run.

'A wyrdlight is just a ball of raw mana. The summoner must transfer mana from the demon to their own body via a mental link, then push the mana through their finger, like so,' Elizabeth continued, brandishing a finger in the air. For a moment, nothing happened, and Arcturus wondered whether she knew what she was doing. Then, in the blink of an eye, there was a blast of light that illuminated the ceiling above her, beaming from her finger.

'The summoner must then control the mana and make it into a ball. By concentrating, they will be able to manage the size, shape and movement of their spell, in this case, a wyrdlight. If they do not, the spell will come out in a blast, wasting a whole lot of mana, as I just showed you.'

'Very good, Elaine!' Elizabeth said, smiling at the girl and holding her hand up for a high five. Elaine rolled her eyes and turned her attention back to Valens, who had settled on her shoulder.

Arcturus stood in awe, his fingers itching to attempt the same feat. He looked to Elizabeth hopefully.

'Well . . . er . . . let's move on to more advanced spellcraft,' Elizabeth said, dropping her hand with disappointment. 'As Elaine said, a wyrdlight is just a ball of raw mana, which can be controlled with a bit of practice. Its only real use is as a light source, a flash to blind your opponent and occasionally, target practice. It disappears as soon as you touch it.'

Elizabeth snuffed out her wyrdlight with a snap of her fingers, which also served to return Elaine's attention back to her once again.

'The real power we summoners wield comes from etching. Please watch closely. I send the mana *to* my finger, rather than through it.' Elizabeth held up her hand. Her fingertip glowed a dull blue, growing steadily brighter until it burned almost white and Arcturus had to shield his eyes.

'When your finger is bright enough, you draw a symbol, like so!' Elizabeth sketched a strange, jagged triangle in the air, leaving glowing blue lines, like the afterglow of a cinder being waved in the air.

'This is the shield spell. It is one of the four battle spells that every summoner uses when fighting. The others are fire, lightning and telekinesis.' She demonstrated by drawing each in succession, the first a flame-like, curling symbol, the next a zigzagging bolt and the final, a hypnotic swirl. Arcturus wished he had pen and paper to draw them, but instead focussed on memorising the shield spell. Better to be able to protect himself than hurt someone else.

'You must hold your finger in the very centre of the symbol until it fixes,' Elizabeth continued, putting her finger in the middle of the shield symbol. It pulsed once, and as she waved her finger in the air, it followed the tip. It was as if it were fixed there by an invisible frame. This time, Elaine watched closely, her eyes wide as she took it all in. Arcturus grinned, glad that this was all new to the younger girl too. It seemed he wasn't far behind her after all.

'You need to maintain a steady flow of mana to your finger, otherwise the spell will disappear,' Elizabeth said, nodding at the other symbols as they faded in the air. 'The most difficult part is pushing mana both *to* and *through* your finger at the same time. Like so.'

Elizabeth frowned with effort, then a thread of opaque material streamed from the symbol, pooling in the air. Sacharissa growled at the strange material, but Arcturus hushed her with a ruffle of her ears.

'You then shape it as you wish, in this case, like a shield.' The pool shifted, then folded itself into an oval that floated in front of her. 'This will protect you from projectiles and other spells, even a sword blow.'

The shield dissolved into a floating globule once again, then she drew it back in through the symbol.

'You can conserve mana by absorbing the spell once you're done with it.'

'Why don't you make it bigger?' Elaine asked, passing her hand through the space the shield had been in.

'The thicker your shield, the more punishment it will take, before it cracks and eventually shatters,' Elizabeth replied. 'If you make it too wide, you lose durability. Too thick and you waste mana.'

'Maybe I can practise with Sacha,' Arcturus murmured, rubbing the demon's head fondly. Sacharissa was his most powerful weapon. He would make sure it was not just he who benefited from his training at the academy. He looked up to see Elizabeth shaking her head.

'Unfortunately, shields are useless against a demonic attack. Should you be attacked by an orc's demon, or any other for that matter, you will be better off using that dirk I gave you than a shield spell.'

Elaine gave a horrified gasp, holding her hands up to her mouth.

'Not that this should happen anytime soon,' Elizabeth said swiftly, as even Arcturus's face paled. 'It will be years before you graduate as a battlemage and face the orc shamans on the frontier. Not to mention that most of their demons are low-level. You and Sacha shouldn't have much trouble fending one off, even now. You too, Elaine, although your Mite is quite young. I can see it hasn't developed its stinger yet. When it does, you'll be able to paralyse an opponent . . . although an orc takes a few stings before it goes down.'

Arcturus hadn't thought about graduating – it seemed so far away. Was that why Vocans was training them? To fight monstrous orcs in the jungles?

'Now, I think it's time you tried to produce a wyrdlight,' Elizabeth said, sensing his mood. 'Learning to shape and control one is the first step to learning spellcraft. It will leave you well prepared for when you eventually start using spells.'

'What, now?' Arcturus asked, his palms suddenly sweaty. 'I haven't even—'

'Exactly, you haven't even tried yet. Learning by doing, that's the summoner way. It's all reflex at the end of the day – there's only so much you can learn from books and lessons. Let's see if you have a knack for it. I'll tell you what, Elaine can try as well.' She looked for the girl and found her on the other side of the room, playing her game of tag with Valens once again. 'Elaine, stop playing with your demon and pay attention! I'm told you still need to practise your wyrdlights too.'

'That doesn't make me feel any better. Now I'll get shown up by a thirteen-year-old girl,' Arcturus muttered.

'So?' Elizabeth asked. 'You're newer to this than she is, of course she's likely to do better. What does age or gender have to do with it?'

'Umm . . . nothing,' Arcturus said, shuffling his feet.

'Too right!' Elizabeth said, arching her eyebrows. 'Now, most novices find it easier when they are sitting down for the first time. Why don't you sit down with Sacha beside you? Your connection with her won't change no matter how far away she is, but it can't hurt.'

Arcturus settled down, cross-legged, and laid Sacharissa's heavy head in his lap. The weight was comforting and he twisted his fingers in her soft, black fur. Her warm, blue eyes gazed at him with trust before she closed them and let out a contented rumble. He followed suit, waiting for the next instructions.

Elaine sat on the ground beside him and he sensed the young girl give Sacharissa's tail a surreptitious stroke. The demon snorted and Arcturus heard the thwack of her tail and a yelp from Elaine.

'Serves you right,' Elizabeth said, tutting.

She kneeled on the ground behind Arcturus and laid her hands on his shoulders.

'Sense the connection, where you feel Sacha's emotions and intentions,' Elizabeth murmured, her voice soft in his ear.

Arcturus searched for the mental umbilical cord that held Sacharissa and him together. As he touched it, he felt Sacharissa shudder, then relax as he gently grasped it with his mind. Instantly, his body began to suffuse with a sensation both cold and hot, rushing through his blood with every pulse of his heart. His breath quickened.

'That's enough – let go for now. It's just a small spell and you don't want to drain her. Now, take the mana and push it through your finger. As it comes out, open your eyes and try to shape it into a ball,' Elizabeth's voice was low and confident, quelling Arcturus's doubts. 'You can do it.'

He pushed the mana out of his finger, the energy rushing through him like a white-water rapid. He snapped his eyes open and contorted his mind, willing the mana into the shape of a rough ball. Light curled, slowly, emerging from his finger and spinning into an orb that hung in the air in front of him.

'Excellent,' Elizabeth breathed, still behind him. 'Now, why don't you try and float it up towards the ceiling.'

Arcturus's mind felt as if it might snap, his brow furrowed so deeply he could feel the muscles cramping. He nudged the orb upwards, and his heart soared as the orb responded to his touch. It spun and ascended, until it touched the ceiling and disappeared.

'Well done. That's better than most students manage their first time,' Elizabeth said.

Arcturus smiled as another, much smaller ball floated aimlessly in front of him.

'I did it!' Elaine yelled, punching the air beside them. Arcturus watched as Valens buzzed around the ball, making mock dives at it.

For a moment Arcturus stared at Elaine's wyrdlight, watching it fly randomly around the room, like a lazy bee on a hot summer's day.

'There ends the lesson,' Elizabeth said, grinning at Arcturus's expression. 'Next time I'll push you harder, but it's a great step for your first day. Before I go, are there any questions you need answering?'

Arcturus tore his eyes away from the wyrdlight and considered it. He had around a hundred, but so many of them seemed like they might come off as stupid.

'Is a low-level demon a weak demon?' Arcturus asked, remembering that as a Canid, Sacharissa was a level-seven demon. A Mite was only level one.

'Yes and no. The level a demon is simply refers to what level of summoner you need to be to summon them: a level-ten summoner can summon a level-ten demon, or two level-five demons. As a rule of thumb, the higher a demon's level, the more powerful it is, in mana, size and strength. That being said, as a demon becomes more experienced, they can improve in all these counts. A well-trained Canid might be able to take on an inexperienced Griffin, which is level ten.' Elizabeth brandished her fingers as she said each number, as if Arcturus might be incapable of counting. He forgave her for assuming – there were plenty of commoners his age, and older besides, incapable of reading or writing.

'Then there's the fact that some demons are simply more powerful than their level might indicate, even if it is roughly accurate. A level-seven Felid will beat a level-seven Canid almost every time, despite them being the same level. It's even capable of beating some higher-level demons. There are also anomalies, such as Golems, which are level eight. When they are young, they are small. But after a few years they can grow to be as tall as nine feet and just as wide, but they will always remain level eight. So you see, it's just a rough rule.'

'I understand,' Arcturus said, trying to internalise it all. 'I can count by the way. You don't need to use your fingers.'

'Sorry,' Elizabeth grinned, lowering her hands. 'My husband wasn't very good at numbers when I met him.'

Arcturus felt a twinge of pride. The workhouse had been hell but at least they had taught him something.

'Right, that's enough for now,' Elizabeth said, standing up and stretching with a groan. 'I still have to move into my quarters.'

Arcturus stood too, earning himself a grumbling growl from Sacharissa as her head flopped to the floor.

'That's great. I haven't even had time to wash yet!' he said, trying to remember which direction the baths were supposed to be.

'I wasn't going to say anything,' Elizabeth laughed, holding her nose jokingly. 'Go wash up and then relax in your rooms. I will make sure someone brings you lunch and dinner. The others will be at training with Lady Faversham all day anyway.'

'When's our next lesson?' Arcturus asked as he hurried to the door, suddenly aware of how close Elizabeth and Elaine were standing to him.

'I'll see you tomorrow morning. I'm assisting in the summoning lesson with Lord Scipio.'

Arcturus spent most of the morning attempting to improve his living conditions, taking spare sheets and broken furniture from the storerooms, creating a makeshift blockade for the window and adding another few layers of cloth to his threadbare blanket. He was exhausted and hungry by lunchtime, but fortunately food was brought up by a waspish Ulfr, who dumped the tray unceremoniously in the room and left without a word.

The food was plain lamb and potatoes, obviously prepared for the servants rather than the nobles, but it was far better fare than Arcturus was used to at the inn, and ambrosia compared to the slops he had eaten at the workhouse. There was even a bowl of mincemeat for Sacharissa, which she gulped down with relish and then nosed the bowl for more.

As instructed, he went searching for Obadiah in the afternoon, but was swiftly herded back to his room by one of the dwarven servants. It turned out that the Provost had been called away earlier than expected and was no longer at Vocans. This was fine by Arcturus. Good riddance to him.

He and Sacharissa spent the rest of the night practising with wyrdlights, delighting in the way they floated aimlessly around the room, as if they had lives of their own. Sacharissa would snap at them in the air, leaping and diving to catch them, while Arcturus tried to nudge them out of the way. Whenever she managed to touch one, her look of complete bafflement at its disappearance and the fresh darkness entertained Arcturus no end.

His room was considerably warmer than the previous night, with no cutting draught to chill his bones. And in that small bedroom at the tip of Vocan's tower, he was lulled to sleep by the gentle rise and fall of Sacharissa's chest, pressed against him among a tangle of blankets.

10

'Wake up, you're late!'

The banging on the door jerked Arcturus from his slumber. The room was still dark, a consequence of his improvised window shade. He had no idea what time it was.

'Wassat?' he mumbled as Sacharissa whined at the noise.

'Summoning lessons started five minutes ago. Rouse yourself, or stay and face the consequences!' Ulfr's voice came from outside the door. His footsteps echoed down the corridor as Arcturus's sleep-addled mind processed the words.

'Oh no!'

Arcturus was glad that he had slept in his uniform, for he was pelting past Ulfr and down the stairs ten seconds later. Sacharissa ran ahead, punctuating each leap forward with a low pant.

He found her nosing at the summoning-room doors, but he paused and composed himself before they entered.

'Not a great first impression for Lord Scipio. Plus we've missed breakfast.' Arcturus groaned, preparing himself for the worst. He turned the handle and stepped inside.

The other students stood in a circle, but they ignored him as he tiptoed into the room. The group was surrounding a low, round table, but Arcturus could not see what was on it. The nobles did not attempt to make room for him, so he looked over Elaine's shoulder, as she was the smallest of the group.

The table was made of pure white marble, polished to be smooth and round as a river pebble, but it was the object embedded in the centre that took Arcturus's breath away: an enormous gem, the size of a large carriage wheel and as black as ink, shone up at him like volcanic glass.

'Nice of you to join us, Arcturus,' a voice said from behind him. Arcturus turned, an apology already forming on his lips.

A man stood in the doorway. He was powerfully built, with lamb-chop sideburns and curly hair the colour of chocolate. He stood with his arms crossed, but the smile on his face showed Arcturus he did not mind his tardiness, so Arcturus cut his apology short. His gold-edged officer's uniform left no doubt as to who he was: Lord Scipio.

'I was just going to go and collect you when you ran right past me,' Scipio said, before turning back to the open door he had come through. He gave a brief, sharp whistle. The hairs on the back of Arcturus's neck stood up as he heard a yowl from outside, then a demon bounded through the door, its tail lashing the air.

Sacharissa growled, her hackles raised at the sight of the new arrival. It looked like a snow leopard, with a dusting of black spots on a thick white pelt. It had two long canines that poked out on either side of its mouth like twin sabres, below a set of four fierce green eyes, not unlike Sacharissa's. Strangest of all, it seemed to walk like a jungle chimp, crouching on two legs and resting on its front paws, almost bipedal, but not quite. It was agile, for it slunk swiftly around the room, its eyes never leaving Sacharissa.

'Calm down, Kali – you'd think you've never seen a Canid before.' Scipio laughed, as the Felid arched its back, snarling at Sacharissa. 'You'll have to forgive her, Arcturus. She's a bit afraid of them.'

Scipio winked conspiratorially at Arcturus. As if she understood him, the Felid froze, then sat back on her haunches. She proceeded to lick her paw, completely ignoring Sacharissa.

Scipio walked over and held his hand out for Sacharissa to smell. She gave it a cursory sniff, then licked it once with her pink tongue to show her approval.

'Canids and Felids, there's always been a bit of a rivalry there. Must be something to do with competing for food sources in the ether.'

'The ether?' Arcturus asked, his curiosity piqued.

'You'll find out soon enough,' Scipio said, looking behind Arcturus at the others. They had been watching the exchange with interest.

'Make room for Arcturus, ladies and gentlemen. He shouldn't have to crane over young Elaine's head. Charles, Damian, there seems to be some room in between you. Budge up,' Scipio ordered, shooing them with his hands.

The two boys stared daggers at Arcturus, who shuffled forward and wedged himself between them. They leaned in, digging their shoulders uncomfortably into his own.

'For the benefit of Elaine and Arcturus, I shall run through

71

what we are going to learn here over the course of this year. It will act as a good refresher for those of you who have neglected your studies since last we met.'

There was an audible groan from the others and Arcturus frowned apologetically. Edmund mouthed, 'It's fine,' at Arcturus and gave him a smile.

'Now, this stone in the centre is the largest scrying stone ever discovered, otherwise known as the Oculus. Are you aware of what a scrying stone does?' Scipio asked, pushing between the Queensouth twins and pointing at the stone.

'Yes, sir. When a demon touches it, the stone will show everything that a demon sees,' Arcturus said, remembering his brief lesson with Obadiah Forsyth. Elaine nodded in agreement.

'Very good. It will keep showing it until the summoner breaks the connection, or until the scrying stone is touched once again. Now, Kali here will demonst—'

Before he could finish speaking, a draught ruffled the hair on Arcturus's nape as the Felid soared over him. It landed with its paws around the stone before nudging it gently with its nose.

'Ahem . . . yes . . . well done, Kali,' Scipio said, as the stone flickered with colour. A moment later Arcturus was staring at a close-up of Charles's face, for that was where Kali was looking. The detail was incredible. Arcturus could even see the pores in the boy's nose. It was not a pretty sight.

'Felids have better eyesight than others. Most summoners prefer to use a Mite to scout the ether first, but Kali is quick enough to jump back through if there's any trouble.'

Arcturus's curiosity quickened as the ether was mentioned again. Jump back through what?

'And, do you know what infusion is?' Scipio asked.

'Yes, sir,' Arcturus said, still mesmerised by the image as Kali switched her gaze from one face to another.

'Good. I shall teach you how to infuse a demon next week perhaps – your demon seems well-behaved enough not to distract you in lessons.'

'Thank you, sir,' Arcturus said. He felt far safer with Sacharissa by his side, and knew that if he were taught to infuse her, she would not be allowed out for most of the day. Still, he was curious about what it felt like to have the demon within him. He almost didn't believe it was possible.

'Now, I shall use one of the keyed pentacles on the floor beside us. Who can tell me what a keyed pentacle is?'

'A keyed pentacle has a symbol on each corner of the star. They act as coordinates that will open a portal to the ether,' Baybars Saladin replied.

'Good. I shall now do so. Pay attention, everyone,' Scipio said, kneeling on the ground. He laid his hands on the floorboards, then grunted as his fingertips began to glow blue. There was a low hum in the room, and slowly but surely the lines of the pentacle Scipio was facing shone with the same electric light. The symbols on each corner pulsed. A pinprick appeared in the air, expanding slowly into a spinning orb the size of a man's head. Still it grew, doubling in size over and over, until it was larger than the table they stood around.

Scipio's face was red with effort, the veins on his neck bulging. He lifted one hand, causing the pentacle to crackle, before removing a wooden spike attached to a roll of leather from his back pocket. He rammed it into the floorboards, then stood, panting, the leather strap gripped firmly in his hand. His fingertips remained blue and Arcturus could tell he was powering the pentacle through the connection.

'There's got to be a better way of doing this,' Scipio muttered, stepping back into his place at the table. 'Kali! You know what to do.'

The Felid yowled with excitement, before leaping over their heads once again. Kali landed in a crouch, then leaped into the orb, disappearing as swiftly as a disturbed wyrdlight. But Arcturus's attention did not remain on the orb for long. The image on the stone had changed. Scipio smiled at him as his mouth dropped open.

'Welcome . . . to the ether.'

11

Arcturus had never seen so much green. The ground was coated in thick, sage-coloured grass, with mossy tree trunks all around them. Hundreds of feet above, viridescent foliage filtered light from the sky, dappling the shadows with green-tinged radiance.

'All demons originate from the ether. Their world is shaped like a giant disk, with a desert known as the deadlands around the edges, and jungle and forests in the outer ring. The centre is more mountainous and dangerous, filled with the most powerful demons, volcanoes, great expanses of water and who knows what else. Nobody has ever been more than a few miles from the area we hunt in, but if you were to fly high enough, that is what you would see.' Scipio was speaking for Arcturus's benefit, for even Elaine seemed unsurprised by the moving images on the stone.

'Using my mind and what I see in the Oculus, or another scrying stone as the case may be, I am able to control Kali's movements.'

Kali's eyes twitched to the nearest tree trunk, then her claws flashed into view as they began to climb. A tiny Mite, almost as small as a normal beetle, crawled from beneath the bark. Elaine gasped as Kali impaled it with one long talon, before spooning it into her mouth. The image juddered as the Felid chomped down.

'Yes, the ether is a brutal place. It's eat or be eaten, and lesser Mites are at the bottom of the food chain. A Scarab Mite, like yours, is not though. I feed Kali well but she does like a taste of her old diet,' Scipio joked, though Elaine's expression remained grim and defiant.

'Stay away from Valens,' she hissed at the stone.

Kali continued her climb, occasionally glancing around to make sure the coast was clear. It seemed strange to Arcturus that such a large, powerful creature was so wary of her surroundings and he wondered what manner of creatures could be a threat to a Felid.

He didn't have to wait long. Kali broke through the canopy, the Oculus's image flashing briefly as the Felid's eyes adjusted to the new light.

The treeline seemed to stretch endlessly ahead, broken only by jagged mountains and the occasional clearing, like reefs and trenches in a sea of green. Each mountaintop smouldered, sending slow-moving pillars of smoke reaching up before dissipating into a pall of ash that filled the cloudless sky. Arcturus could see no sun or moon to speak of, just an orange glow that reminded him of dusk on a summer's day.

As Kali's eyes adjusted further, Arcturus saw swarms of creatures, too far away to make out, forming and reforming in the sky, while larger dots hovered above them, waiting for an opportunity to strike. A Scarab Mite, its carapace cerulean blue, flitted across Kali's vision.

In the distance, Arcturus saw a herd of creatures making their way through the trees. They had the same long necks and large bodies as giraffes but with thicker limbs and a head that reminded Arcturus of a horse's or camel's. Their short fur was grey and mottled with black patches.

'Looks like the Indrik herds are on the move,' Scipio said, pointing at them on the stone. 'Far too big to be practical as a summoner's demon, but I always love to see them.'

They watched for a moment longer as the Indriks made short work of the treeline around them. Judging by the size of the trees, they must have been as tall as ten men standing on each other's shoulders.

'We cannot stay too long. Can anyone tell me why?' Scipio asked.

'You can never stay too long in the ether,' Edmund said confidently. 'There are other demons out there that might eat your own. No matter how powerful it is, there is always something higher up on the food chain. Then there's the fact that your mana levels are dropping every second you keep the portal open. If they run out or you lose concentration, the portal will close and you will lose your demon for ever.'

Arcturus saw Zacharias roll his eyes, then whisper something to one of the twins, Josephine Queensouth. She giggled and Edmund's face reddened.

'Very good, Edmund. You're absolutely right, but that is not what I am getting at. Anybody else?' Scipio asked, looking around the table. There was silence, then Prince Harold put up his hand.

'Is it the Shrikes?' he suggested, unsure of himself.

'Correct!' Scipio beamed, flashing the prince a congratulatory grin. He turned to Arcturus and Elaine. 'Shrikes travel in flocks, led by their matriarch, the dominant female. During the first few weeks of the academic year, they migrate across our hunting grounds. They are dangerous birds, twice as large as an eagle and many times as vicious. That's them, flying over the Lesser Mite swarms in the distance. They hunt alone for smaller prey, but for Kali, they would attack in a group of ten or more. After they make their kill, they impale their victims on tree branches, to hold them in place while they feast. Luckily for us, we seem to have missed the worst of it.'

Arcturus shuddered. He wouldn't want to send Sacharissa into the ether, but he would dearly have loved to capture a Mite for himself. She had spent most of her life there . . . surely it couldn't be that bad.

'Right, I think that's enough for one day. The first and second years will practise demonic control and infusion for the remainder of the day. As for the rest of you, I suggest you practise opening and closing portals, making sure to keep your distance. As you know, the air in the ether is highly toxic to humans. No demons are to enter under any circumstan—'

Scipio froze, his eyes searching the stone, though all Arcturus could see was the tree trunks.

'Something's coming. Kali can hear it. Smell it,' Scipio uttered. The pentacle behind him crackled as his concentration slipped, but he grunted and it returned to a steady glow once more. The acrid stench of burned wood permeated the room, and Arcturus could see the planks at the edges of the pentacle singeing black.

'Another. Two of them. But not the same. Better stay in the trees.' He was muttering to himself, the lesson momentarily forgotten.

Kali's eyes turned to the ground for the first time. Another orb, identical to the one floating in the centre of the summoning room, hung in the air, spinning gently. It must have been what Kali had come out of, and would need to return to if she wanted to leave the ether.

They were above a large clearing of sorts, for the surrounding area was uneven, scattered with tangled branches and lichened rocks. Yet within the vegetation there was a disturbance, shaking the leaves as something made its way towards them. Though Arcturus could only see what was happening, he could imagine the sound of snapping twigs as a beast tore through the foliage.

To the other side, something even larger had almost reached the clearing, for Arcturus could see horns tearing at the undergrowth. Whatever it was, it was enormous, perhaps as tall as seven feet.

'There's going to be a fight,' Fergus whispered, wrapping his arm around his little sister. Elaine ignored him, instead removing Valens from her pocket so he could watch.

A hairless, gangly creature emerged into the clearing. It was long-limbed and skeletal, with elongated claws and splayed feet. It walked much like Kali did, though it was more hunched and bow-legged, with lengthy arms that knuckled the ground with every step.

Gnarled antlers branched from a heavy-browed forehead

above a snout somewhere between a horse's and a wolf's. Its black eyes scanned the ground ahead and it snorted gulps of air as it sought the scent of its opponent.

'A Wendigo,' Scipio whispered, his voice tinged with something between awe and horror. 'I've never seen one in the wild. They're rare in our hunting grounds – in fact, it's virtually unheard of. Only the most powerful of orc shamans use them, and rarely. It has a fulfilment level of thirteen.'

Arcturus felt his stomach turn over, watching as the grey-skinned aberration edged around the orb. With just one leap, it could enter through the portal and into the summoning room.

'Sir, shouldn't we get help? It . . . it might come through,' Arcturus stammered.

Scipio was sweating profusely now, his face gone from the red of exertion to the pale white of exhaustion. He responded to Arcturus without lifting his eyes from the Oculus.

'Don't worry, boy. Wild demons don't like to go near portals. It's strange enough that the Wendigo would get that close at all. Must be starving – that's why it has wandered into our hunting grounds. Still, if it's that desperate, we can't risk sending Kali through until it has gone. It might jump in after her.'

'Can you keep the portal open for long enough? How are your mana levels?' Prince Harold asked.

'If I can keep the flow of mana steady, maybe another ten minutes or so,' Scipio replied, watching as the second creature neared the clearing. 'I exhausted most of my mana yesterday on the battlefield. If the worst happens, I may send in Kali when the Wendigo is distracted. Let's see what the other demon is first.'

As Scipio finished speaking, the second creature erupted from the bushes with a throaty bellow. Yet when it saw the Wendigo, it began to back away, as if surprised to see it.

'Looks like it didn't know what it was tracking,' Prince Harold said, leaning over the table to get a better view.

'Minotaur. Fulfilment level of eleven,' Rook breathed from beside Arcturus, his voice tinged with awe and longing. 'My father has one of those.'

Arcturus examined the creature as the two demons circled each other. The Minotaur was an enormous beast, slightly taller than the Wendigo, but only because it walked upright instead of hunched over. It had a bull's head, with baleful red eyes and a pair of long, curved horns that it lowered at its opponent.

Its frame was covered by a shaggy carpet of black fur over thick slabs of hard muscle. Even as Arcturus watched, the beast scored the ground with its hooves, preparing to charge, the hooked nails on its hands outstretched.

'That's two demons that rarely show up in our hunting grounds,' Scipio said, thinking aloud. 'It must be the Shrikes – they're following them to eat their leftovers. But there's not enough food for both of them.'

'They had better stop this showboating if Kali's going to get out in time,' Edmund muttered as the creatures continued to stare at each other, making mock charges. Then, as if spurred on by Edmund's words, they met in a tangle of claws and teeth.

The Wendigo's antlers locked with the Minotaur's horns as they spun and circled, spitting and slashing at each other. It was immediately obvious that the Wendigo had the upper hand. The length of its arms allowed it to hack away at the Minotaur's chest and shoulders, leaving deep, bloody scores in the flesh. Meanwhile, the Minotaur's reach was too short; the antlers its horns were caught in kept it at a distance. Instead, the Minotaur snatched at the Wendigo's wrists until finally it managed to grasp them. They struggled on, straining against each other, as the Minotaur's blood trickled into the tall grass.

'I'm going to make a break for it,' Scipio gasped, as the pentacle began to crackle. The wooden boards were smoking now, as the unstable connection generated too much heat.

'Now!' he yelled.

Kali somersaulted from the tree, plunging towards the spinning portal. There was a brief image of the two predators, their eyes turning at the sudden arrival of the Felid. Then she was through, slamming into the floor below the summoning-room portal. Scipio released the leather cable and collapsed. The orb shrunk into nothingness and the pentacle faded, leaving a smoking outline of charred wood. The room was cast in darkness as the wyrdlights winked out, one by one.

There was silence.

Then Scipio spoke, a ragged voice in the shadows.

'Let that be a lesson to you. The ether is a dangerous, unpredictable place. Class dismissed.'

12

They trooped out of the room in silence, leaving Scipio to recover on his own. Prince Harold threw some wyrdlights over his shoulder on the way out, allowing Arcturus to catch a glimpse of the teacher embracing Kali with tightly closed eyes. He understood the feeling – if Sacharissa had almost been lost to the ether, he would likely be in tears.

It seemed incredible to Arcturus that the students would be exposed to such danger, especially in their first lesson. Would it be like this every day? He dreaded to think of a time when he would have to send Sacharissa into the ether.

Yet, even as the thought crossed his mind, he could hear the other students talking excitedly about their near miss. Perhaps this was not so normal after all.

'So, Dog Breath. Are you off to hide in your room like you did yesterday?' Charles asked, stepping in front of Arcturus. Rook and Zacharias crowded close to him, but he ignored them and met Charles's gaze with as much confidence as he could muster.

'I wasn't hiding,' he replied, lifting his chin. 'But you don't seem to enjoy my company, so I chose to avoid yours. Maybe you're scared of me.'

'We're of different stock, you and I. A mongrel and a thoroughbred. Yokel and blue blood. Pigswill and upper crust. It wouldn't do for us to mix.' Charles sneered.

Arcturus resisted the urge to punch the boy in his smug face, which was just as well, for Sacharissa's chest was rumbling with a deep growl.

'Oh, leave the boy alone,' Prince Harold called out in a bored voice. 'Zacharias, don't you have better things to do? Edmund and I are going to Corcillum. Will you join us?'

Zacharias dug his elbow into Arcturus's ribs before following the Prince and Edmund through the atrium's entrance doors. The others were already making their way up the stairs, except for Elaine, who was watching their exchange with open curiosity.

'Not invited?' Arcturus asked innocently, noting Charles's disappointed look.

'Shut up,' Charles hissed, shoving a finger in Arcturus's face. 'The prince likes me well enough. Zach and Edmund are his childhood friends, just like my father and the king were. If I was a bit older and didn't live so far north, things would be different.'

'Sounds like I hit a nerve,' Arcturus said, goading the boy. It wouldn't help matters, but Charles already hated him and it felt so good.

'I'll hit you in a minute,' Rook snarled, grasping Arcturus by the collar and raising his fist. A warning bark from Sacharissa was enough to stop him going any farther.

'Don't worry, Rook. This is my fight,' Charles grunted,

laying a hand on his friend's shoulder.

'Yeah, tell your lapdog to stand down,' Arcturus said, smiling at Rook. The boy's face reddened with anger, but he obeyed Faversham without question, releasing the collar and stepping back.

'How about it, Arcturus? Tonight, just you and me. We can meet right there, in the summoning room. Nobody will hear us.'

Arcturus knew he was being baited, but he could feel Sacharissa's eagerness to fight fuelling his own. He remembered Charles's new demon was the Faversham family's second choice, an Arach . . . whatever that was. Surely Sacharissa was more powerful? And it was Charles's first year at Vocans too. He had only just had his first lesson at performing battle spells, so it was unlikely he would be able to do one yet. They would be evenly matched.

'What time?' Arcturus asked, clenching his fists.

'When the second bell rings, open the summoning room door,' Charles said, barging him in the shoulder as he and Rook walked away. 'Don't be late. Again.'

Arcturus waited a few minutes before he followed them up the stairs. He would have liked to go sooner but Elaine took what felt like an age to leave, lounging around the atrium until he pretended to head to the washroom. He wondered if she had heard what they were discussing. Though . . . what difference would it make if she had?

As he trudged up the stairs, Arcturus wondered if he was doing the right thing. At the workhouse, he would never back down, or else the older boys would steal his food. He had to goad his bullies into a fight and make sure he blacked their eyes, even if he lost. That way, his tormentors would think twice about attempting it again – he was not an easy target.

Arcturus didn't need to keep Charles and Rook within sight, so he hung back when he made them out in the gloom ahead. After all, he already knew where Charles's bedroom was. It didn't take long for him to arrive outside the door. Sure enough, he could hear muffled voices behind it. Too muffled.

He tutted with frustration and pressed his ear against the wood, but still the voices were indistinct. He hadn't anticipated that. There was always the possibility that Charles would cheat. That maybe Rook would come at him from behind as soon as he stepped into the room. Maybe they would simply attack him together. If that was the case, there was a good chance they would be discussing it at that very moment.

Sacharissa nosed under the door, as if she could smell the plush carpet she had enjoyed just two days ago.

'I wonder if you can hear what they're saying,' Arcturus murmured. 'You seem to understand me well enough.'

She licked his hand then cocked her head to one side. Arcturus knew she didn't really understand him, but simply sensed his intentions. Still, her snuffling had given him an idea.

'Look at me, Sacha,' Arcturus instructed, lifting her head with his hand. He stared deep into her eyes, trying to catch that brief moment they had shared. In the dim torchlight of the corridor, her eyes shone like shards of blue ice, never wavering from his own.

The world started to shift, the blue becoming a cold grey, the flickering orange replaced by pale shadows. He could smell the oil in the lamps, suddenly bitter and pungent in his nostrils. Most importantly, the voices in the other room came through clear as day, as if he were standing right beside the boys.

'. . . he will find out soon enough. We need to get rid of the evidence, or all will be lost. My father has spent years currying favour with the king. Never has our future been so threatened.'

It was Charles, his voice low and rapid. Arcturus could even hear his panicked breathing.

'Are there others?' Rook asked.

'How should I know? There might be!' Charles snapped.

'What good will it do then, if there are others?'

'They won't know where to look for them . . . yet. My father has already taken care of the innkeeper and his wife – they were the only others who knew where the urchin came from, before he was a stable boy. Father sent word that Provost Forsyth will return tomorrow to interrogate the boy. We cannot let that happen. A few words from him and all might be lost.'

Stable boy? They had to be talking about him. As he tried to make sense of it all, Arcturus's concentration slipped and the world turned colourful again. He gritted his teeth and grasped Sacharissa's head in his hands, forcing the connection. He had to know more.

'. . . tonight. I'll tell dog breath what he is before we begin. I want to see the look on his face,' Charles snarled, followed by the sound of cracking knuckles.

'There's a chance he might win, you know that, right?' Rook warned. 'Your demon is the same level as his and neither of you can cast any spells.'

Charles laughed scornfully, 'Don't you worry about that. The battle we witnessed today has given me an ide—'

Sacharissa whimpered. Arcturus realised he was gripping her head, his fingers tightening like a vice as he concentrated on the connection. He could suddenly feel her pain, fierce pulses of agony that she had borne stoically.

'What was that?' Rook hissed. There was the sound of feet thudding to the ground.

Arcturus released Sacharrissa and they sprinted away, dodging around the corner just in time. The door slammed open, the bang echoing down the corridor.

'Nobody here,' Rook grunted.

'Well, close the door, it's freezing out there,' Charles called.

The door closed and Arcturus breathed easy once more. He let himself slide down the wall, until he was sitting on the cold paving of the floor.

'I'm so sorry, my darling,' Arcturus whispered, gently stroking Sacharissa's back. 'I didn't mean to hurt you.'

She lapped at his hand, as if to say she still loved him.

'I wasn't so sure if I was going to go tonight – if I do, it will put us in unnecessary danger. But now I know I have to. Lord Forsyth will interrogate me tomorrow, and we know what that could be like.' He remembered the pain of Sacharissa's whipping. The darkness of the cell.

'Charles said he would tell me what I am before the duel. I won't even fight, I'll just hear what he has to say and then we'll leave Vocans. Maybe we can make it to the Elven lands in the north. It'll be safer than this place.'

Sacharissa yawned, and rested her head in his lap. Arcturus laughed as she began to snooze, half closing her eyes.

'You're right, you lazy thing. Let's get back to the room, pack our bags and rest up. We've got to be ready at the second bell and as far away from Vocans as possible by first light.'

13

Arcturus didn't sleep. His bag was packed, his meagre possessions in the satchel and ready to go. He would take it with him when he went to the summoning room. As soon as he was out of Vocans he would need to change into his old clothes. The uniform would be too conspicuous. Then again, with Sacharissa by his side, it wouldn't really matter what he was wearing – they would stand out like a sore thumb. Once he had put a few miles behind them, he would need to somehow teach himself infusion.

For a while he had debated whether to keep the dirk strapped to his boot or to stash it in the bag for his meeting with Charles. He had been wearing it over the past two days, but nobody seemed to mind – it was a military academy after all. If it did come to a fight, he would prefer there to be no weapons involved. At the same time, if Charles planned to use one, it would make no difference if Arcturus was visibly armed or not.

'I'd rather have it and not need it than need it and not have it,' Arcturus reasoned to Sacharissa, listening for the dull sound of the second morning bell. His mouth was dry and the evening meal Ulfr had brought him remained untouched beside his bed. Even Sacharissa had refused to eat it, although that might have had something to do with it being a salad. Arcturus suspected that, to her, it might as well have been a pile of grass.

The knell of the bell echoed down the corridor, leaving his heart thundering as he realised the moment had arrived.

'Come on, Sacha,' Arcturus murmured, opening the door. 'Let's hear what he has to say and then leave as soon as possible. We'll run back to the room and lock ourselves in for half an hour, then make our escape when the coast is clear.'

They hurried down the corridors, feeling their way in the darkness. Arcturus didn't risk a wyrdlight, for it would be too bright against the pitch black of the castle interior. If any of their teachers caught him out at night, his chances of meeting Charles would be scuppered, not to mention any possibility of escape.

It felt like an age until they reached the atrium, and for a moment Arcturus was worried that he was too late. It was only when he saw a bright light flickering beneath the summoning room's door that he realised that Charles was waiting within.

'OK, Sacha. This is it.' He took a deep breath and pushed open the heavy door.

For a moment Arcturus didn't understand what he was seeing. After being in darkness so long, the light within half-blinded him.

It was a portal, the blue orb hanging in the air like a miniature sun. Rook was kneeling beside it, pulsing mana into the violet pentacle beneath. This wasn't right.

Arcturus turned to run, but Charles was standing in the

doorway, a nasty smile on his face. He swung the door closed with a kick of his heel.

'What's going on here, Charles?' Arcturus growled, gripping Sacharissa by the scruff of her neck. She was preparing to pounce on him, driven by equal parts of fear and fury.

But before Charles could answer, Arcturus felt something wet and sticky whip around his body, trapping his arms to his chest. Sacharissa leaped, but Charles was already rolling out of harm's way and the Canid slammed against the door. Another thread hissed through the air, glowing like a shield spell. This time, it wrapped around Sacharissa's hind legs.

'Trussed like a chicken, ready for the kiln,' Charles cackled as more threads shot out of the shadows, swathing Sacharissa as she scrabbled at the oak floorboards. Another lashed around Arcturus's neck, tighter than a hangman's noose.

Arcturus fell to the ground, bringing his knees up to his chest. He gripped the dirk in his hand and eased it from the scabbard, even as he became entangled by more of the deadly strands. Soon he could barely move, only watch as Sacharissa howled and snapped at the strange fibres that constricted her. A few moments later, a last thread encircled her muzzle and tightened, reducing her noise to a strangled growl.

'Beautifully done, Anansi,' Charles called. 'You can come out now!'

Charles's Arach crept out of the shadows, the strange glowing fluid dripping from the back of its abdomen, beneath a deadly stinger. It was an enormous black spider, with a body as large as a human head and long spindly legs that scuttled along the floorboards. It had a cluster of beady eyes set in the centre of its forehead and a swollen body peppered with stiff brown hairs. The mandibles that served as its mouth clicked menacingly as it circled around Arcturus to return to its master.

'You know, I think you did me a favour, stable boy, by taking that pathetic Canid from me,' Charles sneered, hunkering down to bring his face close to Arcturus's. 'The Arach is a glorious specimen, able to trap its prey with a mana web, inject them with its stinger and then consume them at its leisure. Anansi can even scratch away at his hairs, which float into the air to blind and irritate his victims – as his owner, I'm immune, of course. He is versatile, agile and deadly. I couldn't ask for a better demon.'

'Thanks for the demonology lesson,' Arcturus said sarcastically, though the tremor in his voice revealed his fear. 'Why don't you tell me what all this is about. You're taking a great risk, trapping me like this. When the king finds out—'

'The king won't find out,' Charles interrupted gleefully, slapping Arcturus lightly on the face, just because he could. 'You won't be in a position to tell him, or anyone else for that matter, what with you being dead and all.'

Arcturus's heart lurched as Charles's eyes bore into his, their murderous intent as plain as the words he had just spoken. Twisting his hand beneath the webbing, Arcturus began to gently scrape at the gossamer with the dirk's blade. It was hard to tell if it was having any effect, but it would not do to reveal his weapon to Charles. His only chance now was the element of surprise. He had to keep the young noble talking until he was free.

'How's it looking, Rook?' Charles called, for the pentacle was

93

spitting and sizzling behind them. Arcturus twisted his neck to see Rook's kneeling figure, beads of sweat trickling down his forehead.

'Five more minutes. I've found the Minotaur's corpse. The Wendigo only took the heart, liver and kidneys. The flesh must have been too tough – it will still be hungry. There's a trail of blood.'

Arcturus saw a shard of scrying crystal on the ground between Rook's hands, flashes of green reflected in it as his demon hunted in the ether. Why on earth were they hunting for the Wendigo, and now of all times? Even Scipio had been afraid of it.

Arcturus turned back to Charles, who was gently stroking the Arach's abdomen.

'Why am I here? You said I did you a favour by taking Sacha, and I've caused you no other offence.' Arcturus felt the first strand of gossamer part, leaving him more room to manoeuvre the blade.

'It's not what you've done, but what you are. In more ways than one.' Charles plucked a patch of hair from Anansi and stroked it along Arcturus's bare arm. It raised a welt of red as it stung the skin, as if he were being stroked by a nettle. 'Commoners should not be summoners. It upsets the natural order of things. Any commoner planning a revolt against the ruling classes knows they are doomed to failure. But throw common summoners into the mix and suddenly our spellcraft and demons aren't so intimidating any more. That alone should be enough reason to kill you. But it's not the only one.'

'Enlighten me then,' Arcturus said, gritting his teeth as the pain in his arm began to throb. He didn't want to think how much it would hurt if a hair found its way into his eye.

'Do you remember how a firstborn child of a summoner will always inherit the same gift?' Charles asked, allowing the Arach's bristles to fall to the ground.

'I do,' Arcturus grunted.

'Well, a summoner can have several firstborn children with different partners, as long as it is the first child of that partner. So a man might father several firstborn children with various women. As long as one parent is a summoner and one has never had a child before, the offspring will inherit the gift.'

'I understand, get on with it,' Arcturus snarled, redoubling his efforts with the dirk. The blade scraped along his skin painfully, but he didn't care. He had only a few more minutes to make his escape.

'So eager to die, Arcturus?' Charles laughed. 'Don't worry, you'll hear the whole story before you've breathed your last.'

Arcturus wondered what he would do when his arms were free. Would there be time to release Sacharissa, or would he have to kill the Arach first? Sacharissa was quiet now, as if she could sense what he planned to do. Another thread parted, and Arcturus felt like he could tear himself free if given enough time. But he needed it to be fast.

'I see it!' Rook shouted from behind. 'Not long now!'

'All right, looks like I'll have to make this quick,' Charles snarled, taking a handful of Arcturus's hair and drawing him closer. He took a deep breath and began to speak.

'I don't like the rumours going around.'

'What rumours? I don't know what you're talking about.'

'Don't you see, Arcturus? You grew up in Boreas, the same

95

city my father lives in. Born with the power to summon. Abandoned as a child at an orphanage. You are proof of my father's infidelity. You are his bastard, and it won't be long before someone else comes to the same conclusion.'

'No . . .' Arcturus stammered, his escape forgotten as understanding began to dawn on him. Could it really be true? He pictured the beady-eyed man who had imprisoned him in that cell, without food or water for days. He shuddered with horror. Not him. Anyone but him.

'Your mother was nothing but a common courtesan, who whelped you and abandoned you for the state to raise. If only she had left you out in the cold to die. But no matter. I will take your life instead, before Obadiah has time to find out where you came from.'

Sacharissa was struggling now, grunting as she strained against her bonds. Her claws scratched on the wood, but all she managed was to shuffle a few inches closer to them.

'You're my *brother*?' Arcturus cried. Charles planted his knee in Arcturus's stomach and began to twist his head. Arcturus felt his spine creak under the pressure, as if Charles were trying to snap his neck.

'Half-brother,' Charles hissed in his ear, pointing at the floating globe. 'I guess this only makes this half-fratricide. Now look. See what fate we have planned for you.'

The portal spun in the air, crackling with energy. Rook had stabbed a leather tie into the pentacle's edge and was standing just a few feet away from them now. He looked exhausted, yet he was in a sprinter's crouch, as if ready to run from the room at any moment.

Suddenly, a demon hurtled from out of the portal, gliding out in a flutter of wings. It looked like a large, red-feathered owl with four legs. Arcturus caught a glimpse of round black eyes before it flew over him. A spatter of blood struck his face, and he realised the bird must have attacked the Wendigo with its talons before coming through.

'Will it follow a Strix? Strixs aren't known for being prey,' Charles wondered out loud as the portal continued to spin.

'If it doesn't, no matter. We'll just stick a blade between his ribs and throw him through.' Rook panted, his breathing heavy with effort from keeping the portal open.

'Too risky. Father said it has to look like an accident – that's the whole point of this. Someone might find his body if they go demon hunting. Not usual this time of year what with the Shrikes, but still a possibility.'

'The Wendigo will dispose of the body,' Rook snarled.

'You're going to make it look like I tried to capture a Wendigo, alone, *and it killed me*?' Arcturus said with horror.

'A living demon not connected to a summoner fades back into the ether within a few hours of entering our dimension,' Rook laughed, glancing back at Arcturus. 'They'll never know what killed you, but they'll have their suspicions.'

Even as he spoke, the Wendigo emerged from the portal in a tumbled clatter of claws and antlers, dripping blood from scratches across its muzzle.

'Have a nice life, *brother*. All thirty seconds of it,' Charles whispered.

14

Arcturus was shoved to the floor, his nose thudding into the floorboards. The door slammed and the room was cast in pitch darkness as the portal disappeared, its power source gone with Rook.

Salty blood gushed from Arcturus's nose as he struggled to get upright, ripping at his weakened bonds with all the strength he could muster. As the dirk sliced through the mana web, it dissolved into nothingness – no evidence to prove what Charles had done. They had planned his murder well.

As quietly as possible, Arcturus shuffled back and began to work on Sacharissa's bonds, all the while impressing the need for silence on her with his mind. She barely breathed, even when he sliced her in his blind rush to get her free. Every moment mattered, for the gossamer still glowed just enough for the Wendigo to track in the darkness.

He could hear it now, its claws slipping and scraping on the floorboards. Arcturus could remember the way its hooked claws had dug into the earth for purchase when it had battled the

Minotaur. It was a wild animal, completely new to such a smooth, hard surface. He would use this to his advantage.

The final thread was sliced away and Arcturus helped Sacharissa to her feet, now in total darkness. The Wendigo was snorting lungfuls of air, hunting for them by scent alone. For the first time, he was glad of the stench of burning wood that polluted the air. It would help keep them alive.

First, Arcturus tried the door. It was locked, but he could feel the keyhole, so large that he could stick two fingers through it. The lock was rough and simple, a relic of the old times the castle had been built in. If he was lucky, a bit of jimmying with the dirk might get the door open.

As his eyes adjusted to the darkness, Arcturus saw that there was dim light from beneath the door, enough to see Sacharissa's eyes. Instinctively, he re-formed their connection. Her black-and-white vision would not make much difference in the gloom of the room; hearing and sound would be key.

The scratch of claws against the wood was sickening, like nails against a chalkboard. But it was nothing compared to the smell that the Wendigo gave off. It was like rotting carrion, thick and ripe in the air. Arcturus felt as if it coated the back of his throat, so strongly did it reek of death. He sensed the demon was creeping towards them, cautiously. Arcturus supposed that it must have not recognised his scent, since humans were not native to the ether. It was suspicious of the unknown – yet it approached nonetheless.

'Get back!' Arcturus yelled, slamming the dirk through the keyhole, twisting and scraping at the mechanism within.

He heard the skitter of claws as the Wendigo leaped away,

like a startled bird. Even so, it was but a moment before he heard the slow creep once again.

Strangely, it did not seem to be approaching him this time, or at least, not that he could hear. Instead, the Wendigo appeared to be heading towards the lockers on the other side of the room. As Arcturus honed in on them, he could smell a trace of something he hadn't before: a mix of bath soap, sweat and leather. Perhaps both he and the Wendigo could smell the aprons within, and the creature had decided they were easier prey.

Arcturus didn't care, as long as it was moving away from him. He could feel the lock in the door clicking with every rattle of his dirk, until finally, a dull clunk told him that the latch had popped on the other side. With a last wrench, he dragged the door open, tumbling through with Sacharissa just behind him.

He slammed the door closed, threw the latch back in place and pressed his back against it.

The Wendigo rammed against the door, its predatory instincts telling it to chase that which ran away. The door shuddered but stayed firm against the demon's onslaught. Perhaps it had been made thick and sturdy for that very reason.

Arcturus felt a rush of hot, moist air against his ankles as the Wendigo snorted beneath the door, smelling him. He slid down and raked the dirk through the crack, and was immediately rewarded by a grunt of pain. The blade tip came away sticky with black blood. Then there was a clatter of claws as the demon crawled away in search of less dangerous prey.

Arcturus took a deep breath and assessed his situation. His satchel was still attached to his back and Rook and Charles were nowhere to be seen. They must have returned to their rooms, in case someone heard Arcturus screaming.

It had all turned out better than expected in the end. There was blood on the floor from his nose and Arcturus was sure that if they found no body, Charles would assume that the Wendigo had eaten him entirely, then faded into the ether.

He had inadvertently faked his own death. It was perfect.

Sacharissa nosed against his palm and he gave her a brief hug. He only wished he had time to try to infuse her before he disappeared into the night. She was in enough danger, and it would save him feeding her. She was already hungry, for Ulfr had only brought her one meagre portion of mincemeat in the afternoon.

Suddenly, he heard a bellow from inside the room, like the last breath of a wounded bull. Then a scream, so loud and full of horror that it cut him through to his very soul. There was no doubt in Arcturus's mind who it could be.

'Elaine!' he gasped.

15

He threw open the door, the darkness inside suddenly lit by the dim light of the atrium. Wyrdlights flew from his fingers, zooming in to reveal the monstrous figure at the other end of the room.

Elaine lay curled up on the floor in front of a broken locker, covering her head with her hands. Brave little Valens was buzzing around the Wendigo's head, stabbing his undeveloped stinger at its eyes. With each swipe of the Wendigo's claws, the Mite dodged into the maze of antlers that branched from the monster's forehead, so that his attacks clattered ineffectually against them. Arcturus realised that Elaine must have overheard him and Charles, and then hidden in a locker to watch their fight.

'Elaine, get out of there!' he yelled.

But Elaine didn't move. She was motionless, as helpless as a newborn lamb.

'Fetch her, Sacha,' Arcturus ordered, running towards the Wendigo, his dirk outstretched. Sacharissa bounded beside him, skittering as she struggled to find purchase on the smooth floor.

It was a good fifty yards to run, but it felt like a mile as the Wendigo flailed its claws around the room, each step dangerously close to Elaine's prone figure beneath.

Sacharissa reached her first, snatching Elaine's shirt collar and dragging her to the open door of the summoning room. It was slow going and they had barely made any progress when the Wendigo spotted his two new opponents.

Enraged by the stinging insect, it bellowed a challenge at Sacharissa, raking its claws along the ground to leave deep scores in the floorboards. Sacharissa paused, lowering her head and crouching against the floor. Arcturus sensed her intent: to meet the Wendigo head on.

'No, get her out of here,' he yelled, stepping between them. 'I'll keep it busy.'

He held the dirk in front of him, cutting back and forth at the air. It looked tiny next to the long talons that the Wendigo bore. One blade against ten.

A wyrdlight drifted between them. For a moment the Wendigo's eyes were transfixed upon it, then it was gone, floating past them.

'How about this,' Arcturus yelled, shooting a wyrdlight from his finger to zoom around the Wendigo's head. It blinked stupidly, then swiped its claw at it, just as it had done with Valens. The wyrdlight was extinguished, but another few seconds had been bought. Valens took this opportunity to sting at the Wendigo's eyes again. The monster swiped blindly at its face and left a groove of raw flesh in its own skin before the Mite was forced to take refuge in the antlers once again.

'Take this, this and this,' Arcturus yelled, sending one

wyrdlight after the other to circle the Wendigo's head. The Wendigo staggered in confusion, slapping at them like flies on a hot day. Arcturus glanced back to see Sacharissa was almost at the door. That was his mistake.

The Wendigo lunged, its claws slicing through the air to grasp for his throat. It was only by sheer luck that Arcturus managed to dive aside, but a grasping claw sliced him at the hip.

He was barely up and running before the next claw came slashing towards him. This time, there was no time to dodge. Instead, Arcturus blasted wyrdlight in a thick pulse of mana, a beam that left the Wendigo staggering as it clutched its scorched retinas. The claw knocked Arcturus flying, but the bulk of it was caught in the satchel on his back. Still, as he landed on the ground he could feel blood trickling down his spine and a streak of fierce pain across his shoulder blades.

Then he was running again, driven by adrenaline and fear as the Wendigo roared behind him. Valens zoomed over his shoulder, abandoning his perch to return to his mistress. Sacharissa was moments from the door, but Elaine was fighting against her now, oblivious that the Canid was trying to help, beating at Sacharissa's snout with her fists.

It was the blood that did it. The puddle of blood Arcturus had left on the ground from his nosebleed, wet against the smooth surface of the oak floorboards. His boot slipped from under him, no more than a few feet from the entrance. His head cracked against the ground, blackening his vision as the senses were knocked from him. So close. He had been so close.

He could feel Sacharissa dragging him, and the dull vibrations as the Wendigo approached from across the room. There was a strangled snarl and the pressure on his leg loosened. Then Sacharissa was leaping over his body, claws outstretched.

'No,' Arcturus whispered weakly, forcing himself to his knees.

But Sacharissa was already there, dodging beneath the Wendigo's outstretched claws to bite at the legs beneath. She took a calf in her teeth and shook her head violently, tearing into the hard flesh. Even as the Wendigo lashed at her, she had disappeared between its legs, only to swipe at its thigh with her claws. But as Arcturus rejoiced, the Wendigo kicked blindly like a mule, catching her in the chest and hurling her across the room. She lay there, barely able to breathe. Arcturus heaved with the pain of it, and knew her ribs were broken.

The Wendigo advanced upon her, saliva dripping on the floorboards, ready for the killing blow. It raised its hands high in the air, claws pointing down, like a mad pianist ready to play his first note.

Arcturus roared, leaping on to its back and burying the dirk up to the hilt in its spine. The Wendigo screeched like a banshee, spinning and slapping at him. But Arcturus was well placed, right in the small of its back. He clung on to the hilt, swinging back and forth as it leaped this way and that. Valens was there too, burying his mandibles in the Wendigo's ear.

It couldn't last though. The Wendigo bucked, breaking Arcturus's grip and sending him tumbling away. He fell in a tangle of limbs, right on top of Elaine. She sobbed beneath him, still frozen in fear. The end was near now. There were no cards left to play. He barely had the strength to walk, let alone drag Elaine out of the door.

He climbed on to his feet unsteadily and held up his fists.

The Wendigo limped towards him, its leg in tatters, yawping with pain as the dirk twisted in its spine.

'It hurts so much,' Elaine gasped beneath him. He saw the blood then, trickling from her head. She hadn't been paralysed with fear. The Wendigo had knocked her unconscious.

'Get out of here, Elaine. I'll hold it—'

The Wendigo's claw flashed out, slicing him across the face. He could not see, but punched out, connecting with the cold, hard flesh of its chest. He could hear Sacharissa howling, then he collapsed as another blow whistled over his head. A kick then, like a sledgehammer in his stomach. He puked.

He could see Sacharissa crawling towards them. She leaped, though the pain that ripped through her in doing so was like a knife in Arcturus's heart. Her tackle did nothing but cause the Wendigo to stumble. Then a bellow. Blood, dripping on his face. Flashes of light.

Then darkness.

16

A glimmer, flickering in the black. He was so close to letting go. There was so much pain. It would be easy to drift into the abyss.

The light was relentless, darting back and forth to keep his attention. It wanted him to follow.

'He's waking up.'

It tugged at him, insistent in its need. It knew him, this light. It was his friend.

'That's it, come back to us, Arcturus. You're going to be all right.'

Sacharissa was calling to him. He could feel her love, tugging him through their connection. She was the light in the darkness. The only one left in the world who cared for him. He struggled back, wading through the void, though it lay heavy, as if Anansi's tendrils gripped him still. He opened his eyes.

Three faces looked down at him. Elizabeth. Scipio. Obadiah. He groaned as he saw the Provost's face.

'Not you. I'll do whatever you want. Just don't hurt Sacha,' he croaked, grasping Obadiah's jacket.

'He's delirious. Thinks you're the Wendigo,' Scipio said, sponging Arcturus's forehead with his sleeve.

'Did the healing spell not work?' Elizabeth asked, her eyes filled with concern.

'It worked perfectly, but he took a knock to the head.' Obadiah lifted Arcturus's eyelid and peered close. 'Nothing a healing spell can do about concussion.'

'I'm fine,' Arcturus said, slapping Obadiah's hand away and sitting upright.

The room was filled with rows of beds, just like the one he was on, but from the masonry he knew he was still at Vocans. Bandages, bedding and medical instruments were stacked on shelves nearby. Elaine lay on the bed beside him, but she looked asleep. They were in the infirmary.

Sacharissa was curled up at the end of his bed, covered by a warm blanket. Arcturus could feel a fierce ache through their connection, which told him her ribs were still broken.

'Heal her,' he ordered, shuffling closer to Sacharissa and stroking her ears. 'Heal her and I'll tell you everything you need to know.'

'It's dangerous to use the healing spell on broken bones, Arcturus,' Elizabeth said gently, laying a calming hand on his shoulder. 'It can only be used safely on flesh wounds. We have to let nature take its course. She needs rest.'

'How did I get here?' Arcturus asked, blinking tears from his eyes. Sacharissa was so quiet, her chest barely rising and falling. How could he have let this happen to her?

'Ulfr woke us, told us he had heard unusual sounds from the

summoning room. We got there just in time to fight off the Wendigo. I left it locked in the summoning room, while we tended to your wounds.' Scipio looked reproachfully at the Provost. 'Obadiah arrived as we dragged you out. He is going to harness the Wendigo later.'

'You're going to make that thing your demon?' Arcturus cried. 'After what it did?'

'It's a powerful demon, and weak enough to capture now, thanks to you,' Obadiah stated, unashamed. 'I will bend it to my will and use it against the orcs. I have given my Hydra to my son, Zacharias. This demon will take its place.'

Arcturus leaned away from him, disgusted. What manner of man would want that monstrosity as their demon, powerful or not? He was so lucky to have Sacharissa.

'I want to know what you meant when you said you'd tell us "everything you need to know",' Elizabeth said, tactfully changing the subject. 'Is that why your bag is all packed?'

'I overheard Charles saying that the Provost was coming back to interrogate me – I wasn't going to hang around for that,' Arcturus muttered.

'Interrogate is a strong word. I wanted you to confirm my theory, that's all. I suspect that is why Charles and Rook tried to kill you. Little did they know, I had already guessed the truth.' Obadiah's face darkened with sudden anger.

'How do you know they were involved?' Arcturus asked, dumbfounded.

'Ulfr saw them leaving the summoning room,' Obadiah said. 'Of course, the word of a dwarf will never stand up in court, especially against two nobles, but it is enough for me. The half-men are malicious little creatures, but this particular one had no reason to lie. The two boys will be expelled from the school, to be privately tutored at home. It is as harsh a punishment as I can give them.'

Arcturus nodded, unsure of whether to be pleased or angry. It could have been a lot worse – their actions may never have come to light. But expulsion . . . was that all? Even when caught red-handed, their high birth had protected them.

He felt a flash of gratitude for Ulfr. Were it not for him, Arcturus would be slowly digesting within the stomach of a monster. It was unfair of Obadiah to speak of him in such a way.

'Lady Faversham is dealing with them now,' Obadiah said, lowering his voice and leaning closer. 'It is a good thing she is not here, for what we are about to discuss must never reach her ears.'

'What do you mean?' Scipio asked. Even Elizabeth looked perplexed. Clearly, this was news to all of them.

'As soon as I heard of the mysterious fire that killed the innkeeper and his wife, I suspected foul play. Yet, they were the only two that knew where you came from. I already suspected you were Faversham's bastard son – hell, that's why the king put me in charge of the investigation in the first place. He suspects the same.'

'He's Faversham's son?' Scipio groaned, laying his face in his hands. 'This is going to cause a mess. Lady Faversham is going to be furio—'

'Lady Faversham will know nothing,' Obadiah snapped. 'Now keep your tongue still until I have finished speaking. What

110

we are about to do amounts to high treason, but it is the only thing we can do to save hundreds of lives and prevent the kingdom from tearing itself apart.'

Scipio fell silent, though his face reddened with anger at being spoken to in such a way. Elizabeth squeezed his shoulder and nodded at Obadiah to continue.

'I searched for mysterious deaths in the local area. Faversham wouldn't stop at the innkeeper, he had too much riding on it. So when I discovered that the owner of a workhouse had been mysteriously murdered, I knew where to look.'

'Smart,' Arcturus said, but he shook his head in disgust.

'But that's not all. When I visited the workhouse, I discovered something else there.'

He leaned even closer, his voice barely more than a whisper.

'There were others. Like you. More of Faversham's brood.'

Arcturus was stunned. Lord and Lady Faversham were obviously covering up an unhappy marriage if there were other illegitimate sons out there.

'I tested them, the same way we do with non-firstborn noble children, in case they have inherited the ability to summon. Two others, plus one more in another workhouse.'

'Three of us,' Arcturus murmured.

'All boys, believe it or not,' Obadiah chuckled. 'But that was not all. You see, I had sent my most trusted officers to test other children, to keep up appearances, you understand. They flew from village to village, lining up the boys and girls and checking one by one. They have been through thousands of them, testing each and every one. It was only on my way here that I received the message. There are more of them.'

'What does that mean?' Elizabeth asked. 'Other illegitimate children?'

'No, not bastards,' Obadiah stated, sneering as Elizabeth winced at the terminology. 'The officers confirmed it. The village they found the first common summoner in was hundreds of miles from the nearest noble estate. The mother is a brunette who had never been more than a mile from her village. The local baker was the father, and the boy had his red hair and green eyes. There was no doubt of parentage there.'

'So . . . it's not just illegitimate children. Commoners are manifesting the ability independently,' Scipio gasped.

'Not so loud,' Obadiah hushed. 'Yes, that is the case . . . and that is the story we are going to tell the king. Nobody must know that Lord Faversham cheated on his wife. There will be other bastards out there, just like Arcturus. Scores of them. Maybe hundreds.'

Arcturus thought about all the other 'bastards' out there, left to rot while their noble fathers lived the high life, careless of their children's circumstances. Obadiah was sweating now, and Arcturus grimaced as he realised that perhaps even Obadiah himself had worries about illegitimate children of his own.

The noble and his ilk were selfish brutes, the lot of them. Even speaking to the man left a bad taste in Arcturus's mouth, but he forced himself to listen.

'Imagine what would happen, if word were to get out. The orphanages around the country would be tested immediately, proof of every infidelity across the country revealed. Noble houses would split apart, Hominum's aristocracy shattered in an instant. Right when we need to be strong.'

Elizabeth and Scipio were nodding, though most of the conversation went over Arcturus's head. All he knew was that they were going to keep his origins a secret.

'The dwarves plot another rebellion as we speak. The orc raids become more frequent each day. Hell, the commoners themselves are becoming despondent, furious at the way the king has bankrupted the country. There is even talk of the king giving up his throne so that Prince Harold can take his place, just to placate the people!'

'All well and good,' Elizabeth said, holding up her hands. 'I agree that we must keep illegitimate children a secret and tell the world that Arcturus simply manifested the gift independently, as the other commoners you found did. But I have two questions for you. How will we keep him safe? As long as Arcturus is here, Lord Faversham and Charles will try to kill him, to get rid of the evidence. Also, how will we keep this a secret? Let's not forget that if Lady Faversham finds out, she *will* kill him.'

'Now, I want you to stay calm,' Obadiah said warily, backing away from the table. 'But I have made a deal with Charles and his father.'

'You did *what*?' Elizabeth snarled, her eyes blazing with anger. 'After what they tried to do to Arcturus?'

'I said calm yourself!' Obadiah growled back. 'It had to be done, to keep the boy safe. In exchange for Arcturus's safety, I promised that I would remain in charge of the search for the commoners for as long as the king will allow me to. I will conceal all knowledge of the clusters of adept commoners in the workhouses and orphanages from the world, and keep Lord

Faversham's shameful secret. I was going to do it anyway – we might as well secure Arcturus's safety out of it. All I need from you three is to keep your mouths shut about this whole thing.'

'But what if you die, or the king decides to place you somewhere else?' Scipio asked. 'What if he creates a grand inquisition to investigate the whole affair? You said yourself he has his suspicions.'

'At that point, Arcturus will hopefully be a graduated battlemage, capable of taking care of himself and away from Lady Faversham's wrath. Do you agree to this plan?'

'I do,' Arcturus said, despite his disgust. But it was not like he had any other choice.

'As do I,' Scipio agreed in a low voice.

Elizabeth paused for a moment, then nodded.

'If it keeps Arcturus safe,' she said.

'Good. Now, let's allow the boy to have his rest.' Obadiah clapped his hands together with finality. 'You should be happy, Arcturus. Your year is just beginning.'

'Rest up,' Elizabeth said, following Scipio and Obadiah as they filed out of the room. 'I'll bring you breakfast in the morning.'

The door slammed behind them, leaving Arcturus sitting in silence. Even Sacharissa was asleep, despite the discussion that had been raging above her head. He lay back and tried to do the same.

'Well, I thought they'd never leave!'

His eyes snapped open to see a grinning Elaine, her tresses falling over him and tickling his nose.

114

'I thought you were unconscious!' he spluttered, pawing her hair out of his face and sitting up.

'So did they,' Elaine giggled.

Arcturus's heart began to thunder. A secret that could tear apart the empire, in the head of another student.

'What did you hear exactly?' he asked carefully.

'I don't know. After they said Charles was expelled, I stopped listening. Too confusing.' She shook her head, then winced and rubbed the back of her skull. 'It still hurts.'

'Serves you right, listening in on people's conversations. You'd think you would have learned by now, after that Wendigo almost killed you,' he growled.

'Oh poo. Sacha was there to protect me, weren't you, beautiful?' She stroked Sacharissa's neck fur.

'Stop that!'

She snatched her hand away and crossed her arms, giving Arcturus a grumpy look.

'If we're going to be friends, you can't talk to me that way,' she said haughtily, turning her nose up at him. 'You have to say please.'

'OK. *Please* don't do that. It's not polite.'

'Good,' she said, instantly forgiving him. 'I'm a good friend, you know, I promise. We can talk whenever you like. You're not alone any more.'

Arcturus shuffled over to make room as she sat beside him. He smiled as she surreptitiously flicked the end of Sacharissa's tail.

Arcturus then thought of the risk his teachers were taking to keep him safe. The feeling of being protected was new to him.

His mind turned to the brothers and sisters he might have out there. Then the other common adepts, illegitimates and randomly gifted alike.

'You're right, Elaine. I'm not alone. Not any more.'

17

Arcturus spent two weeks in the infirmary, claiming dizziness from his concussion – though in truth only Sacharissa needed healing. It was a relief, to be away from the noble students – he was sure they had all heard about what had happened in the summoning room, and had no desire to face them until he was ready.

His only visitors were Elizabeth and Elaine – the former to bring him food and tutor him while he was unwell, the latter to pester both him and Sacharissa, and gossip about what was happening in the academy.

As the days passed by, Arcturus was pleased to discover that as far as anyone knew – Ophelia Faversham included – Charles and Rook had been expelled for duelling each other, and that he had been injured in the crossfire. A few students harboured suspicions, but the boys had not been particularly popular and after a few days of gossip things had died down.

According to Elaine, only Zacharias seemed bothered by the loss of Charles and Rook, so Arcturus endeavoured to stay away from the Provost's son as much as possible. He suspected that somehow, Zacharias would blame him for the pair's expulsion – especially if his father had chosen to trust the boy with the truth about that night.

By the end of the fortnight, Arcturus was pleased to see that Sacharissa was almost fully healed, her recovery sped up by her successful infusion a few nights before. Elizabeth had spent many hours teaching him the technique, and had even given him an old summoning leather of hers to practise with while she was busy downstairs.

Still, he had to rejoin the world eventually, and Sacharissa was becoming boisterous now that she was recovered. So, almost two weeks after that fateful night, he decided to go down for breakfast, though he infused Sacharissa first – standing her on the summoning leather and absorbing her into his body. He didn't want to get in trouble for having his demon out before lesson time.

As he did so, Arcturus remembered the first time he had infused Sacharissa, guided by Elizabeth in the infirmary; the euphoria of her being merged with him, and the strange knowledge that she could now see through his eyes.

It felt strange to leave the infirmary. Of course he had left the room before, to use the facilities and wash, but he had purposefully chosen to go when lessons were in progress, and he was yet to see any of the students.

For that reason, Arcturus was somewhat surprised when he found the dining hall mostly deserted when he entered – even if, to his dismay, one of the few people there was Zacharias. Edmund, the boy who had shown him some kindness on that first day, was also there, as well as the Queensouth twins and Prince Harold. When they noticed his presence, the group fell silent, following him with their eyes as he crossed the room.

Arcturus took a tray from a waiting dwarf servant, and sat himself down beside them. He focussed on eating, ignoring their stares.

'So . . . are you going to tell us what happened?' Josephine Queensouth asked after a moment's pause, giving him a nudge.

'I don't want to talk about it,' Arcturus mumbled through a mouthful of eggs.

'Leave him be, Josephine,' Alice, her twin sister, said. 'It's not our business, and we already know what happened anyway.'

'But not the juicy details,' Josephine moaned, rolling her eyes.

Alice ignored her. She leaned forward and gave Arcturus an encouraging smile.

'Are you feeling better, Arcturus?' Alice asked.

Arcturus looked up and gave her a quick nod, forcing a smile of his own.

'Jolly good,' Edmund said loudly, putting his arm around Alice's shoulders. 'Glad to have you back. Now, where were we? The weekend, right?'

'That's right,' Zacharias said, his eyes fixed on Arcturus. 'We were saying we should probably avoid Corcillum, after the protests last week.'

Protests?

'Riots, more like,' Prince Harold muttered, half under his breath.

'It can't be helped,' Josephine sniffed. 'The plebs just don't understand the pressures of ruling.'

119

But Harold shook his head.

'They're right to be angry,' he said, stabbing a sausage with his fork. 'My father was a fool to spend so much of their taxes on building his palace. There are people starving across the kingdom and he plants roses and builds fountains.'

There was an awkward pause, and understanding dawned on Arcturus then. Obadiah had said something about this – how there was growing unrest because of Harold's father, King Alfric, bankrupting the country.

'I say we go to my place,' Edmund broke the silence, leaning back in his chair. 'My parents are on a trade mission with the elves, so we have the run of the estate. We can go hunting for buffalo.'

The room rang with agreement, and Edmund turned to Arcturus.

'What do you reckon, Arcturus?'

Arcturus stared at him blankly, yolk dripping down his chin.

'That sounds . . . like fun,' Arcturus said, after a moment's consideration. Was that an invitation?

'So it's agreed,' Edmund said, clapping his hands together. 'Carriages arrive tomorrow morning at first bell. Don't be late.'

Arcturus sat speechless as the benches were scraped back and the group began to head out. Only Zacharias remained, glowering at him, his square jaw set with anger.

Arcturus met his gaze head on, keeping his apprehension hidden with a steady stare. Finally, Zacharias broke the stare and stood too, barging Arcturus's shoulder as he strode past.

Alone, Arcturus quickly finished his breakfast, wolfing down the last of his eggs and toast, but not before making sure to pocket some sausages for Sacharissa to eat later.

His belly gurgled at the sudden influx of food. In just one meal he had eaten as much as he would have in a week when he had been a stable boy. He had forgotten how it felt to *feel* full.

Since he had arrived at Vocans, he had more energy, more strength, and even the cold didn't bother him half so much. But he couldn't allow himself to become complacent.

And what had Elizabeth told him? Trust no one. Yet . . . he felt like he could trust Edmund, not to mention both Elizabeth and Elaine. Although, now that he thought about it, he wondered why his new friends had not told him about the riots.

More to the point . . . where were they? Elaine and her brothers should have been at breakfast, and Elizabeth had not come to see him the night before for their usual summoning lesson. In fact, she was supposed to have been there that morning too, to help Arcturus with his demonology studies.

Arcturus knew that Elizabeth was housed above the servants' quarters, so he set out across the atrium and up the east staircase. As he made his way up the winding steps, he felt the temperature drop. Clearly, this side of the building did not benefit from the roaring fireplaces that warmed the west wing, where the noble students and wealthier teachers slept.

Still, even if the servants' quarters were colder, they were decorated as ostentatiously, and Arcturus could see passages lined with paintings, tapestries, even suits of armour and racks of gleaming weaponry, as the winding stairway took him higher and higher.

When he reached the top floor, Arcturus paused, wondering which way to go. A long, darkened passageway stretched in front of him, while the balcony overlooking the atrium lay to his left and right, with doors studding its walls.

An idea came to Arcturus, and he smiled. He kneeled and unravelled the summoning leather that Elizabeth had given him, leaving the square of pentacle-embossed leather on the ground in front of him.

Moments later, Sacharissa materialised into existence, her tail wagging like a metronome. She whined and nuzzled against Arcturus's palm, then nipped him lightly for keeping her confined for so long.

'I'm sorry, Sacha, but you'd better get used to it,' Arcturus smiled, ruffling her ears. 'Now keep quiet. You're not supposed to be out.'

The dog demon rolled on her back, whining hopefully as she waited for a belly rub. Arcturus obliged, shaking his head ruefully as she wriggled with pleasure. She was still a puppy at heart.

'Can you smell Elizabeth for me, girl?' Arcturus murmured. 'I need you to find her.'

Instantly, the demon was on her feet, her ears upright and alert, nose close to the ground. He could sense her excitement, pulsing through him like a rush of adrenaline. A hunt. It was what she was born to do.

Already she was snuffling the ground, prowling forward with the low gait of a lion stalking a gazelle, the soft padding of her feline feet barely making a sound in the echoey hollow of the murky passageway ahead.

'Attagirl,' Arcturus said, rolling up his summoning leather and following her into the ill-lit corridor.

He could almost smell the scent that Sacharissa was pursuing, just as he had smelled Elaine in the summoning room. It wasn't as powerful as when he looked directly into Sacharissa's eyes, but it seemed as if the demon's senses were bleeding into his own.

Elizabeth's scent was like a symphony of notes in Sacharissa's mind, and Arcturus found it hard to concentrate as the new sensation wafted through him.

And yet, there was another, stronger smell breaking through, made up of leather, musk and soot. Even as it became stronger, Arcturus thought he could make out a short, stocky figure in the gloom ahead, a flickering light hanging in the air beside it.

It was Ulfr, squinting at them beneath his bushy eyebrows as the pair approached. Arcturus stepped into the light of Ulfr's lantern, and was suddenly suffused with guilt. He had not thought to thank the dwarf – he owed Ulfr his life, after all. If the dwarf had not gone for help when Arcturus was under attack, the young summoner would likely be Wendigo droppings by now.

'I . . . I wanted to thank you, for fetching the teachers,' Arcturus stammered, suddenly shy under the dwarf's glower. 'I should have come sooner. I'm sorry.'

'No thanks or apologies needed,' Ulfr muttered, turning aside. ''Twas not for the love of you, but to get back at those noble brats. Many's the time they've taunted me. Now who's laughing?'

The dwarf broke into a grim smile.

'You have my thanks all the same,' Arcturus replied, his heart sinking at Ulfr's words. 'We are not all like them.'

'Aren't you?' Ulfr growled, his brows beetling as his face darkened with anger.

He grabbed Arcturus's arm and pulled him a few steps up the corridor, ignoring the warning growl from Sacharissa. The dwarf spun Arcturus around and stabbed a stubby finger at a painting hanging on the wall.

'This is what humans do.'

It took a moment for Arcturus to register the scene before his eyes, for the image was cracked and faded. Then his eyes widened in horror.

A column of dwarves were depicted mid-march down the centre of a parade, complete with a pennant-waving crowd on either side. They were naked and soil-stained, with metal collars around their necks and heavy chains kept taut between them. Behind, men on horses were frozen in the act of flailing whips at their bare backs, and if Arcturus looked closely, he could see red-furrowed wounds on the dwarven skin and the red rivulets of blood that streamed beneath them.

'They hang these in the servants quarters, especially the dwarven floors. "Lest we forget", so we're told,' Ulfr spat. 'Well, I won't forget, they can be sure of that.'

'Who are they?' Arcturus asked.

'The captives from the last dwarven rebellion, many years ago,' Ulfr said through gritted teeth. 'They want us to remember that we lost the last one. And the one before that.'

'It's cruel,' Arcturus said, horrified.

'Aye. Like all your kind,' Ulfr said.

Before Arcturus could think of an answer, someone cleared their throat behind him. He spun to see a thin, yellow-toothed man standing behind him. The newcomer wore the robes of a servant, and his expression turned to one of surprise as he took in Arcturus's uniform.

'Are you lost, my lord?' the man said with a bow, his voice nasal and obsequious.

'No need to bow, Crawley, he's no lord,' Ulfr said derisively. 'He's that commoner.'

'Indeed?' Crawley's eyes lit up with sudden interest, and he leaned in to examine Arcturus closely. 'Fascinating.'

He furrowed his brows, cocking his head to one side, and his eyes flashed hungrily to Sacharissa.

'I had not thought . . . perhaps . . . yes . . .'

He trailed off, but continued to stare at Arcturus, his eyes roving back and forth. Arcturus coughed awkwardly, eager to get away from the strange man.

Remembering himself, Crawley smiled and nodded at Arcturus before turning to Ulfr.

'Ulfr, I was looking for you—'

'We've nought to talk about,' Ulfr interrupted, shuffling uncomfortably. 'You've heard my answer and that's the end of it.'

The dwarf caught Arcturus staring at him and his face darkened.

'Don't you have somewhere to be?' Ulfr snapped.

Sacharissa growled at the dwarf's tone, and Arcturus was forced to grip the mane along the ridge of her back.

'You had better hurry along,' Crawley said, still giving Arcturus that strange, inquisitive look.

'Come on, Sacha,' Arcturus said, calming his demon with a

thought. She had become extremely protective of late.

They continued down the corridor, following Elizabeth's elusive scent. Behind them, a whispered argument echoed eerily, though Arcturus was unable to hear what was being said.

He glanced over his shoulder as they turned the corner, catching the silhouettes of the two servants.

'I wonder what that was all about?' Arcturus pondered aloud, scratching Sacharissa under her chin. It was strange, but she had grown almost a half-foot taller than she had been when they had first met, and was now almost as large as a miniature pony.

As she looked up at him, her eyes half closed with pleasure and their gazes met. Arcturus felt himself slipping into the grey-tinted world that Sacharissa inhabited, complete with intensified sounds and smells.

He did not break the connection – it was an experience like no other. Scents were so intense it was as if he were tasting the air itself, and he could even sense its ebbs and flows and determine its direction. Still, it was not all good.

A stale aroma of body odour leaked beneath the door they stood beside. It made Arcturus gag with every fresh waft, while Sacharissa snuffled at the door with an inquisitive nose, fascinated.

He looked away from Sacharissa's eyes, and was relieved to find that with a bit of concentration, he was able to continue the ability independently.

Intrigued, he took a few steps away. Along with the marginally fresher air, sounds of a whispered argument around the corner reached his newly sensitive ears.

'. . . I say again, the dwarves will not join you in this folly.'

It was Ulfr, his words rapid and angry. 'Nor will I have any part in it.'

'You're making a mistake. Grant me an audience with your elders. I know I can make them see reason,' Crawley growled. 'This is happening with or without you.'

'I cannot help you,' Ulfr replied.

'If the dwarves will not aid us, I cannot guarantee their position when the sun rises three days hence,' Crawley said, his voice taut and threatening.

'So be it,' Ulfr snapped.

Arcturus heard footsteps as Ulfr strode away.

'Wait!' Crawley called. 'There's something else.'

The footsteps ceased.

'The boy. You know him, yes?' Crawley asked.

'What of it?' Ulfr replied warily.

'He could be useful. Perhaps you could turn him to our cause. If you did, our leaders would look more kindly on the dwarves.'

Silence.

'You leave him out of this,' Ulfr said.

The footsteps continued until they had faded from earshot.

18

Arcturus hurried down the corridor, Crawley's footsteps following behind him. The man was cursing under his breath, but Arcturus did not wish to listen any further. Nor did he wish to run into him, especially after what he had just heard.

His mind was in turmoil. Their conversation had made little sense to him. Crawley needed the dwarves' help to do something secret . . . something that would take place in three days' time. And somehow Arcturus was involved. But why? Why *him*?

Arcturus's thighs thudded into Sacharissa's side, nearly tripping him on to the floor. The demon was sitting beside a wooden door, one of many embedded in the walls of the maze of corridors.

He realised that they had arrived at Elizabeth's room. As Crawley's footsteps neared, Arcturus banged on the door with his fist, looking furtively down the gloomy passageway.

Moments later, the door swung open, revealing a dishevelled-looking Elizabeth, her uniform rumpled and soot-stained. Her eyes were red-rimmed, as if she had been crying.

'What are you doing here?' she asked, confused.

Arcturus barged past her, catching a brief glimpse of Crawley rounding the corner. Sacharissa bounded in behind him and Elizabeth closed the door, a puzzled look on her face.

Arcturus breathed a sigh of relief and collapsed on to a stool in the corner of the room. He had not realised how panicked he was until that very moment, heart hammering in his chest.

'Arcturus, I did not invite you in,' Elizabeth said reproachfully, surreptitiously flicking her blanket over her unmade bed. 'I know you were raised in an orphanage, but surely you know this is unacceptable.'

Embarrassed, Arcturus lowered his head. The room was barely furnished, with a few dirty plates piled on a rickety desk, alongside a stack of books, parchment and a stub of candle. A large wardrobe was the only other piece of furniture, leaving Elizabeth to sit down on the bed.

'I'm sorry, I was just . . .'

He stopped. Something held him back from mentioning Crawley. Ulfr was involved somehow, unwillingly or not, as was he. Was he keeping quiet to protect Ulfr . . . or himself?

'. . . worried about you,' he muttered lamely, twisting his hands in his lap.

Elizabeth's face softened at his words, and Arcturus felt a twinge of guilt for lying to her.

'Well, something to keep in mind next time,' she said, giving him a quick smile. 'I'm sorry I wasn't there this morning. Unfortunately, I've been ordered to report to the palace, so I won't be able to come and tutor you in the afternoon. After the weekend you'll have to rejoin normal lessons – Provost Forsyth's orders.'

Arcturus's heart sank, dreading his next encounter with Lady Faversham – he had just got her son expelled after all, and who knows what Charles had told her. He didn't want to think about it.

'What happened to you?' Arcturus asked, staring at Elizabeth's blackened uniform.

Elizabeth sighed and brushed ineffectually at the soot on her trousers, but only managed to spread it further.

'There was trouble in Corcillum last night,' Elizabeth replied, rubbing her eyes wearily. 'Some of the common folk set fire to the barracks. They're not happy with how their taxes are being spent. There was some looting, even some fighting. Most of the teachers were called in to manage the situation – lessons have been cancelled today since we were up all night fighting the blaze.'

Of course, he should have known – Zacharias had mentioned the riots. Arcturus stood and shook his head apologetically.

'I'm sorry, I must have woken you. I should go,' Arcturus said, standing.

'It's fine. Here, take this,' Elizabeth said, reaching across to her desk and picking up a slim volume. 'It's the demonology textbook. All the demons that we know of are in here, along with their stats and abilities. This one's out of date – there's a new edition each year with updated illustrations and newly discovered demons – but it should give you something to read if I can't make it this afternoon.'

'Thank you,' Arcturus said, clasping the book gratefully

to his chest. 'I'll study it today.'

He slipped out the door, giving her an apologetic wave.

Only to find Crawley waiting for him.

'Ah . . . there you are,' Crawley said, putting an arm around Arcturus's shoulders and propelling him down the corridor. 'We haven't been properly introduced.'

The servant ignored a warning growl from Sacharissa, who paced along beside them with her teeth bared. There was a strange scent emanating from the man, masked with what must have been a liberal splash of cheap cologne – Arcturus couldn't place it.

'Arcturus, right?'

Arcturus nodded mutely, trying to shrug off the iron grip that now encased him.

'I'm Crawley, head steward,' the man continued, turning Arcturus down another passage. 'You might say I run the show where the servants are concerned. I want you to know, if you need anything, anything at all, you just let me know.'

'Thank you,' Arcturus said guardedly, finally managing to extricate himself. They had arrived in a small alcove with a bookcase and two armchairs. He could see the balcony further down the corridor, and the area was lit by a rainbow of light from a stained glass window in the wall.

'This is my favourite place. Please, sit.'

The hand that pushed Arcturus down gave him little choice.

Crawley settled opposite him, and gave him a calculating look over steepled fingers. This time, Arcturus was angry. They might both be commoners, but that gave the man no right to manhandle him that way.

'What do you want?' Arcturus said, lacing his voice with a measure of the anger he felt.

Crawley only smiled and continued staring. Even another growl from Sacharissa couldn't shift his eyes. It was as if he were deciding something.

Finally, after what felt like an age, he spoke.

'Do you like it here, Arcturus?'

Of all the questions, that was what Crawley wanted to ask him?

'I like it well enough. I mean, I almost died last week, but that's over with now.'

'Ah yes. The supposed duel . . . I think we both know that's not exactly what happened. They tried to kill you, didn't they? For being a commoner. Don't deny it.'

Arcturus blanched at the accusation, and Crawley smiled at his reaction, nodding to himself.

'I thought so.'

Unnerved, Arcturus made to get up, but Crawley raised a warning hand.

'I know you were forced to keep it quiet. I'll keep it our little secret. I mean, they wouldn't want the story that some nobles had tried to assassinate the first common summoner getting out to the masses. Not in the current climate.'

Arcturus didn't like where the conversation was heading.

'Look, whatever you want from me, I don't want any part of it. Leave me alone and we won't have any problems.'

This time he stood and began to walk away. Crawley snatched his wrist as he hurried past, holding him in place for another moment.

Crawley glared up at him, and this time Arcturus saw a fanatical, mad look in the servant's eyes.

'You're going to have to pick a side one day, Arcturus,' Crawley snapped, 'and you may not have a choice when that day comes. Think on it.'

Sacharissa barked, flecking the man's face with saliva. He didn't even blink. It was all Arcturus could do to stop her from latching on to Crawley's forearm, his mind twisting to hold her in place.

'I . . . I will,' was all Arcturus managed to say.

Crawley let his arm go and Arcturus rushed away without a backward glance. He felt sick to his stomach, the world spinning as he sprinted down the stairs.

It was only much later, reading his new demonology book beneath a glowing wyrdlight, that Arcturus realised what Crawley had smelled like. The fires in Corcillum sprang unbidden to his mind.

He had smelled like lamp oil. Flammable, raw lamp oil.

19

When Arcturus woke to the first rays of morning light streaming through the open arrow slit, the previous morning's events felt like a bad dream.

He had hidden there for the rest of that day, only opening his door to accept cold sandwiches of salt pork and cheese from an impatient servant boy, feeding half to a hungry Sacharissa.

Now he pushed the memories from his mind, packed up his meagre possessions and headed down for breakfast, wondering if Edmund's offer had been genuine . . . or even directed at him at all. He kept Sacharissa infused once again – she had come so close to attacking Crawley, Arcturus was worried he might not be able to stop her from attacking the next time he was being threatened. And that was happening far too often these days.

His heart dropped when he stumbled into the dining hall. It was empty but for a single, bored-looking servant hunched beside a platter of bread and bowls of jam and butter.

Arcturus felt a strange mix of relief and disappointment. In some ways he had been scared of joining these rich, confident nobles on a weekend jaunt. But still . . . he had been looking forward to making some friends – or at least, friends his age. If the day before had taught him anything, it was how alone he really was.

'There you are,' a voice called out from behind him. 'Honestly, where are your chambers? We've been banging on every door in the west wing looking for you.'

Arcturus spun, only to find a grinning Edmund, standing with his hands on his hips.

'I'm in the tower,' Arcturus replied, smiling himself. The young noble's grin was infectious.

'The carriages are waiting outside. I say, is that all you're bringing?' Edmund looked pointedly at the small bundle of possessions on Arcturus's back.

'Errr . . . yes,' Arcturus said.

'Jolly good, no need to call the soldiers in to help move your stuff,' Edmund said, heading for the double doors in the atrium. 'I swear, Zacharias brought his entire damned wardrobe.'

'Soldiers?' Arcturus asked, hurrying behind him.

'Ah . . . yes, well, what with the riots last night and Prince Harold coming with us, King Alfric has sent some of Hominum's finest to escort us,' Edmund replied.

A chill ran through Arcturus at the reminder of the riots. He didn't want to think about it . . . things would sort themselves out.

Edmund heaved the heavy double doors open, and Arcturus followed him into the brisk morning air. To his surprise, the courtyard was a hive of activity. Servants ran back and forth, lifting and tying an assortment of trunks and bags on to the tops of two carriages. In front of each vehicle stood a pair of sleek, black horses, snorting gouts of steam into the chill, morning air.

'Zacharias has taken up most of the room in one of the carriages with all his damned bags – and you're the last one here. You'll have to ride with the soldiers,' Edmund said, grimacing apologetically.

He pointed beyond the carriages, where a squat, canvas-covered wagon sat beside the drawbridge. A dozen soldiers stood outside, stomping their feet to stay warm.

'We'll have plenty of time to catch up when we get there,' Edmund said, giving Arcturus a gentle push. 'Go ahead, I told them to make room for you.'

Arcturus turned to thank Edmund, but the boy had already disappeared into one of the carriages. Through the darkened glass, Arcturus could see Zacharias and Harold there too, the spare seat piled high with cases and furs. As he looked, Zacharias turned towards him and gave him an icy glare, before tugging the curtain closed.

'Great,' Arcturus mumbled, trudging towards the wagon.

As he came closer, he was surprised to see the military's horses were of a far poorer quality than those on the nobles' carriages. The two specimens before him were swaybacked nags, the fur around their muzzles dusted with the grey of old age, though his experience as a stable boy told him they were well fed and groomed.

Now that he thought about it, the soldiers were not in the best shape either. All wore a hauberk of chainmail, but the metal links were stained with the tell-tale red-brown of rust. Their boots were cracked and worn, and most of their clothing looked as if it had not been washed in weeks.

And yet . . . there was an air of cool professionalism about them. They held themselves with confidence, and their eyes roamed the surroundings in a habit clearly born of long practice, even as they puffed tobacco from pipes and cheroots.

'Well, lad, are you coming or not?' a grizzled sergeant called from the driver's bench at the front of the wagon. The middle-aged man patted the seat next to him, and though Arcturus looked longingly at the relative warmth within the vehicle's canvas shell, he leaped up at the front.

'All ready!' called a voice from behind them, as dwarven servants scattered to make a path.

The wagon shook as the soldiers leaped in behind them, then they were trundling over the drawbridge, while Arcturus looked nervously at the murky waters on either side – knowing that if they tipped in, he would sink like a stone. He had never learned to swim.

'So, they've saddled you with our little band of ruffians,' the gruff sergeant beside him said, clicking his tongue as he turned their wagon on to the dirt track outside Vocans.

'Well, there was no room so . . .' Arcturus mumbled.

'Aye, that Zacharias boy brought enough garments to clothe half of the King's Army,' the sergeant grumbled. 'Though truth be told, we could do with them, fancy though they may be.'

The sergeant grimaced, picking at a loose thread on his breeches. Arcturus maintained a diplomatic silence, looking out at the rolling countryside.

'We'll not be seeing any orcs around here,' the sergeant said, misunderstanding Arcturus's gaze. 'They don't raid this far north. Nor would a gang of brigands attack a convoy under our protection, not to mention one carrying a group of novice summoners. You're safe, lad.'

Arcturus was not so sure: Edmund had told him that the need for an escort was related to the riots. Still, it was a relief to hear that they were not in danger of orcs. He had never seen one, but the fearsome creatures were the stuff of nightmares, used to scare naughty children into behaving.

'You fight them?' Arcturus asked. 'The orcs, I mean.'

'That's the long and short of it,' the sergeant said. 'Raiders mostly, after cattle. The southern villages are all but empty now – nobody wants to live there any more. There's only so much our soldiers can do.'

Arcturus shuddered at the thought, remembering the tales he had heard from the wounded veterans that had passed through the tavern, trading their tales of horror and bravery for a few pennies and a bed.

'How many of you are there?' Arcturus asked, remembering the paltry number of men in the wagon behind them.

'There's maybe a few hundred of us,' the sergeant said. 'A score or so of squads like mine. Hard to say really – we lose a lot of men, and recruit a lot of volunteers. Poor buggers. When they find out the reality of it, it's too late to change their minds.'

'Is it really so bad?' Arcturus asked.

If he ever graduated from Vocans, he assumed he would be on the front lines with men like these. At least, that was the case for the lesser nobles who had no money to raise their own soldiers, and instead became officers in the King's Army. It was a few years away yet, but that did not change the dread that suddenly seized his heart.

'Not for my lads,' the sergeant replied, a hint of pride in his voice. 'We haven't had a casualty in almost six months. It's why our squad got picked for this escort mission, even if it is a babysitting job.'

'That's a relief,' Arcturus replied, but the sergeant remained unconvinced.

'Don't be fooled by our appearance. We do our best with what we have. Our generals equipped us with hand-me-downs of hand-me-downs, rusty old swords and half-rotted crossbows. But you'll find my men know how to use them. I keep them on a tight leash.'

'The tightest,' came a voice from behind them, muffled by the canvas. 'He's a harsh taskmaster, that's the truth. Drills us night and day. It's a miracle we even get any sleep.'

'Quiet in the ranks!' the sergeant barked, but with a grin on his face.

A head popped out between Arcturus and the sergeant, pushing through the parting of canvas behind them.

'Bloody hell, sarge, you don't half blather on. We're trying to get some sleep back here.'

The soldier who had spoken was surprisingly old, aged at what Arcturus guessed was in his thirties. He had light-brown hair and a wide, infectious grin.

'Private Rotter, you will get back to your station,' the sergeant growled, pushing the private's head back with his elbow. 'Or you'll be digging our latrines for a week.'

'Right you are, Sergeant Caulder,' Rotter replied, saluting smartly and retreating back inside.

Sergeant Caulder shook his head and gave Arcturus a wry smile.

'Despite appearances, Rotter's a damned good soldier,' Caulder whispered. 'I'd have recommended his promotion a long time ago, if he weren't so damned immature.'

The muffled sound of a raucous, curse-filled shanty emanated from behind them.

'Shut it, Rotter,' groaned another soldier.

The singing only got louder.

Arcturus grinned. Maybe he hadn't pulled the short straw after all.

20

As Arcturus gazed at the slow-changing surroundings, the gentle, green-carpeted fields filled with sleepy hamlets and lowing cows receded into the hills behind them, replaced by something wilder.

Untended, overgrown hedges began to mar the landscape, which was now scattered with outcrops of rocks and sprawling brambles. It was only when they began to see the first ruins of burned-out and abandoned houses covered with invading tendrils of ivy that they turned off the main path, forking to the south-west. The convoy was on the edge of orc-raiding territory now, and the sergeant laid a crossbow upon his lap, his eyes scanning their surroundings for signs of an ambush.

Already the weather was becoming warmer, and the sun was high in the sky when they reached what Sergeant Caulder told him was Raleighshire's edge, the border marked by a bridge of wide stone, arched over a rushing river.

Beyond, a savannah of yellow long grass swayed in the breeze. The horizon was broken by a row of jagged mountains, with the plains beneath populated by herds of four-legged creatures that Arcturus could not see clearly from where he sat. It was a marked difference – shocking in the contrast between green and yellow, and separated only by the broad river of dark water.

On they went, the wheels rattling along the cobbled bridge and on to the hard-packed mud path on the other side. To Arcturus, who had never been so far south, the warmth was a miracle. To have to undo the top few buttons of his jacket at this time of year? Unheard of.

Now he could see the animals, like the deer of the north but with twisting horns and a ribbon of black separating their white-furred bellies and the sandy coat above. They were strange creatures to be sure, and he had no idea what they were.

'Gazelles,' Sergeant Caulder said, smiling at the look of wonder on Arcturus's face. 'You'll be hunting them soon enough.'

'How?' Arcturus breathed, watching as the beasts cavorted in the sun, springing as high as a man was tall and dashing back and forth just for the joy of it. Nearby, a pair of males rutted, their sharp horns locked as they butted and shoved each other for supremacy, their short black tails wagging frantically in the excitement of it all.

'Crossbows, most likely,' Sergeant Caulder said. 'Or with your demons, if they're fast enough.'

Arcturus smiled at the frolicking animals, knowing he would find it hard to bring himself to kill one.

He closed his eyes to enjoy the warmth of the breeze and smell the tang of the new world. Somehow, the anxieties of his new life seemed to fade away, replaced by the gentle creak of carriage wheels and the soughing of the breeze.

* * *

'Wake up, lad!'

Arcturus opened his eyes, only to find himself slumped against Sergeant Caulder, his head resting on the man's shoulder.

He jerked away, embarrassed, but the grizzled soldier only smiled and pointed at the carriages, where Alice and Josephine Queensouth were standing, rubbing their eyes.

They were in the middle of a town square, surrounded by stonewalled houses. Men and women stared out from windows, curious at the visitors, while others called in greeting as Edmund Raleigh strode about, organising rushing servants who were removing the luggage from the carriages.

Arcturus felt as though he had slept for hours, but the sun hadn't set, and it cast the world in a dim, orange glow as it hung above the horizon.

'Wake up, or we'll miss hunting this evening,' Edmund called out to the still sleepy Queensouth twins, stepping aside as a pair of overzealous servants tried to lift a heavy trunk.

He barged one of the servants accidentally as he passed and the trunk tumbled to the ground, spilling its contents.

'Watch it,' Zacharias yelled out from within the confines of his carriage. 'If anything's broken, I'll take the skin from your back as payment.'

But there was nothing to break within . . . because a skinny, pale-faced girl lay sprawled on the ground.

'Owww,' she groaned, rubbing her head.

'Elaine?' Arcturus asked, unable to believe his eyes.

'A stowaway,' Edmund said, smiling with amusement. 'Would you look at that.'

Elaine scrambled to her feet, her thin arms crossed defiantly as she glared at them. Her chest heaved with emotion, and her face was red and sweaty from her confinement within the trunk.

'I'm not a stowaway, I'm a visitor,' she said, narrowing her eyes at Edmund. 'It was rude of you not to invite me. Everyone else was. Even Arcturus, and Zacharias doesn't even like him.'

Arcturus reddened at Elaine's bluntness, even as Edmund chuckled at her shameless attitude.

'You're right,' he said gently, putting an arm around her hunched shoulders. 'It was jolly rude of me. Only . . . your brothers told me your family was going home this weekend, and I assumed that meant you too. My mistake.'

'Big mistake,' she huffed, even as she allowed herself a small smile.

Edmund knelt down and unravelled a small summoning leather from his pocket, no larger than a handkerchief. A flash of white later and a purple-shelled Mite demon had materialised in the air, its beetle-wings buzzing as it hovered in front of Edmund's face.

'What are you doing?' Elaine asked as he rummaged through his satchel and began to scribble a rough message on a scrap of parchment.

'Your parents must be worried sick,' he said, signing off his message with a flourish of his quill. 'Especially with all the riots yesterday. I'm sending my Mite to let them know you're safe – I bet they have half of Vocans looking for you by now.'

She blanched at his words and lowered her head. Arcturus couldn't help but feel sorry for the poor girl. He could imagine it was hard for her, being the youngest with three older brothers.

She was probably left out all the time.

'Are you going to send me home?' Elaine asked in a small voice.

'No,' Alice said firmly, stepping away from her carriage and giving the girl a hug. 'You can stay in my room this weekend.'

'Well, glad that's all sorted,' Edmund said, tossing the Mite into the air, the scroll tied to its back. 'Right, Zacharias, get your lazy arse out here. Daylight is fading. We've a few hours of hunting before it's time to turn in. I've got a craving for fresh gazelle haunch.'

'But . . . I want to get dressed for dinner,' Josephine said plaintively, as Zacharias stumbled from his carriage.

'No buts!' Edmund said, beckoning a nearby servant over. 'Fetch the crossbows, there's a good lad. We'll be feeding half the town tonight with any luck.'

'Right you are, my lord,' the servant said, scurrying off into a nearby building.

'We're coming back as *soon* as it gets dark,' Alice said, looking worriedly at Elaine. 'Elaine's far too young for this kind of thing as it is. There are hyenas, cheetahs, leopards, even lions out there. We might run into one.'

'I'm not too young,' Elaine protested. 'Valens would stin—'

'Oh, I hope we do run into one,' Zacharias said, talking over Elaine's protests. 'I'll take its head as a trophy for my wall.'

'You're so brave,' gushed Josephine, taking the noble's arm.

Arcturus resisted the temptation to grin as Alice performed the world's most exaggerated eye roll. The two sisters might look identical, but he was realising more and more that they were two very different people.

145

As Edmund reluctantly agreed to Alice's demand, Arcturus noticed the servant returning, pushing a rattling cart over the cobbles.

'About time,' Zacharias grunted, shoving the servant aside to pluck a crossbow from within. 'Thanks for looking after it for me, Edmund.'

Arcturus could see the Forsyth family crest carved into the weapon's stock, a strange, four-legged demon with three intertwined heads on long, snake-like necks.

Then it was the twins' turn to delve into the cart, revealing a matching pair – elegant pieces that they loaded with practised efficiency. They had done this before.

Edmund gave Arcturus a curious look as the young commoner peered into the cart, and leaned in to pull out his own crossbow. It was made of black, polished wood, and the stock was carved to fit the owner's shoulder. Arcturus resisted the jealousy that surged through him, even as he wondered for a moment if he had been brought to load Edmund's crossbow for him.

'Made from ebony, grown right here in Raleighshire,' Edmund said, brushing an invisible fleck of dirt from the beautiful weapon. 'Made by the finest dwarven bowyers. You load it by pulling back on this lever, here.'

Edmund heaved on a metal spar that sat crosswise beneath the crossbow's string and eased it back, until the string clicked into place and the lever laid flat against the stock.

Arcturus blanched. Maybe he *was* going to be the loader after all.

'Then you place a bolt – sometimes called a quarrel – here,' Edmund continued, tugging what, to Arcturus's eyes, looked

146

like a short, fat arrow from a quiver in the cart, and laying it in a groove in front of the taut string.

'When you've got something in your sights, you place the butt against your shoulder, look down the bolt, and . . . pull the trigger.'

Edmund swung up the crossbow in one smooth motion and the weapon twanged, sending the quarrel whistling through the air. Arcturus ducked instinctively, but the projectile was aimed well above him. There was a thud, and then Arcturus saw the sign that hung outside a nearby tavern swinging back and forth.

'Edmund,' Alice chided, looking at the splintered sign. 'They won't be able to fix that.'

'Good riddance,' Edmund replied, grinning. 'It's got our family crest on it. Hate the damned thing.'

Arcturus squinted and could just make out what appeared to be a Manticore in its centre – a hybrid of scorpion and lion. He couldn't help but agree with Edmund – it was an ugly looking creature.

Edmund handed the crossbow over, and Arcturus looked at it dejectedly. He guessed he'd be carrying Edmund's crossbow as well. Still, at least he was here, away from Crawley and in the sun. It wasn't as if he wanted to kill any gazelle anyway.

'Well, don't look so glum,' Edmund said, a hint of a smile playing across the raven-haired noble's lips. 'Don't you like it?'

'What do you mean?' Arcturus asked, confused.

'It's yours,' Edmund said, tugging another crossbow from the cart and hefting it. 'Just make sure you don't let the teachers see it when we're back at Vocans.'

'Bloody hell,' Elaine said, as Arcturus stared at the weapon in amazement. 'Where's mine?'

'How about you share mine for now,' Alice offered.

Arcturus turned to thank Edmund, but the boy was already walking away, a bundle of crossbow bolts in a quiver over his shoulder.

'Come on, grab a quiver and let's get moving,' Edmund called over his shoulder. 'We've got dinner to catch.'

21

Arcturus crouched low in the long grass, sweat dotting his brow as he sighted down his crossbow at the grazing beast ahead of him.

'Don't hold your breath,' Edmund whispered beside him. 'Pull the trigger as you breathe out. Easy does it.'

The tip of the quarrel swam in and out of focus, the black-and-white stripes of Arcturus's quarry blurring in the background. Perspiration trickled down his spine, pooling in the hollow of his back.

Arcturus closed his eyes and fired, and the crossbow leaped in his hands, thudding into his shoulder as it spat the bolt with a dull twang. It whistled harmlessly over the zebra's head, disappearing into the long-grass beyond.

The creature froze for a moment, blinking its long eyelashes as it looked in their direction, then went back to cropping the grass with its buck-yellow teeth.

Edmund squeezed his shoulder, even as Arcturus was flooded with relief. He hadn't wanted to kill it. It reminded him too much of the horses he had cared for in the past. They were probably the closest things he had ever had to friends.

'It's all right, old chum,' Edmund whispered. 'There'll be another chance tomorrow.'

There was a rustle as the young lord raised his own weapon.

Arcturus tried not to breathe, watching as Edmund's crossbow eased upwards, then hung perfectly still in the air. The boy had barely broken a sweat, squinting down the quarrel with a practised eye.

The zebra bolted, galloping towards its nearby herd. Then, in a shifting mirage of black-and-white stripes, the herd itself moved on in a tumult of thundering hooves.

Edmund cursed, but Arcturus was already up, his head cocked to hear the noise that had startled the zebra. There it was again. A scream in the distance, somewhere to the east.

He turned and saw Elaine running towards him, her black hair streaming as she twisted her head to look behind her. It was then that he noticed the demon.

It was green-brown in colour and as large as a stallion, with hooked claws and snake-like fangs. It chased Elaine, lumbering across the plains like an iguana, its three heads swaying on their sinuous necks with every step. Arcturus recognised it immediately as the demon he had seen but an hour before on the stock of Zacharias's gun. Arcturus could now see the boy beyond, doubled over in laughter as Elaine's shrill screams rang out. Zacharias was tormenting her.

Without thinking, Arcturus tugged free his summoning leather and unleashed Sacharissa. Then the two were running, and Arcturus was cranking back his crossbow with strength born of fury.

He waited for Elaine to rush past him, before kneeling and loading the crossbow. His eyes focused along its length, narrowed against the setting sun on the horizon. Sacharissa crouched beside him and he laid the stock against her back, steadying his aim as the demon trampled closer and closer.

It was only now that Zacharias seemed to notice and the demon faltered as its master ordered it to turn back. But it was too late. Arcturus took a deep breath . . . and fired.

The bolt whipped into the air, striking the beast square in its chest. Its front legs collapsed on impact and the demon twisted and fell, throwing up the dry savannah dust as its trio of squeals echoed across the plains.

'Trebius!' Arcturus heard Zacharias scream his demon's name.

He looked up at the boy, now no more than a stone's throw away. The young lord's eyes were blazing with hatred and he raised his hand and traced a symbol in the air.

Then the world flared with light as a ball of fire erupted into existence, streaking across the savannah and setting the long grass ablaze.

Sacharissa covered Arcturus with her body, for all the good it would do. He closed his eyes. Stupid. He had been so stupid. Injuring a noble's demon, when Elaine had never been in any real danger.

The world roared hot, and beneath his eyelids his vision seared white at the intensity of the blaze. And yet . . . no pain.

He cracked open his eyes, only to see the flames buffet harmlessly around them, stopped by an opaque wall that seemed to hang in the air ahead of him. Tiny cracks appeared along its surface, but it held strong. Soon the fireball dissipated, until the only sign of its existence was the channel of blackened, smouldering grass left in its wake.

Sacharissa whined and licked his face, her fear and confusion mirroring his own feelings.

'Zacharias!' Edmund shouted, and now Arcturus knew the source of the strange spell that had protected them. A blue symbol hung from Edmund's outstretched finger.

But the blond noble ignored him, instead running over to his collapsed demon and tugging at the bolt stuck in its chest. It had barely penetrated the thick chest muscles, and came out with little more than a wiggle. Zacharias tossed it aside, then there was a flash of white light as Zacharias performed a second spell, sketching a heart shape in the air. Moments later the wound was gone, and the only sign it had been there at all was the bloodstained projectile in the grass beside it.

'Zacharias,' Edmund repeated, squaring up to the boy opposite him, rigid with anger.

'Why did you stop it?' Zacharias growled, standing and facing Edmund. He was a full head taller than the raven-haired boy, but that did little to faze his opponent.

'You mean why did I stop you from *murdering* my guest?' Edmund growled, shoving Zacharias back.

Zacharias stared back at him, confusion spreading across his handsome face. It was as if nobody had ever pushed him before.

'He's a commoner. Who tried to kill my demon,' Zacharias said, as if he were explaining something to a child. 'It was a joke, for heaven's sake.'

'I didn't know it was yours, and I was protecting Elaine,'

Arcturus yelled, the half lie coming easily to his lips.

'Whose did you think it was then, you stupid fool?' Zacharias roared, raising his fingers again. Edmund knocked his hand back down and shoved him again. This time, Zacharias shoved back.

'Boys, no!'

Beyond the pair, Alice, Josephine and Prince Harold had arrived on the scene.

'I thought it was an orc's demon . . . or a wild animal,' Arcturus said lamely. The words were unconvincing in his ears.

'You were being cruel to Elaine,' Edmund said, and it was strange for Arcturus to see the happy-go-lucky boy so angry. 'It seems to me you deserved this.'

Zacharias raised his fist, but then Alice was standing between them, her chest heaving with exertion.

'Don't . . . be . . . so . . . stupid,' she managed. 'You're . . . supposed to be . . . friends.'

'What gave you that idea?' Zacharias spat.

He turned and stalked away, his back stiff with anger. The demon followed, but not before one of its heads hissed threateningly in Arcturus's direction. Josephine stood for a moment, undecided.

'Wait up, Zach!' she yelled, jogging behind him.

As Zacharias walked out of earshot, Edmund deflated and ran a hand over his face.

'That was unfortunate.' Prince Harold shook his head, a grim look on his face. 'Arcturus, over here, please.'

Arcturus approached him, wincing as the soles of his ragged, stable-boy shoes sizzled in the still-burning grass.

'I'm sorry, Harold . . . I wasn't thinking,' Arcturus muttered.

153

'Well, why don't you *try* thinking next time,' Harold snapped. Arcturus stared at his feet, kicking at the sooty ground.

Harold sighed.

'Forgive me. You have to understand, Zacharias is—'

Then he stopped, staring past Arcturus, his eyes widening.

Arcturus spun, his heart racing at the thought that Elaine might be hurt. But she was fine, sitting cross-legged just a few paces behind him, wiping at her tear-streaked face.

No, it was the figure staggering towards them behind her, his face and uniform covered in blood.

It was Rotter. Even as he neared them, he fell to his knees.

'Help me,' he gasped. 'For heaven's sake, help me.'

22

It took only a few seconds for Alice to heal Rotter, wiping away the deep cut in his ashen forehead like wine spilled on a table. But in that time it seemed the world became darker, the sun halfway through its descent beneath the horizon.

'What happened?' Prince Harold asked, handing a flask of water to the exhausted soldier.

'Men from the north,' Rotter gasped after a deep draught. 'A few hundred of them. Came at us with swords while we set up camp outside Raleightown. I was on the edges, played dead . . . waited till they'd moved on.'

For a moment the group stared at him in shocked silence.

'Did any of your comrades survive?' Edmund asked, gripping Rotter by his shoulder.

'Aye, Sergeant Caulder,' Rotter said, his eyes darting furtively behind him. 'Sarge fought like the devil, but there were too many. One snuck up from behind, knocked him out with a club. I think they kept him alive for interrogation.'

'Is the town being pillaged?' Edmund demanded, his eyes

turning in the town's direction. 'I don't see flames.'

Arcturus could see the glow of the town's torchlights in the distance, suddenly visible in the growing darkness.

It didn't seem real. It was so quiet. Were there dead men over there, cut down in the dusk light?

'What are they doing here?' Alice murmured. 'No pillaging . . . and there are too many of them to be bandits. A dwarven uprising?'

'They were no dwarves,' Rotter growled. 'Too tall. But they wore matching cloaks and covered their faces with scarves. Like they were organised. Like someone might recognise them.'

Arcturus felt a chill take hold of him then. Could this be what Crawley had been talking about?

'The riots,' Arcturus said, his voice barely more than a whisper.

'What of them?' Zacharias snarled from behind him, making Arcturus jump. He had not heard Zacharias and Josephine return. The boy's demon was gone – infused into Zacharias's body.

'Arcturus is right,' Prince Harold said, holding up his hand. 'They are here for us. This is an uprising. Just not a dwarven one.'

'It's the commoners,' Edmund said, his face filled with sudden understanding. 'The ones who started the fire in Corcillum.'

'What are you saying?' Josephine asked. Her voice quavered and Arcturus could see her face was pale in the dim light.

'They are here for us,' Edmund explained, loading his crossbow with grim determination. 'The prince, the nobles. All of us.'

'No!' Elaine gasped and rushed over to grip Arcturus's hand.

'Why?' Alice asked. 'What good are we to them?'

'Because we are weak,' Prince Harold said. 'Weak enough to capture. All of us are novices, with our first demons and the most basic grasp of spellcraft. We have not had the time to grow our summoning levels or capture more powerful demons. With their numbers . . . they could defeat us without too much trouble.'

'What good would capturing us do?' Josephine demanded, her words verging on a wail. 'Our parents control everything, not us!'

'Exactly,' Edmund replied. 'With a knife to our throats, they would be able to make our parents do whatever they wanted.'

'Not mine,' Harold said, shaking his head. 'My father would never bow to their demands, the stubborn old goat. I'd die for sure.'

'Even if our parents did not love us, the consequences of our deaths would be too costly,' Edmund said, shaking his head. 'We are not just their children – most of us are their heirs, their firstborn.'

'Only the firstborn are guaranteed to be born summoners,' Arcturus murmured, understanding dawning on him. If the firstborns were killed, the ability to summon might be lost to their families for ever.

'I'm not a firstborn,' Elaine whispered, nudging Arcturus. 'My brothers can summon. Will I . . . ?'

'No,' Arcturus said, forcing a smile. 'Your parents would never let that happen.'

Elaine gripped his hand and he felt the weight of her Mite,

Valens, alighting on his shoulder. Sacharissa nuzzled the young girl's waist and she stroked the demon's shaggy coat.

'So what's the plan?' Josephine asked desperately. 'Shall we head for the bridge?'

'No,' Edmund said. 'There are two ways into Raleighshire. One is across that bridge to the north, and the other is a pass south through the mountains, which will lead us into the orc jungles anyway. With an attack this well organised, we can assume they will have blocked both routes.'

'Well, whatever your decision, you had better make it soon,' Rotter snapped. 'They'll be sending out search parties the moment night falls, if not sooner. And they have hunting dogs with them.'

Prince Harold cursed.

'We won't last more than a few hours – the dogs will follow our scent right to us. Not nearly enough time to send for help.'

'So do we fight?' Zacharias said.

For all his bravado, the blond noble looked terrified. But Arcturus could take no satisfaction from it. Not in their predicament.

'There's a rocky outcrop not too far from here,' Edmund said. 'If we run we might be able to make it there, fortify it.'

'With what, sticks and rocks?' Josephine muttered. 'That's suicide. I'd rather surrender and let our parents deal with it.'

'It's your father's fault anyway!' Zacharias pointed an accusatory finger at Harold. 'So what if he has to give up the throne? That's what they want, right?'

'I don't deny it,' Harold said simply.

More silence, broken only by Zacharias's angry breathing.

'Let me think,' Edmund murmured, gripping the bridge of his nose with his fingers.

It was almost dark now and Arcturus could see the sun was just a sliver of orange on the horizon. Despair gripped him as the light faded and his thoughts turned to Crawley's offer. What if he surrendered . . . would he have to join the rebel commoners? Should he?

But how could he betray his friends . . . and who knew if the rebels would succeed? If they did, he would be hanged as a traitor with the rest of the nobles.

'Doesn't your family have men protecting the mountain pass?' Zacharias asked Edmund, interrupting Arcturus's thoughts. 'Maybe the rebels haven't got to them yet.'

'Even if that was the case, there are barely a score of them, mostly retired soldiers that my father didn't have the heart to fire,' Edmund replied. 'His personal guard went with him on his trade mission. They timed this attack well.'

'Do you have any better ideas?' Zacharias snapped.

Edmund gazed towards the town, his brows furrowed.

'There's something else. But . . . no.'

'Tell us,' Alice said. 'If there's even a chance . . . we should take it.'

Edmund sighed, indecision plain on his face.

'Hurry,' Rotter hissed. 'We have to go!'

'There's a secret passage,' Edmund said. 'Beneath a statue opposite the old church in Raleightown. But . . . it leads into the orc jungles, beyond the mountain pass.'

'You want us to go *towards them*?' Zacharias snarled. 'And then into orc territory? Are you crazy?'

'The dogs aren't tracking our scent yet,' Edmund said. 'If we go back to the town, they won't have a trail to follow. Maybe we can hide in the passageway until help arrives.'

'The path back is clear,' Rotter said. 'I just came from there.'

'So that's it?' Alice asked, gazing back at the town's distant lights. 'That's our best plan?'

Edmund turned to Harold, and the prince gave him a grim nod.

'We go back,' Edmund said firmly. 'And hope we survive the night.'

23

The group crouched in the long grass outside the town, staring into the glow of torches. The air was filled with the barking of dogs and the shouts of angry men.

Arcturus tried not to look at the blood that stained the dry soil, or the wide, staring eyes of the men that lay dead around them. And the soldiers were not the only corpses that had been left to the wild jackals.

Sergeant Caulder's squad had sold their lives dearly, leaving over a score of enemy bodies scattered on the battlefield. The courage to stand against such odds astounded Arcturus, and he felt ashamed that his first instinct had been to turn on his friends.

The dead rebels were clad in different shades and styles of dark, hooded jackets with scarves across their faces. Their weapons, along with those of the soldiers, had been taken, much to Prince Harold's dismay. The nobles had but a single sword and a half-dozen crossbows between them.

As they waited, Arcturus wished that Sacharissa could smell the bodies, to see if Crawley was among them. But all of their demons had been infused – a precaution in case their scent attracted the rebel hunting dogs. All but one, anyway.

Edmund lay on his back beside Arcturus, his scrying crystal held up to his nose. His demon, a strange hybrid of owl and cat, was gliding over the town, scouting a safe route to the secret passageway. Through the corner of his eye, Arcturus could see the image on the shard of stone, where rooftops and ill-lit streets flitted by.

Arcturus rolled on to his side, to see where Rotter sat with Elaine, his sword drawn. Edmund had tasked the soldier to look after her, and Arcturus was surprised to see that Elaine seemed almost amused, their situation forgotten as Rotter whispered some joke in her ear.

'They're busy rounding up all the townsfolk into the town square. I think there's a way,' Edmund hissed, alerting the others. 'Quietly now. Make sure your crossbows are loaded.'

Then they were up and running, their bodies crouched as if it would somehow hide them entering the town's edge and into the cobbled streets.

Lanterns lined the road on either side, and Arcturus could hardly believe that they were heading towards the shouting voices in the near distance. They turned down an alley, then another, and somehow the walls that pressed in on either side gave comfort to Arcturus, as if they were safer here than in the wider streets.

'Wait,' Edmund growled, stopping and staring at his crystal. Above, Arcturus saw a flash of fur and feathers as the demon swooped by.

The young noble kneeled and levelled his crossbow down

the passageway. The others followed suit, preparing a row of projectiles held back by nothing more than a twitch of their fingers.

'Fire on my command,' Edmund said, and suddenly Arcturus's vision blurred, his heart pounding in his chest.

Seconds ticked by and all Arcturus could think of was how much he didn't want to be there.

'Now!'

Arcturus fired without thinking, his nerveless fingers jerking at the sound. He barely saw the two rebels round the corner, nor did he know which one his bolt had struck. All he saw was the men hurled back against the brick wall. And the blood pooling as they choked their last breaths, their chests pin-cushioned with the broad shafts. It was an ugly, horrible death, and Edmund did not waste precious seconds to end their suffering, urging the group on down the next street.

'Take that, you rebel scum,' Zacharias snarled, and Arcturus heard a thud behind him as the noble kicked one of the dying men.

But Arcturus felt no triumph. Only shame and horror.

What if he went back, tried to heal them? Edmund's plan would never work. But it wasn't too late to join the rebel cause.

'Hellfire, they've sent out the hunting parties,' Edmund cursed, looking up from his crystal. 'Come on!'

On they went, running faster now, accompanied by the sound of their footsteps and the rattle of the loose crossbow bolts in their quivers. They turned down another street, eerily empty, while the howls of the dogs swirled around them like the baying of wolves.

Then they saw it: the town hall, a round building with a wide set of double doors, set on the corner of a crossroads. Two rebels stood guard outside the entrance, oblivious to the approaching nobles.

They were armed with the most rudimentary of weapons, and now Arcturus understood how Sergeant Caulder's soldiers had managed to kill so many of them. One held a makeshift spear, constructed from what might have been a rake's handle and a kitchen knife nailed to its tip. The other held a cleaver in his right hand, the lid of a cooking pot in his left.

The spearman did a double take as they approached, then pressed his back against the wall, terrified. The other seemed frozen to the spot, unable to move even when Edmund's crossbow pointed directly at him.

'Stand aside, gents,' Rotter said, pushing past Edmund and Prince Harold. 'I'll handle this pair.'

His sword held unwavering in front of him, Rotter approached the two rebels. Suddenly, the spearman yelled and charged him, his spear lowered at the soldier's gut.

With practised ease, Rotter sidestepped the skewer and hammered the man's head with the flat of his sword. The rebel collapsed, sprawled unconscious on the cobblestones, his spear clattering until it settled against Arcturus's feet.

'Drop it,' Rotter barked to the other man.

The cleaver and pot lid fell to the ground with a clang, and the rebel's knees followed soon after, his hands clasped in supplication.

'Please . . . I didn't mean it . . .'

Rotter leaned down and inspected the cleaver.

'No blood,' he said. 'You're lucky.'

He lifted the hilt of his sword and slammed it down, knocking the rebel out with a sickening crack.

'Amateurs,' Rotter spat. 'Where to now?'

But Edmund made no move to leave. Instead, he turned to face a statue that stood opposite the town hall entrance.

'We're here,' Edmund said.

It was an unassuming structure, perhaps small for a statue, depicting a man whose appearance matched Edmund's closely, if not for the moustache and lamb-chop sideburns that adorned the figure's features. The man's body was clad in chainmail and he carried a sword.

'My father had this put up to cover the tunnel,' Edmund said, crouching at its base and fiddling with the stone plaque there. 'It's of himself. Bit self-indulgent if you ask me, but it did the trick – half the town hate the damned thing, don't go anywhere near it.'

There was the sound of grinding stone, then Edmund stepped away and revealed a hole where the plaque had been before.

'Come on, in you get.'

He didn't need to say it twice – the barking of the dogs seemed to be getting louder. Zacharias barged past the others in his haste to get through, wriggling his broad shoulders through the gap. Elaine, the twins and Prince Harold followed in quick succession.

But then Edmund hesitated, looking over his shoulder at the two unconscious men in the doorway behind him.

'What are you waiting for?' Alice hissed, poking her head up into the gap.

'They might wake up, tell their friends we were here,' Edmund replied, pointing to the two rebels. 'We should take them with us.'

'And the dead bodies around the corner, what about them?' Alice asked, exasperated. 'They'll find them eventually.'

'They wouldn't know who killed them,' Edmund replied. 'These guys actually saw us. Come on, Arcturus, help me.'

Arcturus hurried forward and together with Rotter, they managed to manhandle the bodies into the hole beneath the statue. Arcturus pushed through the spear and cleaver for good measure, and resisted the urge to grin as Zacharias swore, the spear haft hitting the noble on its way down.

'What were they guarding anyway?' Arcturus asked breathlessly. 'Why aren't they with the rest of them?'

'Do you want to stay and find out?' Edmund asked.

But something stopped the young noble even as he spoke, and he turned to stare at the town hall's doorway.

'Sergeant Caulder,' he uttered. 'Maybe they were guarding him.'

'Leave it, you fool,' Zacharias called from within the passage. 'We're almost away!'

Arcturus looked desperately down the street, where the glow of lights seemed to be becoming brighter, as if blazing torches were being carried towards them. He could hear raised voices now, breaking through the incessant howling of the dogs.

But Rotter didn't wait to hear Edmund's decision. Throwing caution to the wind, the soldier kicked open the door, rushing in with his sword held aloft. Arcturus charged after him, brandishing his unloaded crossbow like a club.

Within the dim room, a man lay tied up, a flour sack pulled over his head. Rotter kneeled and began to slash apart his bindings, revealing a bloodstained Sergeant Caulder.

'What took you so bloody long?' Sergeant Caulder growled, forcing a weak smile.

'Hurry!' Alice's voice came from behind.

There was a mad, stumbling rush into the night air, Arcturus moving with Sergeant Caulder's arm thrown around his shoulder. For a moment he glimpsed hooded figures, rounding a corner on the road to his right. Then he was in darkness, tumbling through empty space.

24

Arcturus groaned and rubbed his head. For a moment, his breath caught short, the darkness overwhelming. Was he blind?

A light flared into existence, bathing the world in a pale-blue glow.

'Quiet,' Edmund whispered, holding a finger to his lips. Beside him, the wyrdlight he had cast floated aimlessly, shifting the shadows around them.

Voices called out above them, barely audible over the barking of the hounds. Then . . . snorting above them too. The snuffling of a dog and the scratching of its claws against stone.

'Gerroutofit, stupid mutt,' a gruff voice shouted, filtering through the garbled noise on the other side. Still the dog scratched, until they heard a yelp as it was kicked.

They sat and listened, holding their breaths in the darkness.

'Find 'em, lads,' the same voice called. 'They're out there somewhere.'

Slowly – ever so slowly – the noise began to fade.

Finally, they were in stillness, broken only by the dripping of water somewhere deep in the cavern.

Now that Arcturus could breathe again, he was able to see that they were in a rough-hewn tunnel, approximately as wide and tall as one of Vocans's corridors. Here and there, patches of wet seemed to shine on the walls, as if they were sweating. Underfoot, pools of dark water had formed, and Arcturus could see they would have to wade in parts if they were to advance further.

He hoped it would not get deeper. Being unable to swim, he'd sink to the bottom before anyone could save him. Arcturus supposed he could hold on to Sacharissa, though the thought of drifting half-submerged in the darkness filled him with fear.

'How long do you think it will take for help to arrive?' Arcturus asked, first to break the silence, if only to escape his own thoughts.

'Athena is on her way to the palace now,' Edmund replied, lifting his scrying crystal and peering at it. 'She has a scroll attached to her foot, explaining our predicament. A Gryphowl flies pretty swiftly, and the Celestial Corps will be even swifter. Perhaps at midday tomorrow, if all goes well.'

'What do you mean, if all goes well?' Zacharias groaned.

Edmund bit his lip. Prince Harold answered for him.

'If my father is not there, she'll have to search Corcillum until we find him . . . or one of our parents . . . or a general,' he said.

Arcturus looked at his feet, wondering what it would be like to have a parent, someone who would do anything to protect him. He felt the sudden urge to summon Sacharissa. She was the closest thing he had to family.

'It could take for ever to find someone,' Alice whispered.

'Can the rebels get in if the dogs lead them back to it?' Sergeant Caulder asked, wincing slightly as he stood. 'Through the secret entrance, I mean?'

Edmund floated the wyrdlight towards the stone tablet that covered the hole they had come through. There was a strange mechanism built into the rectangular tablet that covered the entrance, all cogs and hinges.

Arcturus peered closer and saw a word engraved in the side. *Thorsager*. A dwarven name . . .

'My father hired a dwarven smith to build it,' Edmund said. 'It will only open if someone presses the right places in the right order – but a few blows with a sledgehammer and they'll be through. It was designed to be hidden, not to hold back an army.'

'Dwarves?' Zacharias spat, incredulous. 'You've doomed us all. A dwarf would sell its own mother for a bent penny!'

'Oh Zacharias, you're so bad,' Josephine giggled.

Alice shook her head in disgust at her twin sister.

'We should get moving,' she said, summoning her own wyrdlight and sending it down the passageway. 'The dogs could bring them back here eventually – let's not make it easy for them.'

The tunnel yawned ominously as the blue ball of light floated deeper, before disappearing around a winding corner. Arcturus couldn't help but feel a sense of dread. Somewhere on the other side lay the wild jungles of the orcs.

He set his jaw and forced himself to step deeper into the darkness. He could not show weakness in front of the others – they would abandon him if he slowed them down.

'What do we do with this pair of idiots?' Sergeant Caulder asked, pointing at the two rebels lying unconscious on the floor.

'We should—' Prince Harold began, but Sergeant Caulder held up a finger.

For a moment he peered at the pair, then picked up the spear that laid on the ground. He prodded the nearest rebel and was rewarded with a yelp of pain.

'Cheeky bugger,' Rotter grinned, kneeling beside the rebel and tying his hands with a strip of cloth.

'Help! Hel—'

Rotter clamped a hand over the rebel's mouth, and together with Sergeant Caulder they succeeded in gagging the struggling man. Rotter followed suit with the second rebel, and then the pair were lifted on to the soldiers' shoulders – one wriggling like an eel, the other a motionless sack of potatoes.

'Right, let's get out of here,' Rotter growled.

The nobles released a stream of wyrdlights from their fingers, illuminating the passageway in ethereal blue light. The new glow did little to calm Arcturus's nerves – the gloom still wavered in the moving light, and the stalactites and stalagmites that pierced the air reminded him of the maw of a giant beast. Worse still, the path angled downwards, as if they were descending into the bowels of the earth.

He hesitated as the team moved forward, his earlier courage dissipating as quickly as it had arrived, but soon fear of being left alone in the dark stirred his feet, sending him stumbling forward over the uneven ground.

Finding himself shrouded in darkness at the very back of their band, he released his own wyrdlight and guided it ahead of him.

He concentrated on keeping it steady, distracting himself from the walls that seemed to close in on him with each step.

For a moment he was tempted to summon Sacharissa to keep him company, but after his foot slipped and he found himself knee deep in a pool of water, he thought better of it. Why subject her to the same for no more than a modicum of comfort?

Moreover, the others might see it as a weakness – the only other summoner who still had their demon out was Elaine. Better to push on ahead and only summon Sacharissa if he needed to swim. He shuddered at the thought.

'How much further?' Prince Harold's voice echoed from up ahead.

'An hour or so, if I remember correctly,' Edmund replied. 'In truth, I have never come this far, or seen the exit on the other side. But the dwarves mapped it out for us.'

'Are you serious?' Zacharias moaned. 'What if they lied? What if we're trapped down here?'

'Better than being trapped up there with the rebels,' Alice snapped. Clearly, the blond-haired noble had worn her patience thin.

So they walked. It seemed a never-ending procession of warped walls and undulating ground, coupled with the echoes of their footsteps and the ceaseless trickle and slosh of water. It was a wonder to Arcturus that the entire place didn't flood, for the drops of water from the porous rock above soon left him bedraggled. As for his boots and trousers, they were soaked through – the group had been forced to wade up to their waists more than once. Every step then had been a moment of terror, as Arcturus imagined plunging into a hidden pool below.

On and on they went, any attempts at conversation forced, and soon cut short by the gut-churning dread of their predicament. It seemed they were now as deep beneath the ground as Vocans was tall, and Arcturus felt as if the ceilings could collapse, swallowing them in a jumble of jagged rock and creeping water.

Only Rotter seemed in good spirits, though if it was just an act to calm the others, Arcturus could not tell. Whatever the reason, the jaunty tune he began to hum halfway through their journey was swiftly silenced by a cursed order from Zacharias.

Just under an hour later, the tunnel began to bend upwards, and Arcturus was not the only one to thank the heavens out loud. It was a blessed relief to begin their ascent, away from the oppressive darkness and the walls that seemed to shrink towards him with every step.

Even so, it soon became hard going, the angle so acute that it became almost a climb. More than once, Arcturus found himself using a stalagmite as a handhold, heaving himself up another steep incline, his hands slipping against the smooth limestone.

Elaine had to be hauled up by Edmund, and Arcturus could see even her little Mite, Valens, tugging at her collar valiantly as he hovered above her.

'Is that light?' Prince Harold called hoarsely.

It was. Barely more than a dim glow, filtering through a crack in the wall of the passageway. And beyond, a solid wall of rock – the end of the line. They had made it.

25

The team collapsed on the ground, careless of the scattered puddles, groaning with relief.

'I tell you what, I'm not looking forward to going back,' Arcturus panted. 'The Celestial Corps can pick us up on the other side of that crack.'

'Agreed,' Edmund said. 'I'll have Athena guide them to us when the time comes.'

He tugged forth his scrying crystal and peered into it. Within the image, Arcturus could see rolling green hills as the young lord's demon flew over Hominum's landscape.

'Guide us where?' Alice asked. 'We don't know where that comes out.'

She sent her wyrdlight to hover beside the crack, a jagged tear in the rock, where Arcturus could see the first signs of life – plush moss living off the meagre light from outside.

'Those dwarves did a shoddy job,' Zacharias said, still breathing heavily. 'An orc could fit through that gap.'

'My father said it's well hidden,' Edmund vouched, though

his voice was laced with doubt. 'And how would an orc know where it leads? If one wandered in here, it would look like this goes down into the depths of the earth.'

To illustrate his point, he threw a stray pebble down the way they had come. There was a faint rattle as it fell, fading but still sounding as the rock bounced deep into the earth.

'One word from those dwarves to the orcs . . .' Zacharias muttered.

Arcturus ignored him and turned to look at the others. Rotter had been forced to leave Elaine to her own devices as he dragged the rebel he had been carrying into the darkness to tie and gag him. There were groans coming from where the soldier was hunched over, and Arcturus realised the second captive must have regained consciousness.

He scooted over to Elaine, who had wrapped her skinny arms around her knees and was rocking back and forth. Even Valens could do little to distract her, though he buzzed to and fro in front of her as if he wanted her to play.

'Hey, you OK?' he asked.

'Yeah,' she replied in a small voice. 'Just thinking.'

'We're going to be fine,' Arcturus said. 'We're miles from the rebels by now.'

'It's my brothers,' Elaine said, shaking her head. 'Our estate is even smaller than Edmund's, and my parents were away too. This might be happening in my home right now.'

'I'm sure they're fine,' Arcturus thought aloud, putting an arm around her shoulders. 'They attacked us here because it's so far from civilisation, and there are half a dozen noble children here, including the prince. I doubt they'd split their forces to catch a few sons of an impoverished noble family.'

Elaine smiled at that.

'Sometimes being poor has its advantages,' she said. Arcturus thought she didn't know what poverty *was*, but kept it to himself. After all, she would have some idea if they survived the night, when hunger gnawed at her belly and the next meal was nowhere in sight.

She was cold and he wished he had a jacket to keep her warm. Instead, he pressed his side against her and they huddled for warmth as their wet clothes sapped the last of the heat from their bodies. The dim glow of sunlight from the crack beyond looked so inviting . . .

'Right,' Sergeant Caulder said, breaking the silence. 'I think it's safe to take this off now.'

Arcturus turned to see the sergeant tearing away the gag from his own rebel – the same one who had tried to disembowel Rotter with his makeshift spear, and who had been pretending to be unconscious earlier.

'What's your name, son?'

The rebel took a deep breath, then spat in the sergeant's face.

'You little . . .' Rotter growled, lunging for the rebel, but Sergeant Caulder held up his hand.

'Full of vim and vinegar, aren't ye?' Sergeant Caulder growled, wiping his brow. 'No need for any unpleasantness. You just tell us what your friends are after, and Prince Harold over there will put in a good word with his father when we're rescued. Maybe you'll avoid execution, eh?'

'Ye don't have the guts to kill me,' the man yelled, struggling against his bonds. 'Ye would've done it already . . . I won't tell ye a thing.'

'Just give me a few minutes with him,' Rotter growled. He was holding the cleaver from the other rebel, twirling it in his hand. Arcturus gulped, surprised at the sudden change in the happy-go-lucky soldier.

'I don't think—' Edmund began, but Sergeant Caulder held up a hand.

'Ask the other one first,' Sergeant Caulder said, his voice low and dangerous. 'Maybe he'll be more obliging.'

He left the spitting rebel wriggling on the ground and snatched the other trussed-up captive's feet.

'What do you reckon, Rotter?' Sergeant Caulder asked. 'Do you reckon he'll talk?'

'Oh, he'll talk,' Rotter said, licking the back of the cleaver with an evil look in his eye. 'They always do . . .'

With that, the pair dragged the other rebel into the darkness of the tunnel, rolling him down until all Arcturus could hear was the frantic moaning from their captive, his attempted screams muffled by the gag.

'Dominic . . . Dominic!' the rebel near Arcturus yelled. 'Leave 'im alone, you monsters.'

'Let's take this off,' Arcturus heard Rotter say.

'Help me!' bellowed a voice. 'Hel—'

The voice was cut short. Then . . . a blood-curdling scream, one of a man suffering unimaginable pain. It tore at Arcturus's heart, but he could not bring himself to put an end to it.

'Stop,' Elaine cried. 'Stop it!'

'I say, that's enough now,' Edmund called out.

But they went on. Behind him, Arcturus heard Zacharias retch, the sound of liquid splattering on the stone. The acrid stench of vomit filled the air.

'Who do you work for?' Sergeant Caulder barked.

Another scream, higher pitched than the last. It went on and on, so long that Arcturus thought the rebel's lungs would burst.

'Give him some more encouragement,' Sergeant Caulder yelled. 'Again!'

But there were no more screams now, just a raw, throaty sobbing, punctuated by the occasional animal yelp of pain.

Arcturus turned to look at Edmund – the boy seemed frozen in place, his face white as a sheet in the ethereal blue glow of the wyrdlights.

'He's not going to talk,' Sergeant Caulder said. 'Put him out of his misery.'

Arcturus heard a final, desperate yell . . . that swiftly devolved into a terrible, spluttering gurgle. Finally, silence reigned once more, but for the dripping of the water and the horrified breathing of the nobles.

He felt sick. He had respected the two soldiers. But . . . they were monsters. Worse than monsters – they seemed to enjoy the torture they had inflicted upon the poor man.

Sergeant Caulder reappeared, climbing back out of the darkness. There was blood on his hands, and even a stain on his forehead where he had gone to wipe his brow. He tugged the red-stained cleaver from his belt, and put it against the remaining rebel's throat.

'What's your name?' Sergeant Caulder said, hunkering down beside the man.

'Tim,' the rebel stuttered, his eyes glazed over with fear.

'Who are you?'

'I . . . nobody. I'm just a shoemaker. I went to a few meetin's, down the pub. Complainin' about the king and the like. His damned taxes were killin' me business, ye know? They said to wear a black hood, come by one night, armed. I thought it was gonna be another riot. But then they put us on a bunch o' carriages, said we were gonna change things. I didn't have anythin' to lose . . .'

Arcturus's heart twisted. This rebel was no soldier. He was just a desperate man, pushed to breaking point.

'Who's *they*?' Sergeant Caulder snarled, digging in the edge of the blade.

'I don't know, I swear it,' Tim cried, trying to squirm away. 'They always hid their faces. But they came up from the south. I saw 'em arrive one night.'

Vocans. Vocans was to the south. Arcturus knew for sure then. Crawley was involved.

'That doesn't help us,' Sergeant Caulder growled. 'Give me something useful.'

'They're after the common boy!' Tim said frantically, his eyes rolling into the back of his head with terror. 'Him and the Prince Harold. The rest of you were just a bonus.'

Cold fear pooled in the base of Arcturus's stomach, trickling down from his spine.

'I'm a nobody,' he whispered. 'What could they want with me?'

But Tim had no answers for him. He had passed out from sheer fright, his head lolling to the side. This time, Sergeant

Caulder didn't try to prod him awake. Instead, he sighed and got to his feet.

'All right, you can come back now, Rotter,' the sergeant called.

'About bloody time,' Rotter replied from the darkness. There was a grunt of exertion, then Rotter emerged from the dark incline, dragging Dominic's body with him.

But . . . the body was moving. Struggling in fact, with Rotter's hand clamped firmly over Dominic's mouth. At the sight of the unconscious Tim, Rotter released his grip, and the rebel unleashed a tirade of curses.

'Better make use of that gag again, eh, Rotter?' Sergeant Caulder grinned.

'Blimey,' Elaine said, amazed at the endless string of swearwords emanating from the rebel's mouth.

'Wait . . .' Prince Harold said, staring at the rebel as Rotter gagged him once again. 'You didn't kill him?'

'Cor, what he must think of us, eh?' Rotter said, shaking his head with a rueful smile.

Arcturus felt a wash of relief flood through him. Yes, these rebels had wanted to capture him, maybe even end his life. But after hearing them speak, seeing they were *real* people . . . he could not have wished such a fate upon them.

'Rotter makes for a great actor, don't you think?' Sergeant Caulder laughed. 'We used to do this with the new recruits, only we'd pretend it was punishment for falling asleep on watch. Works every time!'

''Course, the blood was a new addition,' Rotter said, grimacing as he rolled up his chainmailed sleeve to reveal a shallow cut there. 'I drew the damned short straw.'

'You scared the living daylights out of us,' Harold said. 'We thought you were . . .'

'Slaughtering a man in cold blood?' Rotter asked, his eyebrows raised.

'I thought it was revenge,' Arcturus said, feeling a twinge of guilt. 'Your friends . . . the rebels killed them.'

Sergeant Caulder twisted his hands, his eyes downcast.

'I blame nobody but myself for that,' the man said. 'Maybe if I had . . .'

'There was nothing you could do, Sarge,' Rotter interrupted. 'There were too—'

'Silence,' Sergeant Caulder said, holding up his hand.

'I'm sorry, I—' Rotter began, a hurt look on his face.

'Quiet, I said,' Sergeant Caulder snapped, standing. He cocked his head to one side and peered into the darkness. 'Can you hear that?'

Arcturus strained his ears. There was a sound beyond, deep in the black interior of the cave. High-pitched. Almost like . . . howling.

'We have to go,' Sergeant Caulder growled, snatching up the cleaver. 'We have to go now!'

26

'Let's go, let's go!' Rotter shouted, shoving them one after another through the gap.

'What about the rebels?' Alice asked, stumbling as her sister dragged her out of the darkness.

'Leave them, they'll only slow us down!' Sergeant Caulder yelled.

Arcturus grabbed Elaine's hand and pulled her through. He caught one last glimpse of the two rebels, trussed up in the gloom, then he was blinking in the dawn light.

It was all so green. Bright sunlight filtered through the leaves of the canopy, catching the motes of dust that floated in the air. Vegetation surrounded them, a tangled snarl of branches and viridescent fronds, growing from the black earth beneath. Birds squawked and trilled in the distance, signalling that it was early morning still.

'Where now, sergeant?' Prince Harold emerged behind Arcturus.

'We split up,' Sergeant Caulder said, shading his eyes from

the brightness. 'It will confuse the dogs and they'll spend time deciding which path to follow.'

'Are you serious?' Edmund asked. 'There are too few of us as it is.'

'We've no choice,' the sergeant replied. 'It's our only chance.'

'Where are we even going?' Alice asked. 'We're in orc territory now.'

Arcturus was hardly listening. He needed Sacharissa, danger be damned. She was straining within his consciousness, eager to return to the real world.

It took but a moment for him to unravel his summoning map and bring Sacharissa into existence. Then his face was buried in her fur, hugging her for dear life.

She nuzzled against his chest, whining. Arcturus resolved he would not infuse her until this was over. She was the only one he could truly trust, especially after what their captive had said – he would not be the only one wondering why the rebels were after him.

'Let's head deeper into the jungles,' Sergeant Caulder shouted, throwing his voice towards the crack they had come out of. 'We can hide near the mountain pass.'

Then he leaned in, beckoning them closer.

'We'll go east around the mountain, then head north to Corcillum,' he whispered.

'I'll take Edmund, Josephine, Harold and Sergeant Caulder,' Zacharias said, shoving Elaine away from him. 'Come on, let's move.'

Arcturus clenched his fists and looked at what was left . . . only him, Alice, Rotter and Elaine. Definitely the weaker of the two groups, with Alice the only summoner with any experience and Elaine without a crossbow. Sacharissa whined, sensing his anguish. At least Rotter had a sword.

'I'll stay with Alice,' Edmund said in a low voice, stepping away from Zacharias with a look of disgust.

Sergeant Caulder peered into the sky, staring at the mountains above them. Arcturus realised they had emerged from the range's southern side.

'We'll hug the mountain's side – it should lead us back to Hominum's territory,' Caulder said, half to Rotter, half to Prince Harold. 'You go a bit deeper and angle around.'

'Do you think they'll even follow us in here?' Prince Harold asked. 'This won't be what those men signed up for.'

'Does it matter?' Zacharias snapped. 'They'll be here any minute – we have to go.'

Prince Harold hesitated, his gaze lingering on Alice for what felt to Arcturus like a moment too long. There was something in that look, a raw emotion that Arcturus could not read.

Then Sergeant Caulder was pulling him away, and the four were gone, disappearing into the jungle with a crackle of branches.

'We should go too,' Rotter said, handing the makeshift spear to Elaine and drawing his sword. 'Keep your crossbows loaded.'

He pushed his way through the brambles and Sacharissa prowled after him, her nose low to the ground, hackles raised. Concentrating, Arcturus could sense the alien smells of the jungle blazing through her consciousness. The rich odour of the black soil beneath his feet, the fragrance of exotic fruit and flowers, even the stench of animal droppings somewhere in the distance.

Arcturus could only follow, wanting to take Elaine by the hand to keep her close, but instead holding his crossbow, swinging it back and forth as the green leaves slapped against his face. It was useless – he could barely see Rotter's back ahead of him, let alone make anything out through the thick vegetation.

Behind, he could hear Edmund murmuring to Alice and wondered if they were talking about him. Were they plotting . . . ? Would they use him as a bargaining chip, hold a knife to his throat if the rebels caught them?

This was his best chance – he could lose the nobles in the foliage and circle back to their hunters. It had to be safer with them than striking out into the orc jungles, whatever they wanted of him.

He looked back and caught a glimpse of Elaine staring at the spear in her hands as if it were a venomous snake. He smiled at her with as much encouragement as he could muster, then stumbled and was forced to turn around once more. No . . . he couldn't leave her.

'Have you ever been in the jungles?' Arcturus asked Rotter, hoping to distract himself from the hopelessness that seemed to grip him tighter with every step.

'Aye, we pursued an orc-raiding party here once, after they'd slaughtered an entire village. Lost two men that day,' Rotter growled. 'Never saw the brutes neither. Only the javelins that pinned my mates to the trees.'

That did not make Arcturus feel better, so he concentrated on following Sacharissa's bushy tail as it swept back and forth in front of him, wagging frantically as she took in the new world. Despite their predicament, the boisterous creature was enjoying herself, and soon Arcturus could not help but smile as she snuffled back and forth along the ground, sneezing once as she accidentally snorted the dusty pollen from a bulbous flower.

Then the leaves fell away, and Arcturus stumbled into an open space, interweaving branches arching to form a loose thatch roof along what looked like a corridor into the forest.

'An animal trail here,' Rotter said, helping Elaine through. 'We should follow it while it goes in the right direction. We'll move faster, even if it gives the dogs an easier job following us.'

'Just a second,' Edmund said, peering into his scrying crystal. 'Athena has arrived in Corcillum. There's smoke in the air . . . Looks like there were riots last night.'

'A distraction,' Alice said, leaning in to look. 'Our parents would have spent the entire night helping fight the blazes.'

'She's heading for the palace,' Edmund sighed. 'If we're lucky, King Alfric will be there, staying safe.'

'Where else could he be?' Arcturus asked.

'He might have left Corcillum and gone into hiding until the riots have ended,' Alice replied.

Rotter groaned with frustration.

'None of this will matter if we can't get away from the dogs. We can discuss this later,' he said.

Already Sacharissa was roaming down the path, her nose seemingly affixed to the ground. There was a veritable bouquet of animal scents on the ground, made obvious by the many prints that littered the soil.

But instead of following her, Rotter crouched, holding his

hand up to stop them. He beckoned them nearer, and put his hand close to the ground, his fingers splayed. Beneath it, Arcturus could see a footprint, complete with five toes. Only . . . it was huge, as wide as Rotter's hand and longer than the dirk still strapped to Arcturus's boot.

The print belonged to an orc.

27

Arcturus stared at the imprint, struggling to fathom the size of the creature that made it. He had heard that orcs were enormous beasts, standing seven feet tall when full-grown. But to see it . . . it boggled the mind.

'It's a bull orc from the size,' Rotter said, his breath catching in his throat. 'They must use this path. Arcturus, can your demon pick up its scent?'

Startled, Arcturus called Sacharissa over with a thought, and the demon immediately sensed his intentions, putting her wet nose to the footprint and sniffing deeply. Within his consciousness, the scent swirled about Arcturus's head . . . it was a pungent smell, all body odour and sweat, with a distinctive tinge that he could not place.

Worst of all, Sacharissa was already nosing the ground in the direction they needed to go, tracking the spoor like one of the hunting dogs that followed them.

'It was headed the same way,' Arcturus said, trying to hide the apprehension in his voice.

'Well, we'll keep our wits about us,' Rotter said. 'If there's just one, I can probably handle it, but you'd better release your demons now, just in case. Hurry, we need to move – they'll follow our scents easily enough now, demons or no demons.'

Arcturus looked on as Edmund and Alice delved in their quivers where they had stored their summoning leathers in a handy compartment. The pair kneeled in the moist earth and unravelled them, then, together, they summoned their demons in a flash of white light.

It was with some surprise that Arcturus saw Edmund had a second demon – a Canid. It was a lean, long-legged beast with a pelt of slate fur and a long muzzle, not unlike a giant greyhound. The demon was almost large enough for Elaine to ride, with its back reaching the height of Arcturus's chest.

Mere moments after it had materialised, the demon hared towards Sacharissa, its tail wagging excitedly at the sight of another Canid.

'Back, Gelert,' Edmund called, as the two Canids crouched on the ground, paws extended, play fighting as dogs are wont to do. 'Leave that pup alone.'

But Arcturus was not looking at Gelert – for Alice's demon had brushed against his legs.

He recognised the creature from his demonology book – in fact it was one of the first he had learned of, but it made the beast no less fascinating to his novice's eyes. It was a Vulpid, and he was instantly smitten.

Its lustrous fur was a yellow-white, like finely threaded gold, coating what appeared to be the body of a fox, complete with the animal's narrow muzzle and broad triangular ears. But most beautiful of all was its tail, or, rather, tails – three of them, in fact. Each was as thick and bushy as the real-world counterpart, and the trio of brushes whirled excitedly with every step.

Arcturus had to resist the temptation to stroke the beautiful creature, and suddenly understood Elaine's obsession with Sacharissa.

'She's beautiful!' Elaine said, hugging her arms to her chest. 'What's her name?'

'His name,' Alice corrected. 'It's Reynard.'

Arcturus smiled. Sacharissa had competition.

Even as Arcturus watched the three demons meet ahead of them, circling each other with excitement, the faintest echo of a sound broke through. Barking, drifting on the wind.

It pricked up all three of the demons' ears, and Arcturus spun round, looking in the direction they had come from. His view was obscured by the vegetation, and their pursuers were too far to see regardless, but now he saw the trail they had left – the broken stems and parted vegetation they had pushed through. There was no doubt in his mind which group the hunters would follow.

There was no need to say another word. Together, they turned and ran. It seemed endless, hearts pounding, breaths coming thick and fast, quivers rattling and bouncing along their backs. Rotter was setting an impossible pace, the hardy veteran used to marching long hours.

Elaine was the first to go down. Arcturus knew she had tried, tried harder than any of them, for he had kept a watchful eye on her as they had sprinted along the uneven ground, ducking low-hanging branches and hacking through where the path had become overgrown. There was no room for stealth now – they knew the hunters were chasing them. The barking seemed to be getting louder.

He did not see it, but heard her fall, tripping on an errant root worming its way across the path. She had been too tired to notice it. Too tired to get up.

'Elaine!'

Arcturus ran to her side and hauled her to her feet. She could barely stand, hanging off his arm like a sack of potatoes.

'We need to take a break,' Arcturus gasped, at the others.

Rotter turned and held up a hand, chest heaving.

'Let me think,' the soldier said, looking back behind them. 'They're already faster than us, even if I carry her.'

He looked around, then fell to his knees, pushing his hands deep into the dirt. The ground he kneeled on had been torn up by the thoroughfare of animals, and puddles had formed in their tracks, creating a makeshift waterhole. The air was tinged with the smell of animal faeces and urine.

For a moment Arcturus thought he was praying. Then the soldier pulled out a dollop of mud and kneaded it in his hands.

'Take off your clothes,' he said, standing and removing the red-cloth surcoat that covered his chainmail.

'Are you joking?' Edmund said.

'There's no bloody time – take off as much as possible. Do it, quickly!'

Arcturus stared at the soldier as if he were mad, but still he did it, tearing at the metal buttons of his uniform and pulling at his shirt until he stood, bare-chested beside Edmund. The two girls still wore their lace undershirts to protect their modesty, but their jackets and overshirts were off.

'Wipe your sweat with them – get as much on there as you can,' Rotter growled, mopping at his brow with the surcoat.

In truth, Arcturus was soaked in sweat from his run, and it was a relief to wipe away the salt that had been stinging his eyes.

'Which of your demons is fastest?' Rotter said after they were finished.

'Gelert can run like the wind,' Edmund said proudly.

'Good,' Rotter said, bundling the clothes together in a makeshift knot with his surcoat. 'I need you to give him these and send him running down there for as long as you feel comfortable with. Then order him off the path, get him to bury the clothes and roll around in the mud, and take a roundabout path through the bushes before coming back to us. Can you do that?'

Edmund nodded grimly, and the large Canid took the clothing in its mouth. Then, after a quick hug from Edmund, it was off, haring down the path faster than Arcturus thought possible. Soon the demon was out of sight.

'The rest of you, infuse your demons, and I mean all of them.' Rotter looked pointedly at Elaine, who, despite her exhaustion, had surreptitiously hidden Valens behind her back. 'Their smell is distinctive.'

'All right,' she groaned, removing a handkerchief-sized summoning leather from her pack.

Arcturus grimaced as he called Sacharissa, who reluctantly allowed him to infuse her once again. Perhaps if the dogs were not so close, she would have refused him, but the barking was so loud it sounded as if they were just around the corner of the pathway.

'Now, cover yourselves in mud from head to toe,' Rotter said, digging thick dollops of mud from the ground and smearing himself all over. 'We haven't much time.'

So they did, being careful not to take it all from the same place. It was not perfect, but soon they were almost entirely covered by the foul-smelling sludge. Arcturus suspected that other, less savoury substances had been mixed in with the mud.

'We're downwind, so this may just work,' Rotter muttered. 'Now follow me.'

They ran further up the trail, then suddenly Rotter pushed his way into a thinner patch of vegetation, walking along the top of a fallen tree trunk and slipping into the bushes at its end. Arcturus and the others followed, until they were all crouched behind a screen of waxy leaves, watching the path ahead.

'Here, rub these on yourselves,' Rotter murmured, crawling a little way back and tugging a few handfuls of leaves and tubers from a nearby plant. 'It's wild garlic, I think . . . might help mask the smell.'

They did so, hearts pounding in their chests as the sound of the rebels' dogs became louder and louder, and the distant chatter of voices could be heard.

Then they saw it. The first dog, scampering past with its nose to the ground, tongue lolling out, tail wagging. But even as Arcturus allowed himself to feel relieved at its passing, it returned, called back by a sharp whistle.

'Look here, footprints,' shouted a voice. 'The dogs 'ave slowed. Summat's changed.'

'Keep it down,' growled another. 'There're orcs here.'

'Like the dogs aren't making enough of a racket?' one more replied. 'This is a fool's errand. We'll never find them in this mess.'

Now Arcturus could hear the jingle of metal and the panting gasps of men who were nearly out of breath. And there were dogs passing ahead of him, a whole pack of them, panting as they loped by their hiding place. For a moment one paused, a mangy, flea-bitten thing, its nose snorting in their direction. It growled, its lips curling back to reveal a row of yellowed teeth.

'Gerronwithit,' a voice shouted, and the hound yelped as a hobnailed boot kicked it ahead. 'They're close, I can sense it. Hurry up, lads, we're catching up to them!'

Arcturus caught a glimpse of several hooded figures running past them, then behind followed a straggled line of others, clutching assorted weapons to their chests.

They remained crouched in the bushes, holding their breaths as more and more rebels thundered past. Arcturus could hardly believe how many of them there were. At least a hundred men had followed them into the jungle. All to find Harold . . . or him.

It felt like an age until the last rebel had stumbled by, and even then Rotter kept them silent and still for a full five minutes before he allowed them to move.

'I was wrong – 'twas a bloody bad idea following the trail,' he finally whispered. 'I thought there would be but a dozen or so of 'em. We should cut through the jungle. There's too many of 'em to keep up with us – they'll get separated and lost.'

Edmund cursed, swiping a curious insect from his face.

'Damned vermin,' he growled, waving his hand. 'We can't cut through the jungle now, our rescuers will never find us. The trail is the best marker we have for the Celestial Corps.'

'We haven't much choice,' Rotter replied, getting to his feet. 'We've bought ourselves some time, but they'll be back this way when the trail runs cold.'

'Something's wrong,' Edmund said, clutching his brow. 'Athena's angry! Wait . . . I can hear something.'

He tugged the crystal from his pack and the group leaned in to see. Only . . . it was black.

No. There was a dim glow, filtering through.

He closed his eyes and cocked his head to one side.

'A man is speaking . . .' he whispered. 'Athena can hear him. They've got her trapped somewhere, I can sense it. A cupboard or something like it.'

'What's he—?' Rotter asked, only to be silenced by a raised finger from Edmund.

'It's one of the king's guards,' Edmund said, his brow furrowing. 'He's telling someone that . . . it was a good thing they read the note before they sent her on her way. That General Barcroft will be pleased.'

'Barcroft?' Alice whispered.

'They must be rebels,' Edmund said. 'I can hear footsteps . . . the bastards are leaving.'

He cursed and smacked the ground with his fist.

'To hell with them!'

But Arcturus was barely listening. They were being hunted deep in enemy territory. And nobody was coming to save them.

28

The sun was setting by the time Rotter allowed them to make camp. He had pushed them hard all day, hacking a path through the undergrowth with his sword, taking them away from the trail and then curving to follow its direction around the mountains.

Now they huddled together, deep within a broad-leafed bush, eating the squashed remains of some guava that Rotter had found on the ground and saved in his pack.

'What if I send Valens,' Elaine said, speaking up for what seemed to Arcturus the first time that day.

'No paper left. I used it all with the scroll for Athena and the message to your parents,' Edmund said, poking dejectedly at his mud-stained boots with a twig. 'I thought of that already.'

Alice hugged the sad-faced noble, and kissed him on the cheek. Gelert had not returned – as far as Edmund could tell, the demon was lost, wandering aimlessly in the jungle, attempting to catch their scent. A Canid's sense of smell was far more powerful than a dog's, but it was still a dangerous situation.

'What do we do now?' Elaine whispered, shuffling closer to Arcturus and laying her head on his shoulder.

'We could wait it out,' Rotter said. 'Hope that Harold and the others make it back and send rescuers searching for us. We could survive a day or two in the jungle, if we find a water source.'

'They may be in a worse spot than we are,' Edmund muttered. 'We saw a hundred rebels following us. But there are at least another hundred unaccounted for. Maybe they followed Harold and the others.'

'We can't rely on anyone to save us now,' Arcturus said firmly. 'The only ones who are getting us out of this are ourselves.'

They looked at him, surprised at his candour. He realised he had not spoken for quite some time – but he was getting sick of letting others decide his fate. Noble or not, trustworthy or not, they were all in the same boat. Or bush, anyway.

'So what do you suggest?' Edmund asked. 'We head for the front lines? Hope we don't run into the rebels ahead of us?'

'Yes,' Arcturus said. 'That's what the plan was anyway, right? The rebels and Athena's capture haven't changed that.'

Edmund grunted and went back to cleaning his boots. Arcturus did not take offence – both the boy's demons were in jeopardy. He was not sure how he would cope if Sacharissa were lost in the wilderness, or trapped somewhere by rebels hell-bent on his destruction.

'There's something else we need to speak about,' Alice said, changing the subject. 'Arcturus . . . why are the rebels looking for you?'

197

Arcturus felt icy fear surge through his veins.

'I don't know,' he said, hugging his knees closer to his chest.

'Isn't it obvious?' Rotter asked.

Arcturus stared at him. How could Rotter know? Even Arcturus didn't know, and that was after his strange conversation with Crawley.

'A common summoner. He could be the rebel figurehead. Even their leader. The nobles would not seem so high and mighty when commoners can summon too.'

'But—' Arcturus began.

'They could take him around the land,' Rotter continued, 'proving that some commoners can summon. It is only the fear of your demons that keeps the common man down.'

'I'm *not* a commoner!' Arcturus snapped.

He regretted his words as soon as he said them.

'What do you mean?' Edmund said, looking up from his boot. Alice simply stared at him, wide-eyed.

'I'm . . . I'm not what you think I am,' he muttered, avoiding their eyes.

Silence. Arcturus paused, his heart twisting with instant regret at his outburst.

'I'm Lord Faversham's son. His bastard son. That's why I can summon.'

He cursed himself silently. Telling them that didn't help . . . it probably made things worse.

'I . . . I didn't know,' Edmund said.

'It's why they tried to kill me. Charles and Rook. So nobody would find out that I'm Faversham's bastard.'

'That makes two of us,' Rotter said, patting Arcturus's back.

'Never knew my father either. 'Tis nothing to be ashamed of.'

'And we won't tell a soul, will we, Edmund?' Alice said firmly.

'Of course not,' Edmund said.

Arcturus didn't know what to believe, but that was the least of his concerns.

'It doesn't matter,' Arcturus sniffed, feeling the hot sting of tears at the corners of his eyes. 'They don't know that. They'll want me anyway.'

'Well, at least they don't want to kill you,' Elaine said brightly, looking up at him.

That didn't make Arcturus feel better. But in that moment he knew he had to choose a side. He had shared too much with his impulsive outburst already, but the nobles would need more if they were going to trust him.

In for a penny, in for a shilling.

'I may be a half-noble, but Provost Forsyth says there are true commoners out there who have manifested the ability to summon,' Arcturus said, the words spilling out after keeping them pent up inside for so long.

He knew it was a secret, but he'd be damned if he was going to keep it now. He didn't owe the Provost a thing.

'What . . . how?' Alice said, her brows furrowing in disbelief.

'I don't know. I don't even know if it's true. It's only what he told me.'

'Look, I don't know about you, but this can all wait for another time,' Rotter sighed. 'It's irrelevant. What matters now is that we get ourselves out of this mess.'

Edmund nodded.

'I agree with Arcturus's assessment. Nothing has changed.

We get to the front lines, only instead of waiting for rescue, we meet up with a band of soldiers like yours, Rotter. Then head for Corcillum.'

'What if the soldiers are rebels, like the king's guards that captured Athena?' Alice asked. 'What if they're working for General Barcroft too?'

'Who is that, anyway?' Arcturus asked. The guards who had captured Athena had mentioned that name.

'He's the general that commands the south-western portion of the front lines,' Rotter answered. 'He's my boss, technically, about a dozen ranks above me anyway. A good man, so I'm told. Petitions the king to get us the supplies we need to keep on fighting.'

'Well, he's a traitor, if those guards are working for him,' Edmund said. 'Maybe he got sick of asking, thought he could do a better job.'

'Can you blame him?' Rotter said, lifting a flap of rusted chainmail. 'This could have been my grandfather's.'

'That's dangerous talk,' Edmund warned.

'After all I've done for you . . .' Rotter began angrily.

'That's enough!' Arcturus said, holding up his hand. 'It's been a long night, we're all tired, and we all know we're on the same side. Let's just get some rest and make it to the front lines. We can decide if we can trust the soldiers then.'

29

Sleep did not come easily that night. Hunched in the darkness, with nary a wyrdlight to illuminate their makeshift shelter within the bushes, Arcturus could hardly see his own hand in front of his face.

And the noises. Arcturus had never thought the jungle could be so loud. Grunts, howls and screeches filled the air around them, accompanied by the incessant chirr of crickets and the whine of mosquitos. It was all he could do not to despair, and nobody begrudged him when he summoned Sacharissa later that night, pressing himself against the curve of her back to take comfort from her warmth and feel the slow rise and fall of her chest.

It was only when morning came that Arcturus allowed himself to end his attempts to sleep – all he had managed was a cycle of jerking awake in fear, only to sink back into the darkness and let exhaustion drag him over the edge of slumber once more.

Yet, as the first tendrils of light filtered through the trees, and the birds began their morning calls, the world lost its hard edge. He could see pink flowers opening to catch the morning glory, and the sweet scent filtered through the trees, lingering in his consciousness as Sacharissa breathed in the myriad of smells that greeted the sun. Tropical birds flitted in the branches above, their feathers fanned out in a blaze of yellows, reds and blues.

As the night terrors faded from memory, Arcturus felt a sudden tightness of his bladder and the dryness of his throat raged more keenly than ever. Their paltry meal of dank fruit had assuaged it the night before, but now he found himself sitting up and seeking a nearby tree.

The others were still sleeping and Arcturus could not help but smile at the sight of them. Alice and Edmund were curled in each other's arms, while Elaine had surreptitiously taken hold of Sacharissa's tail, curling herself around it like a cuddly toy. Even Rotter seemed oblivious to the world, spreadeagled like a bearskin with his mouth wide open enough to catch flies.

Not wishing to disturb them, Arcturus ordered Sacharissa to stay put with a thought and ducked out of their leafy den, careful not to make too much noise.

Embarrassment at being caught took him further into the jungle, along with the desire to find something to eat. Hunger gnawed at his belly – the thought of the trampled guava they had eaten the previous night seemed like the sweetest ambrosia now.

Once he had put some distance between him and their camp, Arcturus ducked under a sheet of hanging moss and found a nearby tree.

As he sighed with relief, he heard something. At first,

he thought it a bird call, but then it came again, louder this time. A scream. Coming from ahead of him.

Arcturus pulled the crossbow around from the sling across his back, swiftly loading it and levelling it at the thickets ahead of him.

It came again, and now he recognised it was a woman's voice, wailing in agony. Could it be Josephine? Panic thundered through Arcturus's heart. There was no time to get the others.

Indecision froze him still, and now he could sense Sacharissa rising from her sleep to wake the others.

Then Arcturus was running, tearing through the undergrowth in a mad dash, disregarding the thorns and branches that tore at his skin.

It was a root that saved him, tripping him before he reached the screams. Before he reached the orcs. He tumbled as it caught on his toes, ripping through the snarled branches and vines that blocked his path and rolling to a dead stop a few feet away from the clearing where the screams came from.

The wind was knocked from his chest, gusting out of his mouth and leaving him gasping like a beached fish. Perhaps if he had groaned they would have heard him. But as it was, he could only pant noiselessly as he stared through the screen of leaves at the scene in the glade beyond.

There were four of them, standing in a small space among the trees, made possible by a fallen tree. Each of the orcs was a giant, their bodies corded with grey-skinned muscle and adorned with alien swirls of war-paint, daubed on by fingers dipped in ochres of reds, yellows and orange.

Seen from a distance, they may well have been men, were it

not for their monstrous faces. Tusks jutted from their lips, fierce canines as long as curved daggers, making their speech garbled as they talked among themselves. Stranger still were their jutting, gorilla-like brows, sloping back to reach thick tufts of black hair, styled in a broad mix of topknots, shaved patches and bowl-shaped mops.

Arcturus lay frozen to the ground in terror, unable to take his eyes from the creatures as they barked in their strange, guttural language. They were facing in his direction. Directly in front of him, another orc lay injured on the ground.

From her anatomy, Arcturus could tell she was female, though her modesty was covered by the same grass skirt that all the orcs wore, along with a fibre-woven shawl draped across her shoulders and chest.

She was crying, and from his position, Arcturus could see her face was bruised and swollen, with blood dripping from her lips. A large male orc stood over her, his fist raised in the air. The female orc cringed away from him as the aggressor made to hit her, and then he laughed as she tried to drag herself away from him on the mud-slick ground.

The male orc stopped as the crackle of branches resounded in the foliage on the opposite side of the clearing. Arcturus's eyes widened as new arrivals emerged from the trees.

Rhinos. Great, grey beasts with wrinkled skins and small, watery eyes, their long horns pushing through the tangle of lianas and leafage like icebreakers on a northern trade ship. And on their backs rode orcs, each one dressed in rattling animal-bone armour, held together by twisted sinew wound through drilled holes. All wore headdresses of multicoloured feathers and swung wooden clubs nonchalantly in their hands. These were larger, nobler creatures than those already in the clearing.

Upon their arrival, the four orcs turned and fell to their knees, bowing their heads respectfully. The female orc lay forgotten and, weakly, she crawled herself back away from the others. Back towards Arcturus.

Her hand fell a foot away from Arcturus's face, and he could see the black nails digging into the ground as she tried to reach safety. Then she stopped, her strength failing her as she gasped for breath.

Arcturus tried to retreat in terror, only to find his back pressed against a sapling, his skin grazing against its rough bark. Beyond, more orcs emerged from the trees.

Even with the female orc so close, he could not tear his eyes away from the new arrivals. For these were not just rhino riders, but also younger, smaller orcs, their necks lassoed tightly in a long rope chain, stumbling along the forest floor, dragged by their mounted captors. They were prisoners, their faces badly bloodied, some limping from wounds, others nursing broken bones.

All of the captives were adolescent males, if the size of their tusks and relatively smaller stature were a sign. Of course, even these young orc pups would stand head and shoulders above Arcturus, but from his vantage point in the bushes, he couldn't help but pity the poor creatures as a rhino-rider lashed them forward with a long, curling whip.

Then his view was obscured as the female orc pulled herself into the bushes, and suddenly Arcturus was staring into her dark, tear-filled eyes. She stared at him, shock plain across her swollen features. Frantically, Arcturus held a finger up to his lips, hoping she would understand.

Still she stared, and beyond, Arcturus could hear the leader of the rhino-riders snarling orders. The four orcs that had been assaulting the young female stood, and one yelled out in annoyance and strode towards them.

For a moment the female stared at him, her eyes wide with panic. Then she was being dragged back into the clearing, the male orc laughing as he pulled her by her foot.

The female clawed wildly at the vegetation around her, her hands tugging up roots and snapping young boughs as the orc heaved at her legs. Then, suddenly, Arcturus was jerked after her, her hand curling around his ankle like an iron shackle.

Sobbing with terror, Arcturus grasped at the sapling behind him, and it felt as if his arms would tear from their very sockets as the bull orc heaved.

He kicked out, looking down at the female and shaking his head in a desperate plea. Their eyes locked for a split second . . . and she let go.

Then she was gone, back into the clearing, where the thud of flesh against flesh could be heard, the male orc's fist rising and falling over and over. It was a pitiless, sadistic display of violence, and Arcturus could do nothing but watch in horror as the female's raised arms fell away, too weak to defend herself against the blows that rained down upon her.

In his mind, Arcturus could sense Sacharissa now, following his scent through the undergrowth. He could feel her panic mirroring his own, and shared the flashes of pain as she ripped through thorny branches. The Canid knew he was in trouble. She was coming for him.

The rest of the orcs were almost gone now, disappearing back into the jungle in a tumult of snapping branches and guttural yells from the riders. Still the bull orc continued his beating, laughing as the female's head lolled to the side.

Arcturus's anger rose like bile in his throat, sickened by the display of cruelty. How could the bull orc do this to one of his own?

The bull orc lifted the female by her hair, clutching at the long, black braid that fell down her back. She hung there, limp, as the orc raised his fist once more. It was the killing blow.

Arcturus could not watch. Would not. Instead, his hand scrabbled at the ground beside him. Met the stock of his crossbow.

He didn't think. Didn't even aim. He just raised it and shot in one smooth motion, yelling through the fear, ignoring the madness of it all. The weapon's butt slammed into his shoulder, and the male orc fell back, a feathered bolt seeming to grow out of its eye.

Arcturus scrambled through the leaves, the dirk from his boot clutched in his hand. He half lunged, half fell on to the male orc, stabbing down, cursing with every breath, plunging the dirk again and again into the orc's chest. The orc writhed beneath him, his hands slapping at Arcturus, scratching at his bare chest.

Arcturus felt the orc's fingers around his throat, and suddenly the world was darkening at the corners of his vision, his breath caught in his lungs as the orc's hold tightened. The dirk fell from his fingers and he fell limp, held up only by the orc's grasp.

A dark shape crashing through the trees. Hot spray across his face, the metal taste of blood on his tongue.

He was falling.

Then nothing.

30

Arcturus opened his eyes to Sacharissa's rough tongue licking his cheek. He couldn't have been out for more than a few moments, for he could still hear the crashing of branches in the distance as the orc horde pushed on through the trees beyond. He sat up, panicked.

Had they heard him?

He was beside the corpse of the male orc, sitting in a spreading pool of blood emanating from its neck. A deep furrow had been slashed across its throat where Sacharissa must have savaged the beast as it choked the life from him. He had come so close to death.

And for what?

Arcturus turned to see the female orc staring at him, squinting through her swollen eye sockets as if she found it hard to see. She held his dirk in her hand and was pointing the weapon at him.

The foolishness of Arcturus's actions dawned upon him then. This orc was not his friend. She was the enemy. Her entire species was. What madness had possessed him to risk his life for hers?

Yet the memory of her eyes staring up at him swirled about his head. She had let go of his leg knowing what fate awaited her beyond. The orc had chosen not to take him with her. Hadn't she?

'I'm not here to hurt you,' Arcturus said, holding up his hands. Sacharissa growled beside him, lowering her body into a crouch. Her hackles were raised, the mane on her back standing up like a startled street cat's.

Arcturus tried to calm her with a thought, but the demon's aggression was up and he could taste the orc's blood on her tongue through their connection. Instead, he straddled Sacha's back, forcing her down. As a juvenile Canid, she was still no bigger than an overgrown dog, and she trembled briefly beneath his weight before succumbing and lowering herself to the ground.

The female orc cocked her head to one side, the dirk still extended towards him. She was breathing heavily, as if the very act of being alive exhausted her. Bruises were blooming across her grey skin even as he watched. She had taken a terrible beating – Arcturus doubted any human could have survived what she had endured.

Then he saw it. Her belly had been obscured by the shawl, but now he could see the distended curve of her protruding navel. The orc was pregnant.

'Arcturus, back away slowly so we can get a clear shot,' Rotter's voice called from the trees. 'Three feet should do it, then we'll have it.'

'Don't shoot,' Arcturus hissed. 'She's pregnant.'

'So what?' Rotter snarled from the bushes. 'She'll kill you if given half a chance.'

But Arcturus didn't believe him. In fact, the orc's arm was trembling now, and she let her hand drop to the ground. For a moment she stared at him. Then she shook her head weakly and tossed the dirk aside. The orc let herself fall back, and gazed up into the canopy.

'Get back,' Rotter said. 'It's a trap.'

'Lower your crossbows,' Arcturus said, staring in the direction of Rotter's voice. 'If she had wanted to kill me, I'd be dead already.'

His group must have circled around, for they were somewhere to his right, hidden in the foliage. Alice was the first to emerge, her crossbow still loaded, but aimed at the ground.

'Just leave her,' Edmund's voice called. 'There's nothing we can do for her.'

But Alice sidled closer, looking down at the bruised and broken figure. As a female orc, the mother-to-be was only six feet or so tall, far less imposing than her male counterparts.

'We can't just leave her like this,' she said, biting her lip.

Arcturus rolled from Sacharissa's back and sheathed the dirk in his calf-scabbard. As he did so, Elaine came out of the trees, staring at the orc with wide, curious eyes.

'Keep your distance,' Edmund warned, joining them in the clearing. Rotter followed behind, shaking his head with disapproval.

'She's old for a mother,' Rotter said, hunkering down beside Arcturus and Sacharissa. 'You can tell by the size of her tusks – she must be around my age. It won't be her first child.'

'Does that matter?' Elaine asked.

'No,' Rotter said, scratching at the stubble on his chin. 'Just an observation.'

'Well, she's unarmed now,' Arcturus said. 'We should at least get her out of this clearing. It's too exposed.'

'We don't have the time,' Rotter said. 'I understand your sentiments, but they're not like you and me.'

But Alice had already crept over to the orc and was gently covering her with the shawl.

Then she took the sword from Rotter's hand.

'Aye, we should put her out of her misery,' the soldier said. 'Let me do it. You're too young for this.'

But Alice had other plans.

'We can make a stretcher,' she said firmly, striding into the bushes and hacking at the same sapling Arcturus had used as a handhold. 'Come on, help me.'

Edmund cursed, but at a warning glance from Alice sheepishly followed her example, wandering into the forest to gather vines.

'This is a bloody bad idea,' Rotter grumbled. But he did nothing to stop them.

Within a few minutes, knotted vines had been stretched between two poles, and the orc, now unconscious, had been rolled on to the rudimentary stretcher.

'What now?' Rotter asked.

'We need to find water,' Arcturus said, swallowing drily. The fight with the orc had sapped him of all his energy and the inside of his throat felt like sandpaper. The world was already beginning to spin ever so slightly, and their water reserves were now gone, leaving them with empty flasks.

He turned to Sacharissa, who had finally calmed down and was now sniffing curiously at the female orc's toes. Calling her over with a thought, he looked deep into her larger set of deep-blue eyes and concentrated.

What felt like long ago, but couldn't be longer than a few weeks, Sacharissa had led him to the Vocans baths using scent alone. Now he sought that same smell, that fresh, clear fragrance of water.

In those first moments Arcturus was overwhelmed. Magnified as the smells were, his mind roiled with a miasma of a thousand things. The scent of the orcs was strongest, a great channel of odour that dominated the space. On top, were the sweet notes of fruit and flowers, along with grassy vegetation and the acrid decay of fallen leaves. And yet . . .

There it was. Not so much a smell as a sound, in the distance. The rush of water, coupled with the faintest hint of moisture.

'Find it, Sacha,' Arcturus whispered, sending her his intentions with a thought.

She pressed her head against his thigh, then pushed past his legs and slipped into the jungle.

'Come on,' Arcturus said, not waiting for them to follow. 'There's water that way.'

31

Water.

A river of rushing water, carving its way through the jungle, clear as a mountain stream and wide as a city street. Beneath, Arcturus could see fronds of green, waving as the river ebbed and flowed. Beneath, silver shoals of fish darting back and forth, parting and coming together as long-mouthed river pike swam by.

They did not wait to fill their flasks, but simply buried their faces in its cool shallows, bathing away the sweat and grime and gulping down fresh draughts of clear water until the liquid sloshed in their bellies.

Sacharissa dove in headfirst, splashing happily in a doggy-paddle and snapping at the flashing scales of the fish that swam around her and nipped at her paws.

Arcturus splashed Sacharissa as she returned to the shallows, and the demon sneezed. She sprayed Arcturus back with a flick of her tail, leaving Arcturus spluttering.

He shook his head at the cheeky demon and pulled her

close to him, ignoring the smell of wet dog and ruffling her ears.

'Thank you for saving me,' he whispered, looking deep into her eyes. She stared back with a love and devotion that Arcturus knew he did not deserve. Embarrassed, he looked away.

The orc lay motionless where they had dropped her stretcher, her head lolling to the side. Her eyes were now so swollen it was hard to tell if she was awake or unconscious.

Elaine sat beside the great beast's head, trickling water into the orc's mouth from her flask. The orc gulped it all down, and licked her lips as if asking for more.

'She likes it!' Elaine murmured, using some of the excess to wipe away the blood and grime from the orc's face.

'Aye, and she'd like the flesh from your bones too if she could get at it,' Rotter said, jabbing a finger at the prone figure.

'What do you know anyway?' Alice asked, falling on to her back and clutching at her full stomach. 'All you've done is fight them. Maybe some of them are peaceful.'

'That's right,' Arcturus said thoughtfully. 'Surely they aren't born evil. I mean, I saw some of them were prisoners of the others. Young males, by the look of them.'

'I'll tell you what I know,' Rotter growled, standing and stretching his back. 'Those orc boys you saw can't have been older than ten. Orcs mature faster than we do, and get old faster too. If an orc lives to see fifty, they've done well.'

He strode over to the orc and hunkered down beside her.

'This one, she's past her prime. It's a miracle she's pregnant at all,' he said, examining her more closely.

Rotter narrowed his eyes and pointed at her stomach, where thick ropey scars surrounded by faded white lines extended horizontally above the skirt.

'Old stretch marks and surgery scars. She must be what we call a brood mare. Forced to have children over and over again. She's not had a nice life, that's for sure.'

'Why would they do that to her?' Alice asked, horrified.

'Orc shamans. Their firstborn children are guaranteed to become summoners too, but there's always a chance that a second or third child will inherit the ability to summon, like Elaine. So they travel from village to village, impregnating vulnerable females. The villagers consider it a duty, but it's a brutal life for the chosen girl. She must have run away.'

Arcturus could see pity in Rotter's eyes now, and the soldier sighed and sat back on his heels.

'We're in a tough spot,' he said, rubbing his eyes. 'She needs to be back with her people, but we'd take a big risk heading for a village, if we can find one at all. And who's to say they won't finish what they started, as punishment for running away.'

As he spoke, the orc coughed and groaned, reaching blindly. Elaine fell back, with Valens buzzing protectively above her.

Clutching her swollen belly, the orc moaned again. Rotter looked down.

'Oh . . . damn,' Rotter said. 'I think . . . I think she's about to . . .'

His face whitened and he looked around him.

'What do we do?' he said.

'Stand aside,' Alice snapped, rolling up the sleeves of her undershirt. 'Elaine, I'm going to need your help.'

'What about us?' Edmund asked.

'Get her to the water,' Alice said, lifting the corner of the stretcher. 'It will help with her contractions – she's probably been having them for a while judging from her moaning. Then keep watch for us. From the looks of this, it isn't going to be a quiet affair.'

Arcturus hurried to help, and together they managed to manoeuvre the female orc into a sitting position in the shallows. Her breath was coming thick and fast and she clutched at Alice's hand.

Arcturus sensed the world shifting. Gone was the ogreish savage that he had once seen. Now, a mother. Fighting for her life. To think . . . Rotter had wanted to kill her.

'All right, give her some space,' Alice demanded. 'I'm going to guide the head.'

She didn't need to tell them twice. Arcturus hurried up towards the curve of the river where fronds from a hanging tree drifted in the water. He tried to focus on the bend of the river but could not help but listen to the sounds of the labour behind him.

'All right, Elaine, try to keep her calm,' he heard Alice say. 'Rub her shoulders, there's a good girl.'

'How do you know what you're doing?' Elaine asked.

'I've helped deliver a few calves on our estate,' Alice replied. 'If we're lucky, orc labour will be as quick as theirs.'

The orc's moans became louder. Somehow, the forest had gone completely quiet but for the soft soughing of the breeze.

'Come on, push now,' Alice called out.

Still the orc moaned.

'You've done this before. Push!'

There was a single, drawn-out scream. And then the coughing

cry of a baby, ringing through the air.

'Arcturus, I need your dirk,' Alice called.

He ran back, blade drawn, to where the trio sat in the shallows. For a moment he stood there, confused as to why they needed his blade.

Then he saw the pink, twisted tube of the umbilical cord, and knew what he had to do. It was over in a single slice . . . and then he was staring into the face of an orc baby.

Its little face was crinkled as it wailed at the light of the world, and Alice held the child closer for Arcturus to see, for the mother was too weak to even lift her arms. It had a small patch of curling hair on its head and tiny canines protruding from either side of its mouth.

But for all these details, there was one that stood out to Arcturus the most.

The orc was white. Even its hair was colourless, and its wide eyes were tinged a pink-red. He held out a finger and the baby reached out its hand, taking his finger with surprising force.

'What's—' Arcturus began.

But a shout to his right interrupted him.

'Quickly, into the bushes,' Rotter hissed from upriver, sprinting towards them.

For a panic-stricken moment, Alice and Arcturus stared at each other. The orc was too heavy to move, and Edmund, Elaine and Rotter were already diving into the undergrowth. Sacharissa tugged at Arcturus's wrist, her nostrils filled with a strange, fishy scent.

Then they were running, baby in tow, leaving the exhausted orc sitting in the shallows. What else could they do?

They were not a moment too soon. For within seconds of reaching the safety of the trees, a flotilla came around the bend, the likes of which Arcturus had never seen.

The scrawny creatures within the vessels were short, coming no higher than Arcturus's knee, with bulbous eyes, floppy, webbed ears and long noses and fingers. They wore little more than ragged loincloths and clutched barbed spears in their hands.

They were floating in what looked to Arcturus like large, upturned bowls of varying sizes. Every few seconds, one of the creatures would plunge deep into the water then clamber back out, like seagulls diving for food. With each jump, they would emerge with silver fish spitted on the end of their weapons.

'Gremlins,' Rotter whispered.

Even as Rotter spoke, the gremlins screeched at the sight of the orc, her body motionless in the shallows but for the loose braid of her hair drifting in the water.

'They hate orcs,' Rotter said, a grim look on his face. 'The orcs've been enslaving 'em for centuries. These look like wild 'uns though.'

Indeed, the flotilla had stopped, the gremlins back-paddling with their tiny oars to keep the coracles in place against the currents.

'We have to do something,' Alice hissed. 'They're going to kill her.'

Yet, it did not seem that way to Arcturus. Though they held their spears pointed at the orc, the gremlins were manoeuvring a much larger version of their vessels down the river towards her. What were they doing?

He watched on as the strange little creatures began to tug

ropes from within their boats, swinging them around their heads to lasso the orc where she sat. She moaned as the ropes were tightened, much to the excitement of the gremlins, but still she remained immobile, unable to summon the strength to escape.

Soon she was festooned with cordage, her arms strapped tightly to her sides. It appeared they didn't want to hurt her – but they did want to capture her.

Arcturus unslung his crossbow, unsure what to do. There were as many as a hundred gremlins crouched warily in their boats, their large eyes scanning the surroundings for danger. They were so small . . . perhaps he and his friends could take them.

'Don't,' Rotter grasped his arm with an iron grip. 'There's too many.'

'Are we supposed to just let them take her?' Arcturus asked. He had risked his life for her, mad though it had been.

'The baby's safe,' Edmund whispered. 'Maybe it's better this way . . . there's not much we could do for her anyway, the state she's in. Looks like they want her alive.'

'Her baby,' Elaine gasped. 'We can't take her baby!'

Arcturus looked down at the pale child in Alice's arms, where it stared back at him silently. He thanked the heavens that it had gone silent – Rotter was right. Fighting the gremlins would be suicide – there were hundreds of them.

'I have to give the baby to her,' Alice muttered, but Edmund gripped her knee, holding her down.

'Would you condemn it to a life of slavery too?' he asked. 'Even if they don't kill you on sight . . . That's the fate that awaits it.'

'I . . .' Alice began.

But it was too late. The female orc had been tipped into the wide vessel, sprawled among a bloody pile of silver fish.

Then, with strange, fluting cries that reminded Arcturus of tropical birds, the gremlins slipped away down the stream, their armada hurried along by the rowers within. There was no more fishing now, and the gremlins seemed to be cheering, stabbing their spears into the air.

For a moment Arcturus and the others stared after them, watching as the strange creatures disappeared around the bend. Then, as one, they turned to look at the newborn baby in their midst. It gurgled and glared back at them, jamming its fingers into its tusked mouth.

'Hellfire,' Edmund cursed. 'What are we supposed to do now?'

32

'This is, by far, the stupidest bloody thing I've ever done in my life,' Rotter growled, wringing his hands.

They were crouched on a small, shrub-covered hillock looking downhill into the hollow of a wide valley. Above the canopy of the trees beneath them, they could see a thin stream of smoke, just visible before it dissipated into the clear blue sky. Elaine had sent Valens to spy, and now the group was sitting in a circle around the young noble, peering into the shard of scrying crystal that Alice had lent her.

Within, they could see from the beetle demon's point of view as he flitted between trees, careful not to be seen by any of the wild animals that populated the jungle. The Mite was still a young demon, so it was no larger than a stag beetle and armed only with a weak, undeveloped stinger on its rear. Even a small bird of prey, or wildcat, would make an easy meal of him with one mouthful.

It had taken over ten minutes for Valens to reach his destination, and now he sat on the underside of a waxy leaf, staring down at the source of the flames. Elaine flipped the scrying crystal so that the view was the right side up, and together they leaned in to catch their first glimpse of an orcish settlement.

What was almost immediately clear was that they were looking at no more than a small village made up of wattle-and-daub huts with thatched roofing. In its centre was a pit containing a fire, and surrounding this . . . were orcs.

Yet, these were not the orcs that Arcturus had seen in the jungle earlier – for there were barely any males in sight. Instead, the few orcs he could see were much older, with white hair and hunched, decrepit statures. The remaining orcs were females, dangling babies on their arms or chastising the toddlers that stumbled about the place.

'We're in luck,' Alice murmured. 'No warriors.'

'Any one of those females could rip your head clean off,' Rotter growled. 'Just because the menfolk are out of town, so to speak, doesn't mean anything about this is safe.'

'I think I know what happened to the men,' Arcturus said, thinking of the young captive orcs he had seen earlier that day. 'I don't think they're coming back.'

'Well, I'm going down there wherever they are,' Alice said stubbornly, hefting the baby against her chest protectively. 'We can't take it with us and we can't abandon it either. This is the only way.'

'It's not going to be you going down there,' Edmund said, crossing his arms. 'I'll do it.'

'You'll look like more of a threat,' Alice rebutted, taking a step away from Edmund. 'It's better if a woman goes in, holding the baby as if it were her own. There are plenty of mothers down there. They won't hurt me.'

'Right,' Edmund said, rolling his eyes.

Alice handed the baby to Elaine and took a stick from the ground, then scratched two rough circles into the soil.

'I'll curve around from our position,' she tapped the smaller circle and drew a curved line around to the larger one, 'and enter the camp from the east, where there are fewer orcs. I can leave it on the ground and run into the jungle before they even see me.'

'See, if leaving it on the ground is even an option, why not just leave it on the edge of the camp,' Rotter argued, taking the scrying stone from Elaine and pointing at the forested border of the village. 'They'll find it eventually.'

'Where a wild animal can get to it?' Alice snapped. 'It has to be inside the village itself.'

Rotter sighed and rubbed his beard.

'Wait. Who is that?' Arcturus asked.

He was looking into the scrying crystal, where a much larger orc had emerged from one of the huts. He was an adult male and looked entirely different from all the orcs Arcturus had seen before. His body had been painted pitch black with soot, and the pattern of what appeared to be bones had been smeared over the top of it in a white paste. An outline of a white skull had been drawn starkly against his features, and his head had been shaved completely bald to complement the effect.

Other than his body paint, he wore no more than a loincloth and carried a gnarled staff in his hand. As he walked among the villagers and crouched to warm his hands by the fire, the others shied away from him. The women of the village sent their children scurrying inside and some of the younger females slunk fearfully into the forest.

The orc seemed unperturbed by his effect on the tribe, instead taking a hunk of meat from a nearby elder's hand and gnawing at it as he stared into the flames.

'Damn, what if I run into the ones that are leaving,' Alice muttered, staring down the hill at the smoke, as if she could see the females hiding beneath.

'You're not going,' Edmund hissed. 'Can't you get that through your head?'

Arcturus could not tear his eyes away from the painted orc, for the beast was doing something strange. Though he could not hear the words, the giant was rocking back and forth, muttering something in what he imagined must be the alien, guttural language of the orcs.

Then he saw it, small though it was in the image upon the crystal. A gremlin had limped out of the same hut the painted orc had emerged from, its batwing ears drooping with pain as it scurried towards its master. On its back, Arcturus could see the source of its agony – a bloody mark, carved deep into its very flesh. A pentacle.

Now the others were looking down at the crystal in Rotter's hand. Alice gasped in horror at the sight of the maimed creature, and they watched on as it hobbled its way back to its master.

The white orc lifted the gremlin by its head with a large hand, the fingers encompassing its head as easily as a human might grasp an apple. It hung limply in his grip for a moment. Then, as blue light began to glow from the orc's hand, it wriggled frantically.

Arcturus could almost hear the sizzle of its flesh as the mana burned down the gremlin's back in a jagged blue line until it reached the incisions, suffusing the pentacle until it blazed with the same glow.

White light began to swirl from above the carved symbol, knitting together into flesh and bone.

'It's summoning something . . . this is a shaman!' Alice uttered.

But this was different from when Arcturus summoned Sacharissa. The white light swirled endlessly, growing larger and larger, building up a giant figure beside the flames of the fire.

'What . . . what is that?' Edmund gasped.

Slowly, ever so slowly, the demon materialised.

It was enormous. As large as two orcs and twice as wide, it appeared as a giant, bipedal elephant, with great flapping ears, a powerful trunk and serrated tusks as long as a man was tall.

Finished with the gremlin, the orc took one look at the twitching, burned body, then tossed it derisively into the fire's flames.

'It's . . . a Phantaur,' Alice whispered. 'I've only ever read about those – it's never been seen in the flesh. This is one of the most powerful demons in existence.'

'Well, you're definitely not going down there now,' Edmund said. 'That thing could step on you and barely notice.'

'Nobody has to go down there,' Arcturus said.

He looked at Sacharissa, who had been sitting patiently in the shade of a shrub, her tongue lolling out as she panted in the heat.

'Sacharissa will take the baby. She's fast enough to get in and out quickly, and if we're lucky they'll think she was some kind of wildcat, maybe a panther.'

Edmund stared at Arcturus, then clapped him on the back.

'That's the best damned idea I've heard all day,' he laughed. 'Why didn't I think of that?'

'It's a great plan,' Alice said. 'With one minor difference. Reynard will go. He's faster and more mature than your Canid – plus he's larger.'

Arcturus flushed with relief, though he felt a twinge of guilt as he nodded in agreement. Edmund had lost both his demons, with Gelert still hunting for them in the jungle and Athena diligently screeching every few minutes in the hope of rescue.

Alice was taking a big risk with Reynard, and he was grateful that Sacharissa would not need to go down there.

'Elaine, can you fly Valens to the east side of the village?' Rotter asked. 'We need to scout Reynard's path.'

Silence.

Arcturus looked up from the crystal, searching for Elaine.

But Elaine wasn't there. She was gone . . . and the baby with her.

33

Arcturus was running before he had a chance to think, pacing through the undergrowth with Sacharissa racing beside him. He could smell Elaine's path ahead, meandering through the bushes in the direction of the village.

'Arcturus, wait!' Alice called, and he saw a flash of white light behind him as Reynard was summoned into existence.

He ignored her – every minute counted. Every second. Elaine didn't know that there was a shaman down there.

This time, Arcturus slowed as he neared the edge of the village, hunkering down at its edge and catching his breath. He took a deep sniff and could smell the animal scent of the Phantaur thick in the air.

'Where is she, girl?' Arcturus said, tilting his head to listen for any telltale sounds. When he concentrated, he could hear and smell better, though not nearly as well as when he looked into Sacharissa's eyes.

But now he needed his own eyes for scanning the surroundings, so he relied on Sacharissa as she snuffled her way around to the east side of the village. Arcturus followed, careful to place his feet in the soft soil, away from crackling leaves and brittle twigs. The Phantaur's ears were enormous and he did not doubt that it could hear every sound in the jungle.

As he made his way around the edge, he could see the shaman and his demon. The painted orc had been lifted on to the beast's shoulders and he was shouting orders to the villagers around him. One handed him up a woven basket of fruit, while another scurried into a hut and emerged with a fly-ridden haunch of meat.

'Elaine, where are you?' Arcturus mouthed, not even allowing himself to whisper.

Then he saw her, crouched beside the village edge, the white orc infant clutched to her bosom. Her eyes were wide with terror, staring at the Phantaur. She appeared frozen to the spot, and now Arcturus could see Valens buzzing around her face, tugging at her hair with his mandibles in a bid to make her move.

Arcturus crept towards her on his hands and knees, moving as quickly as he dared. Any minute now an orc would see her. She was crouched in plain view, just within the village border.

He was a mere stone's throw away from her when it happened. It was a toothless orc elder that saw her, and time seemed to slow down as he raised a trembling finger and cried out hoarsely at the sight.

In that moment, Arcturus hurled himself out of the bushes and sprinted towards her. He took her shoulders and pulled her away. For the briefest of seconds he tried to tug the baby from her hands, but she would not let go – it was all he could do to get Elaine to stand up and walk. It was only when an earth-shattering trumpet of noise blasted from behind him that she snapped to attention, but by then it was too late – they were already deep in the trees.

They ran, ripping through the snarled bushes and shrubs in their path, blinded by the beams of sunlight that filtered down through the canopy. There was no time to find their way back to the others. Arcturus could hear the thunder of great footsteps behind him, the noise reverberating through his chest as if the very ground were shaking.

'This way,' Arcturus gasped, gripping her undershirt and pulling her off to the left. They ran on, deeper into the jungle, but the footsteps only seemed to get louder. The shaman was gaining on them.

There was only one chance. A mad idea drifted across his consciousness as he saw an enormous fallen trunk, its insides hollowed out by years of rot, one half buried beneath a pile of fallen branches and creeping vines. Its fall had created a clearing of sorts – enough to see its open end.

'In!' he gasped, shoving Elaine after Sacharissa as the demon ran full tilt into the hollow tube of desiccated bark. He followed moments later, crawling for a few panicked moments until he bumped into the young noble, then pressed his knees tight against his chest as he turned himself into a sitting foetal position. He swivelled his head and looked down into the circle of green-yellow light at the end, the dark tunnel broken only by hairline cracks in the wood above, leaving filtered shafts of light along its length.

'Quiet,' he gasped, trying to slow his breaths, a combination of exertion and terror pounding his heart so hard he felt like he could hear its echoes within the log itself.

So they sat there in the cloying darkness, staring at the opening a half dozen feet from where they hid. All was silent.

Until they heard it. Another thud.

It was slower now, as if the Phantaur had stopped lumbering after them, instead taking its time as it swept the area.

'I'm sorry,' Elaine whispered.

'Shhh,' Arcturus replied, rubbing her shoulder to keep her calm.

Immediately the footsteps stopped. Arcturus cursed inwardly. Had it heard them?

Still . . . nothing. Silence, but for the soft rattle of branches in the afternoon breeze.

A shadow, falling across the circle. Then, the crackle of wood, as if a giant had slowly set its foot down on a forest trail.

The world flipped sideways. One moment they were staring in silence, the next they were screaming as the tree trunk was lifted high. Blue-green flashing as the trunk's end faced the canopy.

Next a stomach-churning drop and a bone-juddering crash that spun Arcturus on his side. The bark held – but more cracks appeared along its length.

There was no time for planning. Arcturus had barely a moment to draw his dirk before a snake of leathery grey flesh wriggled its way through the opening. The Phantaur's trunk darted at him, two powerful fingers closing like a snapping mouth grasping for its prey. The world darkened as the demon placed its face against the opening to push its trunk further still, and suddenly it was within inches of Arcturus's face. He stabbed at it, barely making a scratch in the thick skin. The fingers closed on his hair, jerking him a foot towards it before his scalp burned and a tuft of hair ripped free.

He rolled as the trunk slammed down, splitting the wood further so that he felt wet soil against his bare back. He stabbed again, directly at the trunk's tip. This time he was rewarded by an ear-splitting squeal of pain, and the trunk withdrew a few feet. He stabbed it again, drawing blood. This time he felt the blast of air as the beast trumpeted in agony. The tip was sensitive.

Mere seconds of respite followed.

'Valens,' Elaine called desperately. 'Valens!'

But if the little Mite was attacking the demon, Arcturus could not see it. They were on their own. He could hear Sacharissa whining, desperately trying to push past Elaine's body to fight, but the space was too tight.

Crash!

Splinters of wood sprayed, throwing sawdust and a spattering of soil into the air. A great pillar of grey flesh and bone had slammed down on the end of their tree trunk, crushing the end, bringing the circle of light ever closer.

Crash!

Again, the Phantaur's foot slammed down, crushing the end of the trunk.

Crash!

Arcturus closed his eyes, wishing he had had time to learn a spell, any spell that might save them. But all he could do was flash wyrdlight. Useless.

Crash!

The foot was but an arm's length away now, working its way up the tree-trunk. He would be first. One more stomp before it was over. Arcturus brandished his dirk, ready to stab it when it came. He would go down fighting.

He could almost feel the shift of weight as the Phantaur raised its foot. In that moment, Arcturus jammed the hilt of his dirk into the crack in the wood ahead of him, pulling his hand away in the nick of time. The foot slammed down, impaling itself on the slim blade.

For a second there was silence. Then a scream of agony unlike anything Arcturus had heard before, so loud and high-pitched his ears sung with pain at the noise.

'Now,' Arcturus cried out, grasping the leg as it withdrew. 'Run!'

He was pulled through the splintered hole, holding on for dear life as the Phantaur lifted its leg in the air, the delicate pad of its elephantine foot pierced deep by his dirk. He felt himself slipping and let go, landing among the fragmented wood as Elaine and Sacharissa rushed past. Above, the foot hovered in the air, a pillar of grey with the hilt at the bottom.

Growling, Arcturus took the handle and twisted it with all his might, and the resultant scream of agony nearly deafened him as he pulled his blade free in a spray of crimson.

Then he was running, sprinting towards a gap in the foliage, where Sacharissa's tail swished as she flew into the undergrowth. He snatched a glance as he ran, saw the shaman on the demon's shoulders, hands in the air, sketching a symbol in blinding blue light.

He ran on, leaping for the undergrowth . . . only to slam into an opaque barrier. He fell, near stunned. Upside down in his vision, he saw the beast approaching in a limp that shook the ground with every stomp. On its back, the shaman howled murderously, its staff pointed directly at his face.

Arcturus struggled to his feet and clashed his dirk against the barrier, but its tip slipped along the surface like wet ice. He could not penetrate it.

Then Sacharissa was sailing through the air and the shield dissolved as she passed through it, her demonic essence ripping through the mana like rice paper. But even as she leaped for the Phantaur's leg, the demon's trunk whipped out, hurling her body in a tumble of limbs into a nearby tree.

Arcturus fell to his knees, the pain of Sacharissa's injury flaring like lightning across his brain. He could barely see through the agony, only feel the tremors of the Phantaur's approaching steps.

The grey snake of the trunk encircled his neck and lifted him. He kicked his legs as it tightened, and suddenly he was staring into the orc shaman's eyes, bloodshot and black in the dark pools of the skull paint's eye sockets.

The orc grinned a sabre-toothed grin, and the trunk brought Arcturus closer until the yellow tusks scraped his ears and he could smell the shaman's foetid breath.

Pain. He saw Sacharissa pulling herself towards him, dragging her injured body over the dead leaves. But the trunk gripped tighter and he could feel the veins throbbing in his temples.

The shaman laughed as Arcturus's boots struck the thick skin on the Phantaur's skull. It was like kicking a rock. He lifted his hands and scraped at the leathery surface of the trunk.

It did nothing. He didn't have the strength.

The orc lifted a black-nailed finger and brushed hair from Arcturus's face, the gesture unnervingly intimate. He stared deeply into Arcturus's eyes as the grip slowly tightened. He wanted to see the life drain from him.

Arcturus choked breathlessly, desperate to pull some air into his lungs. He could feel himself letting go, his chest burning, the corners of his vision darkening.

He was going to die.

'Stop!'

The relief was almost immediate, the trunk loosening just enough to allow him one ragged breath. The orc cackled and Arcturus spun dizzily as the Phantaur turned his body to face the speaker. His heart dropped when he saw her.

Elaine. She had made her way back.

In one hand she held his crossbow, fallen from his back in the mad scramble within the tree trunk. Its tip wavered in the air, for her other hand still clutched the baby orc to her chest.

The Phantaur's grip continued to loosen and suddenly he was falling. He collapsed to the ground and groaned, gasping much needed breaths through his swollen throat.

He rolled on to his back and saw the shaman staring at Elaine. His skull-painted visage was a picture of surprise, as if the sight of her was the biggest shock of his life.

Arcturus didn't care. All he could focus on was dragging breath after gulping breath into his lungs, and he pushed out with his heels, trying to get away from the demon.

The orc's staff fell, landing beside him in a spatter of soil. Above, the orc had spread his hands wide, palms open. And strangest of all, he looked afraid. Terrified even.

Arcturus managed to struggle to his knees, twisting his body and crawling towards his erstwhile saviour. When he reached her, he took the crossbow from her hand and fell on to his back once more, aiming the bolt directly at the orc's face.

Now the orc had the same opaque barrier hovering in front of his body in a concave oval. Cursing, Arcturus turned his sights on to the Phantaur's face instead, aiming at the small watery eyes on either side of the demon's trunk.

'Sacha, get into the trees,' Arcturus yelled. Out of the corner of his eye, he could see the injured Canid still dragging herself towards him. She ignored him and continued on, whining through the pain.

'Arcturus, are you all right?' a voice shouted from behind him.

It was Alice. Arcturus breathed a sigh of thanks – the others had arrived. The odds of winning the battle were still very much stacked against them, but it was no longer suicide.

'I'm fine,' he wheezed, not daring to look back and break his aim. 'Just get Sacharissa to safety.'

There was the patter of paws along the ground and Arcturus caught a flash of white at the edge of his vision dragging Sacharissa into the bushes. The pain of it made his vision swim, but he kept his weapon steady, the tip hovering just above the Phantaur's eyes.

But the orc seemed to hardly notice. Stranger still, he was not looking at Arcturus or his crossbow. The shaman's eyes were still firmly fixed on Elaine, and his hands were still held high in the air.

He spoke. Not in any language Arcturus could understand, but it seemed like a question. Almost as if the orc was beseeching them. Begging them.

'What's it saying?' Edmund's voice came from the bushes behind.

'Hell if I know,' Rotter growled. 'Just back away slowly and then we can run like the clappers.'

Arcturus slowly got to his feet. The orc repeated himself, more insistently this time. What did he want? Arcturus didn't care – he just wanted to get to Sacharissa. He could feel her pain, a dull ache that flared every few seconds.

He took a slow step back. Now he could see Elaine, shaking as the orc yelled at her again.

'Elaine, move into the trees,' Arcturus hissed. 'More orcs could arrive any minute.'

With a trembling foot she took a step back. Immediately the orc broke into a tirade of guttural ululations, and now his finger, glowing with blue light, was pointed at her. She whimpered with fear and stood still once more.

'Wait,' Arcturus said. He took another step back. Then another. The orc did nothing.

The orc pointed at her again, jabbing at her chest with his finger. The baby. He wanted the baby. Of course.

'Elaine . . . I want you to very, very slowly, leave the baby on the ground,' Arcturus whispered. 'Then I'm going to take your hand and we're going to walk into the jungle. Are you ready?'

'Yes,' Elaine whispered in a small voice.

'OK. Easy does it,' Arcturus replied, watching as Elaine lowered herself into a crouch. She laid the baby in among the leaves. It gurgled its annoyance at being left on the cold wet ground, its little face screwing up to cry.

'All right,' Arcturus said, hurrying forward and taking Elaine's hand. It was clammy and she trembled as he pulled her back with him.

The orc ignored them completely, his only acknowledgement of their existence being the shield that floated in front of his face. Instead, his Phantaur kneeled in the dirt and the orc stepped down from its shoulders and into the grass, absorbing the shield into his finger as he did so.

For a moment Arcturus felt the urge to fire but thought better of it as the orc fell to his knees and prostrated himself on the ground, his arms extended palms down in supplication. Then Arcturus's view was obscured by the vegetation.

And they ran.

34

It was only an hour later, when light had almost faded, that they allowed themselves to stop running, collapsing together in unanimous exhaustion in the shadow of a moss-laden boulder.

For a few sickening minutes they panted, gasped and gulped water from their flasks, catching their breaths. Arcturus had never felt so tired, or so hungry. His stomach cramped and gurgled as he lay there, and even the water he drank did little to assuage its ravening.

'What the hell was all that about,' Edmund groaned, the first to speak. 'It was like the beastly thing was worshipping the baby.'

'I don't care,' Arcturus replied. 'We're alive and it's not our responsibility any more.'

Silence reigned for a few moments longer, then Elaine spoke up in a small voice.

'I'm sorry. I thought I was helping . . . I didn't want you guys to argue.'

Arcturus felt the strange dual sensation of wanting to harangue her and hug her at the same time.

'It was an extremely foolish thing to do. We could have all died. Never do that to us again, all right?' he said, his voice angry.

She lowered her head and hugged Valens close to her chest.

'I know,' she whispered, a slow tear rolling down her face. 'I just wanted to do something brave. You're all so brave all the time . . . I wanted to be too.'

Arcturus shook his head. It was hard to stay angry at her. Still, he forced himself to let her stew for a few more seconds before he gave her a tight hug. She sobbed once and then pulled away, rolling over as if going to sleep.

'Any news from Athena?' Rotter asked, tugging off a boot and turning it upside down. A stream of pebbles and twigs trickled from it and Rotter groaned with relief.

'No sign,' Edmund said, giving his scrying crystal a cursory look. 'I'd have felt it if something changed.'

'Maybe Harold and the others managed to get a message out,' Alice said. 'They might even have escaped the jungles by now.'

'If they haven't been captured or worse,' Edmund said. 'For all we know, the rebels could have taken over Hominum already.'

'There's nothing to be gained by thinking about that now,' Arcturus said. 'The best we can do is concentrate on getting out of this hellish jungle.'

'So, where are we then?' Edmund asked, pressing his back against the boulder's edge. 'Were we at least running in the right direction?'

'Roughly,' Rotter said, staring up at the canopy.

'How do you know?' Alice asked. 'We could have been running in circles.'

'The stars,' Rotter said. 'The Elven Arrow always points north. Here, look.'

He used his fingers to trace three bright stars in the sky, and if Arcturus squinted he could make out a cluster shaped not unlike an arrowhead at one end.

'Well, that's a relief,' Edmund said. 'With any luck we should reach the southern border of Hominum tomorrow afternoon.'

'Aye,' Rotter said, laying on his back. 'And not a moment too soon. The orcs will know we're in the jungles by now if that shaman has any sense – they'll be sending search parties out soon enough. We should get some rest.'

Arcturus shuddered at the thought of the orcs hunting for them in the dark. He couldn't help but stare into the surroundings, focusing to use Sacharissa's night vision. All he saw were the scurrying of jungle rodents and the swooping shapes of fruit bats. Somehow, the animal noises comforted him, even as they grew louder in the ever-growing gloom. He felt they would be silent if orcs were approaching. Or hoped, anyway.

Turning away from the surroundings, Arcturus summoned Sacharissa in a flash of white light and wrapped himself around her. She whimpered as his hand pressed against her wounded side, and he hushed the Canid with an apologetic kiss on the nose.

Even in their haste to escape, Arcturus had found time to infuse her – she would never have been able to keep up with them after her injuries. He knew she would heal faster while within him, but he could not help but summon her, for he had felt her battering his consciousness in her desire to be physically close to him. It was a slightly selfish decision, but he had no regrets as he cuddled her.

'You did well to survive the battle with the Phantaur,' Alice whispered from the darkness. 'In case you didn't know, I can't heal Sacharissa. It's a bone injury . . . it has to heal naturally. Sorry.'

'It's OK, that's why I didn't ask,' Arcturus said. 'But . . . I do have a question for you.'

In the background, Arcturus could hear Rotter and Edmund snoring and could make out the forms of the two propped against the boulder.

'What is it?' Alice asked.

'I haven't been taught proper spellcraft. If I had known some, I might have been able to use it against the shaman or his demon.'

'That's true,' Alice replied. 'Although, spells don't work as well against demons, just so you know – the shield spell in particular. That's why Sacharissa was able to break through the shaman's shield during your battle.'

'Even so, I'd like to learn,' Arcturus said. 'I know the symbols for the four main spells – Lieutenant Cavendish taught me, but he never showed me how to use them.'

'Well, there's not much to it,' Alice whispered back. 'You simply channel mana to your finger until the tip glows. Then you draw the symbol in the air and hold your finger in its centre until the spell "fixes" itself in place, moving in tandem with your hand as you move it around. Finally, you maintain the flow of mana both to and through your finger at the same time, and as the mana pushes through the symbol, it will perform the spell.'

'That simple, huh,' Arcturus muttered semi-sarcastically,

trying to keep her instructions in his head.

'Of course, then you can control the direction of your spell with your mind, in the same way that you can control a wyrdlight. That's how you shape a shield, or decide if you want to send out a stream of fire or simply a ball of it.'

'Right,' Arcturus said. 'I'll just try it, shall I? You can tell me if I do something wrong.'

'Maybe tomorrow,' Alice whispered, patting him on the shoulder. 'Whatever spell you use, it will make light and noise – better not to signal our presence to any orcs out there.'

'Of course,' Arcturus said, feeling a hint of disappointment.

Still, now that he knew the basics of spellcraft, he could teach himself. He just hoped that he wouldn't need to use it before the morning.

35

They smelled it before they saw it. Or at least, Arcturus did. It was metallic, so strong he could almost taste it on his tongue as they pushed through the trees, blinking in the dawn light as the vegetation thinned.

Sacharissa noticed it first. Arcturus almost fell as her consciousness was suffused with a sudden horror. Then he saw it too. The bodies. Scattered like ragdolls on a nursery floor, their dead eyes staring through him and into oblivion beyond.

Rebels. At least a hundred of them, their corpses adorned with gaping wounds, or their bones caved in by enormous force. The team stood frozen and Arcturus heard Elaine retching as she emptied their meagre breakfast of wild berries on to the blood-soaked ground.

That was what the smell was – blood. Only now it was tinged by the barest hint of putrefaction, and the air hummed with the buzz of a thousand flies and the croak of carrion birds as they hopped among the feast laid out before them.

Arcturus's gorge rose, but he forced it down, eyes watering

as he staggered against a tree.

'Orc handiwork,' Rotter growled, and Arcturus heard the rasp of the soldier's sword being drawn. 'There.'

He jabbed his blade, and Arcturus followed its point to see the body of an orc among the humans, its grey skin stark against the damp soil, a ragged wound to its throat showing the reason for its demise. Now that Arcturus looked, there were half a dozen others, though their corpses were surrounded by the scores of humans they had taken down with them.

'How many could have done this?' Edmund said, his voice uneven in his distress.

'Twenty, maybe fewer,' Rotter replied, edging forward. 'However many, they won.'

The field of battle was in a clearing of sorts, scattered with the occasional sapling and tree stump. Beyond, Arcturus could just make out what looked like green fields of long-grass – where the jungles ended and Hominum's territory began. He tried to resist the urge to run for it. The area was still with nary a breeze to stir the leaves.

'They don't leave their dead if they can help it,' Rotter said, turning his head and body slowly as he walked further into the battlefield. 'They'll be back for them soon enough. Must've looted the weapons first. We'd best be on our way quickly now.'

Arcturus didn't need telling twice. He took a moment to grab Elaine's hand and then he was pulling her along, wending a path through where the bodies were thinnest on the ground.

'It tells a story, this,' Rotter said, walking backwards now as he watched the forest behind them. 'They came from the back, took the rebels by surprise. Some others . . .'

He turned and stared into fields beyond. The bodies were thickest along its edge.

'They came from that way too,' he said. 'Must've been tracking them. Set up an ambush, hid in the long grass. Hit 'em from both sides.'

'It's a good thing, right?' Elaine said, her voice still weak from throwing up. 'They're not hunting us any more.'

'There's nothing good about this,' Arcturus whispered. He tried not to look at the eyes. Somehow there was accusation in their gaze.

'Do you think this was the group who were following us, or were they following Prince Harold and the others?' Alice asked.

Her question went unanswered because Rotter had frozen, his eyes bulging from his head as he looked into the trees beyond him.

'Don't look behind you,' Rotter growled, walking backwards once again, 'Just keep doing what you're doing. But when I say run, you run like the dickens, understand?'

Elaine whimpered and Arcturus gripped her hand, if not for her comfort, then for his own. Sacharissa growled beside him and it took all of his control to keep the demon from turning around to look behind them. Instead she looked into his eyes . . . and suddenly he could smell them. Orcs, yes, but something new too. Something animal, with breath that stank of rotting meat.

'What . . . is it?' he managed to say, the words catching in his throat, breaths coming in short bursts.

'Orc scouts,' Rotter replied. 'There's three of 'em. But they've got hyenas with 'em. Big buggers, chests like carthorses. Easy now, they're just watching us at the moment. 'Tis a good thing you and Alice have your demons out, they'll know you're summoners. Might spook 'em.'

Arcturus could almost feel the orcs' eyes on the back of his neck, and he pulled Elaine closer to him as they staggered over the bodies on the edge of the grasslands.

'Run!' Rotter yelled, turning and sprinting into the fields.

They ran. Sacharissa flattened a path through the grass ahead and it was all he could do but follow her, dragging Elaine stumbling behind him.

They were a stone's throw into the grasslands now and ahead, Rotter had turned, his sword extended at whatever followed them. Pushing Elaine behind him, Arcturus stood alongside Rotter, tugging frantically on the crank of his crossbow in his haste to load it.

'Hide in the grass,' Arcturus snarled to Elaine over his shoulder. 'And don't you dare come out.'

He heard the telltale click as the string fell into position and he fumbled a bolt into place from the rattling quiver at his back. It was only then that he allowed his eyes to dart up towards the jungle's edge, and the horrors running at them.

The bull orcs were charging through the field of corpses, resplendent in great swathes of green paint daubed across their grey skin. Racing ahead of them were their hyenas, four barrel-chested beasts with slavering mouths, baying for blood with every leap across the ground.

'You'll only have one shot,' Rotter shouted, 'so make it count. Wait for it . . .'

Arcturus glanced over to see Edmund and Alice with their own crossbows pointed, their only other weapons the cleaver and spear.

'Now!'

He barely had a chance to aim before his shot was whistling through the air, and the nearest hyena was tumbling as the shaft hit it. But even as Arcturus whooped in triumph, it was back up and running, the bloody bolt dangling and bouncing from its shoulder as it ran on and on.

'Hellfire,' Arcturus cursed, kneeling to pull out his dirk. From the corner of his eye, he saw another hyena writhing in its death throes on the ground, while another limped and the third raced towards the others. Then his vision was filled with the piebald body of the creature ahead of him leaping for this throat.

He fell back, only to hear Sacharissa's deep roar as she met the hyena in mid-air above him, slamming into it and falling to the ground in a maelstrom of claws and snapping teeth. She was smaller than the hyena, and injured, but Arcturus had no time to worry for her, rolling away from them and to his feet, blade clutched in his hand.

Because beyond, another orc was charging directly at him.

It was almost on instinct that his hand flew up. Swirling the air with the tip of his finger, blade clutched in the remainder, Arcturus sketched the spiral of the telekinesis spell. Over and over his finger circled, while his mind tried desperately to pulse mana through his body.

He could hear the wet slap of the orc's feet on the muddy field, see its red-rimmed eyes boring into him. His mind was suffused with terror, even as he felt the mana roil in his veins, pulsing alongside Sacharissa's consciousnesses with jolts of pain, anger and fear.

Still he stood firm, gasping as his finger took on a blue glow. The symbol hung in the air as he traced its outline, then he felt a shudder through his hand as it fixed in place, following the motion of his arm as he pointed it at the orc, now so close he could smell its musk.

His mind twisted as he tried to push the energy through his fingertip, struggling for the briefest of moments until it suddenly jetted through in a shimmering ball of swirling, translucent energy. He let it gather, even as the orc bellowed, lifting a long, stone-studded club high above its head.

Yelling through the sheer terror of it all, Arcturus unleashed the spell, sending the churning ball of energy directly into the orc's midriff. To his surprise, the giant orc was hurled back, lifted off the ground as if a huge fist had struck it in the chest. Then the ball imploded, and the giant was thrown head over heels in the air, the force of the blast rippling across its body like a rock thrown into a lake.

Arcturus didn't stay to watch it fall to the ground, instead running to the still-fighting beasts, following the bloodstains on the grass to where Sacharissa tussled with the hyena. A dozen paces beyond them, Alice's Vulpid, Reynard, had the throat of its own hyena clutched between his jaws.

Before he had a chance to intervene, he saw Sacharissa had the upper hand, the claws of her back legs scratching the lower half of her opponent to ribbons as their jaws snapped at each other on the ground. Their rolling bodies were moving too fast for him to get a clear blow – all he could do was watch and wait for an opening.

But before one presented itself, there was a scream. Arcturus looked up, and his heart froze. An orc, its shoulder and chest a blackened mess of burns from the battle, clutched Edmund by his throat, lifting him high above the ground as if he were no more than a piece of fruit plucked from a tree. Alice lay some distance away, dragging herself towards them, her face bloodied, eyes dizzy, a cleaver clutched in her hand. Behind them, Rotter and a third orc battled back and forth across the ground, the bold soldier leaping and thrusting, oblivious to what was about to happen.

Arcturus lifted his finger, but the spell had faded and the mana no longer flowed through his veins. Not enough time. His crossbow lay a dozen feet away, forgotten. Instead, he ran.

The grass snatched at his heels and in those panicked moments it was as if he were wading through treacle. All the while, Edmund struggled and kicked, and the orc laughed throatily as it swung back its club, ready to bring it down on the writhing boy's head.

Time seemed to slow. Back the arm went and Arcturus knew he wasn't going to make it. Instead, he hurled the blade in his hand with all his might, and his heart sank as the dirk tumbled pitifully through the air.

Still, even as the orc began to swing down, the weapon slapped across its face, slicing open its cheek and thudding across an eye with its hilt. The orc flinched just for a moment. Enough time for Arcturus to tackle its legs, slamming his shoulder against its knee with all the strength he could muster.

It was like running into a stone pillar. He barely shifted the orc an inch before it kicked him, throwing him head over heels into the long grass. He gaped and gasped like a beached fish, barely able to take a breath, his midriff a band of red-hot pain searing across his stomach and deep into his insides.

The orc laughed again, raising its club once more. Arcturus could see Alice, her finger tracing in the air, the fire symbol spluttering and fizzling as her concentration wavered. He raised his own hand, knowing he would never make it in time.

Then it happened.

A great silver beast hurtled out of the jungle, sailing through the air and landing on the orc's back. Blood sprayed as it ripped at the orc's neck with its teeth and the club fell from nerveless fingers. Edmund followed moments later, crumpling to the ground.

The orc spun and twisted for a half-dozen seconds, flailing its arms as the slavering creature savaged its head, the fangs sinking deep into its prey's skull. Then it fell, lifeless, as the demon took a deep, savage bite out of its neck.

Gelert. Covered in mud and grime, his eyes bloodshot from exhaustion, legs trembling as he pulled himself towards Edmund's inert body.

There was a garbled bellow of pain, cut short, as Rotter skewered his own orc through the throat, withdrew and sliced the tusked head from the giant's shoulders. Behind him, Sacharissa licked her wounds beside the corpse of the hyena – a deep bite on her haunch seemed to be the worst of the damage.

Seeing the pair were now safe, Arcturus headed to Edmund first, where Alice had finally reached him. Tears cut runnels in the blood that smeared her face, the source of which Arcturus saw was a split lip and a copious nosebleed.

She was frantically sketching a heart shape in the air, the healing symbol fizzling as she struggled to keep it in place. Her breathing was thick and fast.

'Slowly.' Arcturus kneeled beside her and laid a hand on her shoulder. 'Show me how to do it.'

The girl gulped and nodded. Slower now, her finger carved through the air, leaving a glowing blue line in its place. Beneath, Edmund wheezed through his wounded throat, his eyes closed, body near motionless. The only sound was Gelert's whining as he nuzzled his master's boots.

The heart symbol pulsed once as it fixed to Alice's finger, then Alice and Edmund gave a mutual sigh of relief as healing white light streamed through the symbol and flowed around his wounded neck. Slowly, the red bands of swollen flesh shrank and paled until it looked good as new, and Edmund breathed easy once more, though his eyes remained closed.

A scream broke into the moment. Arcturus spun round, only to see the orc he had blasted barrelling towards him, its body hunched over in pain, a muddied tree branch clutched in its giant fist.

Arcturus fell back, his hand grasping for the dirk, meeting nothing but wet grass. Sacharissa was limping towards them with Reynard hard on her heels, but they were too far away. Rotter could do nothing but yell.

Gelert struggled to his feet and staggered in front of them, his chest still heaving with the exertion. He wouldn't last long. Arcturus pulled on his mana reserve, his finger twisting in the air once more. The orc was but a dozen paces away.

Gelert leaped, only to be slammed away by the tree branch, yelping in pain as he tumbled into the long grass. The orc roared in triumph, spewing blood from its lips – Arcturus's spell must have damaged its insides. Yet it charged on, even as Arcturus's spell flickered and died.

The orc's head jerked sideways. It fell and rolled along the ground, sliding the last few paces to press up against Arcturus's feet. Its glazed eyes stared up at him, and it was only then that he saw the bloody bolt that had pierced its skull from temple to temple. And beyond, Elaine, a crossbow in her arms.

36

Edmund remained unconscious, even when they splashed water in his face. Despite this and their injuries, they only allowed themselves a few minutes to regroup before they decided to move on. Rotter knew more orcs would follow soon enough.

Still, before they left, Rotter sent Alice and Arcturus among the bodies to salvage what they could. Arcturus found himself wandering among the many corpses, trying to avoid their dead stares while searching the ground for anything useful.

Though they were leaving orc territory, there was no telling if there were more rebels hunting them. Hell, for all they knew the kingdom had been overthrown and the rebels had taken power. They needed to defend themselves . . . and clothe themselves for that matter. Now that they had left the warm confines of the jungle, it would become colder as they moved north, back towards Corcillum.

As he stumbled through the corpses, Arcturus tried to read the battlefield the same way that Rotter had. At first, it seemed random, bodies scattered like seeds across a tilled pasture. But his eyes were soon drawn to the orc bodies, for their skin was stark against the black soil of the jungle's edge.

There were as many as four of them in a group, lying together in the shadow of a dead tree, split down the middle where lightning had struck long ago. Now that he looked closer, there was a cluster of human bodies there too, fallen in a rough semi-circle.

Arcturus stopped on his way, removing an undershirt from a rebel boy roughly his height – the cloth miraculously unsullied by blood from the owner's head wound. He pulled it on, and found it to be a good fit.

As he approached the tree, Arcturus saw a man better dressed than the rest among the bodies. The leader of the group, Arcturus thought. He crouched beside the body, examining it.

The man was of a solid build with a bushy beard that obscured the bloody throat wound that had taken his life. He wore a black cloak of fine wool that fell to his knees, complete with a deep hood to keep the wearer warm – a guardsman's cloak by Arcturus's guess, proofed against the rain and wind. Arcturus pulled it from the corpse's shoulders and threw it around his own. Instantly he warmed, and it was a blessed relief from the cool wind that chilled his flesh.

'We're leaving soon,' Rotter called. 'Grab what you can and get away from there.'

Arcturus looked up to see the soldier tugging on a bloodied black cassock from a body on the border of the grasslands. Beside him, Alice and Elaine had found dark overcoats of their own and were in the process of constructing a hasty stretcher from scavenged clothing and two spear hafts.

Arcturus turned back to the bodies, searching for a new weapon. His dirk was sharp, but short and useless for parrying. He needed something with more stopping power.

'Now, Arcturus,' Rotter called again.

There were no swords among the rebels' weapons nearby – the orcs must have looted the best of them. Most seemed to be farming implements or kitchen utensils – scythes, billhooks, skewers and knives. In fact, there was not one true weapon among them – even the leader appeared to be armed with little more than a makeshift spear, similar to the one they had picked up earlier.

Arcturus sighed and moved to pick up the spear . . . only to see a wooden handle sticking out beneath one of the orc bodies. Curious, Arcturus tugged at it, struggling as the other end was prised loose from the orcs flesh. It came free in a spatter of blood, and Arcturus grinned as he held it up to the light.

It was an axe of some kind, perhaps once used as a felling axe. The handle was made from a dark, solid wood, with a leather grip wrapped around the bottom. The head itself was a gleaming single-edged blade, perfect for splitting logs . . . or an orc's ribcage, as the case may be.

Arcturus hefted it to feel the weight, letting it rest on his shoulder. It felt familiar, and so it should – he had known axes for as long as he could remember. Splitting firewood for the tavern's hearth had been one of his most onerous chores, along with his stable-boy duties. It had given him a wiry strength to his arms and he reckoned he could wield this one as well as any warrior.

He removed his quiver and slid the axe handle through a

leather loop on the back. It fitted well beside where the crossbow slotted, and though the wooden butt occasionally knocked against his lower spine as he walked, it seemed as good a place for it as any.

Smiling, Arcturus hurried back to the others, where they were busy lifting Edmund on to the stretcher. His weapon choice earned him an approving nod from Rotter.

Arcturus looked down into Edmund's face. The boy looked almost peaceful, and someone had covered his body with a bloodstained fur coat.

'Bad business, this,' Rotter said, looking down at the unconscious noble. 'He'll slow us down, sure enough. We may be at Hominum's border, but orc raiders roam far and wide here.'

'Not to mention there might be other rebels about,' Arcturus said. 'We can't be certain that this lot were the ones chasing us.'

'Do you think Prince Harold made it?' Elaine piped up. 'If these rebels were the ones chasing them, then they might be ahead of us.'

'Let's hope so,' Arcturus said, giving her shoulder a squeeze.

'I think my arm is fractured. Are you able to help carry him, Arcturus?' Alice asked, wiping at the blood on her face. 'Perhaps the demons can pull him along, like a sled.'

'I've got no broken bones, but those two do,' Arcturus said, looking at where Gelert and Sacharissa were curled up together. 'I think they'd struggle to keep up with us, let alone pull a sled.'

Both demons had almost definitely suffered broken ribs, and he could feel a constant dull ache of pain in his consciousness. He had only dared to heal Sacharissa's back leg, performing his first healing spell moments after the battle.

'Bugger it. Grab that end,' Rotter said, picking up the front of the stretcher and turning around. 'If we were going to drag him we'd have built a sled, not a stretcher. Careful with the spear points.'

Arcturus did as he was bid, wincing slightly under the weight.

'Elaine,' he called, half turning his head to catch a glimpse of the younger girl, who had armed herself with a spear. 'Thank you for saving us. We'd all be dead if it wasn't for you.'

'Any time,' Elaine said, and Arcturus couldn't help but mirror the grin that spread across her face.

Then they walked on, into the rolling hillocks. Back to civilisation.

37

There was a biting chill to the air as they trekked across the open countryside. It was a strange world, so close to the jungle's edge, yet immeasurably different from the tropics it bordered. What had once been a land populated by orchards, farms and homesteads had long been abandoned, leaving dense hedgerows, copses of fruit trees and ruined cottages.

They searched each ruin they came across, only to find little of use, the insides already looted by orc and bandit alike. Their only real find was a cart, the wheels loose and rusty, but still serviceable, giving Edmund a bumpier ride but providing a welcome relief for Arcturus and Rotter's blistered hands as they travailed the overgrown cobblestone roads that criss-crossed towards the horizon. Soon Reynard was hitched to its front and the Vulpid pulled it faster than any carthorse would.

It was difficult to keep track of their direction, since they were forced to follow the various winding roads. Elaine was pleased to send Valens ahead to scout their course, borrowing Alice's scrying crystal and calling out directions as the trails split and split again.

Though Sacharissa could be infused, Gelert could not, and his broken ribs hindered him. This forced them to stop for rest regularly, while Rotter climbed nearby trees, and even the steeple of a nearby crumbling church, to scout for pursuers – Valens was too far ahead to see behind them. It was at the first of these stops that Arcturus infused Sacharissa, saving her strength for whatever new dangers they might encounter.

They slept that first night within the church Rotter had climbed, for its stone roof was intact, unlike the other rotted ruins they had come across. Exhausted, they cleared aside broken glass and piled the pews against the door, shivering as the wind gusted through the gaping windows. A paltry meal of under-ripe apples was their only sustenance, and the small fruits were sour and unappetising.

Arcturus was used to hunger but the others could not continue on without a proper meal the following morning. Fortunately there were still vestiges of crops now growing wild and untamed beyond the parcels of land they had been seeded upon. Though much of the land was filled with thick clumps of wheat grass that Arcturus's friends had neither the time nor inclination to grind into flour, they were fortunate enough to see a cornfield in the distance. Soon enough they were burning their lips on blackened ears, cooked hastily over a small fire.

Rotter estimated that they would reach Vocans at midnight, though they had yet to decide upon their approach. Valens might have gone ahead to spy, but it was possible the Mite would be recognised, and they needed him to scout the paths just ahead of them. It was during this discussion that Arcturus felt the most guilty.

He wanted to tell them about Crawley – how the servant had asked him to choose a side, but he knew they would resent him for not telling them sooner. So he kept silent and hoped that Crawley was away making trouble in Corcillum and that the teachers and other students would already have secured Vocans. Then the others would never have to know . . .

The sun was nearly set when they saw it – or rather, Valens did. Soldiers; setting up camp in the roofless husk of an old barn, a dozen or so men warming themselves beside a fire. Arcturus and the others were crouched in the tall wheat grass a few hundred feet away, listening to the distant sounds of laughter.

'They've got a sentry,' Rotter murmured, pointing at a shadowed figure in the scrying crystal. It was a man leaning against the wall outside. A glowing ember seemed to hover in the air beside his head, then Arcturus realised the soldier was smoking a rolled cheroot.

'Do we go to them?' Alice asked. 'If this General Barcroft has joined the rebellion, then these soldiers could be working for him.'

'Aye,' Rotter said, peering at the image. 'But then, Sergeant Caulder and I weren't. I reckon if these lads were rebelling, they'd be in Corcillum causing mischief.'

'We don't need their help,' Arcturus murmured, though he was half-hearted in saying it. The fire looked so warm, and Rotter had argued against lighting one of their own so far for fear of alerting the world to their presence. There were at least a hundred rebels unaccounted for, if indeed a second group had

261

gone after Prince Harold, and then there were marauding orcs and brigands to worry about.

'Maybe we do,' Alice said, chewing her lip. 'We're vulnerable right now. I've fractured my arm, and with Sacharissa and Gelert injured, and Edmund . . .'

Her voice broke with emotion as she looked over at the unconscious noble. He had remained asleep even after two days of travel, and their attempts to pour water down his throat had nearly choked the poor boy.

'Plus, you and I are probably nearly out of mana,' Alice continued, 'and Elaine hasn't learned to do more than wyrdlights yet.'

Her words earned her a scowl from Elaine.

'We'll be far safer walking into Vocans or Corcillum with this lot than alone,' Rotter agreed. 'Let me greet them, see what they're about. If I feel we can trust them, I'll call you in. Otherwise, I'll say I'm going out for a piss, then we'll bolt.'

'It's as good a plan as any,' Arcturus said, thinking longingly of the fire inside. Even at the stable he had slept beside the warm horses, buried in their straw. His new cloak was thick, but he still shivered as the wind gusted past them, carrying the sound of the soldiers' laughter.

'Go on,' Alice said, looking at Edmund. 'The sooner we get Edmund to safety, the better.'

'Right, wish me luck,' Rotter whispered.

He gave them a wild grin, then stood and held his sword high in the air, approaching the barn slowly.

'Ahoy,' he called. 'Have you a place by your fire for a lost comrade.'

'Who goes there?' the sentry shouted, and Arcturus could see the man shuffle forward, a crossbow pointed at Rotter's face.

'Private Rotherham of the tenth platoon, under Sergeant Caulder,' Rotter said. 'We were ambushed a day's march from here. I'm the only survivor.'

The man kept his crossbow up.

'Who ambushed ye'?' the man asked. 'That's no uniform I recognise.'

Arcturus cursed under his breath. Rotter was still wearing the black cassock he had taken from a rebel. They had been too tired to realise.

'Sarge,' the sentry called. 'You'd best come out here!'

In the scrying crystal, Arcturus saw the soldiers swiftly emerge from the barn, weapons drawn. Each one wore chainmail with a red surcoat over the top. More crossbows were raised, their points all centred on Rotter's chest.

'Says he's from tenth platoon,' the sentry said. 'But look, he's—'

'I know,' one of the soldiers said, stepping forward for a closer look at Rotter. Arcturus saw the sergeant's chevrons glinting on the man's shoulder.

'I'll get to the point,' the sergeant said, raising his sword and pointing it. 'There's bad business going on to the north. Agitators and rebels, all wearing black. So you had better explain your garb.'

'It was rebels who ambushed us,' Rotter said, his arms still in the air. 'I had to dress as one of 'em to escape, took this off a dead body in the night.'

The explanation did not seem to please the sergeant. The crossbow stayed pointed.

'A likely tale,' the sergeant growled. 'I've an inkling you're on your way to join your rebel friends in the interior.'

Rotter shifted on his feet and now Arcturus could see the worry on his face. They hadn't thought this through.

'Now . . . let's not be hasty,' Rotter stammered, his confidence evaporating as the reality of the crossbows hit home.

Arcturus cursed under his breath and began to etch the shield spell in the air. It was a complex spell, one that required both shaping and moving the substance of the shield itself, but he had to try.

Then a voice called out from the back of the assembled soldiers.

'Rotter, is that you, ye daft bugger?'

'Frank?' Rotter said, peering into the gathered men.

'Lower your weapons, lads, I can vouch for 'im.'

Frank stomped out of the group and Arcturus saw he was a bearded young man with a lazy eye.

'I oughta let them put ye' down, ye' still owe me a shilling from that card game,' Frank said, with mock anger.

'I thought it was the other way round,' Rotter grinned, slowly lowering his sword.

'This ugly mug is a scoundrel, and I wouldn't let 'im within a 'alf mile of me wife, but he's no rebel,' Frank said.

The pair embraced, slapping each other on the back with gusto. Arcturus breathed a sigh of relief and let the floating glyph on the end of his finger fizzle and die.

The sergeant grimaced and signalled to his men to lower their crossbows.

'All right, now, don't overreact,' Rotter said, extracting

himself from Frank and addressing the platoon. 'But I'm not alone.'

'More survivors?' the sergeant asked, sceptically.

'Something like that . . . it's a long story,' Rotter said. 'Just don't shoot anyone.'

He turned to the fields behind him.

'Arcturus, Alice, Elaine . . . you can come out now!'

38

They were welcomed with open arms. Food was broken out as they settled around the campfire. The simple fare of cheese, bread and cold meats was like ambrosia to the half-starved group of summoners. They even provided some of the less appetising cuts of meat for Gelert and Reynard, though they turned their noses up at the bread.

Still, Arcturus's relief was stymied by Edmund's continued unconsciousness, though the boy still breathed easily despite his lips being a little chapped from dehydration. Alice busied herself by trickling droplets of water into Edmund's dry mouth as Rotter told their story.

To Arcturus's surprise, the man was a natural storyteller and he felt himself strangely captivated by Rotter's words, hanging on every sentence despite knowing each twist and turn already.

By the time the tale was finished, the night sky above was pitch black, the stars obscured by the glow of the fire. Silence reigned as Rotter stopped speaking and Arcturus shuffled his feet uncomfortably. Now that he thought about it, the sergeant had yet to say a single word, and had asked no questions before Rotter had launched into his story.

'You've come a long way,' the sergeant finally said, warming his hands by the fire. 'I am Percival, and these are my men. You were lucky to have found us – most of the platoons in this area have abandoned their posts.'

Rotter frowned at the man's words, but said nothing.

'We are thankful you were here,' Arcturus said, smiling gratefully. But his smile was not returned, and he felt a twinge of unease. The men sitting around them were grim-faced, and their expressions had only darkened as Rotter told his story.

'We'd heard rumblings of a rebellion from the local farmers,' the sergeant continued. 'Rumours mostly, about men in black burning buildings and disappearing into the night. And then we received this by carrier pigeon . . .'

He pulled a scroll from his jacket and unravelled the tight roll to reveal a scrawled message.

'King Alfric is at war with the common people of Hominum, stealing their hard-earned livelihoods and starving our poor to line his pockets,' he read aloud. 'This cannot stand. All men loyal to General Barcroft are to turn their coats to the black and march on Corcillum at the soonest opportunity. Further instructions will follow to those who take up the sword.'

Arcturus stared at the message, his mind reeling at the implication. The General had laid his cards on the table. There was no backing out for him now. He'd lead his soldiers to the bitter end.

'Turn your coats to the black?' Alice asked, looking up from her ministrations.

'Aye, the lining of our coats is black,' Frank said from beside Arcturus, opening his coat and showing the dark cloth within. 'We turn them inside out on night missions so we blend in. It'll help the General tell friend from foe when the soldiers reach Corcillum.'

'When?' Elaine piped up. 'Are they not there now?'

'The message arrived but a few hours ago,' Percival growled. 'By my estimate, most soldiers will be arriving within the next few hours.'

'But not you?' Rotter asked, his brows furrowing. 'Why?'

'We took a vote. Barcroft may be a good man and Alfric a greedy git, but we'll not throw away our lives for either of them, or betray our solemn oaths. Our duty is to protect the people of Hominum and we'll not leave the borders undefended.'

'We're lucky to have men such as yourselves protecting us,' Alice said. 'Thank you for your service.'

'Aye, well, don't thank us yet,' Frank said. 'Your arrival has put us in a tough position, so it has.'

'What do you mean?' Arcturus asked, the lump of unease moving from his stomach to his throat.

'Whatever the outcome of this rebellion, we didn't choose a side, so to speak,' Percival said, looking at his men. 'We voted to stay out of it, and can argue we decided to stay and protect the borders. But now I have to decide if we will help you.'

Arcturus felt Sacharissa's consciousness pulling within him, begging to be summoned. She could sense the threat, and his apprehension. He soothed her with a thought, trying to concentrate on the matter at hand.

'It's my call,' Percival said, after a moment. 'And I reckon we should help these youngsters get to safety. So, if anyone has something to say, I suggest you do so now.'

The last of his words were addressed to his men, who seemed to be avoiding looking at Arcturus, or anything other than their feet. It seemed there was little enthusiasm either way.

Finally, Frank spoke up.

'If their parents find out we didn't help them and the rebellion fails, we're sunk anyway,' he said, giving Arcturus a surreptitious wink. 'At least this way we might get them to safety and get back to our posts without the rebels being any the wiser.'

'It's decided then,' Percival said firmly. 'We'll escort you from here on in, at least until your friend here has received the medical attention he needs.'

'We'd appreciate that,' Rotter replied.

Sergeant Percival nodded, then gestured to his men.

'Don't blame my soldiers for being so hesitant. It may seem like cowardice, but we have our families to think of. If we choose the wrong side, they may suffer as a consequence of our decision. And in truth . . . we don't care enough about either side to put our loved ones at such risk. King Alfric is not forgiving, and if these rebels are burning and killing innocent people, I doubt they will be either.'

'We understand,' Rotter said. 'I'd feel the same way if I had any family. I've heard of your platoon, Sergeant. The twenty-fourth, right?'

'Aye, that's us,' Frank said.

'You're an unconventional unit, if the rumours are true,' Rotter continued, and Arcturus could tell the soldier's words were calculated, though he wasn't sure why.

'So we are,' Percival replied, his voice betraying a hint of delight at being recognised. 'We fight the old way. The way King Corwin fought when he first came upon these lands.'

The sergeant pointed at the back of the room, where Arcturus could see a stack of concave, rectangular shields, with spears leaned against the wall beside them.

'The shield wall is a forgotten art. But I've trained my men to be experts in it.'

Arcturus could see the men lifting their heads, and the pride in their faces was evident. Now he understood what Rotter was trying to do. The men were warriors. But they had forgotten it, in the face of events beyond their control. They needed to be reminded.

'I should like to see it someday,' Arcturus said. 'I'm just surprised the rest of the army doesn't use it.'

His words elicited a groan from the rest of the men, but he saw they were nodding in agreement with him.

'If the damned generals had any sense, they would,' Percival said enthusiastically. 'Of course, none of them are willing to listen.'

'Maybe we could change that,' Alice said. 'Our parents are officers of the highest order, some of them generals themselves. I'm sure they'd grant you an audience to demonstrate.'

'I would like that very much,' Percival said.

'I promise you once this is over, it's the first thing I'll do,' Alice said.

'Good,' Percival said, clapping his hands. 'Now, the sooner we get you out of here, the better. Twenty-fourth, get ready to move out!'

Arcturus stared into the flames as the men around got to their feet, ignoring the clatter of metal as they armed themselves once more. The next few hours could determine the future of the empire. And somehow, he was stuck in the middle of it.

39

They were going to Vocans. The instructions on the scroll had been clear – traitor soldiers were to go to Corcillum, and that meant that it was the most dangerous place in the empire at that moment. Not to mention the rumours that claimed, as Percival told it, the city's street fighting and fires had turned it into a hellscape.

So they marched. Rotter had the bright idea that they should turn their coats black, not only to avoid being seen, but so that if they came across any rebel soldiers, they too would appear to be rebels.

But there would be no nobles on the rebels side, so Reynard had been infused and Gelert was now in the cart with Edmund, hidden beneath the men's spare cloaks. They went in silence, footsteps muffled on the grass, avoiding the cobbled roads and thoroughfares as the lands gradually became populated once again.

Soon they could see cows in the fields and crops of swaying corn and wheat, neatly parcelled beside sleepy hamlets and the occasional homestead. For the first time in what seemed like a long time, Arcturus felt as if he were back in the world he knew once more. Though how long it would stay that way was a question he didn't want to consider.

Then it was there, rising up out of the darkness. Vocans. So tall that it dominated the horizon, a four-cornered block of crenellated towers and yellow-lit apertures, with the gatehouse and courtyard at its base. The moat that surrounded it shone in the moonlight, like a shiny black snake encircling its prey.

It was quiet as they approached, turning on to the road outside and marching to the drawbridge, ominously left open despite the troubles of nearby Corcillum. The wood creaked as they crossed, and Arcturus knew he had made the wrong decision. He should have warned the others about Crawley. Was the servant going to be waiting for them? His palms began to prickle with sweat.

Yet . . . where else could they go? Vocans had one of the best medical wings in the empire, and from what Alice had told him, it was stocked with equipment specifically for people in Edmund's situation – for the poison of the ether's air paralysed any summoner exposed to it, leaving them unable to take water or food without aid. Just like Edmund, unconscious in his cart.

They were in the courtyard now, surrounded by deathly quiet. The windows and arrow slits were alight, so they knew it was occupied . . . yet there was nobody to greet them.

'All right lads, stay alert,' Percival muttered, his sudden words in the still silence making Arcturus jump. 'We'll make sure the place is secure and then head back to our posts.'

He turned to Rotter.

'Make sure the drawbridge is raised once we leave,' he advised. 'Whoever left it down is a damned fool. This place would have been near-impregnable without it.'

'Agreed,' Rotter whispered.

They mounted the steps and, silently, Percival's soldiers lifted Edmund's cart, placing it in front of the double doors like a miniature battering ram.

Without a word, Percival eased the door open and they made their way inside. The cart's wheels rattled on the smooth marble floors, echoing around the great empty space. Above, the various balconies hung empty and silent. Still no one.

Arcturus pulled down his hood, glad to be in the warmth once more. Across the room, he could see the glint of the bejewelled eyes of the demon carving above the entrance to the dining hall. And there, between the gap in the doors . . . he saw a face staring at him. Ulfr, hidden in shadow, flapping his hands in warning.

But it was too late.

A whistle was blown, the sound a harsh screech that filled the atrium and put Arcturus's teeth on edge. Then rebels appeared as if from nowhere, rushing out of the darkness and resting their crossbows on the railings of the five floors. Scores of them.

'Shield fort!' Percival cried, and suddenly Arcturus was being shoved into a crouch as the soldiers threw up their shields. He fell among their feet, and found himself beneath a roof of wood, so tightly wedged together that he lay in shadowed darkness. The cart containing Edmund was a little island in their centre, where light filtered through and allowed Arcturus to see the nervous faces of the men beneath.

For a few moments he lay there, listening for the inevitable sound of whistling death that would follow. But instead, he heard a strange sound.

Clapping. Long, slow claps, and footsteps approaching.

'Well done,' a voice said. 'Don't worry, we saw your uniforms. You can lower your shields.'

The twenty-fourth didn't move, though in the shadowed light, Arcturus could hear Percival cursing quietly.

'You've come to join us, have you not?' the voice called out, now with a hint of doubt lacing the words. 'I said lower your shields.'

'That we have,' Percival called out, and perhaps it was only then that Arcturus realised how grave their situation was. The twenty-fourth had been forced to choose the king's side through circumstance, and faced now with the hundred crossbows, they had no choice but to pivot to the other.

'We tried,' the sergeant whispered. 'But we aren't dying here, which is what will happen if we fight. Don't betray us. Maybe we can get out of this mess later.'

Arcturus's heart fell and he heard Rotter agree, the reluctance clear in the soldier's voice.

'I'll stay with you, then,' Rotter murmured.

'We don't blame you,' Alice said. 'Tell the king we've been captured, should you get the chance.'

Percival grunted in assent, then raised his voice.

'This wasn't the greeting we expected, after hand delivering the key to the rebellion's victory,' the sergeant called out. 'Tell your men to lower their crossbows first.'

'What are you talking about?' the voice replied. 'What key?'

275

'The nobles you've been looking for,' Percival replied.

'What's he doing?' Elaine hissed, and Arcturus noticed the girl lying beside him, her hair pinned to the ground by one of the twenty-fourth's feet.

'He's pretending they captured us,' Arcturus said.

There was silence now.

'Lower your crossbows, you fools!' the voice called, and there was a rattle of metal as the weapons were taken from their rests on the railings.

'Down, lads,' Percival said, and suddenly Arcturus was blinking in the light, and rough hands were lifting him to his feet. He was shoved out of the group, and he fell to his knees. Only now could he see the face of the voice, and it did not surprise him.

Crawley, flanked by a dozen rebels, their dark cloaks swirling as they marched towards them. These men still had their crossbows raised, the points squared firmly at his chest. Arcturus saw Alice and Elaine thrown to the ground beside him, and heard the rusted scrape of wheels as the cart was pushed forward also.

The servant crouched before him and his long, spidery fingers cupped Arcturus's face.

'Fancy seeing you here,' Crawley whispered.

40

Arcturus managed to pull away, quelling the battering of Sacharissa, her desperation to come out near-blinding him with confusion.

'You?' Alice spluttered in recognition. 'Crawley? How could you?!'

'How could I not?' Crawley replied dismissively, waving two soldiers forward. 'Letting you snivelling brats order me about like a slave. It was high time you were all taught a lesson.'

'Wait . . .' Arcturus began, the shadows of an idea forming in his mind. But Sacharissa's consciousness was distracting him and he was forced to quell its writhing with a thought.

'Tie their hands,' Crawley ordered, gesturing towards them. 'Tightly now, or they'll be able to etch spells with their fingers.'

Rebels approached them and Arcturus heard the ripping of cloth as they tore strips from the hems of their robes.

'Wait!' Arcturus hissed. 'I didn't tell them.'

'Tell them what?' Crawley said, even as a man took Arcturus's hands and began to wrap cloth around them.

'That you were a rebel,' Arcturus growled. 'I kept your secret!'

'You knew?' Alice gasped, her face screwed up with pain as the men jerked her fractured arm in their haste to tie her hands.

Arcturus turned to her, his heart twisting. He wanted to wink at her, let her know he was still on their side . . . but it was too risky. And . . . there was a snake of doubt twisting in his stomach. Was he still on their side?

The king and his nobles had lost. Vocans had been taken and its students captured. Why not throw his lot in with the winning side? He owed Alfric no loyalty, and there was nothing he could do for his friends as just another captive.

'Don't you see, I've . . . I've been loyal to you all along,' Arcturus said, stumbling over his words in his haste to explain. 'A few hours with these spoiled, pampered kids and I knew which side my bread was buttered.'

'We trusted you!' Elaine cried out, while next to her Alice glared at him, her eyes blazing with anger.

'I couldn't get away,' Arcturus said, loudly this time, wincing as his fingers were crushed in the tight binding. 'But I'm here now.'

Crawley stared for a few seconds, but was distracted by a growl from behind Arcturus. Then Crawley was sprinting for the cart, a curved knife clutched in his hand.

'No!' Alice screamed, lunging for him with her feet.

Arcturus spun and saw the Canid struggling beneath the cloaks they had swaddled him in. Arcturus struggled to get to his feet, straining against the rebel's hands that pushed him down, as Crawley began to put the knife to Edmund's throat.

By now Gelert had wriggled his upper body from the cloak

and was snapping at Crawley, but the servant remained calm in the face of it all, lifting Edmund's head and jerking the knife threateningly.

'That's right, you stupid creature,' the servant hissed. 'Daddy goes bye-bye if you don't settle down.'

The Canid's barking stopped. It was replaced with a low growl, hatred burning in his eyes. With one lunge, Gelert could swallow Crawley's head whole . . . but he would not risk his master's life.

'I said, settle down!' Crawley bawled.

The sound stopped.

'Dorcas, bind this monster's legs,' Crawley ordered.

The rebel holding down Arcturus hesitated for a moment, then hurried to do Crawley's bidding. Dorcas was a large man with broad shoulders that made Arcturus think he had once been a blacksmith. But despite his size, the man's hands shook as he tied Gelert's paws, muzzle and even tail together, leaving the demon trussed up like a turkey.

The whole atrium watched as it was done and Arcturus was stunned by the still silence of the hundred rebels above them. Not a word passed their lips, nor did a cloak stir, as if they were gargoyles arrayed across a church roof.

With the Canid secured, Crawley withdrew the blade and strode towards Arcturus. Then it was Arcturus's turn to feel the cold of the knife against his throat, and he resisted the urge to gulp as the point was pressed against his windpipe.

'You did not seem so keen when we last spoke,' Crawley said, his voice low so that only Arcturus could hear. 'In fact, I distinctly remember you being insolent.'

'I . . . didn't . . . know,' Arcturus said, each syllable slicing the knife deeper into his neck. He felt a rivulet of warm blood trickle down to his chest.

Crawley eased the pressure and gripped Arcturus's hair.

'Give me one good reason why I shouldn't kill you right now,' Crawley asked. 'I could say the nobles killed you. Killed the first common summoner. That would get the people on our side. It was what we were going to do anyway.'

'Leave him alone!' Elaine yelled, and Arcturus heard a slap, then a whimper. He felt the hot rage stir in him then, and he quelled it as best he could.

'I can find more,' Arcturus managed, looking Crawley in the eyes.

'More what?' Crawley asked, twisting the knife's point cruelly. 'Choose your words more carefully, Arcturus. They may be your last.'

'Common summoners,' Arcturus mumbled, feeling faint. 'You need a summoner to test for them.'

Crawley pulled the knife away and tapped it against his chin thoughtfully, leaving a bloody mark on his skin.

'Keep talking,' he said.

'Where are you going to find another summoner to work for you? They're all nobles,' Arcturus said. 'There are more of me out there, the Provost said so.'

'What, more bastards, like you?' Crawley asked, and grinned at the look of surprise on Arcturus's face. 'You thought I didn't know? There's not much old Crawley doesn't know about what goes on at Vocans.'

'Bastards or not, you'll need them in the coming days,'

Arcturus said. He did not mention that he had no idea how to test someone for summoning abilities.

Crawley stared at him with narrowed eyes, and for a moment Arcturus considered telling him about the other common summoners – unrelated to the nobility. But it would not do to muddy the waters.

'All right,' Crawley said, withdrawing the knife. Arcturus felt a flood of relief, and stemmed the flow from the wound on his neck with the rags on his hands.

'Twenty-fourth, you'll wait in the summoning room,' Crawley ordered Percival's men, turning away from Arcturus. 'We'll find a useful task for you when I return.'

If there was any doubt that Crawley was in charge, it was gone now. The man had once commanded the servants here and was clearly used to giving orders. Only now he commanded an army.

Percival bowed in agreement and Arcturus saw the frustration in the man's eyes.

'Like he said, lads, in quick order,' the sergeant instructed, and the men trooped to the open set of double doors that led to the summoning room. Arcturus looked after them, knowing the men might be his only hope of escape.

'You lot, escort the nobles to the safe room,' Crawley barked, snapping his fingers. 'And take their weapons. Dorcas, with me. Bring the common boy, and keep a close eye on him. He hasn't proven his loyalty yet.'

'You must send someone to look after Edmund,' Alice called out. 'He's no use to you dead.'

Crawley paused, then turned and slapped Alice across the face.

281

'You don't give me orders any more, girl,' Crawley snarled.

Then he strode up the winding staircase, and Arcturus was shoved along behind him. He caught one last look over his shoulder and saw Elaine being manhandled into the cart, squashed in beside Gelert. Then they were out of sight.

He gave Dorcas a smile, as if to say they were on the same side. Instead, he earned himself a thick ear and a forceful shove that skinned his elbows on the stairs.

At each floor, Arcturus saw the long row of crossbowmen, standing to attention in the shadows beyond the railings. Not one looked away from their posts, and Arcturus realised they were waiting in ambush for whoever entered the castle. The drawbridge had been left open for a reason.

'Where are we going?' Arcturus asked, wincing as Dorcas thumped his ear again.

'To present you to the man behind all of this,' Crawley said cheerfully. 'He'll decide if you're more useful alive or dead.'

Arcturus stifled a shudder. Then he realised who Crawley was talking about. The man behind all this.

General Barcroft.

41

They reached the top floor and hurried down a corridor, and Arcturus felt strange to be back in a place so familiar, yet different at the same time. The door of every room was open, and within he could see more rebels, some sleeping, others sharpening and oiling weapons. Many of them were soldiers, their jackets turned out and black. This was no rabble, but an army.

For a moment he considered whether the nobility had any chance of defeating the rebellion, even with demons on their side. It was hard to say – he had never seen a full-fledged summoner go into battle.

'Wait here,' Crawley snapped, stopping outside a redwood door, complete with a large lock on the other side. He rapped his knuckles against the wood in a staccato pattern, a secret code of sorts that prompted a rattle of keys, the rasp of a metal bar and finally an open door, where he was met by crossed blades.

'It's Crawley, here to see the general,' Crawley said, rolling his eyes.

'Let him in,' a bass voice growled. 'Crawley, what's this

I hear about new arrivals?'

'Follow me,' Crawley said, and then Arcturus was dragged into a room of plush carpets, a four-poster bed and statues. Arcturus guessed it was the Provost's bedroom and this was confirmed by a large painting on the wall, depicting Obadiah Forsyth with his hand on Zacharias's shoulder.

'The message said for soldiers to gather outside Corcillum,' continued the man who had spoken, and Arcturus was faced with a middle-aged soldier with lamb-chop sideburns, a plum-red nose and a paunch that jutted out over his waistband. Behind him, more than a score of soldiers lined the walls, their crossbows readied to fire.

The chevrons stitched to the man's shoulders confirmed Arcturus's suspicions. This was General Barcroft . . . and he was not much to look at. This was the man who had inspired a rebellion?

'Father, Vocans is on the way to Corcillum for many of your soldiers, is it not?' Crawley said. 'They are not the first group to have stopped here today.'

Barcroft grunted and leaned over a table sprawled with various maps and markers. It took a moment for Arcturus to process how Crawley had addressed the general.

'You're his son?' Arcturus blurted.

'Silence,' Crawley hissed, and Arcturus was rewarded with a slap across the back of the head.

'A bastard son,' Barcroft said, never looking up from his maps. 'Like you, my boy, if the rumours are true.'

Arcturus looked at the thin-faced steward beside him, towering a foot taller than his father. It was hard to see any resemblance.

'Useful things, bastards,' Barcroft continued. 'Loyal and obedient, like a good hunting dog. But only if you catch them young, raise them right.'

Arcturus saw a flash of disdain in Crawley's eyes, but it was swiftly replaced with a forced smile.

'Old Faversham didn't catch you young, did he, boy?' Barcroft asked, finally looking up at him. The man's watery eyes appraised him, and Arcturus stood a little straighter. 'I hear he tried to kill you – is that true?'

'Yes, he—' Crawley began.

'Let the boy tell it,' Barcroft snapped.

It was time to prove his loyalty. For a moment Arcturus considered his chances. They had not stripped him of his weapons, and though his hands were tied, a finger had slipped free. But then he remembered the blade Crawley had pressed against his throat and the row of crossbow men behind him, not to mention the two guards at the door. It would be suicide.

No . . . he would have to talk his way out of this. Sweat prickled his palms, but he took his time and chose his words with care.

'He had his son do the dirty work, and another jumped-up noble boy helped. But I survived,' Arcturus said, as confidently as he could. 'I have no love for him, or any other nobles for that matter. In fact, I despise him.'

It was easy to make his words sincere for most of what he said was true. Even so, the general's eyes narrowed with suspicion and he approached Arcturus.

'So you'd join our cause then, is that what you're saying?' Barcroft asked, prodding Arcturus's chest with a stubby finger.

'I . . . I don't know,' Arcturus said, knowing that they would never believe he had converted so swiftly. 'I would see the commoners rule, if that's what you're asking. But right now I just want a bed and something to eat.'

Barcroft stared at him a moment longer, then grunted and returned to his maps. He muttered to himself and moved a marker a few centimetres upwards. Crawley cleared his throat.

'Father, I have news,' he said. 'We have caught more hostages.'

More? Arcturus's heart dropped. Could it be?

'We have Prince Harold,' Barcroft said, waving Crawley away, 'and a Forsyth and a Queensouth. We have no need of more. King Alfric and his nobles dare not fight back while we hold them. They have not even attacked our patrols.'

So the others had been captured. Arcturus struggled to keep his face blank, even as despair took hold. His newfound friends were all prisoners. And he among them, if he did not play his cards right.

'Indeed, father,' Crawley said, speaking swiftly. 'But now we have a Raleigh, a Lovett and a further Queensouth. It sweetens the pot, does it not?'

'Put them in with the others,' Barcroft said, shrugging his shoulders. 'What matters now is that we take control of Corcillum while the nobles are too scared to attack us. They have already ceded us Vocans and the southern half of the city.'

'What news from Corcillum?' Crawley asked, excitedly. 'Do the people side with us?'

Barcroft sighed and rubbed his eyes.

'Not yet,' he said. 'They cling to their old lives like a whipped dog does its collar. But in time they shall. Once they see the nobles brought low. For now, we must simply make our presence felt, have our men march through the streets.'

'Praise the heavens,' Crawley said, clasping his hands together. He moved towards his father as if to hug him, but was stopped by a look from Barcroft.

'Leave me,' Barcroft said, his face filled with irritation. 'I have work to do.'

'And the boy?' Crawley asked. 'We had plans for him, did we not? A common summoner on our side would sway many to our cause.'

There was a pause, and Arcturus waited, his fate hanging in the balance.

'Put him under armed guard,' Barcroft said. 'I'll decide what to do with him in the morning.'

42

Arcturus shivered in the cold darkness of the room they had thrown him in, rubbing his shoulder where it had hit the cobblestone floor. It was a closet filled with brooms, mops, buckets and the sickly scent of soap.

They had taken his weapons, which were now stacked beside the guard outside. He felt naked without them but armed himself with a broom handle nonetheless.

First he summoned Sacharissa, grateful that the guards had not bothered to take the summoning leather from his pocket. Then, after a moment of excited yelping, wet licks and a shout from the guard outside to keep it down, he settled in the corner with Sacharissa, drifting a wyrdlight around the room and considering his options.

He had managed to free his hands, for their wrapping had been interrupted when he had switched sides. Even so, he knew his mana levels were low, and even if he succeded in overpowering the guard on the door and attempted to escape, there would still be hundreds of rebels to beat, scattered throughout Vocans.

In all honesty, he did not even know if he wanted to escape. The rebels had the king and his allies between a rock and a hard place. Barcroft had said that the nobles were too scared to fight back for fear of hurting the hostages. If he were a gambler, he would bet on the rebels winning. They were the right choice.

But, in the moment the decision solidified in his mind, it instantly dissolved at the thought of his friends. The very idea of joining Crawley and his minions filled him with revulsion.

When he weighed the nobles against the commoners in his life, it was clear to him who had mattered most. He had been made a virtual slave by a common man, and had received little kindness from that tavern keeper and his family. In fact, the only people who had shown him kindness were noble: Edmund, Alice, Lieutenant Cavendish.

And of course Elaine. Twice she had saved his life and wanted nothing but his friendship in return. He could not imagine the terror she was feeling right now, locked away by cruel men who hated her. All he could do was hope she had been able to keep Valens for company, or at least had Alice to comfort her.

No. He was not a rebel. But the only way he could help his friends was by pretending to be one.

'Hey,' Arcturus called, knocking on the door. 'I need to speak to Crawley. I have important information that will help the rebellion.'

'He's busy. Tell him in the morning,' the guard outside snapped.

'I need the toilet too,' Arcturus said.

'Piss in a bucket,' came the reply.

'And I'm hungry,' Arcturus argued. 'I haven't eaten in days.'

'Then another day won't hurt you,' the guard replied. 'Just be quiet. They pulled me out of bed to watch you, so don't make my life any harder than it has to be.'

Arcturus sighed and slid down the door. He pulled his cloak closer around him and tugged the hood over his head. The warmth was comforting, and Sacharissa rested her big head in his lap, looking up at him with her four blue eyes. He kissed her on the snout and sensed that she was cold. Sadly, the room had no linens or towels inside for him to warm her, so instead he flapped the end of his cloak over her shoulders and pulled her in close.

'I wish I had another cloak for you, Sacha,' he said, rubbing the soft fur of her back.

His cloak . . . an idea struck him then, like a bolt of lightning. If he got past the guard outside, he would look like any other rebel, and he imagined that most of the men here didn't know each other. He could hide in plain sight.

The problem was overpowering the guard without any signs of a struggle. Arcturus pushed Sacharissa's head from his lap, earning himself a whine of annoyance. Then he peered through the keyhole.

On the other side of the door, a black-clothed rebel dozed against the wall, leaning on his spear like a shepherd's crook. Arcturus's weapons were stacked beside him.

Arcturus considered his options. He could not pick the lock – there was a spell for that, but he had yet to learn the symbol for it. Nor could he blast the door open with the last of his mana; that would send every rebel nearby running. He might be able to shatter the lock with a controlled kinetic blast – but the sound of it would mean the guard would be ready for him on the other side when they barrelled through.

Ideally, the rebel would come into the room to check on him, but with Sacharissa having made so much noise upon their reunion, the guard would know there was a demon waiting for him on the other side of the door.

A lightning spell was too erratic to aim through the keyhole, and the guard would scream blue murder before a fire spell killed him. A controlled thread of kinetic energy would be the best way to do it. But Arcturus had never tried to shape a spell before. Nor did he have sufficient mana to practise.

The keyhole. That was the solution. If he could get the guard close enough, an uncontrolled blast of mana might do the trick. The question was how.

'Sasha . . . let's make some noise.' Arcturus grinned, still peering through the keyhole.

Arcturus brandished the broomstick and smashed it into a nearby bucket, whooping as he did so. Sacharissa howled like a wolf, though Arcturus kept the sound contained enough that it wouldn't alert nearby rebels.

On the other side of the door, the guard jumped awake, his face twisting into a scowl. He was a mean-looking young man with a potato-shaped nose and beady eyes.

'If you don't shut that creature up, we won't feed you for a week,' the guard growled. 'No water either, and you and that bucket will become very familiar.'

'Help me,' Arcturus wailed. 'My demon's gone crazy.'

Arcturus sent an order to Sacharissa with a thought, and the howl turned into a snarl, low and threatening. She took the end of a mop and began to savage it, and Arcturus accompanied the noise with a choking, gurgling sound.

'Hey,' the guard said. 'Stop that. I know what you're up to.'

Arcturus drummed his feet against the ground, his choking more frantic now. For good measure he scraped his fingernails along the door. Then, with a swift mental order, both he and Sacharissa fell silent, and Arcturus pressed his cheek against the keyhole.

The guard stared at the door, his face a picture of confusion.

'Come on,' Arcturus whispered under his breath. 'Come see.'

His finger swirled in the air, etching the spiral that powered the telekinesis spell. It fixed to his finger, and he held his hand ready beside the keyhole, waiting to strike.

Now the rebel looked up and down the corridor, as if looking for someone to help him. Seeing nobody, he crouched down and shuffled closer to the door. Arcturus held his breath, then grinned as the man lowered his face towards the keyhole. Curiosity had got the better of him.

Arcturus waited. Waited until the lumpy face had filled the small circle of light on the other side. Then he pushed his finger into the lock and unleashed a blast of kinetic energy.

There was a dull *whump* as the spell was funnelled through the mechanism and out of the other side, shattering the lock with a crackle of snapping metal. Arcturus threw the door open and burst through . . . only to find the guard crumpled against the wall, his neck snapped back at an odd angle, eyes glazed over in death. There was no blood – the very force of the blast had killed him.

Arcturus felt the gorge rise in his throat. He ran back into the room and emptied the contents of his stomach into a bucket.

He had not meant the man to die. In truth, he had thought he would knock the man unconscious, or at worst blind him in one eye.

But there was no time to process his guilt. He pushed the body into a sitting position, pulled the man's hood up so it appeared he was sleeping, and laid the spear across his lap.

Then Arcturus strapped on his weapons, infused Sacharissa and pulled his own hood over his head to obscure his face. For all any passer-by would know, he was a rebel now. At most, he had until morning to save his friends. Or die trying.

43

Arcturus stared down the corridor, paralysed by indecision. He needed to find where the nobles were being held hostage, but how would he navigate the maze of rooms and sleeping rebels?

For a moment he concentrated, trying to smell them using his newfound heightened senses. But the myriad of scents that filled his nostrils were confusing – with hundreds of rebels in the building, there were just too many people. Sacharissa might have been able to make sense of it, but she was infused and would need to stay that way.

He considered cornering a rebel and interrogating him for information, threatening death by fireball. But what if the rebel called his bluff and shouted for help? And even if the rebel did give up information, was Arcturus supposed to somehow knock him unconscious, relying on him staying out cold until he had escaped? Or tie the rebel up and gag him with his rudimentary knowledge of knots and hope it worked? He didn't want to think about killing a rebel. It just . . . wasn't an option. The image of the man he had murdered floated unbidden to his mind, and his stomach twisted with guilt and revulsion. No. He would not do it again.

The one thing he did know was that he could not stand there for ever. If he walked purposefully, he could get away with a simple nod and greeting to any passing rebels, as if he had places to be. But if they found him standing like a plum in the middle of the corridor, they might stop and talk to him.

He needed a friend. For a moment he thought about Rotter, stuck with the twenty-fourth in the summoning room. As far as the rebels knew, he was just another soldier in their squad.

If anyone could help him, it was them. The twenty-fourth might be massively outnumbered, but with the element of surprise they might just be able to rescue the nobles and escape. The difficulty would be convincing them.

So he walked towards the atrium, his eyes fixed ahead, his face shrouded by the hood. On either side he could hear conversations, or the clink of metal, but dared not glance into the open doorways. Twice, groups of rebels walked past, but both times they were too deep in conversation to give him a second look.

To his surprise, he reached the balconied floor that overlooked the atrium unnoticed. But that was where his luck ended and he realised just how harebrained his plan truly was.

Crawley had taken him to the top floor of the eastern stairwell and had locked him there too; he knew it best, for it was where the servants' and teachers' quarters were housed. To reach the summoning room, Arcturus would need to go down the stairs and cross the atrium. Only, there were a hundred or so men lined up against the walls of each floor, ready to step out of the shadows and ambush anyone who walked through the double doors.

That meant a hundred eyes watching him as he walked there, and a hundred crossbows ready to be pointed if the squad left without permission.

He was at a loss. For now, he unslung his crossbow and pressed his back against the wall, standing beside the other silent rebels. Now he looked like just another of them.

From his vantage point, he could see the summoning-room door. There were two guards posted outside, their spears crossed in front of it. There was no way he was getting in there, not without being challenged. So he would need to think of another plan.

It was at that moment that he saw him. Ulfr the dwarf, stumbling out of the dining hall at the end of the atrium and heading towards the stairs. He clutched a large tray in his hands, and there were covered dishes piled so high that the dwarf could barely see over the top.

Arcturus waited, hoping against hope that the dwarf would come to his aid. He could smell the food without his new smelling abilities. Bacon and eggs.

The smell grew stronger, and finally he saw Ulfr stomp up the stairs on to his floor, and heard dwarvish curses muttered through his beard.

Arcturus waited until the dwarf walked past then followed, casually breaking away from his post by the wall and walking after him. He could feel the eyes of the nearby crossbowmen on him then, and it was all he could do to keep going. He had somehow forgotten how to walk normally. How was he supposed to move his arms?

To his relief, he turned down the corridor unchallenged, back the way he had come. Again he walked the gauntlet of open doors, but luckily it was Ulfr who got the attention.

'Is that for me, pipsqueak?' called one rebel. 'Let me take some of that load off.'

'It's for the General, you daft git,' Ulfr growled back.

'Well, bring me another when you're done with him,' the rebel replied.

But Ulfr had already moved on, his cursing only getting louder. More calls for food followed, but Ulfr ignored them all.

Arcturus blanched at the thought of returning to that area – Crawley and Dorcas might be prowling nearby, and Barcroft and his guards might recognise him too.

Arcturus's stomach twisted as Ulfr stepped by the rebel he had killed, the man still propped up against the wall, his eyes closed, knees drawn up to his chest. Ulfr barely gave the dead rebel a second look, assuming the man was sleeping. It appeared that so had everyone else who had passed by, but Arcturus's heart still pounded long after they had left the corpse behind.

As he watched Ulfr shuffle down the corridors, he considered how strange the dwarf was. He always treated Arcturus with disdain and his hatred for humanity seemed to run deep. And yet, he had tried to warn Arcturus when the twenty-fourth had come through the door. He had told Crawley to stay away from Arcturus too, and of course he had run to get help when Arcturus was being attacked by the Wendigo.

He was sure Ulfr had a soft spot for him. Better still, he had overheard the dwarf refusing to join the rebels. Perhaps Arcturus could turn him to the right side.

Now they were nearing the Provost's office, where Barcroft had set up camp. Arcturus stopped, sliding into an empty doorway and watching as Ulfr receded into the gloom. It was not long until he was just a hazy figure – the torches in sconces on the walls here were running on a low flame and clearly the servants who usually refilled them had other concerns that night.

As Arcturus leaned out, Ulfr continued right past the office. For a moment Arcturus wondered if he had got it wrong – but no, he was sure of it. Groaning, Arcturus scurried after him, his heart pounding in his chest as he passed the ornate doors to Obadiah's office.

Then Arcturus's heart stilled. Three large rebels dressed in black cloaks lined the end of the corridor. Ulfr stopped in front of them, and Arcturus was forced to hide in a doorway once more. He concentrated, and the world became louder in his ears. He could hear an endless burble of voices, the opening and closing of doors, and the rasp and jingle of metal. But above all else, the conversation down the corridor won through.

'Stop, dwarf. This area is restricted,' one of the rebels said flatly.

'I've brought food,' Ulfr said, and Arcturus could hear the impatience in the dwarf's voice. 'Stand aside.'

'About time, we're starving,' a second rebel said. 'Just leave it here and piss off.'

Arcturus heard Ulfr let out a deep, long-suffering sigh.

'It's not for you, you idiot,' Ulfr said. 'It's for the prisoners.'

44

Of course. There had been too many plates for the general – Ulfr had only said it was for him so the rebels he had been passing wouldn't steal the food. Arcturus knew he should have felt happy to find out where his friends were being held, but instead he felt a lump of dread weighing down his stomach.

He was going to have to get past those guards somehow. The only good news was that along this part of the corridor, there were no open doors. They had moved from the many small rooms of the servants' quarters to the larger chambers where the teachers lived. In fact, there were only two doorways between Arcturus and the three men. If he could act quietly enough, there would be no reinforcements.

Ahead, Ulfr had pushed past them, but they had prevented the dwarf from going further. Lucky for Arcturus, the rebels now had their backs to him.

'Come on,' one of the guards said, grasping Ulfr's shoulder. 'They're nobles. Let them starve. We'll take a plate each, they can share the rest.'

It was going to have to be now. Arcturus's breath came thick and fast as he unslung his crossbow. Sacharissa battered his consciousness, eager to help, but if Arcturus summoned her, the flash of light from the summoning would alert the guards to his presence.

'Let me go,' Ulfr said.

Arcturus walked steadily towards the guards, doing his best to keep his footsteps silent. He was shrouded in darkness, but there were torches on either side of the rebels, and with every pace he knew he became easier to see.

'Three plates,' the central guard said, unperturbed by Ulfr's silence.

'Barcroft said the hostages are to be well looked after,' Ulfr snapped. 'Get your greasy paw off me before I cut it off.'

'Looks like the little half-man has some balls,' the guard on the left laughed.

'We're not asking any more,' growled the central guard. 'Leave it, or we'll take it from—'

'Hey!' the guard on the right shouted, spinning around.

Arcturus cursed inwardly. He did not know what sound he had made to alert them, but now he stood a stone's throw away, his crossbow dangling from his hand. Luckily, it had not been pointing at them, so he did not appear to be an immediate threat.

'Erm . . . I'm here to relieve you,' Arcturus said, his voice weak with fear.

The rebels peered at him sceptically, the surrounding gloom making Arcturus no more than a shadowy figure.

'Just you?' the central man asked, and Arcturus's mind went blank.

The speaker was the largest of the three, and he carried a sword, while the others carried long, black-wood cudgels. The man to his left was tall and slender and the one on the right wide and stocky, but all were well-muscled men and carried themselves with authority. They were the kind of thugs that Arcturus would have avoided if he saw them in the street, for their faces were marred by broken noses and scars.

'He asked you a question,' snarled the thin rebel.

Arcturus took a step back, falling deeper into the shadows. The element of surprise was gone and with every passing moment they became more and more alert. Ulfr stood behind them, forgotten.

'I . . . they're coming,' Arcturus said, looking at a doorway on his right as if it might offer some escape route. 'I think they're in here.'

He stepped into the doorway and turned the handle, only to find it locked.

'I'll go get them,' he said loudly. 'They're late, as usual.'

'Stay right there,' the stocky rebel snarled.

Arcturus heard footsteps approaching. He was obscured from sight, but within seconds the man would be upon him.

He tried to think, but Sacharissa's desperation to be released overtook all other thought. With no other cards to play, Arcturus obliged her.

His hands shook as he unravelled the leather mat, and the flash of light as she materialised was near blinding in the gloom. The demon immediately pressed herself against the door.

'Damned torch won't light,' Arcturus called out unconvincingly.

'What the bloody hell was that?' the approaching rebel bellowed.

His voice echoed down the passageway and Arcturus winced with each reverberation.

'To hell with it,' Arcturus muttered, lifting the crossbow.

Heart pounding, he stepped out of the shadow of the doorway and the stocky rebel squared up to him, a broad silhouette against the torchlit corridor beyond.

'Who—' the rebel began.

Arcturus pulled the trigger, shooting from the hip. It was too close to miss, but too dark to see. He only felt the jar of the recoil against his bicep and heard the man grunt in pain, words dying unformed in his mouth. Then the axe was pulled over Arcturus's head and he was slicing down and to the side.

Arcturus heard the gasp, tasted the spray of blood across his face, felt the sick tug and release on his axe as the man collapsed to the ground. His stomach roiled with nausea, and then he was standing alone in the darkness once more.

He didn't want to be here. He didn't want any of this.

'Roger, what's happening?' the swordsman called out.

Arcturus kneeled and tried to reload, fumbling in the gloom. Bolts clattered to the ground as he tugged one from the quiver, but in the dim light he could not find the slot.

'Get 'im,' the tall rebel yelled, charging.

Arcturus let the crossbow fall to the ground and lifted the axe once more. The approaching rebel was out of the light now and would be on him in seconds.

'Sacha,' Arcturus breathed. 'Now!'

He felt the brush of fur beside him and winced as the pain of the Canid's broken ribs flared in his mind. The scratch of claws skittered on the floor, then the outline of the thin man was gone, replaced by a twisting knot of limbs and fur, accompanied by muffled screams of agony.

But there was no time for triumph – beyond, the swordsman was running to help, his sword extended like a spearhead. No time to etch a spell. No time to load a bow.

Arcturus sprinted to meet his charge. Sacharissa was in danger now, and the thought of it turned his blood to fire. He let the anger take over, replacing the guilt and fear and lending strength to his tired limbs.

'I'll kill you,' Arcturus yelled, enough to turn the swordsman from the tumbling bodies between them. The sword swept high and Arcturus heard the air thrum with the force of it. It passed inches from his face.

Arcturus riposted with a clumsy swing of his axe, but the blow was parried easily, slapped aside with the flat of the rebel's blade. Before he could recover the swordsman jabbed, and now Arcturus felt a sharp pain in his left shoulder.

'Hah!' the swordsman laughed.

Arcturus could feel the warm wetness seeping into the cloth of his shoulder, and the arm fell uselessly to his side. The sword whirled and Arcturus could do little more than jump back, leaving Sacharissa vulnerable, still struggling with the other rebel in the small space between them.

The demon was oblivious, but now Arcturus saw the glint of his opponent's sword as it was raised above Sacharissa.

'No,' he yelled.

Mana roiled within him and he blasted wyrdlight in a solid

beam of blue light. He winced as the sudden glare blinded him, but in his seared vision, he saw the rebel reeling, clutching his eyes.

He swung his axe again, but the man had fallen towards him, tripping over the struggling combatants beneath them. The wooden haft thudded harmlessly into the swordsman's shoulder as the blow passed above his head, and then Arcturus was in his own wrestling bout on the floor, the axe clattering free as he grasped at the hilt of the enemy blade.

But the rebel was too strong. Arcturus was forced on to his back and the man straddled his chest, the weight of him driving the breath in a great gust from Arcturus's lungs.

'I'm gonna gut you slow-like,' the man rasped, and Arcturus could smell the foetid waft of the man's breath as he heaved at the sword clutched between them.

It was all Arcturus could do to ease the blade as it pressed vertically against his chest, the tip slicing into the soft underside of his chin.

Spittle sprayed from the man's lips as he heaved once more. Arcturus craned his neck in desperation and his arms seized in effort, yet still the blade sank deeper. Fresh blood spurted from the wound and Arcturus knew he was going to die.

Then the man stiffened. Arcturus moaned with effort and suddenly the sword was his, and he pushed it up towards the man. His effort did little more than graze the rebel's face, but in that moment the rebel coughed and Arcturus's face was sprayed with crimson. It was only then that he saw a second blade glittering above, and he could finally breathe again as the man's body keeled over.

For a moment he lay there, gulping great gasps of air, ignoring his rescuer. Beside him, he sensed Sacharissa's triumph as she finished her opponent off with a final, savage bite, and the sudden concern as she processed the terror and desperation from her master. She had been oblivious, too focussed on the man beneath her, but now she came, her rough tongue bathing his face as he choked his way back to breathing easy once more.

'You're a fool,' said a gruff voice.

Ulfr. The dwarf stood above Arcturus, his legs akimbo, hands on his hips. He clutched a long knife, the blade red with blood.

'I had . . . to try,' Arcturus managed.

'You should have killed them with a lightning spell,' Ulfr grunted, grasping Arcturus's hand and lifting him to his feet.

Arcturus steadied himself on Sacharissa, his legs wavering like jelly, and Ulfr kneeled, wiping his blade on the dead swordsman's cloak. He had been too low on mana for more than a few, weak spells, but Arcturus didn't have the energy to tell him that.

'Thank you,' Arcturus said instead, 'for helping me. You didn't have to do that.'

Ulfr didn't respond. He simply shook his head and began to drag the swordsman's corpse down the corridor.

'What do we do now?' Arcturus asked.

'Grab hold of a body, get that mutt to do the same, and follow me,' Ulfr snapped, stopping to blow out the torches on the walls. 'If we're lucky they won't see the blood.'

The dwarf stopped to grab his tray and balanced it on the man's crimson-soaked belly. Then he continued on, grunting with effort.

Arcturus sent Sacharissa back to the stocky man he had killed

305

with the crossbow, and tried not to look at the bloodied remains of the rebel beneath him. He could see now that the man had worn chainmail beneath his cloak. It was not a pretty sight.

He looked up the corridor, where Ulfr had already disappeared into impenetrable darkness.

'Hellfire,' Arcturus breathed. 'That was close.'

And followed him.

45

It felt like an age dragging the body through pitch black, and as Arcturus focussed, he could still hear the conversations of the men on the floors beneath them. They swirled around him like the whispers of dead men, but he heard no alarm in them, even if the sound itself sent shivers up his spine.

Then there was a stark voice among the crowd, chiming as an off-key note in the conversation's melody. A bellow of pain, like a boar being speared on a hunt. Arcturus stopped, but it was gone as soon as it came, and he was forced to shuffle on once more.

He had never felt in more danger. It was only the thin light of the moon in the near distance that drove him on, for without it he might have stopped and buried his face in Sacharissa's fur.

With every heartbeat, the wound in his neck throbbed with pain, and he could feel the blood that had pooled on his chest congealing. He only wished he had enough mana to heal it, but he had used the last of it in that last blast of wyrdlight.

Finally, he reached a small pool of light where Ulfr had

already levered open a dust-covered window.

'Help me lift him,' Ulfr said, taking the swordsman's corpse under the arms and heaving its back on to the window. Arcturus took the legs, then the body was gone. It took a long time for Arcturus to hear the distant splash.

The food tray and other bodies followed, and Arcturus felt the blood, sticky on his hands. He felt sick once more – he had no stomach for this kind of killing.

'I took the keys from the big one,' Ulfr said, peering into the gloom they had come from. He held them out and shook them impatiently.

Arcturus took the keys, unsure what Ulfr expected of him. They had likely passed several doors in the darkness, but there was no way of telling which one held his friends.

'Why are you helping me?' Arcturus asked, delaying the task at hand. 'Surely you hate the nobles as much as anyone.'

'Rich humans, poor humans, you're all the same,' Ulfr muttered, avoiding Arcturus's eyes.

Sacharissa whined, sensing Arcturus's fear, and he comforted her with a ruffle of her mane.

'So what's in it for you?' Arcturus pressed.

'If the rebels take power, they won't treat the dwarves any better,' Ulfr sighed, leaning against the wall and closing his eyes. 'We refused to help them.'

'Why?' Arcturus asked.

'We've tried to overthrow the nobles many times, and never won,' Ulfr replied. 'We didn't think they had a chance. Of course, we didn't know the rebels would capture their children. They have a slim hope now, but it's too late for us to join them.'

He stopped for a moment and the dwarf's brow furrowed, as if he were working something out.

'But if a dwarf saves King Alfric's son, the rebels lose,' he whispered so quietly that Arcturus had to strain to hear it. 'Then he would owe us. Give us more rights. Make us equals.'

Ulfr opened his eyes and Arcturus thought he saw the briefest hint of a smile through the dwarf's beard.

'Can you help me get them out of here?' Arcturus asked.

'I can try,' Ulfr said. 'But it's not going to be easy. Come on.'

The dwarf hurried back down the passageway and Arcturus followed. Within moments they were in darkness once more, but soon Arcturus grunted with pain as he ran into Ulfr's back.

'Here,' the dwarf said, guiding Arcturus's hand to the keyhole. 'This is where I brought their food yesterday.'

Arcturus struggled with the keys. There were three of them on a loop and he blindly fumbled one into the slot. It rattled in the lock, but would not turn.

'Try the next,' Ulfr whispered.

On the other side, Arcturus heard the low murmur of voices and his heart leaped at the thought of rescuing his friends. The next key turned, and suddenly the world was bright again as he fell into the room.

He looked up, a grin on his face, but it was wiped away as swiftly as it appeared. Because in front of him, spread in a row, a trio of crossbowmen stared at him down the shafts of their quarrels.

'I'm here to relieve you,' Arcturus said weakly, even as he lifted his bloodied hands, and Sacharissa growled from behind him.

'Don't. Move,' one of the rebels growled through gritted teeth.

'If his fingers so much as twitch . . . shoot him,' another snapped. He appeared to be the leader, for his voice commanded some authority and he wore finer clothes than the others.

Beyond the guards, Arcturus could see the trussed-up bodies of his friends and hear their muffled moans as they tried to speak through tight gags. Arcturus only glanced at them, for he could not tear his eyes away from the sharp points aimed at his chest.

He heard the shuffle of footsteps behind him, though he dared not turn his head more than a few centimetres to look. Ulfr had entered the room, but the dwarf did not have his hands up. Instead, he stumbled to the side and fell.

'Thank you,' Ulfr said, getting to his knees and shuffling away. 'The bastard forced me to bring him here.'

The men ignored him, their crossbows firmly pointed at Arcturus. He was the threat – a single spell from him could take the three of them out. Little did they know, Arcturus had no mana left to use.

'Listen, I can explain,' Arcturus began.

'Save it,' the leader said. 'We know who you are. You're the common summoner. The bastard.'

'We should kill him where he stands,' hissed one of his companions. 'He's a traitor to the cause.'

'Not before Crawley gives the go ahead,' the leader said.

'To hell with Crawley,' the other rebel snarled. 'I'm not hanging around here to get blasted into ash while we wait for permission.'

The leader remained silent but Arcturus knew the man was

calculating the odds. He could almost hear the strings creaking on the crossbows, ready to whip steel-tipped death into his body.

Behind, Sacharissa's growling intensified and Arcturus sensed that she was crouched in shadow beyond the door. Even an order from Arcturus would not quell the noise. Her message was clear. Kill Arcturus and she would tear the rebels apart.

The throbbing of his neck wound grew with the quickening of his pulse. In the corner of his eye, he could see Ulfr had reached the cart where Edmund remained unconscious. Gelert lay prone beside the boy and a slim shred of hope fluttered as Arcturus watched the dwarf draw his knife and begin sawing silently at the demon's bonds, all out of sight of the three guards.

Still, the crossbowmen would fill him full of bolts before either Sacharissa or Gelert got to them, especially now that both were injured. Ulfr might have the chance to help his friends escape, but either way, Arcturus would be dead. He did not see an outcome that had a happy ending.

His only chance was that they missed, but that was not likely at such close range. So he would have to dive aside at the right moment and hope for the best.

'I'll take the boy, you take the demon,' the leader growled.

And fired.

Arcturus tumbled backward, saw the wooden shaft protruding halfway from his stomach, felt the numbness of shock in his mind and the sudden piercing pain in his centre.

Sacharissa. He held her still, though it took every ounce of control he could muster as his body straddled hers in the confusion of the sudden attack.

The crossbows thrummed, one clattering against the wall, another thudding through his shoulder and pinning him to his beloved demon's side. She whimpered but obeyed his command not to attack, even as he lay dying in the shadow of the doorway, the blood pooling in his lap while he grasped the shaft with his hands.

The rebels stared at Arcturus, as if they could not believe what they had done. To his left, Arcturus could make out Gelert, scrambling across the floor, but Ulfr had not had time to free the Canid of his bonds.

'Run,' Arcturus choked, and his consciousness wrenched as Sacharissa was forced to turn tail and disappear into the gloom of the corridors. With any luck he would die soon and she would give in to the ether's call, fading back into her world before the rebels could hunt her down and kill her.

He sensed her anguish but he felt a calm fall over him that stiffened his resolve. They could do no more to him now. He had done his duty.

'Load!' screamed the leader, his hands scrabbling to place another crossbow bolt in its firing slot. The remaining rebels had drawn their swords and advanced on Gelert as the demon snapped and snarled, wriggling as his bonds restricted him to dragging himself forward with a single claw. Within moments they would chop him to pieces.

Blue, bright as a flash of lightning, streaked across Arcturus's vision. The leader, his crossbow half raised, seemed to shudder, then erupted in a sizzling wreath of flashing, jagged energy. Beside him, the other two rebels twitched and jerked on the floor, consumed by the same brilliant light. Their bodies smoked and the room filled with the acrid stench of cooking hair and flesh.

Even as the edges of his vision darkened, Arcturus could see the source of the spell sitting up in his cart, face twisted in a snarl of anger.

Edmund had awakened.

46

He heard the weeping first. Deep, sniffling sobs and wails, and the sound of hushed shushing from the others.

'He's dead,' Zacharias's voice said. 'Just leave him – we need to bar the doors.'

'We're not giving up on him,' Elaine cried, and Arcturus could feel the cool, dainty hands that clasped his own, and the cold of the cobblestones against the bare skin of his back.

He opened his eyes. Elaine and Alice's faces hovered above him, creased with concern.

'He's alive!' Elaine gasped, her pale face streaked with tears.

She hugged him close and Arcturus braced himself for the pain from his stomach. But there was none, nor any from the wounds on his neck.

'What happened?' Arcturus asked. His voice came out in no more than a whisper. Elaine released him and he half sat up. Even that effort was a struggle, so Alice helped him with a gentle arm. He felt as weak as a newborn lamb.

'Ulfr cut Edmund's hands free,' Alice answered, smiling

through glistening eyes. 'He was faking unconsciousness, waiting for his moment.'

'Lucky,' Arcturus managed.

The room was bright from the light of a half-dozen torches. Josephine was sitting in the corner, her knees clutched to her chest, and Zacharias was pacing in front of her, his eyes wild with panic.

Prince Harold and Edmund stood beside Arcturus, though Edmund looked as weak as Arcturus felt; his face was even paler than usual and his eyes were deeply ringed with dark circles.

'I'm sorry I didn't trust you,' Alice said, her voice cracking with emotion. 'You almost died for us. I'll never doubt you again.'

Arcturus looked down at his body, where the crusted red-brown blood had dried against his upper chest and stomach. There were no wounds, and now he realised that Edmund had managed to heal him before he died.

He tried to stand, but a sudden rush of dizziness took him and he fell to one knee. Elaine helped him to his feet and he gave her a weak smile.

'You lost a lot of blood,' Edmund croaked from beside him. 'It took me a while to get to you.'

'A hell of a lot,' Prince Harold said, and now Arcturus could see he was holding Edmund up, just as Elaine was doing with him.

Edmund's eyes were unfocussed and his breathing seemed laboured. Even though he was awake, he needed a doctor, and soon.

'Don't ever do that again,' Elaine said, giving Arcturus a soft punch on the arm.

315

Arcturus looked for Sacharissa, and in his mind he could sense her running back, realising he was safe. She was furious at him for forcing her away from him, but her relief was so palpable that Arcturus found himself grinning stupidly.

'Thank you,' Arcturus said, clasping Edmund's limp hand. 'You saved my life.'

'Yes, yes,' Zacharias snapped, ceasing his pacing to glare at them. 'We're all so glad you're alive, Arcturus. But you've not saved us yet. There are a few hundred damned rebels between us and the front doors, and even if we manage to get out of here, their horsemen will catch us up long before we reach Corcillum.'

Arcturus looked to Prince Harold and the prince nodded reluctantly.

'We're between a rock and a hard place,' he said. 'Even Ulfr doesn't know what to do.'

He motioned with his head over his shoulder, where Arcturus could see the dwarf sitting on Edmund's cart, his face dark and brooding. Beneath him, Gelert was curled up, his dark eyes focussed on his master.

'With our spells, demons and these tight corridors, we might just manage to fight them off,' Arcturus said, thinking aloud. 'Maybe we don't need to leave at all. At least, not until your parents rescue us. They could fly the Celestial Corps in, blast a hole through the walls.'

'No spells,' Alice said, shaking her head. 'They drained us when we came in here.'

'Drained you?' Arcturus asked.

'They used a charging stone on us,' Prince Harold said,

316

lowering Edmund to the ground. The young noble groaned with pain and closed his eyes.

'It's a bit like a fulfilmeter,' Alice explained. 'When you press one on to a summoner's skin, it absorbs and stores the mana within itself to be used later. They forced us to fill it with our mana. We're just lucky they didn't do it to Edmund – he was so weak they were worried it might kill him.'

'So nobody has any mana left,' Arcturus groaned. 'We're—'

Arcturus's words caught in his throat because suddenly a furry ball of muscle erupted from the corridor and tumbled him to the floor, licking his face all over.

He could not help but laugh, and gave Sacharissa a tight hug. He buried his face in the fur of her neck, taking comfort in her solid presence.

'Thank you,' Arcturus whispered. 'For listening.'

Even as he spoke, the licking suddenly stopped and the demon flounced off, giving him a reproachful look and leaving him with a drool-covered face. She was still upset with him, but the anger had been replaced with hurt.

'I'll make it up to you,' he whispered.

She went to curl up beneath Ulfr's cart, her tail between her legs. Gelert dutifully made room for her.

'We're never going to get out of here,' wailed Josephine, finally stirring from her corner.

'At least we're all safe,' Arcturus said.

'Not all,' Alice said. 'Sergeant Caulder.'

Arcturus felt a wave of guilt. He had all but forgotten the brave sergeant who had escorted the other team.

'Where is he?' Arcturus asked, dreading the answer.

317

'They've got him locked away somewhere,' Prince Harold replied, giving Arcturus a grim look. 'They were questioning him.'

'You mean torturing,' Arcturus said.

Prince Harold did not reply, only nodded his head sadly.

'The bastards,' Arcturus said.

There was a miserable silence, broken only by the sound of Zacharias's ceaseless pacing.

'What about flying demons?' Ulfr called from behind them. 'We need to get a message to your parents that we're free.'

'They'll have recaptured us long before rescue arrives, you fool,' Zacharias said. 'If you're going to make suggestions, make sure they're not stupid ones first.'

Ulfr bridled at the insulting tone but Prince Harold held up a calming hand.

'Please, be civil, Zacharias,' Prince Harold said, shooting Zacharias a warning look. 'But it *is* a risk to send a rescue request, at least not until we are safe. If we sent for rescue and were recaptured before they came, there would be a fight and they would kill us before our parents got to us.'

Prince Harold slumped to the ground beside Edmund, pressing his thumbs to his temples.

'There's got to be a way out of this,' he groaned.

'We need to figure out how to walk past the guards without being stopped or questioned,' Arcturus said. 'And find somewhere to hide nearby, where they can't catch up to us once they realise we're missing.'

'Why not add a damned pot of gold and a thousand soldiers to the list?' Zacharias snorted. 'You're dreaming – we're screwed.

Our best hope is to lock ourselves in one of these rooms and hole up until this all blows over.'

'Arcturus will think of something,' Elaine said confidently.

Arcturus *was* thinking.

Soldiers.

They couldn't walk out alone, and disguising themselves with hoods was too risky, even if they did manage to get hold of enough uniforms for all of them. But if they had an escort of soldiers . . . it would be as if they were being taken somewhere more secure. They could walk right out the front door.

And lucky for him, he already had a group in mind.

47

'You're an idiot,' Ulfr said.

Arcturus had just finished explaining his plan, and even Elaine looked sceptical.

'It's the only way,' Arcturus replied.

'The twenty-fourth will be even harder to break out than we are,' Zacharias snapped. 'There's a hundred damned crossbows pointed at them.'

'But they're soldiers, not prisoners,' Arcturus argued. 'As far as the rebels know, they captured four of us and handed us right to them.'

'Even if Ulfr did manage to get to them, they've already said they don't want to take sides,' Alice said, shaking her head. 'It's a huge risk for them to march out with us. What if someone stopped them? What if Crawley saw them? Or a rebel asked them where they were taking us? I assume Crawley hasn't given them permission to leave the summoning room yet.'

It was true, and it was a fact that Arcturus had chosen to ignore. In all honesty, he had not thought the plan through, but it was the best he could come up with.

'Does anyone have any better ideas?' Arcturus asked.

'We lock ourselves in here,' Zacharias said, finally joining the circle. 'Take cover behind the cart, aim the crossbows at the door and summon our demons for battle.'

'Then what?' Arcturus asked.

'We send Elaine's Mite with a note explaining our situation to our parents,' Zacharias said, 'telling them where we are. They can send a demon to scout ahead. If we're recaptured, they won't attack. If we're still holed up, they can rescue us.'

'But we *will* be recaptured,' Arcturus argued. 'We've got a couple of hours at most before they discover our guards are missing. We may take many of them with us but they will beat us eventually, and some of us will die in the process. Your parents can't help us here.'

'The rebels will be too scared to fight us,' Zacharias snarled.

'Don't you get it?' Arcturus snapped. 'We are their entire plan. Us. Our captivity is the only thing that's preventing every summoner in Hominum from tearing this place apart. Without us, the rebellion is finished. Trust me, as soon as they find out we're in here without a crossbow aimed at our heads, every rebel in the building will be pouring through that door.'

'It's a better plan than yours,' Zacharias retorted. 'We can hold out long enough, I'm sure of it.'

But Prince Harold was shaking his head.

'We would be better off surrendering before they start breaking down the door,' he said. 'We would be throwing our lives away for nothing.'

'So we do that then,' Zacharias said. 'But none of this breakout nonsense.'

The noble was breathing heavily now and he glared at Arcturus, daring him to disagree. Despite his lack of support, Arcturus felt his confidence grow. A royal prince, taking advice from a lowborn bastard. They were no better than him.

In the gloom behind, Ulfr spoke.

'I know a place,' he said.

'To barricade?' Prince Harold asked.

'No. Outside,' Ulfr said, pointing at the windowless wall on the far left where an arrow slit had been bricked up with smeared mortar. 'Somewhere we can hide before the rebels catch up with us. Even the hunting dogs will have trouble finding us.'

'Where?' Arcturus asked excitedly.

'Underground. It's a secret place. Not far, as the crow flies.'

'Fat lot of good that does us,' Zacharias smirked, returning to his pacing. 'We're not getting out of here.'

'Shut up, Zacharias,' Harold snapped, his patience wearing thin.

Zacharias held up his hands in mock surrender but remained silent.

'How can we convince the soldiers to help us?' Elaine asked. 'Maybe Harold can offer them a reward or something.'

'It won't work,' Harold said. 'They already knew there would be a reward for helping us, but chose to remain neutral. What we really need is to force them to choose a side. And a way of making Arcturus's plan less risky for them.'

He gave Arcturus an apologetic smile, and Arcturus waved it away.

'Crawley,' Alice suddenly said, looking up. She was cradling Edmund's head in her lap and had been stroking his forehead. The boy seemed oblivious to the conversation.

'What about him?' Arcturus asked.

'If Crawley's with us, nobody will question them,' Alice said. 'We could capture him. Put a knife to his back or something.'

'He scares the hell out of me,' Elaine agreed.

Arcturus considered it. They were really only trading one risk for another, but it took the pressure off the twenty-fourth if they managed to pull it off.

'All right,' he nodded.

'I'll have to come with you,' Prince Harold said.

'You're the most recognisable of us all,' Edmund said, turning his pale face up to the young royal. 'Why?'

'Because the twenty-fourth need to hear their prince ask for their loyalty,' Harold said, tugging a hooded cloak from one of the fallen guards. 'Not a desperate commoner and a servant. When the time comes, they'll be given a choice between helping you or Crawley. It isn't fair or right, but they need a better alternative.'

Arcturus considered him for a moment, watching as the prince slipped the hood over his face and took up a crossbow of his own. In the dim light of the room he could have been any other rebel.

'Fine,' Arcturus said, struggling to his feet. 'You can come with me.'

'And me,' Alice said.

'No,' Arcturus said. 'You've got a broken arm. Plus, you're a woman.'

323

'I beg your pardon?' Alice said, her eyes blazing.

'Sorry, what I mean is, there's fighting ahead if we're to capture Crawley, and there are barely any women among the rebels,' Arcturus explained hastily. 'At least from what I saw. You'll stand out more, and your arm won't let you fight. It has to be me and Harold.'

'Fine,' Alice said, kicking at the paved ground with her toe.

'You're weak,' Elaine said, tugging at Arcturus's sleeve. 'Zacharias should go.'

'And go along with this mad scheme? Not likely,' Zacharias said, crossing his arms.

'It's fine, we'll need my nose anyway,' Arcturus said, pulling his bloodied shirt over his head and using it to wipe away the worst of the blood. 'I might be able to smell Crawley out. We should hurry though.'

With Alice's help, Arcturus managed to remove the shirt from one of the dead guards. It smelled of sweat and charred cloth, and was at least two sizes too large for him, but he cinched it beneath his belt.

'Good luck,' Edmund said, forcing a weak smile. Arcturus grasped the noble's hand and winced at how cold and clammy it felt. The boy needed help soon.

'Come on,' Harold called, already in the corridor. Ulfr followed, his face grim with apprehension.

Arcturus ordered Sacharissa to stay and protect the others, and received a reluctant acceptance in his consciousness. Then he was gone into the gloom. Gone to catch a traitor.

48

They stood among the puddled blood where Arcturus had fought his battle with the three guards. It was sticky underfoot, and Arcturus tried not to look at it as he closed his eyes and concentrated.

Again, his head was filled with the cacophony of conversations, mixed with the snores of a hundred men. The sounds swirled around him in a deafening hum.

He took in the smell of sweat and the metallic, bitter scent of blood from below. It was overpowering and he struggled to sift beyond it and seek what he was looking for.

Cologne. The same cheap perfume Crawley had used to cover the reek of gasoline. This would have been after he had set fires in Corcillum, if Arcturus had guessed correctly. It was there, on the very edge of the myriad of fragrances seething around him.

Then he heard it. Another roar of pain, the same one he had heard in the corridor after his battle. Only this time he knew who it was.

Sergeant Caulder.

Torn between the mission and his pity for the grizzled sergeant, Arcturus felt his mind would split in two as he sought to pinpoint the smell.

'There's only one way,' Harold said, propelling Arcturus along with a gentle shove. 'We can't wait here all day. Work while we walk, the smell will only get stronger.'

Arcturus could not argue with that logic, so he walked on. Now the gloom no longer shrouded them, Arcturus felt as vulnerable as a newborn baby as they walked brazenly into the light. Already he could see men peering at the trio as they walked by, the many doors on either side still left open.

Thankfully, a good number of the rebels were asleep now – they were clearly working on some kind of shift system, and Crawley or General Barcroft must have ordered them to use the corridor to create a gauntlet of men on the way to the Provost's office and the prisoners.

Still, Arcturus's heart beat so hard he felt he might faint as they walked down the corridor, though whether that was from nerves or the blood loss he did not know. Regardless, they made it past Barcroft's quarters undisturbed, stopping at the dead guard propped against the wall. Arcturus felt sick once more, but it was a part of the corridor where there were no nearby rebels, where it was least risky to stop.

Again he concentrated, and now that there was no blood, he could smell the cologne, almost like a trail in the air. The sound of Sergeant Caulder's pain had been reduced to a low moan, barely audible above the clamour of voices around him. And then he realised that the sound and the smell were coming from the same place.

'I think Crawley is directly below us,' Arcturus whispered.

'Follow my lead,' Ulfr said, 'and Prince, do not speak unless absolutely necessary. Your accent will give you away.'

Ulfr strode ahead before they had a chance to reply, so instead they hurried after him. A sleepy rebel stumbled by, rubbing his eyes and yawning. Arcturus withdrew deeper into the hood until he could only see the ground and Ulfr's hobnailed boots stomping their way towards the atrium.

'Come on,' Ulfr growled. 'Mr Crawley doesn't like to be kept waiting.'

He was speaking for the benefit of the rebels around them, for suddenly Arcturus was walking down the winding staircase, catching a glimpse of the iron railings of the atrium's floors on either side. He knew the crossbowmen were behind him now, still lined up in the shadows, and wondered at the discipline these men showed to keep so still and silent. These must be soldiers, well trained in the art of ambush and warfare.

It meant one thing – each and every one of them would be deadly with a crossbow. If they had to fight their way back, it would be like walking into a swarm of steel-tipped death.

They turned on to the new floor. Arcturus was filled with blessed relief when they passed into the confines of the corridor, away from the next row of waiting crossbowmen. This time, almost all the doors were closed.

'Is it this one?' Ulfr asked, and Arcturus was forced to pull back his hood to see the dwarf pointing at a steel-braced door.

Arcturus took a deep sniff and nodded. 'Sergeant Caulder too,' he whispered.

'What's the plan?' Prince Harold asked.

'I was kind of hoping you'd have one,' Arcturus replied.

'Crossbows,' Ulfr said. 'Crossbows and confidence.'

Then he kicked open the door.

Inside was a small, dark chamber, almost no larger than the storage room Arcturus had been kept in. There was a single source of light – a flickering candle on a low table, illuminating a row of gleaming implements on a red cloth beside it.

There were the dim shapes of two men in the room, standing on either side of a third man, tied to a chair. Arcturus aimed at the man closest to him, and Harold did the same.

'Took you . . . long . . . enough,' the third man gasped.

It was Sergeant Caulder. His face was a mess of yellow-tinged bruising and his chin was crusted with red from where his lip had been split. The fingernails on his hands were gone, and Arcturus tried not to look at the pair of cruel metal pliers clutched in the torturers' hands.

Crawley was one of them, while the other was a hunchbacked old man with a scraggly beard and a toothless mouth.

'Step away from him,' Prince Harold barked, jerking the crossbow.

'You . . .' Crawley said, staring at the three of them.

'You'll be quiet, or I'll put this through your head,' Arcturus growled, with as much confidence as he could muster.

Ulfr hurried forward and sawed at the sergeant's bonds where his arms, legs and neck had been tied to the high-backed chair.

'I should have known,' Crawley hissed, staring down at the dwarf with venom in his eyes.

Ulfr glanced up at him, then struck Crawley between the legs

328

with a clenched fist. The steward fell to his knees, clutching himself.

'Always wanted to do that,' Ulfr said cheerfully.

Sergeant Caulder stood shakily and gave Crawley a kick in the ribs for good measure.

'Careful, we need him,' Arcturus said, wincing as the steward keeled over with a grunt.

'Do we need him?' Sergeant Caulder asked, nodding to the other torturer.

'No,' Prince Harold said.

'Good,' Sergeant Caulder said. 'Kill him.'

'Wait—' the torturer began. Prince Harold's crossbow juddered and the man was kicking and twitching his way to hell.

'He . . . he deserved it,' Prince Harold muttered, staring in horror at the dying man. Arcturus recognised the doubt and self-disgust in the boy's voice. A moment later, the prince was emptying the contents of his stomach in the corner and Arcturus felt numb when he thought about what they had done.

But what else *could* they have done? It would have been too risky to tie up the torturer. He tried to shake the guilt from his thoughts, but the feeling remained heavy on his heart.

Crawley stared at the dead man through wide, terrified eyes and Ulfr lunged forward and lifted him to his feet.

'If you don't behave, you'll follow him. Understand?' the dwarf snarled, bringing Crawley's face close. The terrified steward nodded hurriedly.

'You'd better be a damned fine actor,' Arcturus said. 'Because you've had a sudden change of heart. The twenty-fourth are going to escort the nobles to a hidden location outside of Vocans, and you're coming along for the ride.'

'Is that the plan then?' Sergeant Caulder said, removing Crawley's hooded cloak from his shoulders and throwing it around his own. 'We're going to walk out in full view with some friendly soldiers?'

'I'm afraid so,' Arcturus replied.

Sergeant Caulder grinned. 'I like it.'

49

Ulfr led the way once more, with Sergeant Caulder and Crawley behind him and Arcturus and Harold at the back, their crossbows loaded and ready to fire should Crawley get any fancy ideas.

All but Crawley and Ulfr wore hoods, which made Arcturus nervous. Though it seemed that the uniform had been designed for anonymity while inciting riots and setting fires in Corcillum, he had not seen many rebels with their hoods up while inside the castle. It was suspicious for three of them to wear them up, but it could not be helped.

Still, with Crawley walking with them, most of the rebels kept their eyes to the ground – it seemed that Arcturus wasn't the only one who found him terrifying.

Arcturus's back prickled with sweat when they finally made it to the ground level and walked on the marble of the atrium floor. Their footsteps echoed loudly, and he knew the eyes of a hundred crossbowmen were upon him as they headed to the double doors in the side of the atrium.

'Open it,' Crawley ordered, and the steward was indeed a

good actor, for his voice was laced with disdain.

Ulfr pushed open the double doors and then they were through into the leather-covered floor of the summoning room.

Then Arcturus stopped in his tracks. For there were not just the dozen soldiers of the twenty-fourth within the room. There were twice that number.

'Seize them,' Crawley cried out, throwing himself to the floor.

But the heavy doors of the room had been closed just in time, and his voice did not filter into the atrium. Even so, the soldiers, who had been sitting cross-legged in groups of three or four, struggled to their feet and stared at the new arrivals with surprise.

'I said, seize them,' Crawley shouted. 'Or there will be consequences!'

He was rewarded with a quick kick to the face from Sergeant Caulder. Arcturus lowered his hood and stepped forward.

'Where are Rotter, and Sergeant Percival?' he asked.

Rotter shouldered his way to the front of the crowd and hurried to join them. He ruffled Arcturus's hair, and Arcturus grinned, even if it made him look less impressive to the onlooking soldiers. Then Sergeant Caulder and Rotter shook hands, and it seemed to Arcturus that their military ranks were the only thing preventing them from a relieved embrace.

'I'm here,' Percival announced, crossing his arms. 'Here with the thirty-eighth.'

He motioned at the men around him, the soldiers Arcturus did not recognise.

'They wandered in here, just like us. But Barcroft doesn't trust the men who didn't head for Corcillum as ordered.'

'Nor should he,' Crawley snarled, his voice muffled from

where he was holding his injured nose with his hands.

'Why did you come here?' Arcturus asked, pointing to a second man with the sergeant's chevrons on his shoulder. 'To join the rebels?'

The man simply shook his head, as if he did not know the answer.

'We want no part of this,' Percival said, his voice almost despairing. 'We didn't start this war.'

'You're in this,' Crawley hissed. 'Whether you like it or not. And it's time to pick a side. This pack of fools and their forlorn hope, or an organised army of rebels with the imprisoned heirs of the nobility as insurance.'

'The heirs have escaped and are waiting on the top floor,' Arcturus said. 'We need you to escort them out of here, as if Crawley had ordered you to take them to a new secure location.'

Crawley began to speak, but a warning growl from Rotter silenced the man. Arcturus turned to Percival. It seemed the other sergeant was deferring to him, and the men were watching Percival's face expectantly.

'That is a lot to ask of us,' Percival said.

'Help us, and the rebellion will be over. You could go back to your old lives,' Arcturus argued. 'Give us to Barcroft and you'll have joined them. Then you'll be trusting men like Crawley to do right by you . . . if the rebellion even succeeds at all.'

He knew his argument was weak but he spoke with all the conviction he could muster. The fact was, right now the rebels were winning, and he was asking the soldiers to risk it all for the losing side.

Still, Percival hesitated. Doubt was written across his face as

333

clearly as a page from a book.

'You all know me,' Sergeant Caulder said, stomping in front of Arcturus and addressing the crowded soldiers. 'We've fought together. Lost friends together. Stood shoulder to shoulder while the baying hordes of orcdom advanced to take our lives.'

Arcturus could hear murmured agreement and see nods of approval from the watching soldiers.

'But why do we fight?' Sergeant Caulder said. 'It's not for honour. Not for money. Not for the love of battle.'

He paused.

'It's for our families. For our homeland. Our way of life.'

Scattered applause echoed through the summoning room. Though Arcturus sensed a change in mood, he did not dare to hope. Not yet.

'But the rebels do not stand for that,' he said, pointing at Crawley. 'They threaten you for your obedience. They do not ask, they demand.'

He sighed and stepped closer to them, bringing himself into the light of the torches in sconces on the walls.

'They may call themselves our saviours, and preach freedom from tyranny. But would a saviour do this?'

He lowered his hood and held up his hands, displaying his bruises and mutilated fingertips.

'This is the work of tyrants in the making. These are not good men. They are men who want power for themselves.'

'But King Alfric is no better!' shouted a soldier from the back. Men nodded, and Arcturus's heart fell. 'Why should we risk our lives for that bastard?'

'Don't do it for him,' said a voice from behind Arcturus. 'Do it for me.'

Prince Harold stepped out of the shadows and threw off his cloak and hood. He stared out at the assembled soldiers, letting them see him, see the conviction on his face.

'My father is a bad king,' he stated matter-of-factly.

'Hear hear,' a soldier growled.

'He taxes the poor to build his palace – a temple to his own vanity. He underpays Hominum's brave troops who fight for his safety. He drinks and gambles while the country starves. But I will not be that king. So I make you a promise now.'

Harold took a deep breath, and Arcturus with him – he had no idea what the prince was going to say.

'I will replace him as ruler, as soon as I am free. I will feed the poor, bolster the army and cease construction on that damned monstrosity of a palace. This, I swear. Upon my honour.'

The men stared at him in silence. Then a single man began to clap. Another, then another joined in, until the entire room had burst into applause. Arcturus even heard cheering.

Prince Harold turned to Arcturus with a grin then walked to the men and began shaking their hands.

'Looks like we've got an army of our own,' Rotter said, picking up Crawley by the collar and brushing down the steward's crumpled clothes. 'Got to look presentable when we head upstairs.'

Arcturus watched as the men gathered their spears, shields and crossbows, and the wave of relief he had felt was suddenly replaced with apprehension. This had been the easy part. Now they would walk into the belly of the beast and steal the key to the future of Hominum. In full view of the rebel army.

50

They poured out of the summoning room and formed into ranks and files. Percival bellowed orders, sorting them accordingly in the atrium proper. The sergeant ignored the dark forms in the shadows of the floors above, even when a handful of crossbowmen approached the railings and looked curiously below. It was a brazen display – but if they were going to do this, there would be no half measures.

Still, as Arcturus joined the front of the ranks and began the slow march up the stairs, he could not help but look around and see the terrified faces of the soldiers around him. Sweat beaded on foreheads and nervous hands twisted and tapped spear hafts. He imagined the procession through the eyes of the crossbowmen. Would they notice? Or was he making too much of it?

Perhaps he was, because in those nerve-curdling moments of panicked walking, not a single rebel shouted out or spoke. Even Crawley was silent, doing little more than walking beside Ulfr and Percival. It seemed that Sergeant Caulder's loaded and half-lifted crossbow behind him was more than enough of a deterrent.

Time crawled. Every step was agony, every jingle of metal and whispered word seeming to echo deafeningly down the corridor.

Men watched from their rooms, but Arcturus did not risk looking at them. He simply focussed on putting one step in front of another. They passed the dead rebel, then the Provost's office, and finally the sticky patches of blood that seemed to stink like a charnel house in Arcturus's enhanced nostrils.

Then they were there. Thirty-odd men in double file, arrayed in full battle gear outside the room the nobles had been kept in. He heard Elaine's cry of joy and the hiss to be silent from Alice.

Arcturus saw Edmund being helped into line by Prince Harold, the royal's cloak thrown aside. The flash of Gelert being infused, and then Sacharissa pacing beside him, her blue eyes turned up at Arcturus with adoration. He was forgiven. And he was terrified.

In that moment, it was hard to infuse her again – but it would have been too suspicious to have her in view. She reluctantly stood in the pentacle, and then she was within him once more.

Rotter hurried to wrap bindings around the nobles' hands, followed swiftly by Arcturus. Crawley was harangued to the front once more, whispered orders and threats drifting down the corridor.

Arcturus was so tired. So terribly, terribly tired. The blood loss, lack of sleep and hunger were catching up with him. He wanted to fall to his knees and sleep for a week. But Sacharissa's gentle support in his consciousness bolstered his resolve.

They marched. It was a show now. Percival snarled insults at Prince Harold, while another soldier cursed at Zacharias with a vehemence so passionate that Arcturus almost grinned.

Sometimes acting and the truth were closely intertwined.

'Move it!' Crawley shouted just as they approached Barcroft's headquarters. 'Get the prison—'

Sergeant Caulder's bloodied hand clapped to his mouth, silencing the steward before his voice would be recognised. Crawley had been too cowardly to shout a warning, but too treacherous to remain silent. A master stroke.

Arcturus waited with bated breath as they continued on. But there was no movement. Only the sound of Sergeant Caulder's muttered threats, and a whimper of pain and fear from Crawley as the crossbow bolt was pressed into his spine.

Again they moved through the gauntlet of watching eyes. Now the rebels were riled and they cursed the nobles and Arcturus as the procession passed by. Arcturus didn't want to think of the clamouring noise reaching Barcroft's room. Ultimately, the general was the only man he knew of who could supersede Crawley's orders – he or perhaps some of the officers in the army. Where Crawley fitted into the hierarchy Arcturus did not know, and he suspected Crawley didn't either. But they could use this disorganisation to their advantage.

They reached the balcony and the hundreds of crossbow bolts waiting to be hurled into their backs. Then, down the stairs. Arcturus held his breath, waiting for a challenge. But none came. None at all. In fact, the men did not even shout a curse or shift from their positions. They were like living statues, disciplined to the last.

The double doors loomed on the bottom floor. Arcturus's heart leaped as they creaked open, Ulfr heaving them apart with the brute strength of his stocky arms. The men were moving quickly now, eager to escape the waiting ambush.

For once, Arcturus welcomed the biting wind that snatched at his cloak and the grim darkness that enveloped them. They had made it.

'Stop them!'

A scream from above. Barcroft, leaning out over the balcony, a trembling finger pointing at them. The tramp of a hundred rushing feet rumbled.

'Shut it, now!' Sergeant Caulder bellowed.

The doors began to close, ever so slowly.

'Shields!' Percival called.

A dozen men responded to the order, the rearguard turning and kneeling in one smooth motion. Bolts whistled, and Arcturus heard the thunder of the impacts, turning the upraised shields into pincushions of splintered wood. Then the doors crashed closed and they were in pitch darkness.

'Hellfire,' Prince Harold cursed.

Ulfr shoved his way through the shield men, and Arcturus heard the jingle of keys in the lock.

'It won't hold them for long,' the dwarf called. 'We need to move. Now!'

Rotter picked up Edmund, for the boy was barely able to walk, and then it was a mad, bone-juddering rush from the paving stones of the courtyard to the drawbridge. Behind, Arcturus could already hear the pounding of fists on the doors. The rebels would catch up too soon.

The wood of the bridge creaked and shook as the soldiers sprinted across it. For a moment Arcturus thought the platform would snap in two, but then he was across on solid ground once more, and there was Ulfr, leading the way into the low, grassy hills that surrounded Vocans.

Then he stopped. The drawbridge.

That was it.

Arcturus turned and used the last dribble of mana in his body to power up a wyrdlight, barely larger than a firefly. In a rush, he summoned Sacharissa, the pentacle fizzing as her dark form flared into existence. Then he was running across the bridge once more, his axe drawn.

At the base of the bridge, the light revealed two iron hinges embedded in the wood, though the mechanisms were so rusted that it looked like they had not been used in years. These kept the bridge attached to the castle, along with the two thick ropes on the end that raised and lowered the enormous rectangle of wood.

Arcturus drew his axe and hammered it down, sending a shower of sparks flying across the dark water. The light revealed a smear of bright metal where he had damaged the hinge. Barely a scratch.

'Think,' Arcturus cursed.

Sacharissa whined behind him and Arcturus ordered her to begin work on the nearest rope. She snarled and went at it with a vengeance, leaving him to his dilemma.

Beyond, Arcturus could hear the hammer of weapons against the main doors of Vocans. Holes were appearing in the planking, casting beams of light across the courtyard. He had but a few minutes.

He slashed again in desperation and missed completely, instead sinking the blade into the wood itself. It bit deep and was almost stuck, the water-rotted wood splintering easily beneath the cold edge of his steel.

'Wood,' Arcturus whispered.

He wrenched the axe free and chopped down once more, hacking in the dark at the wood that surrounded the hinges. Behind him, there was a snap as Sacharissa's teeth parted one of the taut ropes holding the bridge in place. It lurched to the side, and he fell to one knee.

'Arcturus!'

His name drifted on the wind – someone in the escape party had noticed he was missing. No time for that now. The first hinge broke free from the surrounding wood with a crack, loosened by the shifting bridge. He began on the next one, swinging with wild abandon.

A bolt fluttered past his head, so close that he heard the thrum of its flight loud in his ear. As the atrium doors fell apart, men were firing through a large gap in its centre.

Arcturus sent the wyrdlight flitting there, even as the next man aimed through the hole and fired. The light danced in front of the shooter's eyes, dazzling him, while Arcturus was shrouded in gloom once more. The bolt went wide, clattering into the courtyard wall to his right. Arcturus swung again.

The wood of the second hinge crumbled and the jolt sent Arcturus sprawling, just in time to avoid another bolt that might have skewered him through the shoulder. He crawled for the last rope, where Sacharissa had gnawed it through to the final twisted strand. The platform was in the moat now, but held half-floating in place by this last pulley.

'No!' a rebel yelled, seeing what Arcturus was about to do.

Arcturus swung one last time and felt the bridge was afloat. He sprawled face first to balance it and sent an order to Sacharissa, who dove into the black water and gripped the edge of the drawbridge with her teeth. Even with his weight alone, the water seeped over the edges and on to the front of his shirt. It would not bear the weight of more than a man at a time without sinking.

Sacharissa ignored the pain of her injured ribs, pummelling the water with her feet. Slowly, the long, flat piece of wood floated to the side, out of reach of where someone might pull it back into position and slowly crawl their way across. Arcturus sheathed his axe, and when they had floated a long stone's throw from where the bridge had been, he leaped across, soaking his breeches as he scrabbled against the steep edge of the moat and pulled himself up by handfuls of weeds and grass. Sacharissa clambered out beside him, shaking herself dry in a spray of murky water.

The last-ditch efforts of the crossbowmen thudded into the grass where he had been before and Arcturus laughed at the screams of rage from within Vocans.

Then he was gone. Into the darkness.

51

It was easy enough to find the group's trail – too wet and exhausted to concentrate and pick up the scent, Arcturus simply followed Sacharissa.

He caught up with them within a few minutes, for they had been slowed by Elaine. She was being carried by a big-boned soldier and fighting tooth and nail to go back and get Arcturus.

'Easy there,' Arcturus said, as she jumped free and hugged him tightly. But soon he had to pry her away and take her hand as the group had not waited for their reunion but continued their flight across the rolling hills of southern Hominum.

They were travelling in pitch darkness, for torches would make an easy beacon for any pursuers to follow. So they cursed and stumbled on, skinning their hands and legs on loose rocks as their route twisted into the untamed countryside, away from the pastures and fields.

Finally, Ulfr gave them a brief respite, laying down on his back and waving at the others to take a breather. The dwarf had pushed himself hard, for his shorter legs made him a poor runner.

'Where the bloody hell were you?' Sergeant Caulder panted as Arcturus and Elaine caught up with him.

'I cut loose the drawbridge,' Arcturus said, collapsing beside the veteran soldier.

'Damned fool thing to do,' Sergeant Caulder replied. 'You'd have died if they'd made it through before you'd finished.'

'It bought us more time than we had,' Arcturus said, finally managing to prise his hand away from Elaine's. 'It will take them a while to get enough men across – and I reckon they'll need to wait for at least fifty before they're confident they could beat us. We might have a half-hour's start on them, depending on the number of swimmers they have.'

'We'll see,' Sergeant Caulder grunted. 'The dwarf won't tell us where we're going. But he says we're close. I'll believe it when I see it, though. Even if we go underground, the dogs can follow us in. They'll catch up with us eventually.'

'Could we head for Corcillum instead?' Arcturus asked. 'They can't have more than a dozen horses in Vocans's stables. Enough to catch up with us, but not to beat us.'

He gestured at the thirty-odd soldiers sitting around them, groaning with exertion. They had been carrying their heavy shields, spears and crossbows, as well as the mail and surcoats they wore as part of their uniform. It slowed them down, but made them a formidable force.

At this rate, the lightly armoured and armed rebel foot soldiers would catch up to them eventually. Sergeant Caulder's words mirrored Arcturus's thoughts.

'We're travelling too slow, even their men on foot will catch us before we reach the capital. As for the cavalry, they'll ride by us, and tell every damned rebel in Hominum to watch for our entry on the city's edge.'

'So we're going to be caught either way?' Elaine asked.

'That's the long and short of it,' Sergeant Caulder said. 'But maybe the dwarf can pull off a miracle for us.'

Arcturus didn't have time to contemplate that, as Ulfr led them towards what appeared to be a steep hill, its side so sheer that Arcturus wondered why they didn't go around it.

But then he saw it, as the cloud blocking the moon above finally drifted aside. A cave entrance, as wide and high as two men were tall, its depths shrouded in the darkest shadow.

'This is where we're hiding?' Zacharias announced sceptically. 'We've left enough footprints for them to follow us, even without hunting dogs. We might as well be sitting in an open field.'

'Just follow me,' Ulfr snapped, stomping into the cave. 'And keep your mouth shut if it's only going to spout idiocy.'

Zacharias gazed after the dwarf with malice, but did not respond. For a moment the soldiers hesitated, staring into the blackness. Then a light flared, a beautifully warm orange that drew the wet and freezing Arcturus forward like a moth to a flame. Ulfr held a torch high above his head, and in embrasures alongside him, other torches were held in sconces. He lit these with a sweep of his arm and motioned for the nearest soldiers to pick them up. Then he hurried into the tunnel.

'Come on!' Prince Harold ordered. 'They could be on us any minute.'

'You trust this fool?' Zacharias moaned. 'What are these sneaky dwarves up to, hiding torches in caves? They're as bad as the rebels.'

'Then you can stay here and enjoy the rebels' company instead,' Arcturus said harshly, taking a torch of his own and following Ulfr into the cave. He didn't wait to find out what Zacharias would do. Instead, he relished the warmth that the flame gave off and ran headlong behind the dwarf.

Long, blunt cones of stone grew from the ceilings and floors, some even combining to form strange, middle-pinched pillars scattered along the way. Soon the escape party were straggled in a long line in the cave, following the glow of light from those ahead and slowing to make sure that those behind could still see theirs.

The path split more times than Arcturus could count, and Ulfr led them unerringly one way or the other. It was apparent he knew this place, though for what purpose Arcturus could only guess.

'Ulfr, how much further?' Arcturus called.

For all he knew, the rebels were already in the caves behind them. Though, with all of these twists and turns, it was likely that the rebels would become lost – it was hard to track footprints along a stone surface.

Unless they brought hunting dogs with them, of course. Arcturus hoped against hope that they had been in too much of a hurry to bring them – he had not seen, heard or smelled any when he had been inside Vocans.

But if they waited here, they would be found eventually, by dogs or the rebels.

Still, it seemed Ulfr had a destination in mind. Indeed, Sacharissa was becoming excited, for she could sense the sound and smell of something new approaching. Something that

Arcturus craved, for his throat was parched and his body encrusted with sweat, blood and soil.

Water. Sweet, pure, rushing water, roaring like a river at high tide. It felt so out of place in the deep, dry tunnel they had found themselves in. And when Arcturus turned the corner, he could not believe what he saw.

The passage opened up into a cavern as wide and as tall as the atrium of Vocans itself, though the light from their torches barely reached the ceiling. The chamber's centre was bisected by a broad river, perhaps four times as wide as Vocans's moat, carving through the cave floor and disappearing into the cave walls on either side.

But this was not what amazed Arcturus. It was the flotilla of boats that were beached by the river's side. Almost a dozen vessels were arrayed there, long-keeled and broad, with rowing benches down their centres and oars splayed from their sides like insect legs.

'What are these doing down here?' Arcturus gasped, awed by the strange sight.

'They're for the dwarven servants at Vocans,' Ulfr explained, hurrying to the nearest craft and examining its bottom.

The soldiers behind Arcturus began to emerge from the tunnel behind him, and the air was abuzz with wonder at the strange underground craft. One even had a mast and furled sail, though what purpose it served in the still underground was unclear.

'But why?' Arcturus asked. 'Surely you can walk.'

'By law, dwarves may not congregate in groups larger than three,' Ulfr said, shrugging his shoulders. 'We cannot travel together when making the walk to Corcillum. At least, not in enough numbers to deter robbers and bandits – or drunken humans looking for a fight. We travel together in these instead, away from prying eyes. It's much faster . . . though rowing them back is always a nightmare, with the current against us.'

Arcturus shook his head, disgusted that he was fighting for the man who had created such a law. Even if in truth he was fighting for his friends.

'Come on,' Ulfr shouted, heaving against one of the smaller boats. 'Get these in the water, or the rebels will use them to follow us.'

Arcturus let the soldiers do the hard work, instead sitting on the damp ground and hugging Sacharissa as tightly as he could. Her coat was still musty, but the warmth of her body was a great comfort, even if she smelled like a wet dog.

'Leave that one,' Ulfr shouted, as the soldiers began to manhandle another vessel towards the water. 'We'll need that one.'

It was the boat with the sail. The vessel was larger than the other, enough to accommodate all of them at a pinch.

Ulfr cursed under his breath as the boat he was pushing floated into the water, and the current took it into the dark tunnel in the side of the chamber wall.

The dwarf caught Arcturus's eye and forced a smile.

'The river will eventually take them to the sea,' he said, shaking his head wistfully. 'It took us years to build all these. Such a waste.'

'Why do you have so many?' Arcturus asked. 'Surely there are more than enough for the dwarves at Vocans.'

'They're not just for us servants,' Ulfr said, keeping his voice low so only Arcturus could hear. 'In fact there are not enough of them for their true purpose.'

Arcturus shuffled closer.

'If King Alfric ever chose to exterminate the dwarves, our entire population could use them to escape,' Ulfr explained.

'But how?' Arcturus asked, horrified that Ulfr thought that was even a possibility. 'Wouldn't they have to walk here first?'

'No,' Ulfr said, 'because the river leads somewhere else before it reaches the sea.'

'Where?' Arcturus asked.

Ulfr smiled.

'The Dwarven Quarter.'

52

They heard it long before all the boats had been pushed out into the water. The rebel dogs, their barking echoing eerily in the chamber around them.

'Come on,' Ulfr shouted, pushing aside a soldier and lending his strength to the crowd labouring with the next vessel. It scraped slowly into the river, the current twisting its back half along the edge for a brief moment before it spun in completely.

There were two more boats beside their ship, but progress had slowed – Percival had separated a few of his men to form a barrier across the passage they had come in from.

'Again!' Rotter called, leading the remaining men to the next boat.

Arcturus went to join Percival's men, who were formed six men wide, and three men deep. The first row were crouched behind their rectangular shields, while the second row stood, their crossbows levelled at the dark tunnel in front of them. Behind them, a third row held their shields at an angle above the second row's heads, leaving only a handbreadth of space for the crossbows to fire through.

'We're lucky these men are trained in shield craft too,' Percival said, turning to Arcturus. 'I'm not the only sergeant to remember the old ways. This was how King Corwin took Hominum back from the orcs.'

Arcturus was impressed. Though he could only see it from behind, he imagined any man approaching would be faced with a hail of crossbow bolts, then have to fight his way through a wall of solid wood, while death spat at them from between the shields and long spears stabbed low from the first and third ranks.

'It's done!' Rotter called.

Arcturus turned and was relieved to see that all the boats were in the water. Their own ship had been manoeuvred to where the river was most shallow, and it drifted in the current, held in place by a few of the remaining soldiers.

'Hurry,' Sergeant Caulder ordered, helping exhausted soldiers climb over the sides. 'They'll be here any minute.'

The sound of thudding wood made Arcturus turn. A crossbow bolt had flown from the darkness, burying itself in a shield in the front rank.

'Fire!' Percival bellowed.

The twang of crossbow strings sent a volley into the dim darkness, and the sergeant was rewarded with a scream.

'Back,' Percival shouted. 'To the ship.'

As one, the men eased back, still in formation. It was beautiful to watch, for they moved in perfect time, and the second row reloaded even as they walked.

351

'One, two. One, two,' Percival chanted, setting the pace. Arcturus crouched behind the third rank, his crossbow loaded, but unable to fire through the formation. Instead, he hurled his torch over their heads, illuminating the inside of the tunnel facing them.

Rebels. There were as many as twenty of them, crouched fearfully behind the rock formations that littered the passageway.

'Fire!' Percival shouted again.

Another volley whistled into the darkness. More rebels fell, their paltry cover giving them little protection. But more were coming around the corner now and a scattering of return fire thudded into the shield wall.

'One, two. One, two,' Percival repeated, and the men took up the chant, making their way back to the relative safety of the ship's high sides.

More bolts whistled above him, and Arcturus realised that Rotter's crew on the ship was firing over their heads. The soldiers had almost reached the ship now.

'Hold fire,' Sergeant Caulder's voice floated from behind. 'Give them cover on my command.'

'All right, lads,' Percival said, his voice low so that the rebels could not hear. 'One last volley, then shields on backs and on to the ship. Three. Two. One . . . now!'

Another volley whipped into the tunnel, then Arcturus barely had time to turn before he was swept up in the rush to board.

'Fire at will!' Sergeant Caulder roared.

Bolts whistled into the tunnels, sending rebels diving for cover. Men hurled themselves over the sides of the ship, and Arcturus fell into the bilges, half submerged in the stagnant water slopping there. Even as he lifted himself, Sacharissa's weight fell on his back and he found his face underwater, then he was lurched on to his side as they were launched into the river and the current took the ship.

He spluttered and struggled into a crouch. Quarrels buzzed back and forth as Percival's soldiers fired over the sides, while thuds reverberated along the ship from the rebels' returning fire.

Then their world darkened, the roof of the tunnel looming overhead. Arcturus snatched a glance at the chamber before it was out of sight. Rebels were streaming in, firing desperately as the ship drifted out of range. At the very back, he saw Barcroft emerging red-faced from the tunnel. The general stared after the ship, then threw his sword to the ground in disgust.

Arcturus sat back and let the soldiers take command. Orders swirled around him, and for a brief moment he closed his eyes, letting the exhaustion overwhelm him. Then someone took his hand and led him to the back of the boat. He tripped and jostled his way over the rowers' benches, before being gently shoved into a hollow at the back of the ship, where a pile of dry sacking was stacked.

Prince Harold let go of Arcturus's hand and tugged some sacking over the exhausted boy.

'Get some rest,' the prince said. 'You've earned it.'

53

Arcturus woke with a start. At first, his eyes saw only darkness, but then he registered the undulating ceiling of the tunnel and he remembered where he was.

'How long was I out?' Arcturus asked, rubbing his head where it had pressed against the ship's side.

'Less than an hour,' Prince Harold said.

The young royal was on the rower's bench in front of Arcturus, heaving at the long oar with another soldier. He looked exhausted, but his eyes were wide and alert. It was bitter cold and as the prince spoke, his breath misted the air.

Arcturus winced as he sat up, feeling the aches and pains of several days on the run. Still, the short rest had given him a new burst of wakefulness. He felt something shift beside him, only to see Crawley, bound and gagged. Sacharissa brought her snout close to the steward's face and growled. He wriggled away, whimpering.

'Did you send a message to your father?' Arcturus asked.

'No ink and paper,' Prince Harold said, shaking his head

miserably. 'They still think we've been captured.'

Arcturus pushed Sacharissa off his lap and stood. The only source of light was a single torch on either end of the ship, and the tunnel seemed to stretch for ever both behind and in front of them. The soldiers were sitting two to a bench all the way down, rowing slowly in the dark water.

At the very front, Arcturus could see Elaine and the others, curled up in the space beneath the prow. Only Alice was awake – tending to Edmund. Even from the other side of the ship, the boy's face looked very pale.

'Ulfr, how long until we stop?' Prince Harold asked. 'I assume there's a way out on the other side? Perhaps somewhere near Corcillum?'

Arcturus turned to see Ulfr perched on the back of the ship. He was manning the tiller, guiding the boat's path by swinging the rudder from side to side. The dwarf did not answer.

'Ulfr, I appreciate what you've done for us,' Prince Harold said, 'and I will never forget it. But this is the third time I have asked you. I need to know where we're going.'

The dwarf looked away, as if reluctant to speak.

'We're going to the Dwarven Quarter,' Ulfr announced, jerking the nearest soldiers from their reverie of rowing. 'And we'll be there any minute.'

'The Dwarven Quarter?' Prince Harold repeated. 'Is that . . . safe?'

Ulfr stared at him, as if he was scared to speak.

'The rebels won't know you're there,' Ulfr replied. 'These boats could have belonged to anyone, as far as they know. You'll be safe there.'

'What about the dwarven elders?' Prince Harold asked, his face suddenly panicked. 'Will they shelter us . . . or use us?'

'Use you?' Ulfr growled, affronted by the idea.

'There's a war being fought up there,' Prince Harold said, taking a deep breath. 'Hominum's whole political system is on the edge of collapse. With us in their hands, the dwarves would have leverage over both sides.'

'If you hadn't noticed, you've got a small army with you,' Ulfr snapped. 'And our men are not trained warriors – we'd lose twice your number to capture you.'

Harold opened and closed his mouth, unable to answer.

'And you're more trouble than you're worth. If the rebels were to find out we were sheltering you, they'd storm the Dwarven Quarter just to recapture you. Your father would do the same, even if we claimed to be keeping you safe for him. He hates us.'

Prince Harold looked at his hands, ashamed.

'I was scared to tell you because I think the dwarven elders might throw you out, you fool,' Ulfr said, his face red with anger. 'Hurry you out on to Corcillum's streets and stay out of this rebellion.'

'I'm sorry,' Prince Harold said.

'You humans are all the same,' Ulfr said, staring moodily into the darkness.

Then he straightened, peering ahead. 'We're here.'

The boat lurched and Arcturus fell to the side. By the time he had scrambled to his feet, the boat had scraped itself on to a gravelly beach.

They could have sailed by it and barely noticed it in the

darkness, for it was no wider than a man was tall, and there seemed to be nothing discernible other than that small strip of flat land.

'Everybody out,' Ulfr called.

Arcturus gathered his weapons and jumped over the side, landing in the shallows. He winced as his boots filled with water. Sacharissa sailed over him. She landed on the dry sand and gave him a bemused look.

'It's all right for some,' Arcturus grumbled, stomping after her.

It took but a minute for the men to assemble on the beach, stamping and blowing on their hands to stay warm.

'Nobles, if you would,' Ulfr called, motioning for Prince Harold and the others to join him. Arcturus followed, and they stood away from the soldiers.

'We can wait here,' Ulfr said, once they were out of earshot. 'Wait until this all blows over.'

'If our parents don't know we've escaped, the rebels will just keep lying to them and more of Corcillum will burn,' Prince Harold said.

'And Edmund won't last long in this cold,' Alice said. 'None of us will, really. We need shelter.'

Edmund was leaning against her, his black hair plastered with sweat across his forehead. He smiled weakly, unable to speak. Whatever injury the orc had done to his head, it was taking its toll on the poor boy.

'Well then, I can present you to the dwarven council and they can decide what to do with you,' Ulfr said. 'There's nowhere else I can take you.'

'Can't you take us to your home?' Arcturus asked. He had never heard of the dwarven council before that night, but it sounded like a risky move.

Ulfr let out a bitter laugh.

'I live in Vocans now. What, you think they kept a room for me here? We're forced to live in a small circle of land in the centre of Corcillum – there's no space as it is.'

'Family perhaps?' Prince Harold said.

'And put them at risk?' Ulfr said. 'Even if I wanted to, few dwarves own their own homes. Most of us only have a room in a communal dwelling.'

'The dwarven council will want no part in this,' Prince Harold said. 'You said as much.'

'Odds are they will send you on your way,' Ulfr agreed. 'But you'll be on the streets of Corcillum. That's better than you were before, and I'm sure I can find some parchment for you to tell your parents you've escaped. Find shelter there. Surely you have friends.'

'Perhaps . . . I know a few people,' Alice said hesitantly.

'Commoners,' Zacharias interjected. 'We won't know who to trust.'

'Well, we can't stay here,' Alice snapped back. 'It's as good a plan as any.'

There was a sound from Edmund, barely audible over the echoes of their argument.

'What was that, Edmund?' Prince Harold asked. 'Save your strength.'

'Uhtred,' Edmund whispered. 'Uhtred Thorsager. We can trust him.'

'Who's that?' Elaine asked.

'A dwarf,' Alice replied. 'He helped build the secret tunnel under Raleighshire.'

'Do you know him?' Zacharias asked.

Alice shook her head.

'None of us do,' she said. 'But Edmund's father must have faith in him, to trust him with such an important secret.'

'Can you take us to him?' Prince Harold asked, turning to Ulfr.

The dwarf thought for a moment, stroking his beard.

'He owns his own workshop and home. He's a wealthy dwarf, especially for one so young . . . a blacksmith, if I remember correctly.'

'Can you take us?' Prince Harold repeated.

Ulfr sighed.

'Follow me,' he said.

54

There was a crack in the wall – just wide enough to fit a man. They would never have noticed it, for the outside was covered in lichen, but Ulfr swept it aside and beckoned them through.

The entire group followed, the sound of the soldiers' marching echoing like a drum in the depths of the tight tunnel. Inside, it was somehow colder still, and the path was so twisted that the torches did little to illuminate their way. The soldiers cursed as they passed through, but a bark from Sergeant Caulder silenced them once more.

Still, they pressed on despite their complaints, eager to finally reach somewhere warm and safe. As they travelled, Ulfr would stop and peer at dwarven runes carved into the walls. Their path split and split again until Arcturus thought that Ulfr had become lost. But finally, signs of life began to appear.

A cart full of rocks and oars laid on its side down one tunnel, while in another, Arcturus saw a metal door embedded in the wall. He passed too quickly to get a good look, but soon more began to appear. Great iron circles built into the rock itself, riveted and reinforced with a criss-cross of bracing along its centre. Each one had more runes written above it, but Ulfr did not stop to look – he wove his way unerringly through the labyrinth, ignoring the dripping water from above and the squeaking rats that skittered from their path.

It was only when Arcturus thought he could not walk any further and would need to ask for rest that they reached it. Another metal door, this one as large and thick as any Arcturus had seen, with a great pile of discarded leather, rusted nails and other such leavings outside it.

'This is it,' Ulfr said, leaning heavily against the wall. 'Uhtred's workshop. We had better hope he is in.'

Behind, soldiers collapsed to the ground in relief, ignoring the dampness and the cold stone beneath them.

'Edmund . . . what now?' Alice asked.

But Edmund did not reply. The boy slipped to the floor, his eyes half closed.

'I'll have the red one,' the boy muttered, reaching out at the ceiling.

'He's delirious,' Alice said, pulling her damp cloak from her shivering body and wrapping it around him.

Arcturus strode to the door and rapped it with his knuckles. He winced, and the metal rang so softly that he wasn't sure he'd heard it. Growling, Arcturus grasped a nearby rock and slammed it against the door with a clang.

'Hello!' he yelled, hitting it again. 'We're here, hello!'

Silence.

'If you don't let us in, we'll die down here,' Arcturus shouted. He battered the door with the rock until the stone crumbled beneath the onslaught. He let the pieces fall to the ground and pressed his head against the metal. It was warm to the touch, and he revelled in its heat.

'You have to be there. You have to.'

Still silence. Then . . .

'Who is it?'

The voice was deep, but muffled behind the thickness of the door.

'We are nobles from Vocans. We have Edmund Raleigh with us,' Arcturus replied, trying to keep his voice loud enough to be heard without announcing that they were nobles to the echoing cave. Who knew what other dwarves might be listening?

The voice took a while to reply, then said. 'How?'

'Ulfr brought us here,' Arcturus replied.

'I have heard Ulfr hates humans,' the voice replied. 'You're lying.'

'Please, Ulfr,' Prince Harold begged, looking beseechingly at the dwarf. 'Tell him.'

Ulfr shook his head and approached the door.

'Uhtred, it's me, Ulfr. We have not met, but I believe you're courting my cousin, Briss. She likes you.'

The door was silent again.

'Truly?' called the voice.

'Open the damned door, it's freezing out here,' Rotter shouted.

Finally, Arcturus heard some movement on the other side. A thumping sound, followed by the clanking of metal. Then the door slowly rolled sideways, and a red-bearded face peered through the gap.

'Ulfr?' Uhtred said.

'Aye,' Ulfr said. 'See.'

Uhtred stared at the dozens of soldiers shivering on the floor outside, and the waxen-faced Edmund collapsed in Alice's lap.

'Come in,' he said, his face a picture of shock.

'About bloody time,' Rotter growled. He hurried to Edmund and lifted the boy on to his shoulder, then barged past Uhtred into the room behind. Arcturus followed and the soldiers piled in, thanking Uhtred with the exaggerated gratefulness of men on the edge of despair.

But Arcturus was not listening, because he was staring at a roaring fire, and the heat was the most blessed thing he had ever felt in his life. He fell to his knees and spread his arms, while Rotter laid Edmund out beside him.

'Some warmth and rest will do him good,' Rotter said, brushing the hair from the boy's forehead. 'And some soup.'

Arcturus took a few moments to let the feeling seep to his extremities again, before turning to see Uhtred standing morosely among the men who had crowded into what appeared to be a forge.

Metal tools and implements laid in neat rows on wooden benches, and half-finished weapons and armour were stacked like kindling in wooden boxes around the room. In the centre, where Arcturus was now warming his back, an enormous furnace roared within a metal pipe that extended into the ceiling. On the opposite side of the room, a door identical to the one they had just entered from was built into the wall.

'What's wrong with Edmund?' Uhtred said, hurrying over and kneeling beside the stricken noble.

'He was hurt fighting the orcs, and the summoners couldn't

363

heal him,' Rotter said. 'The skull may be fractured.'

'It may be brain swelling,' Uhtred said, stroking his beard with a worried expression. 'The cold from outside has probably helped with that, but he's too weak to cool him any further. We must give him rest – there's nothing else we can do for him now.'

Arcturus was finally able to take a look at the dwarf. It was strange, but the dwarf was taller than Ulfr, reaching as high as Arcturus's chest. His arms were heavily muscled, and his shoulders as broad as two men standing side by side. But despite his beard, he looked young. Arcturus would have been surprised if Uhtred was much older than himself.

'What are you doing here? Did you say he was injured by an orc? And who are all these men?' Uhtred asked.

He was looking furtively at the men around him, as if he was already questioning his decision to let them in. Arcturus doubted he would have had Edmund not been with them.

Nobody replied to the dwarf – instead Sergeant Caulder slammed the door shut and twisted the metal wheel that kept it locked into place. Then the tired man collapsed to the ground and put his face in his hands.

'We did it,' the sergeant said. 'Goddamn, but we kept you safe. It's a bloody miracle.'

Arcturus smiled and hugged Sacharissa close. It was true. They were finally safe.

55

They sat in a circle in front of the fire. Arcturus, the nobles, the two dwarves and the three sergeants. As for the soldiers, most lay sleeping, scattered like dolls on a nursery floor. Snores permeated the room as if it were occupied by an orchestra of broken wind instruments. Of the nobles, only Edmund and Alice did not join their war council, instead resting in a makeshift bed of furs and leathers in the corner.

'How's Edmund?' Uhtred asked, as Rotter came back from checking on the stricken noble.

The dwarf was still in a state of shock from what Rotter had told him of the nobles' escape, and they were the first words he had spoken in quite some time.

'Well enough,' Rotter said, his mouth half full. 'He's talking normally again, and Alice is feeding him. Thank you, by the way.'

He waved a hunk of bread in the air as he sat down. Uhtred had disappeared upstairs soon after they arrived and had returned with enough bread and cheese to feed a small army . . . which indeed it had. There was water enough from a tank in the corner, one Uhtred used for dousing when he did his metalwork.

Crawley had been tied to the tank while Sacharissa kept watch over him. She snarled if he so much as even twitched, so the man lay perfectly still, his eyes darting around the room.

'How's it going over here?' Rotter asked.

In the centre of their circle sat a pair of scrying crystals, and the group had been watching them in relative silence for the past few minutes. Even with two crystals, it was not easy for everyone to see, but the image was clear enough from Arcturus's vantage.

Valens was on the move with a note that Prince Harold had written. Now the Mite flitted from rooftop to rooftop, observing the streets below.

To Arcturus's surprise, they seemed relatively calm. In fact, few people wandered the streets at all and those that did seemed to be in a hurry. It was as if a curfew had been put in place.

The morning light was barely blushing the horizon, for it was still the early hours. But one thing did seem out of place. The great pillars of smoke, scattered across the sky.

'Something happened last night,' Prince Harold said. 'Rioting? Or an invasion from the soldiers.'

'They were told to head to Corcillum,' Sergeant Caulder said. 'But who knows what orders they received when they got here.'

'I know,' said the third sergeant. He was seated between Sergeant Caulder and Sergeant Percival, a round-faced man who had barely spoken since they had left Vocans. He had introduced himself as Daniels, but volunteered little more until that moment.

'We went to Corcillum,' Daniels continued, and he had

the good grace to look ashamed. 'We were on our way back anyway when Barcroft's orders arrived. There were riders skirting the southern entrances – they stopped us before we could go into the city. They said they'd occupied the southern half of the capital and we were to make camp and wait for more orders. But there weren't many other squads there; ours was one of the first. We thought it would be safer at Vocans . . . wait it out, you know?'

He shook his head, and Arcturus could not tell if his expression was one of regret or relief.

'Then one of the other sergeants came over,' Daniels said. 'He told us the nobles had gathered their household troops and barricaded themselves in Corwin Plaza. That we'd be assaulting it at the tenth bell the next day. And to expect heavy casualties, but that we would triumph.'

'They're going to attack?' Prince Harold said. 'Are they mad?'

'No,' Uhtred said. 'They have the numbers.'

'If you think that, you're a bigger fool than I gave you credit for,' Zacharias laughed.

'With respect,' Prince Harold said, ignoring Zacharias's words, 'these are powerful summoners, many with their own, trained bodyguards. Even the squads that patrol Hominum's southern border would not be able to beat all of them.'

'The rebels don't need the soldiers,' Uhtred replied. 'They have the people. There are marches in the streets, flags being burned. The citizens don't even realise that there's a rebellion – they think it's a spontaneous protest. Just a mass of angry people gathered around the plaza, singing songs and waving banners. Thousands of them.'

'How do you know this?' Arcturus asked.

'The dwarves have their friends among the humans,' Uhtred said. 'We know what's happening. Some are even rebels who want us to join them. But we will not risk dwarven lives for a human cause. Alfric may hate us, but these rebels may be no better.'

Ulfr cursed quietly. The rebels were winning. He had chosen the wrong side, and now the dwarves would be punished.

'The soldiers are supposed to start the fight, then shepherd the crowds towards the plaza,' Uhtred continued. 'It's a powder keg, waiting to explode. And they will light the fuse in a few hours.'

'The cowards are going to make the citizens fight their battle for them,' Rotter growled.

'Hang on – they said they would attack today?' Prince Harold said, horrified.

'That's right,' Daniels said.

'We have to stop this!' Prince Harold exclaimed.

'So you can protect your inheritance?' Uhtred said, raising an eyebrow. 'There's nothing you can do. The king will be forced to surrender – even a summoner can't defeat thousands. How can someone rule those who refuse to obey him? It is better this way.'

'We were never the key to the rebellion,' Arcturus said, realisation hitting as if he'd walked into a brick wall. 'We were insurance. To make sure the nobles behave after they surrender.'

'You don't understand,' Prince Harold said, wringing his hands. 'You think my father would surrender? He would never.'

'But—' Arcturus began.

'No!' Prince Harold said. 'He would die first. It will be a massacre. Hundreds, maybe thousands will be slaughtered. He is one of the most powerful summoners to have ever lived. His demons will butcher people in the streets. Blood will run in the gutters and half the city will be burned to ash before he's done.'

Arcturus knew it was true. He had seen the cruelty in the man's eyes.

'Our families have charging stones full of mana,' Zacharias scoffed, misunderstanding Prince Harold's tone. 'We'd win, easily.'

'They underestimate his power ... and overestimate his aversion for killing innocents,' Prince Harold whispered.

'Some of our parents would surrender, they wouldn't want to kill citizens ... but I know Alfric would not fight alone,' Josephine said. It was the first time she had spoken since they had left Vocans, and Arcturus looked at her, surprised.

'The Favershams, the Forsyths, the Rooks, and many others. They would join him,' she continued, tears in her eyes.

'And well they should,' Zacharias said. 'Why should they lie down and let the plebs steal our birthright.'

His words were met with grim stares, even from Josephine. The noble lowered his head.

'Maybe we could win,' Josephine whispered. 'But at what cost?'

'So we have to stop it,' Prince Harold said.

He turned to Elaine. She was sitting cross-legged, her tongue sticking out with concentration as she guided Valens over the roofs of Corcillum, oblivious to the conversation.

'Elaine,' Prince Harold said.

She looked up and blinked tiredly.

'I can't find our parents,' she said, her eyes half closed. 'Can you tell me where the palace is again?'

'It's OK,' Prince Harold said, brushing a smear of dirt from her cheek. 'You can sleep now. We don't need to get a message to them any more.'

'Why not?' Zacharias demanded.

'Because the fact that they think we're still captive may be the only thing that stops our families from fighting back when the time comes,' Prince Harold snapped. 'And maybe they can convince my father, if not to surrender, then to retreat, fly away.'

'Wait . . . so we want our parents to just give up?' Zacharias said. 'You're crazy.'

'Would they manage to convince him?' Sergeant Caulder asked, ignoring Zacharias. 'To run away?'

'Maybe,' Prince Harold said with a sigh. 'I don't know. But we can't take that chance.'

'There's nothing we can do, Harold,' Josephine said, touching the prince's shoulder. 'We just have to hope.'

'To hell with that!' Prince Harold growled, clenching his fists. 'We're going to stop it.'

'How?' Arcturus asked. 'We're a handful of novice summoners with no mana, most of us are injured and our forces are a few dozen exhausted men. What could we possibly do to change things?'

Prince Harold smiled. It was a strange, unhinged smile, and there was madness in his eyes.

'We're going to make me king,' he said.

56

'Tell me the plan again,' Arcturus said, as Uhtred strapped the breastplate to his chest. It wasn't that he didn't understand it. But hearing it said aloud made it seem less crazy.

'We'll fight our way to Corwin Plaza and then I'm going to demand my father give up the throne to me,' Prince Harold said.

They were in the room above the forge, where Uhtred seemed to store all his spare armour and weapons. Strangely, there also seemed to be large piles of what looked like bamboo lying around, though for what purpose, Arcturus did not know.

Zacharias and Josephine had reluctantly joined them, while the three sergeants were busy getting the men downstairs ready for battle.

'What good will that do?' Arcturus asked, holding his arms and legs wide so Uhtred could fix a pair of metal vambraces to his forearms and two greaves to his shins.

'We will do it in full view of the crowds,' Harold said, examining the weapons piled in the corner and selecting a fine

371

sword. 'They know I am not the same man as my father. I have always been popular with the people. In fact, many nobles have been pressuring my father to abdicate the throne to me for this very reason – including Zacharias's father. Is that not so, Zacharias?'

Zacharias looked up from where he had been prodding a stack of shields with his foot.

'He has,' Zacharias admitted. 'Everyone knows Alfric is detested by all common folk, and this makes the nobles' position precarious given their allegiance to him. But Harold's public support of the military, and his opposition to the continued construction of the palace earned him a lot of goodwill there. He would make a more stable king than Alfric.'

'So it would appease them?' Josephine asked. She had barely left the stairwell, and in the dim torchlight, her face looked pale and waxen. 'If Harold was made king the crowds would disperse?'

'They'd have to,' was Harold's only reply.

'They had better,' Ulfr's gruff voice called from the stairwell. He stomped into the light, and Arcturus was surprised to find the dwarf had armed himself with a battleaxe and was wearing a brigandine of mail and a steel helmet.

'Are you joining us?' Harold asked.

'Aye, I've got to protect my investment,' the dwarf said. 'Can't leave you lot to mess it up at the last hurdle.'

'Very noble of you,' Arcturus said, drily.

Still, the dwarf's participation made him feel much better. They would need every fighter they could get.

'You're all set for armour,' Uhtred said, patting Arcturus's chest. 'Any more and you'd be too weighed down, but at least you're protected from a crossbow bolt or a sword blow. How about your weapon?'

Arcturus smiled and tugged his axe free from the quiver on his back.

'Good workmanship,' Uhtred said, examining the blade. 'Sharp as a razor too. Have you used it before?'

'I have,' Arcturus replied, though he wondered whether his frantic skirmish in Vocans or chopping at a drawbridge really counted.

'Best you hold on to it then,' Uhtred replied. 'Now's not the time to get used to the weight and balance of a new weapon.'

He handed it back to Arcturus and moved on to help Prince Harold put on his own breastplate.

'I have something to say,' Josephine announced.

Arcturus turned, startled. The girl was looking at her feet.

'I'm staying here with my sister,' she said in a quavering voice. 'I'm not cut out for it. I'd freeze up.'

Prince Harold's face fell. But then he went over to Josephine and hugged her.

'This is my mess,' the prince said, kissing her on the cheek. 'I cannot ask you to risk your life for me. Not when you've been through so much already. The soldiers below, they swore to protect king and country. But you . . . you're just a student. You didn't sign up for this. That goes for you too, Arcturus. And you, Zacharias. I will understand if you don't want to come.'

Zacharias looked at the prince for a moment, then smiled with relief and dropped the sword he had been holding.

'Well, then I'm staying too,' Zacharias said. 'Someone needs to protect the girls when you and the soldiers have gone.'

Arcturus snorted at this excuse, earning himself a glare from Zacharias. He'd take any of the girls over ten Zachariases.

Arcturus saw the disappointment in Harold's face, but the prince embraced Zacharias nonetheless. Then he turned to Arcturus.

'Are you coming?' he asked.

Arcturus hefted his axe. This was no longer about survival, or commoners, or nobles. No longer about friendship, or choosing sides. This was about saving lives.

'Thousands could die if I don't,' he said, looking meaningfully at Zacharias. 'Thousands. Of course I'm coming.'

Zacharias shrugged and led Josephine down the stairs. Harold watched them go with what looked like regret.

'I didn't think Zacharias would back out,' he muttered under his breath. 'Maybe I should have pressed him.'

'So, just us three, then,' Arcturus said, patting Ulfr on the back. The dwarf glowered at him and edged away, then muttered something in dwarfish under his breath.

'Edmund and Alice are both injured, but we'll have their demons fighting with us, at least,' Harold said, though he seemed to be speaking to himself more than anyone else. 'Gelert's ribs are hurt, but Edmund says he can fight.'

'Sacharissa's hurt too,' Arcturus murmured.

He felt a flash of guilt for he could still feel the ache of pain from the loyal Canid in his consciousness. But he doubted he could get her to stay behind, and even if he managed to, it would take every ounce of his concentration to keep her there. She was coming with him, one way or another.

'The soldiers can take as much ammunition as they like,' Uhtred said, rapping Prince Harold's breastplate with his knuckles. 'I'll see if I can't scrounge up some spare helmets too. Other than that . . . there isn't much else I can do, I'm afraid.'

'You've done more than enough,' Harold said warmly, shaking the dwarf's hand.

'I'll go get the troops ready,' Uhtred said.

The dwarf bowed and hurried down the stairs, stopping on the way to pick up a large box of helmets, lifting it with his muscled arms as if it weighed nothing at all. Arcturus only wished that the kind-hearted dwarf was fighting alongside them.

Then the three were alone, standing in the ill-lit chamber. They stood awkwardly.

'Ulfr . . .' Harold said, after a moment's hesitation. 'You should know, I will protect the interests of your people whether you help us or not. I will not forget. These laws my father has enacted . . . I will work tirelessly to repeal them.'

'Harold, do you *want* to fight alone?' Arcturus asked, exasperated.

'Don't worry, boy, I'm coming,' Ulfr said, spinning the axe in his hands. 'I've never been allowed to hit a human before.'

He chuckled, then grew serious as Harold's eyebrows furrowed.

'I appreciate it,' Ulfr said, nodding his head respectfully. 'But you won't be able to do any of that if you can't reach the plaza. And whatever I may think of humans, I don't want thousands of deaths on my conscience. Not when I could have done something to stop it.'

'Thank you,' Prince Harold said, looking up at the ceiling, as if he could see what was happening above. 'I just hope this works.'

57

It was a cold morning. Frost grew on the dark windows on either side of them, and gouts of steam plumed from their mouths as the men marched down the road in formation.

The three sergeants led the way, followed by a column three troops wide and twelve deep. Arcturus, Rotter, Prince Harold and Ulfr made up the rearguard, along with the two Canids, Alice's Vulpid and the prince's demon. Zacharias and Josephine had chosen not to send their demons, and much to Arcturus's disgust, Prince Harold had not pressed the issue. They needed all the help they could get, but the pair would not even send their demons in their stead.

Uhtred guided them out of the enormous tent that covered his underground home, through the gardened grounds of the Dwarven Quarter and into the dingy streets beyond before saying his goodbyes.

Arcturus was not sure what he had expected to appear when the prince had knelt with his summoning leather on the cobblestones . . . perhaps a Minotaur, or a brace of Canids. But instead, a demon he had never seen before emerged into the dim, dawn light. Even now, as they moved towards the distant roar of the crowds in the city centre, Arcturus could not help but stare at it. Harold had called it a Nandi.

The demon possessed the size and characteristics of an overgrown grizzly bear, but with a leaner, more muscular body, enormous, tusk-like canines and a physique that hinted at a speed and ferocity that would far outstrip that of its earthly counterpart.

Arcturus knew they must have made a strange sight, walking down the empty streets in full battle dress with their four demons in tow. But there seemed to be no alternative, no sneaking in dressed as rebels. Elaine's Mite's scouting had shown them that.

The young noble had been angry at not being allowed to join their mission, so they had been forced to reach a compromise. Valens would go on ahead, guided by Elaine in Uhtred's home, and Sergeant Caulder would carry the second scrying crystal so he knew what obstacles they would face.

But even before they had left, Valens had reached the plaza, and it became immediately apparent that disguise was not an option.

The four streets that led to their destination were blocked off. There were as many as a hundred rebels at each one, scanning the crowds for anything suspicious as the people milled back and forth, singing and chanting their protests. It seemed that General Barcroft had warned the rebels of what had happened at Vocans. Disguises might have got them closer before the fighting started, but Prince Harold had decided the benefit of the demons outweighed this thin advantage.

'Prince Harold, are you sure we're going about this the right way?' Ulfr asked, breaking into Arcturus's thoughts.

'Yes, Ulfr,' Harold sighed, sick of belabouring the issue. 'The southern entrance is our only option. There are no crowds there – which means fewer casualties if it comes to a fight.'

'But don't you think that's suspicious?' Ulfr asked.

'It's likely where the soldiers will attack through. Then the men in the other three entrances will incite the crowds to riot and surge towards the square.'

'So we'd better get there before that happens,' Arcturus said.

He grimaced, thinking on the new plan that they had hurriedly devised in Uhtred's tent. Ever since the rebels had occupied the southern half of the city, the narrow street there that led into the plaza had been kept clear for some unknown reason.

There were a few dozen rebels there, well-trained traitor soldiers keeping the crowds from the area, but it seemed the path of least resistance, and the one that would lead to the fewest casualties. So that was where they would go.

A thousand thoughts continued to spin through Arcturus's mind as they marched. All the things that could go wrong. The many, many ways that he and Sacharissa could die. But he could do nothing about them now. Only walk on and ignore the twitching curtains and scared faces in the frost-chilled windows on either side.

'Almost there,' Sergeant Caulder called. 'Another street over.'

Now, Arcturus was beginning to see people, though they did little more than scurry away at the sight of them. They could hear the crowds chanting now, and it had become a maelstrom of noise. Somewhere nearby, the national anthem was being sung, near drowned out by the hundreds of screaming, shouting voices.

Then . . . a flash of light.

'No!' Harold yelled.

Above Arcturus, a giant dome was materialising in the air. The surface was a shining, opaque white. A shield spell, larger than any Arcturus had ever imagined possible, completely covering the plaza. And somewhere else . . . screaming.

'The nobles are throwing up a shield,' Sergeant Caulder yelled. 'We're too late, the rebels must be attacking.'

Arcturus sprinted to the front of the line, his heart pounding in his chest. Prince Harold followed close on his heels, and Sergeant Caulder held out the scrying crystal for them to see.

Valens flew high above the southern entrance, and from the demon's viewpoint they could see themselves, just around the corner from the thin avenue.

And down the centre of that channel that led directly to the plaza, dark forms hurried: a block of black-uniformed men, two hundred or more – it was impossible to tell. The image panned to the side, where the nearby eastern entrance was visible. There, crowds surged forward, a stampede pushed on by scores of dark-cloaked men, like wolves chasing a herd of panicked deer.

'What do we do?' Arcturus said, watching as their plan fell apart before his eyes. 'There's an army of damned soldiers between us and your father. We were supposed to get there before their army attacked.'

Prince Harold simply stared, his head shaking.

'That shield won't hold for long,' he said. 'Thank god someone has some sense in there, it will keep the crowds off for now. But once they break in . . . my father will start the killing.'

Valens had hovered over the dome. Through the scrying crystal Arcturus could see the personal bodyguards of the various noble houses arrayed in battle formation, just inside the walls of the shield. Behind them, King Alfric and his various nobles sat in the plaza's centre, watching the crowds seething against the barrier from a large platform of wood. Even in the small shard of scrying stone, Arcturus could tell the edges were beginning to crack.

'You need to get past those soldiers . . . and use your demon to tear through that shield so you can reach your father,' Sergeant Caulder said.

'Yes,' Prince Harold said, his voice filled with defeat. 'And hope the people will listen.'

'So that's what we'll do then,' Sergeant Caulder growled.

'We're outnumbered,' Prince Harold said, shaking his head. 'I couldn't ask your men to do this. It's suicide . . .'

'You don't have to,' Sergeant Caulder said, straightening his back.

He turned and addressed his soldiers.

'Men, our mission is to cut our way through those traitor bastards and get our future king to the other side of the shield spell. Are you ready to do your duty?'

'Yes, sir!' the men shouted, and Arcturus was struck by how young some of them sounded. Many were barely older than he was.

'Then let's go,' Sergeant Caulder bellowed, turning and drawing his sword. 'For Hominum!'

'Shield wall,' Percival shouted.

There was a clunk of wood as the men formed up, a wall of flesh, iron, wood and leather. Only their eyes were visible beneath their helmets, staring between the metal rims of their shields.

Arcturus could not believe their courage. They were facing impossible odds, yet here they stood, ready to give their lives.

'Get behind us,' Daniels ordered, his voice emerging somewhere deep within. 'You too, Caulder.'

Harold, Arcturus and Sergeant Caulder did as they were ordered, slipping through the thin gap of space left on the edges of the street and joining Rotter and Ulfr with their demons on the other side.

'Forward . . . march!' Percival yelled.

They were going to war.

58

They turned the first corner and the next, their formation impeccably turning on its axis and up on to the avenue towards the plaza. Arcturus felt helpless, walking at the back. All he could do was stare into the scrying crystal in Sergeant Caulder's hand, and watch as the traitor soldiers turned and saw the approaching shield wall.

'Let 'em know we're coming!' Daniels shouted.

Wood clattered on wood as the men drummed their spears against their shields. With each beat, they chanted in unison, a great outpouring of breath.

Hoom. Hoom. Hoom.

Arcturus could feel the sound deep in his chest, and the men stamped forward in time, as if they could shake the very ground with their steps.

Hoom. Hoom. Hoom.

Suddenly, Sacharissa unleashed a howl, the cry so loud and keening that it hurt Arcturus's ears. The other demons joined in, adding to the din, an unearthly caterwauling that would chill the rebels' blood.

The Nandi's roar seemed to rattle the windows of the dwellings on either side of the avenue, and Arcturus heard the sound of locks being turned and bars being lowered on the lower floors, while terrified faces watched from the windows.

'Hellfire, there's a lot of them,' Prince Harold shouted over the din. In the crystal, the rebels milled around, unsure whether to charge. Behind Harold's men's shields, it was impossible to tell if they were friend or foe.

'They don't know how many we are,' Arcturus yelled. 'Give them a taste of steel and they'll run.'

Hoom. Hoom. Hoom.

Their thin line was so close to the enemy, no more than a dozen steps away. Beyond, the shield's surface glimmered and swirled, casting their battlefield in an unearthly glow.

'Fire!' Percival screamed.

Eleven crossbows jerked, and as many rebels were hurled back into the mass. There was panic as the nearest ranks scrambled to retreat, while those behind blocked their path.

'At will, at will!' Daniels ordered.

More crossbows spat, sending rebels tumbling. They were so close. Now Arcturus could hear the first bolts being fired back, thudding into the wood of the loyalists' shields. But in their formation, it seemed they were untouchable.

Arcturus saw the elbows of the third rank jerking as they stabbed between the shields, their long spears joining those of the first as the sides met. Screams of pain echoed down the street, and now Arcturus could hear weapons thudding on wood.

'Step over them and kill the bastards. Forwards!' Percival cried.

Hoom. Hoom. Hoom.

Their chanting was breathless now, but still the men stepped forward. In the crystal, Arcturus saw rebels throwing themselves against the shields, beating at Harold's men with their swords. But the shields of the third rank protected the heads of the first, while the crossbow bolts whistled through the gaps and the double row of spears stabbed and stabbed again.

Bodies began to appear, trampled underfoot. An injured rebel flailed as a member of the third rank stabbed down, ending the traitor's life before joining the shield wall once more.

'No mercy,' the soldier bellowed. 'For Hominum!'

They were winning. The rebels were falling over themselves in their rush to escape the meat grinder that approached them, and the white dome drew ever closer with every step.

But then Prince Harold let out a gasp and Arcturus looked behind him. Scores of rebels were emerging from side streets, a hundred feet behind them.

'Bastards,' Sergeant Caulder called, brandishing his blade. 'Our shield wall will be cut to pieces from behind. It can't turn around.'

Hoom. Hoom.

Arcturus glanced over his shoulder. The dome was so close – the traitor soldiers in front of it were running around its rim into the corners of the plaza, thinning the mass of men that still fought a running battle against Harold's loyalists.

But the shield wall could only move so fast, one step at a time.

'Good thing we're here to protect them,' Rotter snarled. The soldier drew his sword and pointed it down the way they had come, where the new rebels were still massing. It seemed there might have been as many as a hundred dark-clothed men there.

Hoom. Hoom.

'They're disorganised,' Sergeant Caulder called out, shading his eyes. 'Those are no soldiers. They're citizens.'

Now that Arcturus looked, he could see the different colours of cloth, and the weapons held were mostly kitchen knives and lengths of wood.

'No crossbows,' Ulfr said. 'We might just hold them.'

Then, as if some order had been given, the mass of rebels charged.

'Sacharissa, with me,' Arcturus called, firing his crossbow into the approaching mass and watching the bolt disappear into the crowd. Then he threw the weapon aside and tugged free his axe.

'Come on!'

They were four warriors and four demons, a single line against a mass of snarling men and women. But Arcturus didn't have time to be scared, only to step into his place and scream defiance as they met in a clash of metal.

The frontrunners came first, a scattered handful ten feet in front of the others. A screaming man ran at Arcturus with a broom handle. Arcturus did not think, only fell to one knee as it swung over his head and then sliced deep into the man's waist. The man choked and fell, the handle falling from his hands. Sacharissa finished him with a lunge from her teeth, her ribs flaring with pain at the sudden movement.

Then another, a bearded monster of a man armed with a spear, who slowed down, his spear held in front of him.

But another rebel slammed into him from behind, and Arcturus chopped down once, then parried as a third man slashed a cleaver at his head, cutting a sliver of wood from Arcturus's axe handle before Sacharissa opened the rebel's stomach with a slash of claws.

'Come and die,' Harold yelled beside him, his sword red with blood. 'Come and die!'

The Nandi roared, and the nearest rebels slowed, while those behind shoved them forward to be slaughtered. A great swipe from the bear-demon's claws sent two men flying, and then it pulled another from the crowd and savaged him with its jaws.

'Die,' Sergeant Caulder yelled. He and Rotter held the edges, while Gelert and Reynard flanked them. The two men were like dancers, lunging and dodging back and forth, while men fell and writhed beneath the onslaught of their blades.

A terrified man was pushed on to Arcturus's blade as he hacked down, and blood sprayed the air. He had just killed a man, and he felt sick and angry and scared. Yet all he could do was swing again and again, his axe thickening with blood, the rebels pushing back and screaming as the momentum of the mass shifted them ever closer.

'Prince Harold!' Percival called. 'Your way is clear.'

'Hellfire,' Prince Harold cursed, hurling his sword into the crowd. Then he and the Nandi were gone. Arcturus had no time to turn, no time to see how close they were. Only to step to the side to fill the gap that the prince had left.

Ulfr flanked him now. The broad-shouldered dwarf was red with blood, his own axe making brutal work as men darted close to try their luck. A knife scraped across the dwarf's chainmail, and the axe bit deep, sending another rebel shuffling off this mortal plane.

But they were spread thin now and the crowd lurched forward. Arcturus felt the scrape of a blade along his breastplate, cutting a shallow wound in his side before Sacharissa clawed the culprit's legs out from under him. Arcturus finished him with a swift chop, and his arm sang with pain as a length of wood broke itself on the vambrace on his wrist.

'Back,' Sergeant Caulder called. 'Back, damn you.'

A crossbow bolt whistled past Arcturus and into the crowd, taking a rebel in the neck. Arcturus snatched a glimpse over his shoulder. The third rank of the shield wall had turned and were giving them covering fire.

Arcturus did not need to hear it twice. He stumbled over the bodies of dead rebels left in the shield wall's wake, sprinting for the safety of the line.

A cleaver whirled over his shoulder, and a flash of pain from Sacharissa made him gasp. He spun, only to see the Canid limping after him, a spear through her back leg. The rebels surged.

'No!' Arcturus screamed.

He charged, swinging his axe in a wide arc over the Canid's head, sending rebels tumbling away under his onslaught. He stepped over her, and then he was on his back, a broom handle clattering beneath his feet. A man yelled and raised a metal pipe, only to twist away as a bolt skewered his shoulder.

Arcturus rolled aside, felt a flash of pain as a knife slashed his calf, and another broke on his breastplate. He was surrounded.

The world pulsed. Wind, curling around him like rapids

around a boulder, tore through the mass of rebels and sent them flying back.

A shadow fell across Arcturus and he tried to block the oncoming blow with his hand, but instead he felt himself lifted to his feet.

'Hurry,' Elizabeth said, her Peryton tossing its antlers. 'That was the last of my mana.' Her eyes were wild as she gripped Arcturus by the hood of his cloak and tugged him behind her on to the back of Hubertus.

'Sacha,' Arcturus cried, but the Canid was already nearly at the shield wall, dragged there by Gelert and Reynard.

Then the world was falling away. And he was flying.

59

Arcturus couldn't speak, only watch as the world swirled and tilted beneath him. He could see Sergeant Caulder and the troops pouring through a tear in the shield spell's side, while various bodyguards stood by to reinforce them. And within the shield, on the platform, Harold kneeled in front of his father.

'What's happening?' Elizabeth yelled, the wind nearly snatching away her words.

Far below them, crowds pressed against the dome, battering it with their fists and feet. The anger had reached a fever pitch, and he could see the rebel agitators at the back, shoving people forward, screaming and handing weapons out.

'Arcturus, tell me,' Elizabeth said.

Arcturus choked a breath, his mind still reeling from how close he had come to death. But before he could answer, the world turned a shade darker . . . and the shield began to warp into a thousand different strands of white energy. The strands streamed and flickered, twisting their way down into a cylinder of stone, held in Prince Harold's outstretched fist.

It glowed bright red, flashing with an intensity so powerful that every man, woman and child in the crowd turned away or shaded their eyes from the glare.

Far below, as the afterglow of the light faded from Arcturus's eyes, Prince Harold's fingers traced a symbol in the air. And then . . . he spoke.

'People of Corcillum,' Harold said.

His voice boomed out over the city, so loud that flocks of birds burst from rooftops, cawing in protest at the sudden noise. He had amplified it with mana, so that all the crowds could hear.

'I hear you. I . . . Prince Harold Corwin, heir to the throne of Hominum, hear you.'

Silence. Not even a murmur stirred the watching crowds. At the back of all four entrances, Arcturus could see the Celestial Corps swooping over the rebels' heads, threatening them into silence. For now, the frenzy the rebel agitators had whipped the crowd into had dissipated. The shield had done its job, letting the mob expend their energy on its walls.

'Our military is weak,' Prince Harold shouted. 'Their coffers are empty. They fight to keep us safe with dented armour and rusted swords.'

'What's he doing?' Elizabeth hissed. 'He's making them angry again.'

'Just wait,' Arcturus said, as Prince Harold spoke again.

'Our poor starve, and those who work see even the stale crust of bread they can afford taken from their mouths to pay for the palace that we do not want or need.'

Now there were stirrings in the crowd. Furious shouts and

raised fists. The crowds now surrounded no more than a thin circle of bodyguards, and a few began to spit and curse at them, daring them to raise their swords.

'It is a travesty,' Prince Harold shouted. 'An abomination of greed and hubris.'

The crowd screamed back and now Arcturus could see weapons raised in the air.

'Seriously,' Elizabeth said. 'What is he doing?'

'Give him a chance,' Arcturus replied, though he too began to worry. Hubertus floated lower and Arcturus could see the battered prince, his face bloodstained, his eyes wild with exhaustion. What was his plan? Arcturus could not see it.

'Crime is rife. Bandits roam our lands, and the rule of law is flouted by those who can pay for the privilege,' Harold continued.

He stared out at the crowd, letting his words sink in. Behind him, Arcturus could see King Alfric, glowering at the crowds from the platform on his golden throne. Whatever words the prince and his father had exchanged, it seemed the king had agreed to this speech.

'No king who would do this to his own people deserves to rule,' Prince Harold shouted. 'A king who would put his own pleasure before the needs of his people is no king at all.'

The crowd roared in agreement, stamping their feet with approval.

'And I am ashamed,' Prince Harold said, his voice cracking with emotion. 'Ashamed that I did not stop it. For you are my people too . . . and I stood by and watched.'

The shouts of anger faded, as if the crowd did not know how to react to Harold's words.

'So I say, my father's reign is over,' Harold bellowed, pointing at his father for those in the crowd who might see. 'He will never rule again. Never!'

Cheers now, fists pumping the air.

'But who should rule in his place?' Prince Harold said, lowering his voice.

The crowd died down. These were no rebels. Just an angry mob who had suddenly found the target of their anger, the royal family itself, agreeing with them.

They had no alternative . . . they did not even know who General Barcroft was. Most had never even seen the battle fought at the southern entrance.

'So I ask you. No, I beg you. Give me that honour. For I will not let this stand.'

Still, more silence.

'The palace tax will be lifted and the gold from our own royal coffers will bring our military back from the brink,' Harold promised. 'A new police force shall be formed to keep our lands safe. The poor shall be given work, and the lawless shall be imprisoned.'

He took a deep breath.

'And I swear to you, I will never fail you again. Because I have heard the voice of the people and I will never be deaf to it.'

It began with a clap. Somewhere at the back, alone in the quiet. Then another person joined in, until the smattering turned into a flood. People cheered, and Arcturus could almost feel the tension leaving the crowd.

He laughed and felt tears flow down his face as he realised it was over. They had done it.

This was not a joyous celebration, nor was there a palpable enthusiasm that took hold of the crowd. At worst, it was polite applause, at best one of relief. But it worked.

It worked.

60

Arcturus sat in the waiting room, sinking into the plush red seat of his armchair. It was heaven . . . Just to sit down. To be warm and safe. To have friends, to be alive.

He was in the palace. Elizabeth had flown him there after healing his and Sacharissa's wounds. He had infused the demon so he could bring her with him, but now Elizabeth had taken her leave and he had forgotten to ask her for her summoning leather. Still, the Canid seemed happy enough within him, even if he wanted to hug her close and sleep for several days.

Finally, after an hour of waiting, several others had joined him, also at Prince Harold's request. Or rather, King Harold.

Not all the soldiers were there. Seven had died in the fighting, while another four were too injured to attend. Rotter was one of the wounded, though Sergeant Caulder had assured Arcturus that the young soldier would be back on his feet in no time.

Strangely, none of the nobles were present. Only the commoners – the three sergeants, the soldiers and Arcturus, all sitting and waiting for their audience with the king. And Ulfr was there too, wringing his hands nervously, his short legs swinging above the floor.

So Arcturus waited, looking at the sumptuous marble floors, the velvet curtains that separated each room, and the grand set of double doors that led to the throne room.

'Do you think he's going to give us a reward?' one of the soldiers asked.

'I'll reward you with a boot up your arse if you're thinking of asking for one,' Sergeant Caulder growled, though he spoke with a good-natured smile.

There was a creak and the doors swung open, held by two heavily armoured guardsmen.

'Finally,' Arcturus said, getting to his feet. 'Come on, Ulfr. You too.'

Arcturus put his arm around the dwarf's shoulders, and to his surprise, the dwarf didn't push him away. There was a smile on his face – one of triumph, and pride.

They walked together through the double doors, leading the way into the high ceilinged throne room. A red carpet led up towards a raised dais, upon which two thrones sat. On either side, great pillars held up the ceilings, and a skylight allowed the morning sun in.

It was a sight to behold, but Arcturus took little time to enjoy their surroundings. Because it was not Harold sitting on the throne . . . but Alfric.

'Come on,' the old man called, beckoning them forward. 'We haven't got all day.'

Arcturus felt a rush of relief to see Harold on the smaller throne beside Alfric's. What had he expected, that the old king would just disappear? Perhaps this was the official ceremony, where the crown was passed from one king to another.

As he drew closer, Arcturus saw nobles lined up beside the throne, confirming his theory. Though, to his dismay, he could see Ophelia Faversham there, as well as Provost Forsyth, prominently seated closest to Alfric.

The group stopped in front of the throne and King Alfric leaned forward and examined them over steepled fingers.

'I was wrong about you,' Alfric finally said, his cold eyes flicking between Arcturus and Ulfr. 'You common summoners are perhaps useful after all.'

He clicked his fingers.

'Obadiah, how goes your search.'

'Well enough, my lord,' Obadiah said, bowing low. 'There are more like him, scattered across the land. Vocans will have new students soon.'

'Good,' Alfric said, then pointed at Arcturus. 'You can stay there too, boy. And you can live. That is your reward for the loyalty you showed me today.'

Arcturus felt the blood draining from his face. This was not how he had imagined this meeting would go.

'Harold . . .' Arcturus said.

Harold shook his head silently, as if to tell Arcturus to hold his tongue. But Arcturus would not.

'Who is king here? You or your son?' Arcturus demanded.

'Did I ask you to speak?' Alfric shouted. 'Hold your tongue, before I have it cut out.'

Arcturus could not believe what he was hearing. Ophelia grinned as the two guards stepped in front of Arcturus, forcing him back.

'Since you *must* know,' Alfric continued icily, once he had settled back in his chair. 'We have been planning this "transfer of power" for some time now, is that not so, Obadiah?'

'Just so, my lord,' Obadiah said, bowing his head.

'Only we had to do it a little earlier than I had planned. No matter, there is gold enough left to finish the palace.'

With every word Alfric spoke, Arcturus felt his happiness shrivel and die.

And he remembered. Obadiah, in the hospital wing at Vocans. Telling him exactly that. How the people were angry at Alfric . . . and that Harold might have to take power. But at the time, Arcturus didn't understand that it would be a ruse. That it was all a trick.

'Father, you promis—' Harold began, but Alfric lifted a hand, silencing him.

'We *agreed* you would be king,' Alfric sighed, speaking as if to child. 'Not that you would hold the king's power. You are far too young for that.'

'I must learn to rule by ruling,' Harold argued. 'Father, I am not a puppet.'

'And so you shall learn,' Alfric said, smiling broadly. 'I have appointed a council for you. To advise you, and vote on all matters of state.'

King Alfric gestured at the nobles around him. 'They will serve you well, and I shall be there to guide them, of course. It has all been ratified in the law. The people will accept that, since you are so young, and they will trust you are in good hands.'

Harold's face whitened and Arcturus knew that there was no hope. What could he do?

'And what of the dwarves?' Ulfr demanded. 'What concessions shall you make for their hand in saving your son?'

Alfric's face darkened as Ulfr spoke.

'Who invited this ingrate?' he spat. 'Get him out of here.'

'I did, father,' Harold said, standing. 'He is a friend and we will treat him as such. I owe him my life, as do many in this room.'

'I risked my life for your son,' Ulfr said. 'The rebels offered us equality if we joined them, and we turned it down to save you.'

'You did your duty as a loyal citizen of Hominum,' Alfric scoffed in reply, gesturing for the dwarf to be taken away. 'You've admitted that your people were tempted. You should be thankful we let you live at all.'

The guards grabbed Ulfr by the shoulders but the powerful dwarf resisted, holding steady as they tugged at him.

'You promised,' he hissed, pointing at Harold with a trembling finger. 'You swore to me.'

'I will keep my promise,' Harold replied, his eyes wide. 'As well as I can, I swear it.'

'Liar!' Ulfr yelled, as the guards finally dragged him down the carpet. 'You lying son of a—'

A punch from a guard knocked the dwarf unconscious, the gauntleted hand thudding with a sick sound.

'Give him a beating,' Alfric ordered lazily, leaning back in his chair. 'So he learns his lesson.'

He looked on for a moment, then shouted. 'And wait until you're outside – I don't want blood on our new carpets.'

Arcturus glared at Alfric and the old king laughed at his expression.

'You should never trust a dwarf,' he said. 'Forget him. He picked the right side and nothing more. But he must be punished for speaking so impertinently.'

He sighed distractedly and turned to Lady Faversham.

'Ophelia, how goes the interrogation of the steward?' he asked.

'We have the names,' Lady Faversham replied. 'He gave that one's name as well.'

She pointed at Arcturus.

'I vouch for him,' Harold said swiftly. 'Crawley would say anything under torture.'

Lady Faversham narrowed her eyes, then shrugged and continued.

'Before nightfall, every rebel leader will be captured. By tomorrow night, we will have more names from them. It is a good thing Harold promised to imprison criminals – our prisons shall soon be overflowing with them and their families.'

She laughed, and it echoed hollowly in the open space around them.

'Of course, the soldiers have already surrendered, and General Barcroft committed suicide as soon as news of his failure reached him. But the others . . . we'll find them, imprison them, and throw away the key.'

'And the battle scene, has it been cleaned up?' Alfric asked.

'Not a speck of blood,' Ophelia said. 'If all goes well, the people will not even know there was anything close to a rebellion. Only a simple protest that took a turn for the worse, followed by a peaceful transfer of power.'

'Good,' Alfric said, clapping his hands and standing. 'Then that concludes today's council meeting. Come on, I have prepared a feast to celebrate.'

'Father,' Harold interrupted, raising his voice. 'Are you not forgetting something?'

Alfric paused, then clapped a hand to his head and looked at the soldiers who had been watching the proceedings in horror.

'Of course. Thank you for your service, men. You're good lads. Very good lads.'

He turned to Harold and cocked his head.

'Happy?' he asked. Harold nodded curtly, and Alfric strode away, heading for a door behind the thrones. The nobles trailed after him and a moment later the door slammed, leaving the room in silence.

Only a servant remained, his back straight, eyes staring straight ahead.

'Kercher, find those guards and stop them from beating that dwarf, on my orders. Hurry,' Harold commanded, pointing at the double doors. The servant scurried off and a few moments later the doors slammed shut.

Harold sighed and walked over to the throne Alfric had been sitting in. He sat down heavily and pressed his fingers against his eyelids.

'I didn't know,' he said, shaking his head. 'I'm so sorry, I didn't know.'

Arcturus walked over to him and put a hand on the boy's shoulder. For that was what he was . . . a boy. It was easy to forget sometimes.

'Things can be better now,' Arcturus said, though he himself

401

struggled to believe his own words. 'You have some power. You can make a difference.'

'With those lackeys on the council?' Harold said, gesturing over his shoulder. 'They're the worst of the worst. I'll never make things better for anyone.'

'You made some promises in your speech that they will be forced to keep if they want to avoid another uprising,' Arcturus said firmly, 'and if you bide your time, you will be able to change things. Don't despair.'

Harold looked up and smiled at Arcturus, and Arcturus saw the new king's eyes were filled with tears.

'You're a braver man than I, Arcturus. I am glad to have you on my side.'

'Always, my king,' Arcturus said.

Harold wiped the tears from his face and stood.

'Sergeant Caulder, Sergeant Percival, Sergeant Daniels. Kneel,' Harold commanded.

The three men knelt before their king while their soldiers looked on, bemused.

Harold drew his sword, and for a brief moment of madness, they looked at him with fear in their eyes. Was he killing them, to keep this silent?

'My king, we would never tell anyone about . . .' Sergeant Caulder began.

'Quiet, you idiot,' Harold said affectionately. 'I may be powerless but I can still do this.'

He laid his sword on the sergeant's shoulder and spoke three words.

'Rise . . . Sir Caulder.'

61

'Arcturus, Provost Forsyth wants to see you,' Elizabeth said, knocking on Arcturus's door and poking her head in.

It had been two weeks since the battle and Arcturus was finally getting used to being back at Vocans. He had hoped it might be Ulfr knocking on his door but he had not seen the dwarf since their return.

Harold assured him that the dwarf was unharmed, even if he now hated humans more than ever.

'Do you know why?' Arcturus asked, looking up from his desk.

'He didn't say,' Elizabeth replied, biting her lip. 'But he seemed in a good mood.'

'That could mean anything,' Arcturus sighed, putting aside his quill and blowing on the scroll he had been writing on. It was a treatise on the anatomy of the Nandi, and it was due to be handed into Scipio within the hour. Now it would be late.

It was strange to be back in class. He had thought that the memories of their escape from Vocans would tarnish the place, make it seem darker.

Yet somehow, the old castle seemed even happier than it had been before. No more Crawley, no more doubts about his place in the world. Sure, Zacharias was still there and hated Arcturus with the same passion as before. But he had friends now, and not just Elaine and Elizabeth.

'Mind if I walk with you?' Elizabeth asked.

'Sure,' Arcturus said.

Arcturus had finally been moved from his cold little space in the tower. Not because of special treatment, but because it was being renovated to accommodate the common students who would be arriving any day now.

Of course, there was plenty of room for them elsewhere in the castle, but Provost Forsyth had decided they should not be treated the same as nobles. He didn't want them getting any ideas above their station.

What that meant was that Arcturus was now temporarily in the east wing, so the walk to the Provost's office was not a long one, just a single flight of stairs and a walk down the central corridor of the top floor.

'So . . . we haven't had a chance to talk,' Elizabeth said as he joined her out in the passageway. 'Are you OK?'

Arcturus shrugged and looked at his feet.

'Edmund is fully recovered, and none of my friends died,' he said, thinking of Rotter. The soldier had come by to pay his respects a few days before, but since then nobody seemed to know where he had gone. He would miss the rascal.

'Is Sacharissa recovering well?' Elizabeth asked.

Arcturus smiled and felt Sacharissa twitch with recognition at her name within his consciousness.

'As well as can be expected,' he replied. 'She hates being infused, but I need to keep her that way so she heals faster. I'm told she'll make a full recovery.'

They turned on to the balcony, and far below Arcturus saw Elaine and Scipio. She was clapping her hands with delight, and above her, a ball of opaque energy floated. Her first shield.

'She's coming along well,' Elizabeth said approvingly, mounting the stairs.

They walked on and Arcturus sensed Elizabeth wasn't just there to keep him company.

'Arcturus, you should know,' Elizabeth began, hesitating. 'Rook and Charles . . . well . . . they're being privately tutored by their parents, away from the academy. But you'll likely see them again. There's a tournament before students graduate, in a few years' time. You'll have to duel them – it's a competition for commissions in the army. The whole thing will be under supervision but students get injured every time. I just wanted to tell you.'

Arcturus turned to her and grinned.

'This is great news,' he said as they turned into the corridor. 'I'll be ready for them then.'

'You're happy?' Elizabeth said, smiling back. 'Oh thank heavens. I thought you'd be upset – they'll try to hurt you, you know. And they won't fight fair.'

'I'm more than happy,' Arcturus said. 'Let them try – I'd relish the chance to face them in battle. Now you've given me something to work towards. They'll regret ever coming back here.'

Elizabeth stopped him and gave him a quick hug.

'You're a brave lad, Arcturus,' she said. 'But . . . if you need private lessons, just ask.'

'Count on it,' Arcturus said.

He watched her as she walked away. The woman had saved him several times over. He would never be able to repay her. But perhaps he could look out for her unborn child some day.

Still, there was always a wall between them, for the teacher/ student divide was too great. And he felt the same way with the others, even Elaine. They were nobles and he was a commoner. They would never be truly on equal footing – they led such different lives. Even in these past few weeks, as they laughed and ate together in the warmth of the dining hall, Arcturus felt out of place.

He was not like them and never would be. And there were others like him out in the far reaches of Hominum. Yet there he sat, eating and laughing with the rich, while they starved and shivered in their orphanages.

'Well, let's get this over with,' Arcturus muttered, continuing down the corridor.

As he walked, he tried not to think of what had happened here not two weeks before. How he had killed a man, snapped his neck with the flick of a finger.

Sometimes he would return to that spot, alone in the night, and consider the consequences of what he had done. He would remember the power he held was not to be taken lightly, and that if he had known more, he might have not been forced to kill.

In the early hours, when he lay awake in bed, he would wonder if the world would be a different place had he not taken that man's life. Could you regret something, if you'd been given no other choice? Arcturus thought so.

The Provost's office door loomed, and Arcturus steeled himself and knocked on the door.

'Come!' called a voice.

Arcturus pushed the door open and entered.

It was strange, but the room looked exactly the same. The same desk strewn with papers, and the Provost was even leaning over them in the same way Barcroft had, staring at a long list of names.

But there was something different. There were three boys seated opposite the desk, all of them dirty-faced. They looked terrified and Arcturus assumed they were new servants, there to replace those who had defected to the rebels. But they looked a little young, the smallest looking little older than Elaine.

'Ah Arcturus, there you are,' Forsyth said, beckoning him closer. 'Come here.'

Arcturus walked over and the Provost threw an arm around his shoulders.

'Would you believe it, but that new king of ours has been pestering me about you all damned week,' he said cheerfully, pulling Arcturus aside.

He lowered his voice and gestured to the three servants behind him.

'Not much to look at, are they?' he said. 'But I see some resemblance. Don't you?'

'Resemblance, Provost, sir?' Arcturus asked, glancing back at the boys.

Obadiah gave Arcturus a strange smile.

'If I'm to tell you, I must rely on your utmost discretion, do you understand? If it were my choice, you would not know at all, but King Harold insisted, so here we are.'

Arcturus stared at the Provost, his confusion deepening.

'They're some of our new common students, of course,' Obadiah said.

'Oh,' Arcturus said, still confused.

'And they are your brothers. Well, half-brothers.'

Arcturus's heart stilled in his chest. Could it be?

'I've told them you all probably share the same father,' Obadiah hissed. 'That's it, understand? Nothing about being noble bastards.'

But Arcturus was barely listening. He lurched towards the three boys, and suddenly his vision was blurred, eyes tearing up at the sight of them.

The black hair, that pale skin. He rushed over and felt their arms around him.

He knew what he had to do then. There were more like him out there, scattered across the empire. All he had to do was find them.

'You're safe now,' Arcturus breathed, holding them close. He had never felt so happy.

Because after all the loss, all the suffering and bloodshed, he finally had what he'd always wanted. A family.

DEMON✪LOGY

MITE

Mites are the most common demon in Hominum's part of the ether and are the food source of many demonic species. Though there are several species of smaller insect-like Mites, Scarab Mites are the most powerful of the Mite genus. These demons appear as large, flying beetles and vary from dull brown to brightly coloured. When full grown, a Scarab develops a weapon to complement their powerful mandibles: a nasty stinger, which can temporarily paralyse their enemy. Many summoners use Mites as scouts to explore the ether before sending a more powerful demon in to hunt.

SUMMONER MASTER:
Elaine Lovett

CLASSIFICATION: Arthropidae

SUMMONING LEVEL: 1

BASE MANA LEVEL: 7

MANA ABILITIES: None

NATURAL SKILLS: Flying

RARITY: Very common

DIET: Omnivore

HABITAT: Most land & freshwater habitats

TEMPERAMENT: Varied

ATTACK/DEFENCE 1: Paralytic sting 2: Mandibles

STRIX

Often mistaken for the Gryphowl, the Strix appears as an owlish bird with four limbs. Their feathers are tipped with red, giving them a fearsome appearance. They are common in orcish parts of the ether, and are valued by orcish shamans for their vicious nature. It is not unknown for a Strix to kill and eat its siblings when they reach maturity.

SUMMONER MASTER: Damian Rook

CLASSIFICATION: Aves
SUMMONING LEVEL: 4
BASE MANA LEVEL: 29
MANA ABILITIES: None
NATURAL SKILLS: Flying, Eyesight
RARITY: Common
DIET: Carnivore
ATTACK/DEFENCE 1: Beak 2: Talons

GRYPHOWL

This demon is a combination of cat and owl, and is closely related to the Griffin and Chamrosh, though it is far rarer. Their sharp retractable claws and beak are their best weapons, but it is their keen intelligence and agility in the air that make them such a desirable demon. The Gryphowl is a loner by nature, but will often form a close bond with its summoner and fellow demons, if treated well.

SUMMONER MASTER:
Edmund Raleigh

CLASSIFICATION: *Aves, Felidae*
SUMMONING LEVEL: *4*
BASE MANA LEVEL: *30*
MANA ABILITIES: *None*
NATURAL SKILLS: *Flying, Climbing, Eyesight*
RARITY: *Rare*
DIET: *Carnivore*
ATTACK/DEFENCE 1: *Beak* 2: *Claws*

ARACH

The Arach appears as an enormous spider, almost as large as a wild boar. Its eight dextrous legs are capable of skilful manipulation, allowing the demon to jump as high as ten feet and grasp its opponents by the face. The Arach has three powerful abilities. The first is the gossamer spell, shooting a luminescent web that puts one in mind of the silk of a glowworm — an adhesive that fades out of existence after a few hours. The second is its vicious sting, the venom of which is capable of killing a grown man — if the impalement of the spike does not do the job first. Finally, rather like some breeds of tarantula, the Arach is capable of releasing the bristled hair from its back to float in the air, scourging its opponents' skin and even blinding them. Only its summoners are immune to these bristles, as well as the Arach's venom.

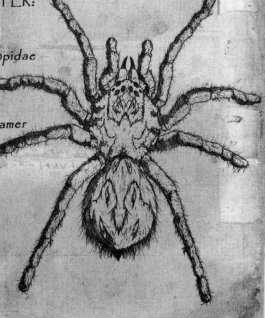

SUMMONER MASTER:
Charles Faversham

CLASSIFICATION: Arthopidae
SUMMONING LEVEL: 6
BASE MANA LEVEL: 45
MANA ABILITIES: Gossamer
NATURAL SKILLS:
Climbing, Jumping
RARITY: Rare
DIET: Carnivore
ATTACK/DEFENCE
1: Venomous Sting
2: Gossamer 3: Bristles

VULPID

A close cousin to the Canid, this slightly smaller, fox-like demon has three tails and is known for its agility and speed.

SUMMONER MASTER: Alice Queensouth

CLASSIFICATION: Canidae

SUMMONING LEVEL: 6

BASE MANA LEVEL: 42

MANA ABILITIES: None

NATURAL SKILLS: Acute sense of smell, Heightened hearing, Agility

RARITY: Uncommon

DIET: Carnivore

HABITAT: Most land habitats

TEMPERAMENT: Loyal

ATTACK/DEFENCE 1: Bite

2: Claws

CANID

A dog-like demon with four eyes, lethal claws, a fox-like tail and a thick ridge of fur down its spine. These demons range in size from that of a large dog to a small pony, depending on the breed.

SUMMONER MASTERS: Arcturus, Edmund Raleigh

CLASSIFICATION: Canidae

SUMMONING LEVEL: 7

BASE MANA LEVEL: 48

MANA ABILITIES: None

NATURAL SKILLS: Acute sense of smell, Heightened hearing

RARITY: Common

DIET: Carnivore

HABITAT: Most land habitats

TEMPERAMENT: Loyal

ATTACK/DEFENCE 1: Bite 2: Claws

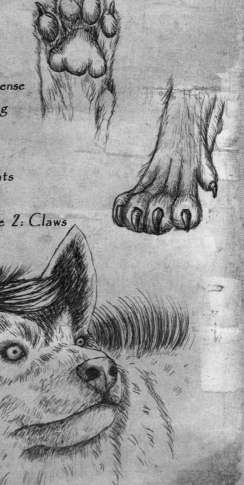

FELID

This bipedal cat demon has four eyes and the stature and intelligence of a jungle chimpanzee. Their breeds vary from leonine, tigrine and leopine, bearing resemblances to lions, tigers and leopards respectively.

SUMMONER MASTER: *Scipio*

CLASSIFICATION: *Felidae*
SUMMONING LEVEL: 7
BASE MANA LEVEL: 50
MANA ABILITIES: None
NATURAL SKILLS: Agility
RARITY: Common
DIET: Carnivore
HABITAT: Most land habitats
TEMPERAMENT: Proud
ATTACK/DEFENCE
1: Bite 2: Claws

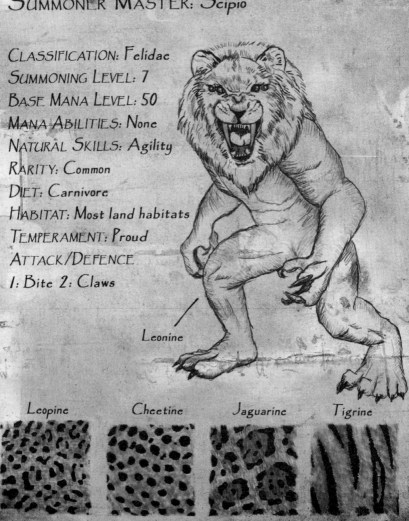

Leonine

Leopine   Cheetine   Jaguarine   Tigrine

Hydra

A Hydra is a large demon with three snake-like heads on long, flexible necks. Its body is similar to that of a monitor lizard, at around the same size of a large Canid. These demons were once more common in Hominum's part of the ether, but are now extremely rare.

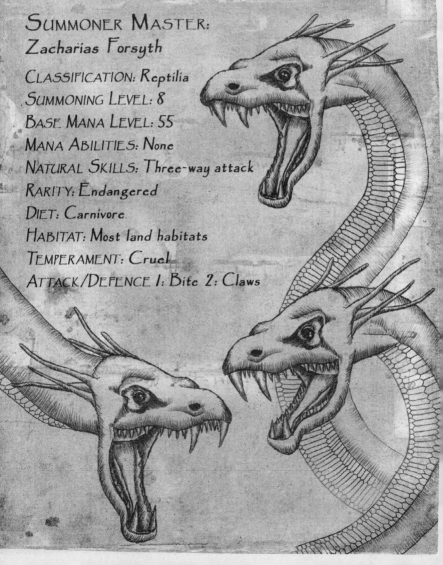

Summoner Master:
Zacharias Forsyth

Classification: Reptilia
Summoning Level: 8
Base Mana Level: 55
Mana Abilities: None
Natural Skills: Three-way attack
Rarity: Endangered
Diet: Carnivore
Habitat: Most land habitats
Temperament: Cruel
Attack/Defence 1: Bite **2:** Claws

PERYTON

The most favoured demon of the Celestial Corps, Perytons appear as winged, horse-sized stags, with majestic antlers branching from their foreheads. Their front legs end in hooves, yet their back legs are clawed like a falcon's, complete with deadly talons that can do serious damage. Instead of the traditional bobtail that most deer possess, these demons have long, elegant tail feathers. Their herds migrate sporadically across Hominum's part of the ether, and they are considered the most common of the flying steeds available to Hominum's summoners.

SUMMONER MASTERS:
Ophelia Faversham, Elizabeth Cavendish

CLASSIFICATION:
Aves, Caprid
SUMMONING LEVEL: 9
BASE MANA LEVEL: 62
MANA ABILITIES: None
NATURAL SKILLS: Flying, Agility
RARITY: Migratory
DIET: Herbivore
ATTACK/DEFENCE 1: Gore 2: Talons 3: Kick

NANDI

The Nandi might be described as a giant, bear-like creature, with powerful jaws and claws that can tear apart most opponents. However, it has a musculature, intelligence and agility more akin to a dog than that of a bear.

SUMMONER MASTER: *None*

CLASSIFICATION: *Megafauns*
SUMMONING LEVEL: *11*
BASE MANA LEVEL: *75*
MANA ABILITIES: *None*
NATURAL SKILLS: *Strength*
RARITY: *Very Rare*
DIET: *Omnivore*
ATTACK/DEFENCE *1: Bite 2: Claws*

MANTICORE

This rare demon has bat-like wings and forelimbs, a
scorpion tail and the body of a lion, though the dark fur
is interspersed with sharp spines. The Manticore's
leonine face can sometimes appear almost human, and
its features are capable of expressing complex emotion.
Its venom is so potent that one droplet will kill a man
within minutes. Members of the Raleigh family are
said to be immune.

SUMMONER MASTER: *None*

CLASSIFICATION: *Arthropidae, Felidae*
SUMMONING LEVEL: *12*
BASE MANA LEVEL: *85*
MANA ABILITIES: *None*
NATURAL SKILLS: *Flying*
RARITY: *Very Rare*
DIET: *Carnivore*
ATTACK/DEFENCE
1: Venomous Sting
2: Bite
3: Claws
4: Spines

WENDIGO

The Wendigo is a rare demon that is known to follow the Shrike migration across the ether, eating the carcasses of its fallen victims. Despite its role as a carrion eater, the Wendigo is a powerful beast in its own right, with corded muscle lining its skinny frame. Standing as high as eight feet tall, it has branching antlers, a wolf-like head and long arms that it uses to knuckle the ground like a gorilla. It is known to have the mottled grey skin of a corpse and the stench to match — most likely from its regular consumption of rotting flesh.

SUMMONER MASTER:
Obadiah Forsyth

CLASSIFICATION:
Canidae, Caprids
SUMMONING LEVEL: 13
BASE MANA LEVEL: 90
MANA ABILITIES: None
NATURAL SKILLS:
Agility, Strength
RARITY: Very Rare
DIET: Carnivore
ATTACK/DEFENCE
1: Antlers
2: Bite
3: Claw

INDRIK

These enormous demons have the long necks and large bodies of giraffes, but with thicker limbs, a long tapering tail and a head that is more akin to that of a horse's or camel's. Their fur is short, grey and mottled with black patches. Travelling in herds of a score or more, Indriks migrate widely, acting as a food source for the large, carnivorous demons across the ether's ecosystem. Given its role as a prey animal and high summoning level, these demons are relatively useless to summoners.

SUMMONER MASTER: *None*

CLASSIFICATION: *Equine*
SUMMONING LEVEL: *14*
BASE MANA LEVEL: *75*
MANA ABILITIES: *None*
NATURAL SKILLS: *None*
RARITY: *Common*
DIET: *Herbivore*
ATTACK/DEFENCE
1: *Stomp*

PHANTAUR

The Phantaur is as much an elephant as a Minotaur is a bull. With its serrated tusks, sturdy fists and a height of over ten feet, it is a force to be reckoned with. Thought to be the rarest and most powerful demon available to orc shamans, only one has ever been seen. Little is known of its behaviours and habitats. It is thought that the one Phantaur to have been captured has been passed down through thousands of generations of shamans, its origins lost to the mists of time.

SUMMONER MASTER: *None*

CLASSIFICATION: *Megafauns*
SUMMONING LEVEL: *20*
BASE MANA LEVEL: *Unknown*
MANA ABILITIES: *None*
NATURAL SKILLS:
Long reach,
Thickskinned,
Strength
RARITY: *Endangered*
DIET: *Herbivore*
ATTACK/DEFENCE
1: Trunk 2: Tusks
3: Punch

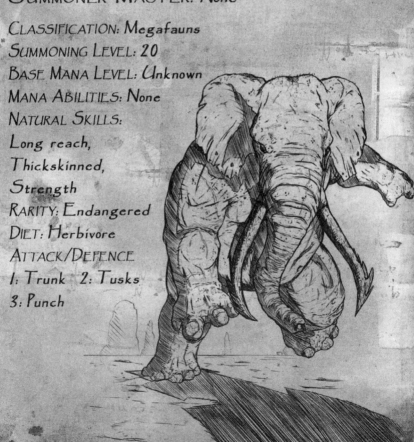

SHRIKE

SHRIKE MATRIARCH

GOLEM

GRIFFIN

MINOTAUR

Acknowledgements

There have been a great many people who I owe a debt of gratitude for their contribution to the creation and publication of the Summoner series.

I would like to thank my UK agent, Juliet Mushens, for all her hard work, teaming up with many amazing publishers around the world. She has been my guiding light throughout the entire process and my life would not be the same without her. I would also like to thank Sasha Raskin, my US agent, for helping take the Summoner series across the pond.

I must also thank both my commissioning editors, Naomi Greenwood and Liz Szabla, for their stellar work in polishing my books into the best version of themselves. Their combined insight has taught me more in one year than a lifetime of my own study of the craft. I owe them a great deal for trusting in me and believing in my writing. Without their support, there would be no Summoner series.

Thank you to the publishing teams at Hodder Children's Books and Feiwel and Friends, for helping bring a beautiful book to as many readers as possible. They have done fantastic work and have stuck with me from start to finish.

There are several artists who I have loved working with to

bring my books to life. Thank you to David North, Malgorzata Gruszka and Michelle Brackenborough for their beautiful artwork.

I would like to thank my friends and family for their on going support, guidance and patience over the past few years. Robert Ayres, Vic James, Dominic Wong, Michael Miller, Brook Aspden, Kash and Emily Siddiqi, Alice Kingsnorth as well as Liege, Jay, Sindri and Raj Matharu, you guys rock.

Finally, thank *you*, the readers, for all you have done. Your comments, reviews, messages and encouragement have meant the world to me. It is ultimately you that made me a success, and you that keep me writing. I will be for ever astonished, honoured and grateful for your support.

Thank you.

THE STORY CONTINUES WITH
A NEW SUMMONER IN

READ ON FOR A SNEAK PEEK OF
THE FIRST CHAPTER...

1

It was now or never. If Fletcher didn't make this kill, he would go hungry tonight. Dusk was fast approaching and he was already running late. He needed to make his way back to the village soon, or the gates would close. If that happened, he would either have to bribe the guards with money he didn't have or take his chances in the woods overnight.

The young elk had just finished rubbing its antlers against a tall pine, scraping the soft velvet that coated them to leave the sharp tines beneath. From its small size and stature, Fletcher could tell it was a juvenile, sporting its first set of antlers. It was a fine specimen, with glossy fur and bright, intelligent eyes.

Fletcher felt almost ashamed to hunt such a majestic creature, yet he was already adding up its value in his head. The thick coat would do well when the fur traders came by, especially as it was now winter. It would probably make at least five shillings. The antlers were in good condition, if a little small, they might fetch four shillings if he was lucky. It was the meat he craved the most, gamy red venison that would drip sizzling fat into his cooking fire.

A thick mist hung heavy in the air, coating Fletcher in a thin layer of dew. The forest was unusually still. Normally the wind rattled the branches, allowing him to stalk through the undergrowth unheard. Now he barely allowed himself to breathe.

He unslung his bow and nocked an arrow to it. It was his best arrow, the shaft straight and true, the fletching from good goose feathers rather than the cheap turkey feathers he bought in the market. He took a shallow breath and drew back on the bowstring. It was slippery on his fingers; he had coated it in goose-fat to protect it from the moisture in the air.

The point swam in and out of focus as he centred it on the elk. Fletcher was crouched a good hundred feet away, hidden in the tall grass. A difficult shot, but the lack of wind brought its own rewards. No gust to jar the arrow in its flight.

He breathed and shot in one fluid motion, embracing the moment of stillness in body and mind that he had learned from bitter and hungry experience. He heard the dull thrum of the bowstring jarring and then a thud as the arrow hit home.

It was a beautiful shot, taking the elk through the chest, into the lungs and heart. The animal collapsed and convulsed, thrashing on the ground, its hooves drumming a tattoo on the earth in its death throes.

He sprinted towards his prey and drew a skinning knife from the slim scabbard at his thigh, but the stag was dead before he got to it. A good clean kill, that's what Berdon would have said. But killing was always messy. The bloody froth bubbling from the elk's mouth was testament to that.

He removed the arrow carefully and was happy to see the

shaft had not snapped, nor had the flint point chipped on the elk's ribs. Although he was Fletcher by name, the amount of time he spent binding his arrows frustrated him. He preferred the work Berdon would occasionally give him, hammering and shaping iron in the forge. Perhaps it was the heat, or the way his muscles ached deliciously after a hard day's work. Or maybe it was the coin that weighed down his pockets when he was paid afterwards.

The young elk was heavy, but he was not far from the village. The antlers made for good handholds, and the carcass slipped easily enough over the wet grass. His only concern would be the wolves or even the wildcats now. It was not unknown for them to steal a hunter's meal, if not his life, as he brought his prize back home.

He was hunting on the ridge of the Beartooth Mountains, so called for their distinctive twin peaks that looked like two canines. The village lay on the jagged ridge between them, the only path up to it on a steep and rocky trail in clear view from the gates. A thick wooden palisade surrounded the village, with small watchtowers at intervals along the top. The village had not been attacked for a long time, only once in Fletcher's fifteen years in fact. Even then, it had been a small band of thieves rather than an orc raid, unlikely as that was this far north of the jungles. Despite this, the village council took security very seriously, and getting in after the ninth bell was always a nightmare for latecomers.

Fletcher manoeuvred the animal's carcass on to the thick grass that grew beside the rocky path. He didn't want to damage the coat; it was the most valuable part of the elk. Furs were one of the few resources the village had to trade, earning it its name: Pelt.

It was heavy going and the path was treacherous underfoot, even more so in the dark. The sun had already disappeared behind the ridge, and Fletcher knew the bell would be sounding any minute. He gritted his teeth and hurried, stumbling and cursing as he grazed his knees on the gravel.

His heart sank when he reached the front gates. They were closed, the lanterns above lit for their nightlong vigil. The lazy guards had closed up early, eager for a drink in the village tavern.

'You lazy sods! The ninth bell hasn't even rung yet.' Fletcher cursed and let the elk's antlers fall to the ground. 'Let me in! I'm not sleeping out here just because you can't wait to drink yourselves stupid.' He slammed his boot into the door.

'Now, now, Fletcher, keep it down. There's good people sleeping in here,' came a voice from above. It was Didric. He leaned out over the parapet above Fletcher, his large moonish face grinning nastily.

Fletcher grimaced. Of all the guards who could have been on duty tonight, it had to be Didric Cavell, the worst of the bunch. He was fifteen, the same age as Fletcher, but he fancied himself a full-grown man. Fletcher did not like Didric. The guardsman was a bully, always looking for an excuse to exercise his authority.

'I sent the day-watch off early tonight. You see, I take my duties very seriously. Can't be too careful with the traders arriving tomorrow. You never know what kind of riffraff will be sneaking about outside.' He chuckled at his jibe.

'Let me in, Didric. You and I both know that the gates should be open until the ninth bell,' said Fletcher. Even as he spoke he heard the bell begin its sonorous knell, echoing dully in valleys below.

'What was that? I can't hear you,' yelled Didric, holding a hand up to his ear theatrically.

'I said let me in, you dolt. This is illegal! I'll have to report you if you don't open the gates this minute!' he shouted, flaring up at the pale face above the palisade.

'Well you could do that, and I certainly wouldn't begrudge you your right to. In all likelihood we would both be punished, and that wouldn't do anyone any good. So why don't we cut a deal here. You leave me that elk, and I save you the trouble of sleeping in the forest tonight.'

'Shove it up your arse,' Fletcher spat in disbelief. This was blatant blackmail.

'Come now, Fletcher, be reasonable. The wolves and the wildcats will come prowling, and even a bright campfire won't keep them away in the winter. You can either leg it when they arrive, or stay and be an appetiser. Either way, even if you do last until morning, you'll be walking through these gates empty-handed. Let me help you out.' Didric's voice was almost friendly, as if he was doing Fletcher a favour.

Fletcher's face burned red. This was beyond anything he had experienced before. Unfairness was common in Pelt, and Fletcher had long ago accepted that in a world of haves and have-nots, he was definitely the latter. But now this spoiled brat, a son to one of the richest men in the village no less, was stealing from him.

'Is that it then?' Fletcher asked, his voice low and angry. 'You think you're very clever, don't you?'

'It's just the logical conclusion to a situation in which I happen to be the beneficiary,' Didric said, flicking his blond fringe from his eyes. It was well known that Didric was privately tutored, flaunting his education with flowery speech. It was his father's hope that he would one day be a judge, eventually going to a lawhouse in one of the larger cities in Hominum.

'You forgot one thing,' Fletcher growled. 'I would much rather sleep out in the woods than watch you take my kill.'

'Hah! I think I'll call your bluff. I've a long night ahead of me. It will be fun to watch you try and fend off the wolves,' Didric laughed.

Fletcher knew Didric was baiting him, but it didn't stop his blood boiling. He gulped the anger down, but it still simmered at the back of his mind.

'I won't give you the elk. There's five shillings in the fur alone, and the meat will be worth another three. Just let me in, and I'll forget about reporting you. We can put this whole thing behind us,' Fletcher suggested, swallowing his pride with difficulty.

'I'll tell you what. I can't come away completely empty-handed – that wouldn't do now would it? But since I'm feeling generous, if you give me those antlers you neglected to mention, I'll call it a night, and we can both get what we want.'

Fletcher stiffened at the nerve of the suggestion. He struggled for a moment and then let it go. Four shillings were worth a night in his own bed, and to Didric it was nothing but pocket change. He groaned and took out his skinning knife. It was razor sharp, but it was not designed for cutting through antlers. He hated to mutilate the elk, but he would have to take its head.

A minute later and with some sawing at the vertebrae, the head was in his hands, dripping blood all over his moccasins. He grimaced and held it up for Didric to see.

'All right, Didric, come and get it,' Fletcher said, brandishing the grisly trophy.

'Throw it up here,' said Didric. 'I don't trust you to hand it over.'

'What?' cried Fletcher in disbelief.

'Throw it up now or the deal is off. I can't be bothered to wrestle it from you and get blood all over my uniform,' Didric threatened. Fletcher groaned and hurled it up, spattering his own tunic with blood as he did so. It flew over Didric's head and clattered on the parapet. He made no move to get it.

'Nice doing business with you, Fletcher. I'll see you tomorrow. Have fun camping in the woods,' he said cheerily.

'Wait!' shouted Fletcher. 'What about our deal?'

'I held up my end of the bargain, Fletcher. I said I'd call it a night, and we'd both get what we want. And you said earlier you would rather sleep in the woods than give me your elk. So there you go, you get what you want, and I get what I want. You really should pay attention to the wording in any agreement, Fletcher. It's the first lesson a judge learns.' His face began to withdraw from the parapet.

'That wasn't the deal! Let me in, you little worm!' Fletcher roared, kicking at the door.

'No, no, my bed is waiting for me back at home. I can't say the same for you, though,' Didric laughed as he turned away.

'You're on watch tonight. You can't go home!' yelled Fletcher. If Didric left his watch, Fletcher could get his revenge by reporting him. He had never considered himself a snitch, but for Didric he would make an exception.

'Oh, it's not my watch,' Didric's voice shouted faintly as he descended the palisade steps. 'I never said it was. I told Jakov I'd keep an eye out while he used the privy. He should be back any minute.'

Fletcher clenched his fists, almost unable to comprehend the extent of Didric's deceit. He looked at the headless carcass by his ruined shoes. As the fury rose up like bile in his throat, he had only one thought in his mind. This was not the end of it. Not by a long shot.

DON'T MISS THE REST OF THE AMAZING SUMMONER SERIES...

THE ULTIMATE BATTLE FOR
SURVIVAL IS ABOUT TO BEGIN ...

CONTENDER
THE CHOSEN
TARAN MATHARU

DON'T MISS THE EPIC NEW TRILOGY FROM
BESTSELLING AUTHOR, TARAN MATHARU

TARAN MATHARU

was born in London in 1990 and found a passion for reading at a very early age. His love for stories developed into a desire to create his own, writing his first book at nine years old. At twenty-two, while taking time off to travel, Taran began to write *Summoner*, which became an online sensation, reaching over three million reads in less than six months. Taran is now a full-time author, and spends his time travelling the world and writing. The Summoner series has been translated into 15 languages and is a *New York Times* Bestseller.

@TaranMatharu1